Tales of Sley House 2023

Edited by
K.A. Hough
&
Lillian Ehrhart

Contents

THE TALES OF CHARLES SLEY

THE TALES OF GENEVIEVE SLEY

THE TALES OF RG SLEY

THE TALES OF CHARLES SLEY

THE TALES OF CHARLES SLEY

My hands are very nearly raw from washing again. Genevieve has provided me with a balm—one I'm not quite sure I trust—that she's witched together in her greenhouse, and I've rubbed it into my chapped hands and topped them with the fine cotton gloves that I use for the most precious volumes in my library. The scent still comes through—something nose-wrinklingly herbal, almost dirt-like. RG had offered a solution as well, but his always have a clinical, chemical sharpness to them, though they *do* work better.

I much prefer the comforting, almost non-scents of my library: the mustiness of the books, heavier with dust than they should be, the beeswax candles that Father always had burning, now standing sentry, cold and unlit, in various heavy sconces. The smells of chalk and salt, sulphur and smoke…

And leather. Father's old desk chair creaks as I take a seat and open this collection on his old, stained, leather-trimmed blotter and page through these new stories, my fingerprints contained in their gloves, leaving no trace, though these tales will leave a mark on my soul for a while yet.

Welcome to Your New Home
Sally Sultzman

Sally Sultzman was a reader first, a writer second, but always a storyteller. She talks writing with anyone who stands still long enough to listen. She lives in rural Illinois with her family, her rescue dogs, and a collection of oversized tea mugs. Find out more about Sally's stories at www.sallysultzman.com.

~

*I*f you're reading this, I'm sorry. I'm so damn sorry."

That's what it said. I stared at the words carved into the wooden door, ice trickling down my back, trying to make sense of them. I'm still trying to make sense of them.

The door was beat up. There were—there were *claw marks* on the door. Underneath the words. At least, that's what they looked like.

But Alice asked, "Mama? Whaizzit, Mama?" as she tried to edge around me, her soft little lisp rounding out the sounds, my special little girl.

"Um," I said, ripping my gaze away from those words, those marks, and grabbing Alice's shirt to keep her from slipping past me. "Not much."

The room was at the very front of the house, so under the entryway? Or the front porch? I wasn't sure. Still not sure. We were down there because I was trying to figure out where the movers had put my food processor. I wouldn't have taken my daughter down there otherwise but it was a basement, you know? Unfinished, full of boxes and random junk. Old paint left over from the previous owners, that sort of thing. Just a basement.

I'd been hefting boxes around when Alice squeaked, "Mama, I finded a magic door!" and I...

I opened it for her.

The little room was just that—little. Maybe four feet wide and three feet deep, if that. The floor was a huge step up, eight or even ten inches high—but it still looked like packed dirt. The ceiling was lower, too—I didn't think I could stand all the way up in the room. It was just this tiny, weird little room. I don't remember seeing a switch or a pull cord or anything but the light was on, throwing shadows around the space and over the only other thing in the room—a workbench, I thought.

The air around me was cold. I remember that. It was…chilly. Wrong. But we were in a basement, so what did I know?

"Ohhhh," Alice said, little-girl longing in her tone as she peeked around me. "Izza magic room, Mama? For *me*!"

"Hmm," is all I said as I backed up so I could close the door.

And the thing is, I can't remember if the door had been there when we'd toured the house. We hadn't had much time, you understand, just half an hour to get in, decide if we wanted to make an offer, and get out. The sellers' realtor was our realtor and the listing was going live in a matter of moments and we'd broken every speed limit known to humankind to make it to town before it hit the market. We didn't have a choice. We were down to a matter of weeks before classes started and we had to live in a hotel.

I don't think I went downstairs. Why can't I remember? The basement is—was—Dan's territory. I claimed the surprisingly roomy kitchen, more than enough space for a small island and a few stools, which was really unusual in a house that old. And a second-floor laundry right next to the master bath? I mean, someone had put some serious money into a one-hundred-and-fifteen year old house but it was perfect for us. Alice had a cute room with a bow window designed for cuddling while reading stories and there was a guest room big enough for my grandmother's bedroom set where my mother could stay with us and Dan's mom's dining room set looked like it was made for the dining room.

And there was a fourth bedroom up there, already painted in shades of blue with a little sailboat border. Just right for the little baby boy we want.

Wanted. I guess that's gone now, too, right?

Like I said—*perfect*. What did I care about basements? We'd been outbid on seven other houses and Dan's new job started in three weeks and at the time, it'd felt like this house had been waiting for us. It'd felt like *home*. So we offered them thirty-thousand dollars over asking and held our breath for four hours until they accepted and—

You don't believe me but I didn't expect you to. I'm telling you, there is—was—something in the basement. A wooden door that opens onto a little room. I don't know if I called it into being? Or if it was Alice? I think it was Alice. I think the room was waiting for her.

She'd said it herself, after all. It was a magic room, just her size.

I had to go downstairs a few times for more boxes, but I always went when she was napping. I didn't look for the room. Why would I? The basement is a dirty, drafty place with bugs, you know? The walls were rough stone, the ceiling was low and Dan thought it would leak in a heavy downpour. There wasn't anything to use it for except storage, okay? And I...

I didn't think about that little room and those scrawled words very much.

Maybe I didn't want to.

So I didn't look for it. I don't even remember telling Dan about finding it. It was just so much work, you know? Unpacking and settling in while a two-year-old 'helps' you. I forgot. I'll never forgive myself.

I don't think Alice forgot.

I know she didn't.

We'd been in the house less than a week when classes started on campus and in addition to two of his advanced electrical engineering classes, Dan also got assigned three sections of the required freshman intro to electrical engineering—new man in the department, I guess. It was a heavy load with one class starting at seven thirty and another one ending at eight thirty at night. He ate lunch on campus because of the required office hours and then scavenged for leftovers whenever he got home, so it was just me and Alice for most of the week.

I had no idea she'd figured out how to pull the little stool we used for washing our hands in the bathroom across the hall to the basement door so that she could reach the little latch we were using to keep it closed. That latch should've been enough but...

But my little girl was too smart for her own good.

The first time I realized she'd gone down into that basement, it's because she came up to me during what should've been her naptime and told me herself. "Mama, I finded the magic room again!"

"You *what?*"

I must've yelled it because the excitement in her eyes turned cautious in a heartbeat. "I, um, I finded the room?"

It took everything I had to stay calm. "Can you show me?"

But it wasn't calm enough because she started pouting and dragging her feet and I know—I *know*—that made it worse. But she still led me to the basement, where the stool she'd used to open the door had been pushed aside and she showed me how she'd scooted down the stairs on her bottom and...

And the creepy wood door was there, exactly as I remembered it from before. "See?" Alice said, excitement crowding back into her tone. "I finded it!"

The door swung open when I touched the handle and I don't know what I was expecting but it wasn't a small rug and a little pillow on the floor that I didn't recognize and some paper and crayons. Alice had been coloring.

But what made it hard for me to breathe was *the door*. I know that the first time I'd looked inside, the words, "If you're reading this, I'm sorry. I'm so damn sorry," had been carved into the door. I *know* that's what it'd said.

That's not what it said this time

Instead, it said, "Get out—if you still can. If it lets you."

I know it sounds crazy. I know you all think I'm insane but I'm not. That's what it said. And I didn't kill my daughter! I would never hurt her! I did everything I could to keep her safe!

I tried to keep her out of the basement. The latch was too easy, obviously, so I bought a slide lock, but a few days later I went down there for yet another damned box and I heard her singing and the room was back and I crept up real quiet like and I heard...

I heard her say, "Oh, that's pretty, too! Mama would..." and then there was another voice or another sound or something, but I couldn't understand it. And she replied, "Can't Mama come with me?"

And I knew. I knew there was something in there with her, something that shouldn't be in my house, much less in a room with my little girl, so I threw open the door and it was just her, sitting on that rug, pictures and crayons scattered everywhere, surprise on her face. She had a strange look in her eyes, almost glazed, and she was pale. Really pale.

And the door? All it had carved into it was, "Too late, too late, why didn't you listen?"

I got padlocks after that. Installed the first at the top of the basement stairs myself, then went down into that basement early the next morning after Dan left. I piled boxes in front of the door up to my eye level, then put a padlock on that door, too. The rest of the boxes covered the lock up. Both keys went on my key ring. Alice was done teething and I never let her drool on the car clicker, anyway, but I started keeping them in my pocket at all times and at night, they were in my bedside table.

Dan didn't even notice when he came home and I...I should've said something. I know that now. But who would've believed me? I didn't believe it myself. And you clearly don't believe me now. Besides, I'd fixed it. Big brass padlocks all over my house, me jumping at every noise, almost afraid to go to the bathroom or leave her alone, even for a second. It's not easy to live in fear.

Despite what they're saying, I'm not a bad mother, okay? It's just hard to keep an eye on a two-year-old at all times and it doesn't make me a bad person to need a break. I hadn't been anywhere but the grocery store and the hardware store and Alice…every time I strapped her into her car seat, she got upset. More upset. The day before she…

That day, Alice threw a temper tantrum so long and loud that she scared me. I almost drove her straight to the E.R. because we hadn't even had our initial appointment with her new pediatrician. She was bright red and screaming so loudly that her voice went raw, clawing at my arms and punching my face, trying to undo the buckles and get out of the car.

So she could go back into the house.

I didn't know. How could I have known?

Why didn't I know?

The old lady across the street came out of her house and glared at me like I was abusing my daughter instead of me getting a bloody nose for trying to safely put her in a car seat. I thought she was going to call the cops on me. Maybe if she had…

But she didn't. And I couldn't deal with the silent judgment. So we didn't go to the store. Alice was hysterical and you can't reason with a toddler. Have you tried?

And I …

I was upset, okay? I was mad that we couldn't go out. Here I was, alone in a new town, stuck in a house that had something seriously wrong with it, where the neighbors were watching me fail. I was functionally a single parent and I know Dan was struggling to fit into a new corporate culture and prep for all his classes, but I felt trapped.

There, happy? That's what you wanted to hear, isn't it? Yeah, I was mad. I wanted to go to the store and get a roast for dinner and buy a magazine I could read while the bathroom door was locked for two minutes at a time and a bottle of wine I could hide in the closet and have a glass after she went to bed and I couldn't even do that, and why? Because a two year old could scream louder than me? You'd be furious, too.

So I took her inside and she calmed down almost immediately but the tantrum had taken so much out of her…I mean, she was just floppy in my arms and I was upset and also scared again because this wasn't like my girl. She had her moments, all kids have moments but I took her up to her toddler bed and rubbed her back but she was asleep within minutes and I…

I left her alone.

I mean, I went to my bathroom and cried, okay? It's not like I got in the car and drove off on a wine bender. I'm not the monster you want me to be. I was forty feet away from her. Two doors separated us. If she'd woken up crying again,

I would've heard her and I would've been there in less than a minute. I cleaned the blood off my face and bandaged up my arms the best I could and then I sat on the toilet and sobbed.

But she didn't wake up crying. And I didn't hear her. Because I was too busy feeling sorry for myself.

Look, I don't know how to explain what happened next to you in a way you'll understand because I don't understand any of it myself and we both know you already don't believe me. But this is what happened. This is the truth.

When I finally calmed down, I went back to her room, but she wasn't in her bed. She wasn't upstairs at all. Or downstairs. Not even in that little closet under the stairs where the vacuum was living—she liked to hide in there.

Not trying to climb up on the counter in the kitchen, looking for cookies.

Not in the backyard, chasing butterflies through the grass or trying to make her own bubbles.

Not racing up and down the sidewalk in the front.

She wasn't anywhere.

And the basement door...

Look, I know you don't believe me, but it was locked. Locked! Shut tight, the padlock clicked into place. There was no way she could've gotten through it. The keys to both padlocks were still on my key ring, which was still in my pocket. I hadn't set it down after we came inside. I'd put it back in the pocket of my jeans and carried her upstairs.

But something felt wrong. Off. And I knew. *I knew.*

I started yelling, started screaming her name. The house—that "magic room" in the basement—it could hear me just fine. The padlock came off easy enough but the basement door? It stuck. It was trying to keep me out and any other day, I might've let it but I knew it had my daughter down there. Somehow, it'd gotten her from her room down two flights of stairs without me hearing her, without removing any locks, and I wasn't going to let it have her.

When the door refused to budge, I panicked. You would've, too, if you'd been there. It wasn't going to let me in and I wasn't going to let it keep me out so I did what I had to do. We'd dumped all our yard care stuff in one corner of the garage and when I went out, the garage door slammed shut behind me, like the house thought it could keep me out but I had a fucking axe. When I hit the garage door, the wood splintered and I swear to God above that it sounded like someone, somewhere was screaming. I didn't stop.

You wouldn't have, either.

The basement door buckled. I just tore that sucker apart. Maybe it took thirty seconds, maybe it was fifteen minutes—I honestly don't know. The house made noises in protest, sounds of pain, but nothing sounded like my little girl. Nothing sounded like Alice.

"I want her back!" I screamed through the gap in the basement door before I took another swing, which was enough to push the thing open and then I was racing down the stairs, kicking and pulling the boxes aside. And…

And…

I'm not fine, okay? Nothing about this is fine! But you have to believe me, the house—this fucking "magic" room, the one you're standing in, if you're reading this—it has my daughter and the longer you stand around, convincing yourself that I'm insane, that I've done something with my precious little angel—the less time we have to figure out how to get her back!

Why won't you help me get her back?

Why won't you help me?

Oh, God, it's too late. She's gone. It won't let her go and now it's too late, why didn't I listen? Why won't *you* listen?

If you're reading this, I'm so damn sorry—but it's too late.

Sleepwalkers
Marie Wendel

Marie Wendel writes stories, poems and novels and lives on an island with tall buildings and abrupt laughter.

~

Weekend service has always been erratic, but never more so than in the past year. Instead of taking a shuttle bus as directed by distorted loudspeaker announcements, you decide to climb the stairs, walk the necessary blocks, descend into another subway stop and resume your journey home from there. Emerging from the station, you pass a restaurant and pause to recall its former incarnation, a dusty cigar shop, its Dominican owner partial to broad-brimmed hats. And over there, that gelato shop? That used to be the store where all the punks bought their Doc Martens. At the corner, you turn down a familiar street just as a girl, the same height as your just-turned 13-year-old daughter, rolls past on a skateboard. Distracted by thoughts of your most recent argument (her plummeting grades), you do not notice where your steps are leading until suddenly it is upon you: the building where you used to live.

Graffiti no longer marks its brick face like pimples. Even the fire escape appears to have been freshly painted. An upscale bistro occupies the storefront space where a Chinese herbalist slash acupuncturist formerly set up shop. The outer door has been changed, too, and a new security camera hides within a black dome above the buzzers. You remain unmoving on the sidewalk staring up at your floor as a cascade of experiential memory slithers through your very being: the taste of a girlfriend's mouth, the style of your bathroom sink, the feel of the fabric of your favorite suit, the colors of broken bottles against concrete.

Behind you in the street, a car passes soundlessly. (In what corner of the city does the sound of reggaeton, forever wafting through open windows of the past, now reside?) An approaching couple pauses, uncertain whether to walk in front of you or try to squeeze between you and the garbage bags at the curb. Decision made, they pass before you and the woman nearest you abruptly spins to meet your gaze.

Immediately it registers. A vivid memory, well-used over the years, stirs in your mind. Sudden desire makes you dizzy. Your hand rises, an unwilled movement, to grasp all that is fleeting. She startles, lurches forward and rushes away, glancing back with frightened eyes.

Tales of Sley House 2023

***

In the city that no longer exists, you live on Chrystie Street. Weekday mornings your alarm blasts Sonic Youth or Nirvana or one of the other bands favored by the DJ whose name you never catch on WFMU. You pee and shower, brush your teeth and shave. Momentarily the lather on your face reminds you of snow in the cornfield beside your hometown football stadium. Your father began to drink after your mother died. You were still in Junior High when he married the woman who flirted anytime the two of you were alone together in the upstairs rooms of your drafty house, the wind seeping in through every seam.

You dress, choosing one of the colored shirts wrapped in plastic from the dry cleaners, and then you collar yourself with a red paisley tie. First you read the sports scores and then the landing strip of information running the length of the front page of the newspaper delivered outside your door. You lock three bolts, walk downstairs, step over a drunk sleeping it off in the foyer, and stride onto the sidewalk.

As usual you see that guy with the vividly expressed death wish and vaguely you wonder: Should I acknowledge him? Twice you've witnessed him stumbling off the curb and just barely avoiding a speeding car. The smoke of his cigarette curled behind him and bathed your face. His eyes exude menace as you pass him. One morning he cursed you and you found the sound of his hatred strangely compelling. A comfort, even. Later you wondered about this, wondered about yourself during an afternoon meeting, weak sunlight spilling onto your gabardine lap.

As you make your way to the subway, plastic drug bags stamped "poison" are crushed beneath your heel. Most days you are not lucky, only occasionally you are, and on those rare days when fortune is in your court you will see one or another of the women who excite you. There are exactly two: one is a blonde, the other a brunette. The blonde is a very young Latina who works at the grocery store. Is she even fifteen? She has blue eyes and a Castilian nose and she is simply and breathtakingly the most beautiful girl you have ever seen and although you have frequently had opportunities to speak to her beyond the moment when she hands you your change, you have not once uttered a word. Now you see her laughing with the boy who stocks the shelves and something icy happens inside your entrails and all the colors of the scene surrounding this couple weirdly ignite. Forcing yourself to look away, you remember how stiff she has always been with you, it is this stiffness that has prevented you from speaking to her, and now, glancing back at her standing there with the stock boy, a simian creature with

16

pronounced brow and biceps, you understand how great is the divide between your world and hers and how much work it would take to bridge that expanse. Pausing for the light to change, you think to yourself that all will continue as it always does. (Probably.) You'll remain paralyzed in her presence and yet you'll think about her each morning as you set out for work and on the nights you are alone in a too-wide bed you'll even dream of rescuing her and taking her someplace far from these streets, someplace like your hometown.

Why do you believe she must be rescued from this? Does it have something to do with the fact that the day after you moved in two guys shoved you against the wall, roughed you up, and then spit "creep" over their shoulders as they walked away? Or is it simply the numbers attached to violent crimes that you read each morning after the box scores? But isn't it also true you feel yourself enlivened in this neighborhood, you've felt that from the start and by now you're completely acclimated, you've adjusted yourself to its rank smells and raw behavior. Sometimes in the break room your co-workers will laugh about your legendarily cheap rent and your quote-unquote *raw* apartment. (Not once have you invited them to visit.) Your father and his flirtatious, pretty/ugly wife and your older sister who never married know your address here but they understand nothing about the city that no longer exists, they've no idea what you've seen since you arrived. Sure, they've heard horror stories on the news, but whenever you surprise them with your annual phone call home (usually on Thanksgiving, though sometimes you wait until Christmas to hear the tightness in their voices, a sound made only in your presence), you like to emphasize that none of *that* happens where you live and then you lapse into silence. If you told your father and his wife and your sister, who maintains a measured distance as if her body is a car and must stay in a lane separate from yours, about the night you came home to junkies fixing on the staircase of your building, a belt, which resembled your own, curling beside them like a snake, what exactly would they say? How about the time you saw a retarded man limping down the street with a knife dangling from his left hand, would they tell you to pack and leave? Could you ever explain that you got a hard-on the first time you saw the transvestites snorting outside the bar on the next block? What would they think?

What do you think? Mostly you don't. Mostly you laugh. It's a free-for-all and you like it like that.

***

It is dark when you arrive home. "We picked up dinner," your wife says and cautiously adds: "Are you ready to eat or do you want—"

17

"I'm ready," you say as if granting a favor.

"Put out chopsticks," your wife instructs your daughter who glances at you and then quickly looks away.

As you eat sushi and tempura, you listen as your daughter explains the science trip her class is planning. *Does she remember…?* Watching your daughter chew, an anxious strain in her eye, you tell yourself it just might be possible that some fragment of what transpired last year awakes now and again, slithers within damp folds of her brain.

"Can we watch a movie tonight?" Your wife's voice breaks your reverie.

"Maybe." Put upon, you are, by such requests.

"And tomorrow can—"

"I'm going to the gym tomorrow," you say in the tone of voice your wife responds to best.

You remember how you'd had to partition her from her small clique of college friends, well-tended girls who never dared to explore the neighborhoods that slouched beyond their manicured expectations. When you first saw her (it happened to be the anniversary of your night with Maxine), she appeared unusually clean and you knew immediately that she would be, as so many have pronounced before you, the girl you would marry. At least that is what you told your co-workers the afternoon they celebrated your wedding with modest sips of cheap champagne in the conference room. Your associates smiled as your words deleted, at least momentarily, any latent suspicions they had of you. But the unvarnished fact you would never confide to your assembled office mates is that you didn't know you would marry your wife until the night you had intended something very different.

"More?" Your wife divides the remaining tempura between the three of you and then chopsticks the final piece of salmon roll onto your plate.

You study the internal black spiral created by seaweed. How long has it been? How long since you lived, a man unburdened by limpid wife, insipid daughter? How long since Maxine?

You laugh. Wife and daughter immediately turn pale. Quickly you say, "I love you," the words intended for both and neither and then you lift the concise morsel of seaweed and salmon, pop it into your mouth and begin to chew.

They both smile yet some shadow of distress is still evident in their eyes.

***

Arriving at work each morning, your city seems to vanish. You come up from the subway in a glossy neighborhood, step into a revolving door, twirl and presto! It's as if you've flown in from, let's say Bogota, while everyone else, well, they've been here all along, striding through corridors smelling of cologne, always smiling those thin smiles as they compete for all that is exquisite and all that can be served to them by others, there must always be others servile and offering themselves with a genteel attitude that disguises fear. Each workday you feel as if you've crossed some invisible border that separates your city from theirs. And every morning you arrive carrying your alternate perceptions and fragmented inclinations, like a passport, with you.

The breakroom coffee tastes like burnt ego. Carrying a mug emblazoned with your company logo, you greet your assistant with a nod. Your last three assistants were temps you slept with and then succinctly fired. Your boss, who commutes from Darien and finds such girls repulsive, thinks you haven't figured out how to delegate properly but this is not an issue with your other subordinates, the full-time permanent associates, all of them similarly educated, though slightly younger than yourself. This thing with your assistants, well, you can't really explain it other than to say when you met each of these girls you understood them immediately. Like you, they reeked of sordid intimacies. They'd grown up in not-so-faraway towns readily escapable, arriving in the city with not much more than a head full of delusions. But unlike you they play bass guitar in jam bands, or they refer to themselves as "improvisational sculptors," or they choreograph experimental dance routines. Each pays rent in some lousy neighborhood similar to your own and once you learned this small detail about them, you knew you were safe and that they'd be unfazed by pretty much anything you could do to them... weren't they wandering around shell-shocked and numb? In any event, when you lied and told them the company needed to cut back two of them seemed too narcotized to even question you. Only one comprehended what was happening to her, she immediately understood that you were discarding her, though really (you wanted oh so badly to say aloud, shout into her face drained now of all color) you were ejaculating her into a filthy toilet. And though you assume she easily found another job, you occasionally nurse a dull worry about encountering her, some primordial boyfriend beside her, on an early morning train.

How you miss your temps now that they are gone! You miss their off-color intelligence and pock-marked temperaments, their particular blend of femininity and anger, their rhetoric of artistic integrity. During lunch as you are checking balances on your accounts, you think you hear the last one's laughter—distinctly un-musical—but when you lift your head you see only the new associate, well-paid and well-esteemed, she is pausing outside your door to wave in a friendly manner. You feel your stomach clench as you stifle some unnamed impulse yet your mouth forms a grinning rictus to show that you are friendly too but then you quickly duck your head into the computer. You sense her self-respecting face ever so slightly hardening before she disappears from your threshold. And so your day begins to crawl like something still-warm but beaten and it is hours later that you detect an odor when you lift a binder to the shelf above the credenza and you understand that all this perspiring fear is the simple result of seeing *her*.

You leave as soon as you are able, just after rush hour. Moving to the edge of the crowded platform just as the train squeals into the station, you feel the inner surge that comes whenever you deny the natural instinct to flee onrushing danger. Within the crush, a man in a cheap suit says, "Let the people OFF first," but you and the others immediately push inside anyway and somehow you end up pressed against a short woman. As the train lurches into motion, you begin to think about your new girlfriend, who is visiting family. (The short woman's tits press into your stomach.)

Your girlfriend's what other women call *fascinating*, other men call *a drag*, but it doesn't matter, you haven't been seeing her long and you've already decided that things won't work out between you. Although she's pretty, she's too… savvy, still there's no need to break up with her, wouldn't it be easier if she's the one to let go first?

Getting off the train, you slowly, slowly climb the littered stairs, you're stuck behind a mother holding the hand of a toddler—like all the mothers in your neighborhood she can't afford a stroller. At the top of the stairs, a homeless man is staring bug-eyed at the crowd emerging from the underworld. His eyes narrow when he identifies you and he hurls a simple invective your way. Crossing the street, you look up just in time to see *her*, your brunette, rushing in the opposite direction. Now you can't help but to inwardly crow. *Both of them in one day!* you tell yourself. A smile lights her face, she's wearing boots and jeans, and a silky-looking white blouse shows through an open jacket. It all feels so natural when you turn around and follow, trailing her by half a block.

***

The blinds are drawn, your daughter has run off with a friend, and you sit alone on the couch beside your dear wife. The two of you watch a movie, her choice, *The Bourne Identity*. You find yourself mildly amused by the film's plot, so obviously a falsified account of an amnesia victim who desperately wants to recover his identity. Meanwhile your wife's excitement steadily grows. You feel her breathing beside you. She gasps. She sighs. You sense how much she loves this guy who is nothing at all like you. In fact, he is the opposite of you; you are the one who bestows the forgetting, you yourself have forgotten nothing. Her eyes widen, they are fastened to the screen as Jason Bourne defends and saves Marie. And so you study this hero, this not-you, while you despise your simple wife as the action escalates and music swells.

She clutches your hand for comfort and you remain untouched, unmoved, until a previously un-thought thought meanders into your mind.

Your wife's fantasy is to be rescued.

Does she even know what that means?

***

Your brunette turns into the alley and then makes a left. Pausing before a small grunge bar, she opens the door with vigor and briefly you glimpse her white blouse, like a flag of surrender. Idling outside, you need less than a moment to decide.

When you open the door, a smiling bartender is pulling beers while she lei-surely arranges her jacket on the back of a barstool just in front of him. There's something of the wife arriving home to her husband about this tableau and you feel yourself seethe. She gracefully spins, walks the length of the bar and disap-pears into the ladies room. You order a beer from the bartender. You sense he's the kind of drunk who boozes steadily all night, a tough guy, instinctive like an animal, who feels an immediate apprehension encountering you, so instead of the stool beside hers you choose a table near the door. There, at a distance, he'll tolerate your presence and there you will be able to observe. And so you're seated before she returns.

With a small sigh, she sits on her barstool. (She is in profile, just ten feet away from you.)

The bartender stands in front of her: "Maxine."

"Ben. How are you?" Her words lilt in a way that might be Southern.

The bartender pours a generous helping of rye over ice. "Work okay?"

"Same. How're things here?"

"Not bad. Good one last night."

"That unusual for a Wednesday?"

"No. The game was on, that helped."

Then the bartender leans in and says something that you cannot hear. Max-ine laughs, throwing back her head; she is a natural beauty and uninhibited and far superior to your careerist girlfriend and you want to do damage to the bartender and then the door opens and a couple enters the bar. The moment ends without so much as a purr. The woman, taller than the man, squints in order to see and points to a stool a few seats away from Maxine. Greetings are exchanged all around and the man smiles wetly and sits between the woman and Maxine.

"You seen Jimmy, Max?" The squinty-eyed woman seems to pounce; like some predatory bird, anticipation seems to hover above her casual words.

Max glances at the bartender whose head is down now, all at once he's vigorously washing glasses. Slowly, she shakes her head. "Has he been around?"

Watching, you hold your breath.

"We've been hearing about some new girlfriend."

Max swings her attention to the bartender. "Have you?"

The bartender focuses on the glass he is dipping in water. "Haven't heard much."

The woman rearranges her ample bottom on her stool. "Well yesterday, who should we run into on Greene Street?"

Max sighs. "I'm guessing Jimmy?" Three words dressed in threadbare hatred.

"Jimmy and his *girl*." The woman's mouth slackens as if she's just finished the task of inserting a dirty needle into a reluctant vein.

Max smiles brilliantly, falsely.

The man, sitting between the two women, breaks the silence. "She's older. Professional-looking." His voice is reedy.

"Blonde. Pretty. Not a girl I imagined he'd choose." The woman's voice is warm and stirring and she's leaning forward to be able to see past the man.

Maxine's suddenly pale face is screened by hair as she bends to search within the depths of her pocketbook.

Just then the door opens as a noisy cluster of twenty-something women enter the bar. Coming straight from work, they begin to debate what's "best" to drink and their small group shifts and rearranges itself near the empty stool between the couple and Maxine who, fully shielded from the couples' view now, allows her shoulders to sag. Meanwhile you wait, watching as the bartender, unasked, refills Maxine's glass. "On the house."

***

Sunday morning. You wake and fling an arm across the cool sheets of a now empty bed and then sink into sleep once again. Waking a second time, you shower and put on sweats and when you step into the kitchen, your daughter is alone studying Biology. She tenses when she sees you. "Mom went out. She said you should drink tea if you need caffeine."

"Tea." You make the silly face that used to amuse her in moments of complicity against your wife. She does not smile. She's ignoring you. Is this part of being a new teenager? "I'll go buy my own coffee."

"You won't need your jacket." Apparently, she cannot resist a wife-like comment.

"You coming with your old man?"

She looks up at you and her eyes immediately lose focus as if she is searching for an answer that cannot be found. "I want to finish this so I can see Marc later."

You try to picture Marc… you come up with nothing but blurred features and designer sneakers. These teenaged boys with their unlimited access to internet porn, their inconceivable norms, all the things you could never have imagined at their age. If they liked, these boys could live each day, every day, in the city that no longer exists. As you put on your coat, you wonder which of them have discovered the same desires you found within you?

Stepping outside you glance up and down the clean sweep of the avenue and inhale deeply with satisfaction. In most locations of the new city, you find it difficult to remember where you are without looking at street signs. Even the most trodden blocks fail to strike a resonant chord. It seems as if all the individual stores and singular restaurants have been replaced by franchises unencumbered by idiosyncrasy. You could never claim that you entirely dislike the standardized seating, lighting and music. Sometimes you even have a taste for their uniform menu selections. These chain stores possess a certain moxie regarding their impersonality that holds a fascination all its own. You enjoy disappearing inside them. They don't require the effort of authenticity.

And so you become one among the many shuffling forward and ordering coffee from some kid from a crummy neighborhood who dutifully mouths the institutionalized greeting. In these places you often feel unmoored. You know exactly what is expected of you… and yet you don't. At the condiment station, you pour sugar into your coffee as a woman and her friend place their cups beside your own. They loudly search for half and half. Glancing up, the profile of the quiet one elicits a quiver. She turns and, seeing her full face, you deflate.

***

Minutes stack up like pancakes. Maxine looks marooned, a lonely satellite pasted onto a starry sky, and whenever the door opens, her head jerks around in a way that appears involuntary. Each time she makes this mechanical motion, her face dissolves into an expression of disappointment. The bar's a turbulent

23

river of sullen regulars and noisy visitors and you are inconspicuous within its flow, just a patient guy with time enough to see a mission through to its natural conclusion. You watch the bartender refill Maxine's glass. She's begun to smile again and so you think, Half an hour?

And then. A guy less good-looking than you though similar in type—late twenties, corporate, a social life consisting of bars—walks through the door. Seeing Max he's obviously thrilled despite her tepid response. (Not "Jimmy," you think.) As he talks, Maxine's sunflower face begins to droop, bending toward the sunset glow inside her glass of rye. Finally, she rouses herself, stands and heads to the ladies, hugging her purse, like a child, to her chest. Slyly, you position yourself next to the jukebox. *This might be it,* you think until some fool asks if you have change so he can play Patsy Cline. *Are you sure you don't have any quarters?* He is badgering you just as she bursts through the ladies' room door. Maxine, freshened though still sodden, heads back to her stool, and seeing your rival talking to the squinty-eyed couple, she swiftly grabs her jacket and makes an Irish exit.

Screened from the bartender's sight by the swirl of after-work drinkers, you follow her through the door.

***

You casually take a seat at the table beside not-Maxine's and her friend and watch them without appearing to watch. You read the free newspaper left behind by another customer and listen and study her movements. In what is said and what is not said you hear: *single woman, decent job, lives alone.* Accidentally-on-purpose you drop the neighborhood newspaper to the floor. Your light remark is answered by the friend, but she doesn't interest you, you're only interested in not-Maxine whose silence turns up a dial inside you.

When they leave, you follow at a distance of a half-block. On a sunny corner, you watch them say goodbye, and then, after more than two hours of lingering outside various boutiques and one putrid smelling pet shop, you trail not-Maxine to a sub-par apartment building where she climbs the stoop and enters through a paint-peeling door.

As you depart from her walk-up, desire stirs your insides like a spoon. You begin the journey home, lingering here and there to pet a tail-wagging dog as you pass in and out of somber shadows cast by random buildings. Nearing your apartment house, you see your wife approaching from the opposite direction. The sun is shining directly in her eyes and, though she squints, you know she cannot see you. You pause now to watch her walk toward, dwarfed by looming giants with steel bones and concrete loins, she appears soft yet oddly brittle. Seeing this fragility, you tell yourself that what's to come with not-Maxine is necessary, required even, if your wife is to remain protected.

***

Maxine slips into her jacket on the sidewalk outside. With a practiced eye, she scans the block before setting forth. Just then, you step forward and present to her a cheerfully wrapped gift: your most winning smile. You see she's taken aback, but still she smiles, almost.

"The music was getting loud in there. May I buy you another drink someplace quiet?" Your breeding, as your maiden aunt would say, is evident.

She hesitates.

Ever so casually, you swivel your head as if following the path of a passing car. Because you've allowed her to discreetly check you out, you know she'll feel relaxed enough to relent.

"I was on my way home, but..." she says and then she shifts her weight, wobbling slightly, and you automatically reach for her arm. "I think I had a little too much." The warmth of her breath touches your cheek. "I'm jus' roun' the corner."

"I live nearby, too."

"Really?" she says, tilting towards you. "I'm on Rivingt'n." As the two of you walk, she staggers slightly so you hold her up, you press her to your side, and soon you are steering both her and her sadness into a bodega where you purchase beer and then swiftly you are out again, walking in the street and then up two flights of shadowy stairs to a silent loft, and somewhere in that brief journey you convince yourself that your intentions are, so to speak, fitting.

Once she turns the lights on, the blue comforter bed becomes visible behind a cloth screen and it beckons like a stream-fed pond on a steamy August day. She removes her jacket and then sits to take off her boots. Maxine, humming, pays you no mind.

You say, "Don't you want one of the beers I bought for you?"

She looks up as if confused. "Who...?"

"A beer," you say gesturing. "Got a bottle opener?"

Dutifully, she steps into the kitchen area and returns with an opener. Still wearing one boot, she has made a clumping sound along the hardwood floor and tasteful carpets, yet without embarrassment she hands off the small metal implement. "Thank you, darling," you whisper as she returns to her chair, and then you open two beers. Two perfectly round pills that resemble aspirin tablets slip into the expectant mouth of one. You gesture towards her and once again it takes a moment for you to capture her attention, apparently she does not even register your existence. Unbidden fury, like the flick of a Bic lighter, ignites within you yet you laugh good-naturedly as you place the bottle before her.

Shaking her head no, she smiles.

"I'm your guest," you say with emphasis as you gesture with your own bottle. "Are you going to make me drink alone?"

Despite her inebriation, Maxine's Southern manners remain intact. She takes a long draught and makes a face. "This doesn't taste good."

You shrug. When you speak again, there isn't even a hint of smile in your voice. "One more sip."

Again she tilts the bottle back and seeing her soft white neck, you finally relax.

She yawns as your eyes focus on the kitchen knives, hanging, blades exposed, suspended within a magnetic fixture nailed to the wall beside the stove. Just then she seems to become aware of you and, pacing the room, she wobbles slightly, glancing nervously your way, and then she suggests it might be time for you to leave? You step over to the wall and purposefully stand beside the knives. She appears a little nervous so you wait until she is near the bed, and then in two quick steps you are beside her. Her eyes widen and her lips form a desperate curl, yet she remains silent. Drool forms on the left side of her mouth. You kiss her neck and as you back her toward the bed, she finally says in a small voice, "I'm going to throw up."

"You're fine." You push her and she falls backward. Now, Maxine appears to be floating on blue waters and her eyes close, she finds it difficult to keep them open, and it isn't easy taking off her blouse as you feel yourself harden. The fabric tears and then you are pulling her jeans down, ripping them off her, you didn't let tight jeans stop you with your second temp. You yank once and then once again. Although her eyes won't stay open, Maxine speaks, an odd assortment of words emerge from her lips: "vomit" and "please" and "why," and "home." Once she is still you have a moment to yourself when you can think and that's when you decide she may not be as pretty as you thought. *Is that a mole on her shoulder?* Against the blue, her hair fans out behind her face, which is floating towards you and away again, towards you and away again, and you think suddenly of your step-mother, what a nerve to call herself that, and just then Maxine moans so you lift yourself and stare down at her floating gently on the surface of a summer pond and now her prettiness has returned, but she's not just pretty, she's magnificent. Oddly, you are reminded of the new associate as you begin to move, that friendly girl who laughed when you accidentally mispronounced a word, she is always flipping her hair and laughing, and you hate the sound she makes, you want it to stop. Now you close your eyes and visualize the word—you knew how to say it all along, you just got nervous in front of your boss. Pausing, you test the word aloud, the only sound in a silent room. "Fungible."

Beneath you, Maxine makes no sound and does not laugh. Pleased, you thrust yourself into her inert form.

"Fungible," you whisper before kissing her goodnight.

***

Your wife remains unsoiled in body and mind by your most authentic self. You've been good for too long a time with barely a single interruption last year, the night of her giggly reunion drinks with her college roommate. Dinner with your daughter—your wife's look-alike offspring—had gone well. She sat primly across from you, a linen tablecloth spread like a sleeping woman between you as the waiter, wearing black and white like a Disney movie zebra, wove in and out of your silly conversation, bending to pour pink juice into your daughter's wine glass. Briefly her eyes had turned bold when she told you her goal in life was to become a Montessori teacher. Your own eyes glistened, which the eavesdropping waiter took for pride. "Daddy's girl," he'd fawned, stooping to pick up a fallen napkin.

At home, your daughter took your wife's place beside you on the couch in front of the TV and she sipped tainted pink fluid from a glass you nudged closer, closer to her hand. Just before the vagueness overtook her and she trespassed oblivion an expression reminiscent of your wife transformed her features. A brain short circuit disrupted your momentum … but then the flower of her face lolled on the stem of her neck in a way unlike anything you'd ever seen—from her, from your wife, from anyone. Some inner volume re-amplified.

Later, you stood alone in a warm shower rubbing eucalyptus scented soap into your skin. All those years ago, what was the expression that had transformed the features of your not-yet-wife. Three dates in, you'd been building to a Max-ine-like crescendo and you couldn't help but smile, thinking of the night's antici-pated conclusion. In response, her usual naïve expression had shifted into some-thing that hinted of the puritanical thoughts titrated into her by spinster teachers and unhappily married aunts. There, then, like a flash of inspiration, the limits of her comprehension had suddenly become clear to you. You understood, you just *knew*, that at her best, at her most imaginative, she might suspect some lyrical in-dulgence on your part (a penchant for business trip flings or visits to a trafficked masseuse), but she would never be capable of comprehending the tastes of the man sitting across from her.

Forever beyond her ken: Y.O.U.

And so in one brilliant moment on that night many years ago you had pivoted (as the cow who is your boss likes to say) and all of your cherished dreams suddenly shifted. New intentions instantly replaced the old lifeless one and so you asked her, right there, to be your wife. She sniffled happily. Ordinarily you'd feel embarrassed, but not that night because you knew the ignorant complicity that she could and would so easily supply was necessary food for you… and you were going to get it.

Now, watching her tiptoe towards you, a somnambulist in showering sunlight, you finally understand what you'd never been able to see. She is the negative space balancing the images you create, each a perfect still life that thrills your soul. It is right and good that, of all the women who slumber on soft beds in this hard city, she alone remains forever safe from what is inside you.

Rushing forward now, you greet her, and though her sunlight-blinded reaction is to lift her hand as if warding off a blow, soon enough she's smiling back at you.

Guardian Angel
Richard Zaric

Richard lives in Winnipeg, Manitoba, Canada. Hiding Scars, *his first book, is a historical fiction novel and was published in 2018. He is presently pitching a young adult novel called* Stealing Amazing Fantasy #15. *He won the Two Sisters Publishing Romance Writing Short Story Contest in 2020. His short stories have appeared in several anthologies. He is just as likely to read the latest hot literary novel as he is to flip through an old comic book.*

~

I step through the shimmering portal and instantly find myself in my basement. There's a party going on. A loud one. The music's cranked. Modern stuff I don't recognize. Fifteen, twenty kids, maybe more are scattered about on furniture and cross-legged on the floor.

Over in the corner I see Jarett. He looks older, filled out. When did he start putting crap in his hair? There was a time I had to hold him down to run the brush through his curly black hair. Now it's short and spiky. This scene must be a few years from now.

The place is soaked in booze. Sure, there's beer, but a surprising amount of hard stuff. Rum, vodka, rye. Some of the girls are holding coolers. Why not stick to beer? It's a hell of a lot easier to manage and tastes better.

But something else catches my eye: drugs. There's a lot of pot, and two people are doing lines of coke in the bathroom. I clench my fist. Where's Lindsay? How can she allow something like this? I relax my grip. Of course she wouldn't. She must be off on another business trip. Jarett must have promised that he wouldn't hold a party and she believed him. She always fell for it.

A pretty barefoot girl with straight brown hair gets up and walks right through me. As she does, I can feel a tingling. It's her emotion, a hedonistic bliss. She's also high as a kite. She pauses and shivers for a moment before continuing on.

I can't hang around for too long. I'm already starting to notice that the back of my left hand is paler than before.

***

It all started the day I died. A massive, sudden heart attack while sitting on the toilet at three in the morning. Lindsay probably didn't notice me in the washroom until she got up. I must have been a sight, plopped down on the ground with my pajamas at my ankles and a dirty bum. Not quite the lasting memory I wanted to leave.

The next thing I remember, I was sitting at a desk in my t-shirt and underwear opposite a man with a thin build. He wore a crisp blue suit. Pencil-thin moustache. Short brown hair cut neat. He looked like an investment banker and didn't display any emotion. All business-like.

"You're dead, you know."

"I kind of gathered."

He raised his eyebrows a touch. "Many don't. They think they're in some dream or nightmare. Sometimes I have to call security."

"So what happens next?"

"Your spirit needs to move on. But that can take a bit of time."

"How long…?"

"When you're ready. Time, at least as you know it, doesn't exist here. It's more of a *feeling*, an *emotion*. You will notice yourself starting to fade. When there is nothing left, then you'll have moved on. But you have a choice." Using his sleek silver pen, the man in the blue suit pointed to a doorway leading to a large sitting room, like in a doctor's office. About half the chairs were occupied. Most of the people looked old, in their eighties or nineties, but a sprinkling of a few younger people rounded out the half-full room. They wore whatever they'd died in, hospital gowns for many of the older folks. One younger guy was head to toe in leather with his motorcycle helmet beside him. Several held cups of coffee or water. A few flipped though magazines or newspapers, fidgeting without hand-held electronic devices; some must feel they were in a type of hell. Sports highlights blared from a television in the background.

"Or," the man raised an eyebrow, "you can make amends."

I frowned. "Make amends? How…?"

"You may use your limited time to affect change on the living."

He went on to explain that spirits can enter doors or *portals* into the future. The doors, which resemble large iPad screens, are in a place called the Room of Tomorrows, the portals arranged like the door displays at Home Depot, where you can flip several to see what you like. A spirit can try to interact with the living by entering a portal—a lot of dead people end up going back to try to scare the willies out of those that had wronged them over the years as a way of exacting revenge. The weepy ones try to communicate with loved ones, maybe to say a final goodbye.

Some spirits, however, try to go back to change something, right a wrong.

Difficult because spirits are generally ephemeral, disembodied entities that can go through walls, and usually have a hard time touching anything, but each spirit is different. Some may appear translucent to the living or become visible in mirrors. Some can move creaky doors, unbolt locks, or make a dish fall and smash on the floor.

***

Jarett had always been a handful for me and Lindsay. He cried all night every night when he was a baby. As a toddler he got himself in all kinds of mischief, everything from rolling around in mud puddles to cutting up the crochet tablecloth his grandma had made. He acted up in school, fancied himself the class clown. By the time middle school rolled around he was getting into fights at lunch. He tried his darnedest to hide his cigarettes, but we could smell it on him. In his first year at Prince Edward Academy it didn't take him long to start hanging around with the bad crowd, including the booze and drugs that came with it. He showed up to class drunk or stoned. I have to admit, the Academy gave him leeway, far more than you'd see at a public school. Maybe that's what you get when tuition is five figures. Not that it mattered because they expelled him before Grade 11 was halfway through.

Lindsay and I wracked our brains. What did we do wrong? We didn't smoke. Hardly drank. Both of us had good jobs, so money was never an issue. We put him in the best school. We provided for all his needs and did our best not to spoil him. As we got older we tried tough love but couldn't bring ourselves to throw him out. The rich kids from fancy schools came with their own set of problems, most of them involving entitlement, boredom, and an inflated sense of superiority. Those kids never had to work hard for anything—drowned in the lavish bounty provided by their parents. Maybe Jarret ended up being one of those snot-nosed rich kids?

After Jarett left school it was one dead-end job after another. His paycheques didn't last long. He partied every weekend. The only thing he got better at was hiding the drug use, but we knew it would come to a head eventually. That was right around when I ended up on the bathroom floor.

***

I pondered the choice provided by the man in the blue suit. I could walk away. Get up from the desk and hang out in the waiting room, watch a little TV or flip through a magazine until I faded away. But guilt overwhelmed me. How would Lindsay deal with Jarett, especially while grieving my death? How would Jarett take it? Would he slide further down the rabbit hole?

I had to make a difference. If Jarett turned it around, then great, I'd hang around until I faded away. No need to interfere. Sometimes bad events change people's lives for the better. But more often, it's the opposite.

It took a while to get the hang of the portals in the Room of Tomorrows. Flipping through the alternatives was daunting at first. It didn't help that there's no sound available when viewing the portals. One time I ended up going too far into the future, something like 350 years.

The custodian, a young, blonde-haired woman in a bright red business suit, showed me how to find where I needed to be. She told me that instead of flipping through scenarios, I had to let go. Close my eyes and *feel* for when and where I needed to be. She giggled when I mentioned that it was sort of like The Force. She'd heard that one a lot, apparently.

If I had still possessed a beating heart, that first portal I stepped through would have made it leap into my throat. The scene was my home a few years into the future. Lindsay was sitting upstairs at the kitchen table. As always, the African violet in the blue ceramic pot at the center of the table bloomed lavender blossoms. But Lindsay's eyes were red from sorrow. Her hair, usually full and lush, appeared scraggly and unkempt. Sad, because she almost always looked good. Her job as a lawyer demanded it. But judging by her sallow cheeks and cracked lips, it looked like she hadn't worked for a while. My first thought was that she was still depressed about my passing, but I took a closer look at the table. She was reading an obituary for Jarett. Her tears had already wrinkled the newspaper. I read over her shoulder. He'd died the week before. No cause of death was listed, but the obituary asked for donations to the Green Spruce Recovery Centre, a local substance abuse facility. That could only mean he took his own life, or his last hit was fatal. Maybe both. Jarret never seemed to be the type of make the final cut, so it must have been drugs. Could my death, coupled with Lindsay's depression, have pushed him over the edge to risky behavior, even by his standards? And if so, could I somehow do something to change Jarret's future, nudge him in a different direction?

Using my emotions as a guide made it more likely to find a pivotal moment, a point in time when a key act or decision will have significant consequences. It's at that point when my actions will have the greatest potential impact. The woman in the red suit explained that a person's life travels one way, or linearly, from start to finish. It's easy to predict where someone's life will be at any moment in time because everything's mapped out. When I asked her who does the mapping, she said, "You know."

But everyone's life has forks at key junctures. Some may seem obvious, like getting a new job or the birth of a child. Others are subtle. It could be a chance meeting. Reading something profound. An inspiring musical piece. Anything, really. The decisions made at those junctures irrevocably change the path of life. You can't go back up the stream, but a fading spirit can encourage or bump someone down a different path.

For me, the trick was to identify that moment in Jarett's life, that key decision, where he ended up going down the wrong path, leading to his destruction. Something must have happened at the party. That's when I discovered the portal to Jarett's basement party.

*****

I mill around the basement. Indeed, Lindsay is in Toronto for work. I overhear Jarret mention it to the girl he has his eye on, the barefoot one who phased through me. People are all over the house. Amorous couples have already paired off into some of the bedrooms.

By midnight Jarret is pickled. The intoxicants pumping through his veins are starting to take a toll. He's lost control of the party. Someone puts a crack in the upstairs bathroom mirror. Another spills rum and coke on the pool table. That stain will not come out. I feel like smacking Jarret in the head, but know my hand would probably go through his skull. So far he's held himself to tequila and some weed. Bad enough, but not hardcore.

Aside from passing through people, I have limited control of what I can do. The more people in the immediate vicinity, the less I am able to interact with the environment. In the basement, where there are about 15 or 20 people, my hand passes straight through tangible items like beer bottles, chip bags and pizza boxes. I find that I can make some items move in places where there are few or no people. I can open and close closet doors. I can move lighter items a few inches, and manage to knock over a small, framed wedding picture of Lindsay and myself off the nightstand beside our bed. I pick it up and put it back. The two young lovers twisting in the sheets don't notice. I can walk on the floor or float in the air. I can pass through some of the walls, but not all. Fickle, this spiritual existence.

Around three in the morning a greasy-looking punk with long black hair motions for Jarret to stagger over. I follow my son into the service room beside the washing machine and furnace.

"I got some for you," says Grease Ball, his lips forming a slight smile. He reaches into his pocket.

"Awesome, how much?"

"This one's on me. But be careful" He hands Jarret a small plastic baggie containing a white substance. "It's way more powerful than H."

Jarret slips the baggie into his shirt pocket.

Did Jarret get into harder drugs like opioids after my death or had he always dabbled? What's in the baggie? His serious drug use issues must have escalated from this party.

I need to stop him from taking the contents of the pouch.

The party looks to be dying down; many have left. Several are passed out. One is throwing up in the corner.

Jarret is on the couch doing tequila shots and passing around a joint with the barefoot girl and another guy. The guy takes a last shot, and leaves the party with a friend, leaving Jarret alone with the barefoot girl. Taking the baggie out of his pocket, he shows it to her before motioning upstairs. She smiles, and he takes her by the hand as they get up from the couch.

In his state, would he even notice anything I did? I could try to make it so he could see me, the full-fledged ghost of his father. But would he just consider whatever he saw a hallucination? Attribute it to the poisons and intoxicants swirling in his brain?

They enter his bedroom, where the dull glow from the nightstand light throws long shadows against the wall. They sit on the bed and start to neck, her hands rubbing up and down his back. She shrugs off her shirt, revealing her black bra. Jarret rises from the bed to clear a few items away from the nightstand. He pulls out the tiny baggie. Gingerly, he taps a few specks of power onto the nightstand, then forms them into two thin little lines using a playing card, an Ace of Spades. I bend down and blow.

Nothing.

I crouch down, phasing completely into the nightstand. Positioned right beside the lines, I close my eyes and blow like I'm trying to expand a hot water bottle, and the dust scatters away from the lines.

"Damn it," Jarett mutters. He picks up the Ace of Spades again and starts to reform the two lines. While he does, the barefoot girl runs her hand through his hair. From her smile I can tell she wants something a little more intimate than nose candy.

Distracted, Jarret turns around to kiss the girl, and I manage to grab hold of the playing card and push the two lines off the nightstand. The evil dust falls, hidden in the white carpet. Neither Jarret nor his female friend will be snorting those lines.

But swiping away a drug won't change Jarett's opinions and lifestyle. That requires an intervention. A *real* scare from the ghost of his father. To do that I have to make my body visible. I concentrate in front of Jarett's closet door, which also happens to be a full-length mirror, but can only produce a faint silhouette glow.

Meanwhile, Jarett breaks away from the barefoot girl and looks over to the nightstand. He raises an eyebrow, likely wondering what happened to his lines. He opens the baggie and plops more powder than last time.

"Let's do some of this. It'll make the experience out of this world."

"Do we have to?"

"C'mon, just take a little. It can't hurt…"

The girl smiles and accepts a small straw from Jarret.

I try to block everything out of my mind to make my body appear. He has to *see* me. *Hear* me. Blowing dust around is not enough. As the girl drops the straw on the ground and bends down to reach it, I see myself in the mirror. I'm whole!

"Leave them alone."

My concentration punctures and my image melts away. I look up. There, above the bed, hovers another spirit. This dead man sports a tattoo of an eagle on his neck. His large arms are also intricately tattooed. Definitely tough-looking.

"It's my son," I say. "I have to stop him, nudge him down a different branch." I get up and try to materialize again. The girl is already snorting the white powder off the nightstand.

Mr. Tattoo swoops down and holds me back. "No, let them be."

"Let go! This might be my only chance." I grapple with Mr. Tattoo. We phase in and out of each other. Occasionally a hand or an arm gets stuck inside the other before loosening. I got a few shots in, but the man succeeds in preventing me from distracting Jarret. My son snorts a line and snaps his head back, wide eyed.

Too late. Damn! I drop my head down. No sense in fighting any longer. Mr. Tattoo sits beside me on the ground near the bed. His determined frown dissolves into something resembling grim relief.

"Why did you do that?" I yell. "I was trying save my son's life. I might not get another chance." Already my left arm looks paler than it had before I entered the portal. The right hand is also starting to show signs of fading.

Beside us, Jarrett and the girl had already shed their clothes and became a mass of writhing limbs. Mr. Tattoo gets up. "Let's leave them alone. I don't want to see this any more than you do."

I reluctantly him follow through several walls into Lindsay's office. A trio of kids are sitting on the chaise lounge in the corner sipping dark drinks, probably rum and Cokes.

Mr. Tattoo faces me. "Sorry, that's my daughter in there. I had to stop you, or Emma would end up going down the wrong path."

I frown. "Wrong path? She just did a line of hard drugs with my son and now she's getting banged by him. You think that's the *right* path?"

"It might not seem like it, but yeah." Mr. Tattoo folds his thick arms across his muscular chest. "I know what happens if your kid sees you. But your appearance and the little speech you were about to give to him wouldn't have mattered to *him*. Actually nothing you could do will matter. It will end badly for him anyway."

I clench my fist, emotion exploding in my skull.

Mr. Tattoo unfolds his arms and tenses, his bulging biceps as big as cantaloupes. "You wanna fight, then let's fight. Bring it on. I don't give a shit."

I unclench my fist and snort as I look away. "What do you mean it'll end *bad?* You couldn't let me try?"

He narrows his eyes. "As much as I don't want her doing drugs or screwing around, she had to do it on this night. Your son ends up forgetting about her because he gets too high. He eventually gets addicted and then ODs a few years later. What just happened here leads Emma down a road to chemical dependency that lasts almost five years. But at the end of it she comes out a better person, meets someone nice and life goes on for her. If you prevented your son from taking that hit, or any of the others that followed, he ends up dragging Emma down with him. And it all would have started tonight."

I shake my head. It doesn't make sense. "But if I don't do anything, Jarret dies."

"Did you even bother looking at the future scenarios and potential branches in the Room of Tomorrows? The chick in the cowboy boots and Daisy Dukes showed me how to check the likelihood of events taking place."

"Daisy Dukes? Mine wore a red business suit and didn't show me anything about event probabilities. The guy in the blue suit behind the desk gave me a choice to fade away or affect change, but he didn't really explain anything either."

Mr. Tattoo's face scrunches into bewilderment. "Blue suit? My guy behind the desk had a leather jacket and a ball cap. He set a couple of thugs on me, too. Anyway, it doesn't matter what you do. Your kid's a prick. He always was, always will be. You might love him to pieces, but it doesn't change what he is."

"What gives you the right to condemn my son? Maybe he'll turn things around."

"No, he won't. I looked. Every scenario ends the same way: He packs it in. The only difference is he either dies sooner or he dies a little later but in the process brings ruin and destruction to other people's lives." He pauses for a moment. "Look, just before I died I had a moment of clarity and knew I had to make a difference. Emma never really knew me. I took off on her and her mom when she was just a rug rat. I skipped the country to avoid support payments and did some real shit. That clarity bought me more time than what most spirits are given. I spent the equivalent of years looking at all the different scenarios in the portals. And in every case, your kid screws up. No way am I going to let him wreck Em's life."

Mr. Tattoo drifts through the wall, leaving me staring at the ground, the three kids sipping their rum and Cokes in the corner of the room.

***

Mr. Tattoo is right. Back in the Room of Tomorrows I scan different scenarios in alternate time branches. In each one Jarett ends up either dying really young or hanging around a little longer and buggering up other people's lives before meeting an untimely end. I feel a lump form in my fading throat.

I sit in the lone chair in the Room, my head down in my translucent hands. I can see straight through portions of my body, including my arms and legs. The rest of my body exudes an opaque glow like from a weak low-wattage nightlight. My time is coming to an end. Just as well. It never really amounted to much. Lindsay and I must have raised Jarret wrong, right from the start. Maybe he had too much attention, being the only child? Or maybe we weren't on him enough? It doesn't matter now. I'm a loser and waiting to move on. Might as well spend the remaining moments in the waiting room. Maybe watch the last bit of TV before my spirit vanishes forever.

I walk past a bank of portals and flip through them randomly. The scenes all seem so sad. Funerals, accidents, losing a job, dead pets, speeding tickets. I don't look up, but I can hear high heels clicking on the tiled floor. The woman in the red suit tells me that it's my mood. The portals are tied to my melancholy feelings. I pause and close my eyes, trying to think happy thoughts and memories. It takes a while.

When I reopen my eyes, the portals have changed. Cheerful. Fun. Carefree. Lindsay is in most of them. In one she looks twenty years older, her hair cut short, and she's let it go grey. She's with another man, and they're both wearing wedding rings. We never brought it up that much, but on a few occasions we

37

agreed that if one of us went, the other should move on.

The woman in the red suit points out that it's an alternate reality. That scene *might* occur, but probably not. "See the percentage at the bottom of the portal." The screens have numbers and statistics along the sides and bottom; numbers, letters and percentages that appeared random—I hadn't paid attention to them until now. This one reads 12.3%. The woman takes me to another bank of scenarios and picks another. It features Lindsay, attending a concert at the symphony. The woman runs her index finger along the bottom of the scenario until her red fingernail comes to a number. 6747. She then walks back to the portal with Lindsay happily married with a new man and enters the number into the portal. For a few seconds the percentage changes from 12.3% to 13.4%. The woman points to the number. "See… if your wife attends the symphony on that particular night, the chance of the future event occurring—the one where she re-marries—only goes up a percentage point." Attending the symphony doesn't cause a major shift in her stream.

That's how Mr. Tattoo must have done his research. He mixed and matched different events and outcomes to see what was most likely to occur. "Why didn't anyone tell me how this room worked?"

The woman in red smiles. "You never asked. But I can see you're near the end of the line, so it doesn't matter much anymore." She walks away. Great, even here there's crappy service. I look down at my fading body, feeling a twinge of sadness in the pit of my stomach.

There's no time to affect any change and even if I did, it wouldn't matter to Jarret. I can't help him and the devastation cripples Lindsay. A crushing sense of defeat cuts through my soul, and the portals change. I flip back to the scene of Lindsay crying over Jarett's obituary. I look at another one. I can't tell when it took place, but it had to be some time after, judging from the African violet in the middle of the table. The plant looks a little larger and thicker. Is it six months later, or a year? The window is open and there's a healthy breeze bouncing the curtains, twitching the leaves of the African violet.

Lindsay's cell is in her hand, and she is entering a number from a piece of paper on the table. I hover over for a closer look, but when she gets to the last digit, a stiff gust blows the scrap of paper to the ground. She starts to bend down, but then pauses and straightens up. Leaving it on the ground, she exits the room, and reenters carrying an empty clothes basket, stepping on the scrap of paper before continuing on down into the basement. I glance at the scenario number, 78345. I pause for a moment to think cheerful enough thoughts to locate the alternate scene in the distant future where Lindsay is happily re-married. I enter

78345 at the bottom of the portal. 5.2%. This future scene has an even worse effect.

I flip over to the very next scene, number 78346. It looks similar. Same setting in the kitchen. But in this one Lindsey enters the entire phone number. She paces back and forth while talking to someone. Damn, I wish I could hear what she's saying. The conversation is short, only about a minute. When it ends, she puts the scrap of paper on the table and leaves the room. Just like in the other scenario, a gust of wind blows the piece of paper onto the floor. But this time, when Lindsay comes back with the laundry basket, she picks up the paper and puts it in the front pocket of her jeans. I enter 78346 on the touch screen at the bottom of the distant future scene where she's remarried. 95.7%. Bingo.

The problem is that the original scene of her leaving the paper on the ground and not making a call is part of the current time stream. I have to do something to bump her into the other possible future reality. She has to make that call.

I go through the portal of the main time stream, the one most likely to occur. Lindsay is still downstairs with the laundry basket, likely folding clothes or something. I look down at the paper still on the floor. *Grant* is written just above the phone number—perhaps her potential future second husband. I try to pick up the paper, but I can't see my left hand, much less touch anything with it. My right isn't much better. At most, the paper flutters gently as my fingers pass through it, and even that small movement might have been from the wind.

Never did care much for open windows. Lindsay always liked having them open. In the height of summer she'd open everything up in the morning, letting in all the humidity. By one or two in the afternoon the A/C would work overtime getting the house back to a reasonable temperature, only to repeat it again the next day. She especially liked everything open on exceptionally windy days, like on this one; papers and anything else that wasn't tied down would float around or get knocked to the floor. I told her that one day something big would fall over.

Something big. The African violet on the table. The velvety leaves and lavender blooms are jiggling like Jell-O from the stiff breeze. I try to use what remains of my right hand and arm to move the plant. Nothing. I'm too late. I hear her close the door to the laundry room downstairs. She will be upstairs in a moment.

I phase into the table and try to push the plant, but again, my hand passes straight through it. I concentrate harder, but still nothing. I look at my belly. It appears more solid than my extremities. Positioning my stomach behind the African violet, I close my eyes and slowly walk forward. I can feel the pressure of the pot against my gut. It's working. The plant skitters toward the edge of the table.

Lindsay reaches the top step just as the blue pot smashes on the floor. Mud and ceramic fragments explode in all directions.

"Damn it," Lindsay says. She places the filled laundry basket near the top of the stairs and grabs the broom from the narrow storage closet beside the pantry. "He always said something would fall over. He was right."

Lindsay throws the plant in a black garbage bag and sweeps the mess on the floor into a pile, including the phone number that had fallen to the ground. She notices it while sweeping debris into a dustpan and reaches for the slip of paper. At that very instant, I make another decision. I phase into her body.

She shivers. I can feel the deep sadness and grief of her empty heart. Her loneliness and yearning for compassion and companionship. She wants to move on. *Make the call, Lindsay. Make it.*

I phase out of her. Lindsay's face is pale. Her beautiful blue eyes are open as wide as they can go. She looks back down at the phone number and wipes away bits of mud.

She closes the kitchen window, dust and dirt from the smashed plant swirling around the room behind her. "It's a sign," she whispers, picking up a broken piece of the blue ceramic pot from the pile. "No way this should have fallen off the table. It's too heavy." She looks back to the note in her hand. "He always said that if anything happened…"

She palms her moist eyes, regains her composure and then grabs the phone from her back pocket. I look down but can barely make out my body. I smile and let myself fade away into nothingness.

Stuffing Bodies
Michael Craigwell

Michael Craigwell is an American author who lives in Scotland. Originally from Kentucky, he has lived in cities across the U.S. and abroad, from Birmingham, Alabama to Chicago, Paris, Providence, Rhode Island and New York City. When he's not writing, you can find him walking his Great Dane puppy with his family in Edinburgh, where he owns a pub. He is represented by Lynnette Novak of the Seymour Literary Agency.

~

Marianne stopped the rental car, double-checked the address. The great antebellum house on her right was surrounded by a hedge and electrified perimeter fence. A uniformed guard approached from the gate. Was this it? Yellow leaves—almost neon on the grass—piled at the base of a big tree in the front lawn. There were still leaves in the trees here, not like in Central Park, where by early November, most were already bare. She rolled down her window. The guard sniffed, red-cheeked in the chill.

"Help you?" he said.

"I'd like to see the Governor," she said gave him her New Jersey driver's license.

He checked with a video intercom and finally came back to the car, returned her license. "Straight through there."

She thanked him, the gates opened, and she drove along a cobblestone path to the front steps and marble columns. A secret service agent took her keys, and a Black, uniformed butler opened the front door. Inside, Marianne walked from the mirrored entry hall to a parlor of flowery couches and marble tables with busts of Robert E. Lee and Ronald Reagan. The Governor sat in a chair near the far wall, speaking into a hands-free telephone as a bald aide asked for his signature on papers, shuffling folders and paper-clipped packets to and from nearby piles.

"I understand, certainly," the Governor was saying. When he saw Marianne, he gestured to the couch, mouthed, *Sit, please,* and said, "Well. Check the third district." Still signing papers, he continued, "Those numbers don't match, that's all I'm saying. Listen, I've got to run. I'll have Tony schedule us for next Tuesday. The Italian restaurant in Louisville—that's the one. Okay, 'till then."

As the Governor approached, Marianne's first thought was that he was bigger than he looked on television, and his handshake was soft. In a blue sweater and jeans, he might have been a local history professor—was there even a university in Shelbyville?—but yes, she recognized the confidence and easy smile that had won him the last debate. Marianne felt as though she already knew him. Of course, Thomas, her husband and editor, had warned her about Morris's charisma, but to sit beside the Governor felt familiar—as if she hadn't been herself until now.

"Please, sit—sit," he said, and to his aide, "We'll pick it up tonight, thanks Tony." When Tony left, Morris said, "Tony is the Kingmaker here. I'm sure you two will chat later. He found me in a Church one day, showed me his credentials, and here we are. Can I get you anything to drink?" he asked, and before she could respond, he was walking her through a cherry dining room, into a granite-steel kitchen. Two days before Tuesday's election, the Governor had returned to Kentucky to spend Sunday with his family: it had earned him another two percentage points in the latest polls.

Morris opened the refrigerator. "*Colleen?*"

A Black woman appeared at the door. "Sir?"

"Do we have any more of that Paté from last Friday?"

The woman laughed. "Mr. Morris, Angela ate that the next morning."

Angela was the Governor's oldest daughter, and now he made a face. "Ugh. Paté for breakfast—I suppose they're only teenagers once." He took an apple.

Colleen said, "That's right, sir. Get you anything?"

"No thank you, Colleen. I think we're fine." To Marianne, "Every once in awhile, the girls need a break from the campaign trail. You don't mind if we take this to my private office?"

"Please—wherever you're most comfortable." A door opened to carpeted basement stairs, and at the bottom, a table was heaped with papers and shiny instruments. Marianne saw bolt cutters, stained, as if had been used to chop brick. At the far corner of the table, she glimpsed a grid gameboard set with odd, glistening pieces in the center, surrounding by whiteish stumps. Through another passage, the Governor finally stopped at a heavy door locked with three bolts.

"Sometimes even I need privacy," he said. One by one, he unlocked the bolts, then opened the door to a small room with bare walls, a vacant desk, and a black couch. "Here we are."

Marianne sat on the couch. "This is your private room?"

He sat at the desk. "You don't use a recorder?"

"No." She rubbed tension from her forehead. "I have a few starter questions if you don't mind. Let's begin with the New Hampshire primary, and . . . I'm sorry."

He took a bite of his apple. "Is something wrong?"

"I'm sorry, sir. I feel like—you've probably heard this before . . . We don't know each other. We've never met, have we?"

"I do meet a lot of people."

"I apologize. Thank you again for agreeing to speak with the *Times*. In New Hampshire . . ."

He adjusted the apple, swallowed. "I didn't agree to speak with your paper. I agreed to speak with you. I know I shouldn't—sentiment is for the weak and all that—but I still don't sleep soundly thinking about your mother."

My *mother*? Marianne hadn't thought about her mother in a year, maybe longer. Not since . . . wait. A knot tightened in her mind when she focused on the memory. Mom left, didn't she? Like Dad.

No.

Thomas would have called this another of her 'brain farts' or 'early onset dementia.' Not funny, but he always chuckled when she suddenly couldn't recall something obvious. She was just tired.

The Governor was still smiling, holding the apple, waiting. What was this? Two days before the election he would never—Governor Morris was too intelligent to sabotage his career. Was this about sex? Jesus Christ. "Governor, perhaps I should have a pen. I'll only be a minute out to my car . . ."

He set the half-eaten apple on the desk. "So you're not interested anymore?"

"In New Hampshire—"

"No." He stood. He wasn't smiling anymore. "You called me."

Marianne's voice was weak, "I'm sorry?"

"One week ago, you called." He went to the door. "Didn't you?"

Get up, Marianne told herself. "Yes."

"You asked me a question on the phone. Do you remember?"

"Who is Anne Mallory?" she said.

"Who is Anne Mallory," he repeated, and as she stood, he stepped out and slammed the door. Marianne heard the bolts lock, but she didn't scream. Not yet.

***

Near the metal detectors at Louisville Muhammad Ali International Airport, a thick man in an untucked suit held a sign that read, *Anne Mallory*. Anne waved—the driver saw her. She passed an elaborate display of Jim Beam bourbon bottles, a chain restaurant, and a vast horse sculpture on her way down to the baggage claim. When Anne collected her suitcase, she followed the driver to a key-scratched town car, and they started to her hotel. Her cellphone rang: her mother thanked Anne for a vase of flowers that had just been delivered.

"Happy birthday," Anne said. "I'm sorry I can't be there tonight."

"Everyone has different priorities," her mother said. "Family isn't as important to you as it is to others. Some of us build our lives around our family. Golden handcuffs."

That phrase always grated—and it wasn't even original. Mom cribbed it from Nan, who used to say in her Irish lilt, '*Your mother was my golden handcuff, Anne-Marie-dear, but we love our children anyway …*' When Anne was just a kid herself, she remembered Nan told her that. Maybe it was Nan's accent or the way her stare could brighten into an easy smile without warning, but growing up, Anne never knew if her grandmother was serious. Never really found out either—and didn't want to. Especially at the end.

Anne took a slow breath. "I'm in Kentucky for my job, Mom."

"Your *job*," her mother said, as if it were a bad word. "When you find a coin, give it away."

Anne remembered that old saying from childhood, too. Mom's birthday was making her nostalgic. She was playing her greatest hits today. Christmas at Nan's second-floor walkup out in Marine Park, maybe twenty years ago: back then, Nan stood over the stove, lecturing Mom about how working too much brought bad luck. '*Evil smells greed. If you find a coin …*'

"But hey," Anne's mother continue on the phone, "I'm only your mother, what do I know?" She asked Anne about Thomas, as she always did. At least once a week, her mother wondered aloud when Thomas would finally propose.

"We're fine," Anne said. "Look, I have to go."

"Okay, I love you, Anne-Marie."

"Love you too, mom."

At a hotel in downtown Louisville, she collapsed onto a thick mattress and called the Councilman's campaign manager. "Hi, is this Tony? This is Anne Mallory from the *Times*. Yes, just this minute . . . . Well tonight, if you don't mind. Great. See you then."

She hung up and watched a *Gilligan's Island* rerun, showered, then put on a purple dress and her wool coat. The Councilman was waiting in the lobby. Perched in a high-back chair, he frowned at a coffee-table chessboard that looked like it had been arranged as short-hand for 'cultured guests only.' He doesn't look like a politico, Anne thought, not like the local papers had depicted him. He might have been a therapist or an off-duty fireman, not a ruthless fundraiser and dynamic—"ground-shaking," they called him—public speaker.

"Councilman Morris," Anne said, and when he smiled, she understood:

this is what they meant. This is what worried the incumbent Governor. At the University of Michigan, Anne had majored in ancient history—not communications—and, guided by a socialist advisor, she had learned to argue in favor of the economics of world events, against the personalities of the actors. Caesar had been a product of his times, no more ambitious or capable than hundreds of similar, long-dead aristocrats. The underlying economy and the mass-movement of social fault-lines had brought down the Republic. Now, Anne knew better.

"It's so wonderful that you could be here, Ms. Mallory. I hope you had a safe flight."

"Yes, thank you." She scanned the lobby. "I spoke to your campaign manager on the phone . . ."

"He'll be along shortly. Do you play?" He nodded to the chessboard.

"No." She did but not since NYU—and not well enough to let this turn into some kind of pre-interview test.

"Do you know they have names for all the pieces?"

"I'm sorry?"

He crouched by the chessboard table, as if he wanted a better look. A nice set, sure, but it was clearly decorative. What was this?

"Is it too much of a cliché to talk chess during a political campaign?" He shrugged. "The pawns look identical, don't they?" He lifted a white pawn from in front of the queen, then a second pawn from its place by the horse-shaped knight. "Same pieces, different identities." Carefully, he swapped the pawns. "Queen pawn—or D-pawn—becomes knight pawn. Same pawn, same purpose; different identity." He straightened again, wiped off his hands, and smiled. "Forgive my little eccentricities. You must be hungry. In my experience, reporters always are."

She laughed, and they walked outside like old friends. Anne had only been promoted from an assistantship two years earlier; she'd never covered national politics, and this—a city-councilman's challenge to the mighty Governor of Kentucky—was hardly a serious assignment. The real action was elsewhere. This would be a week in Kentucky to watch the leaves change; just long enough to post a handful of Page 13 stories, which might or might not be dumped to the website. 'If national elections are theater,' Thomas had told her. 'Regional elections are cable-access. And remember, the theater is dead anyway.' The white-linen restaurant, *Vincenzo's*, was full of candlelight and Italian-accent waiters. After they ordered wine and antipasto, a bald man joined them. "Ms. Ellis, I'm so happy to meet you," the man said with a soft accent—not southern. What was it? His fingers were cold.

"Mallory," she said. "Anne Mallory."

He smiled. "That's a strong, old name. What luck meeting you here."

"Anne," Morris said, "let me introduce my overworked campaign manager, Tony—you two spoke on the phone."

Tony poured himself a glass of wine. "The veal is excellent," he told Anne. "The way you can really *taste* the meat . . ." He kissed his fingers. "It always makes me laugh."

That's when she tasted the smell. An antiseptic cleaning odor, it reminded her of a janitor's bucket; the scent of a grammar school cafeteria after a child vomits. Anne held the wine to her nose to settle her stomach—the taste of meat is *funny?* she thought—and as Tony spoke to the Councilman, she tried to place his accent. Almost Irish, his voice sounded strangely Brooklyn on a handful of words. Like Nan's old neighborhood.

". . . fliers will be done by morning," Tony was saying. "I have five-hundred more volunteers delivering yard signs through the end of the week, and I'm working to double the call center rotations, but the national funds still haven't cleared . . ."

Morris nodded to Anne. "Is something wrong?"

The waiter returned and they placed their orders: Morris asked for the lasagna; Tony ordered veal; and Anne chose chicken parmigiana with a side of steamed broccoli. The waiter filled their glasses, and when he left, Anne turned to Tony.

"Your accent isn't Kentucky," she said. "Where are you from, if you don't mind?"

Tony shifted, as if his chair were too small. He glanced at Morris, who shrugged, still smiling pleasantly. "Hell," Tony said, "my accent is from Hell."

Anne's stomach clenched, and they all laughed. But the choke-pain in her lungs didn't go away. She took a slow breath, finished her wine. They talked poll numbers and the business of newspaper consolidations for the rest of the meal, and when Anne returned to her hotel room at 10:32, she took a digital recorder from her purse, pressed Rewind. It was all official, after all. Subjects tended to speak more freely when they thought she would be relying exclusively on her memory for quotations. She hit Play.

". . . allory." The rattle of dishes and background rumble of dinner table conversations. "Anne Mallory."

Static, then Morris's voice: "Anne, let me introduce my overworked campaign manager, Tony." Murmuring voices in the backdrop. "You two spoke on the phone."

The sound hissed with white noise, as if the hard drive were damaged. The hotel room suddenly felt very small, the lights too dim. The walls were black-shadow.

The static broke—Morris said, "Is something wrong?"

The waiter's voice: "Have we decided? Councilman, would you like to start?"

Morris: "Certainly. I'll have the lasagna."

The hotel phone rang. Anne let it ring again.

"And you, sir?" Static on the recorder, and then the waiter said, "Very good, sir. Ma'am?"

Anne's voice: "Can I have the Chicken Parm—does that come with a side?"

The phone rang a third time. She turned off the recorder. Just Tony's voice. Sound cut-out when he spoke, as if he'd been speaking through an electronic scrambler or—

She picked up the phone. "Hello?" Wind and a soft gurgle, like water down a pipe. "Hello?"

". . . Anne-Marie?"

The voice was far-away, as if she'd imagined the word. "Hello?" Anne sat on the edge of the bed. "Mom?"

"Anne-Marie . . . he found me . . ."

"Mom? What's wrong, are you . . ." A dial tone: there hadn't been anyone there. She hung up, and, fingers shaking, misdialed—"Jesus, stop it. You're tired. It's nothing—stop."—she punched her mother's home phone number. The line rang. Again. Mom always answered after two rings. The answering machine clicked on.

"Hello, you've reached Margaret Mallory. I can't come to the phone right now because I'm being raped and murdered . . ."

Anne balled her hands into fists. What the fuck? Mom's voice was casual, almost bored.

". . . he's forcing me to watch as he feeds my intestines to a dog. Please leave your name and number at the beep and I'll call you back as soon as I can. Thank you."

Beep.

"Jesus Christ, mom—what was that? If you're there, answer the phone. Mom? Why did you change your—that's not funny. I'm calling Doctor Norman in the morning. You're going to scare people with that message. Pick up the phone." Anne waited, the phone trembling against her cheek. "I'm at a hotel called the Seelbach. Call me back."

Anne hung up and sat for a long moment watching the receiver. She'd forgotten the garbled voice recording. She grabbed the phone again, called the police. They transferred her to the Hoboken police department. Two hours later, still dressed and staring at a late night talk show, Anne heard the phone ring, and she started to cry.

***

The apple was long-gone. On the couch, one arm over her eyes to block out the overhead glow—no light switches—Marianne told herself again that she was in no real danger. Realistically, what could happen? *My voice*, a part of her said, *but it was my voice. And his, and*—stop it. *He can't keep me here*, she told herself. *Thomas will wonder why I don't check-in tonight, and tomorrow he'll ask questions: the police will trace my rental car here. And then? Governor Morris might invent a story, but the police will press on, and someone—a secret service agent?—will remember seeing me enter the house, never leave. They'll search the mansion, they'll find me here.* Marianne tried to ignore the urge to pee.

A bolt clicked.

She held her breath, a second bolt clicked, and now the third bolt. Marianne rolled over, started to stand—stopped. An old woman stood in the doorway. She was pale, bright blue veins in her cheeks and neck, and she wore a green bathrobe. Her fingernails and her lips were purple. The woman stared at Marianne—the basement behind her was dark—and Marianne heard a rough *scrape-scrape*, as if someone were sawing a log in half.

"I . . ." *Move.* Marianne stood. "I have to go."

The old woman looked confused. "Where?"

"My car." She approached the woman. "Thank you for opening the door."

"He's going to make me vote on Tuesday," the woman said. Her teeth were nicotine-yellow. "I voted for Dick Nixon in '68, but I don't want to vote for the Governor—the laughing man will make me." She took Marianne's arm, her fingers rough. "Your grandmother warned me never to listen to his song. She said he danced while her brother burned alive. He's not a god, she told me . . ."

"I'm sorry." Marianne stepped past the woman. "I have to go." One hand on the wall, Marianne walked into the darkness.

The old woman called, "Lorrie-Anne knew him. On the green hills, they all knew him. Morris is just a man, but *he* is something else. Please don't go, Anne-Marie."

Marianne looked back. "What did you call me—" And ahead, the bald aide—Tony—looked up from a couch. He held a hacksaw, and there was something big on the table in front of him.

48

"She let you out?" he asked with an Irish accent—no, not quite Irish.

The old woman started to shake. "Please Anne-Marie, help me."

"That's not . . ." Marianne watched Tony circle closer. "Stop," she said.

Strangely, he did. The thing on the table stirred. Oh Jesus.

"Please let me go," Marianne said.

A body pulled itself up from the table, its head drooping sideways on a gaping neck. Ignoring Marianne, Tony raised his eyebrows at the old woman, and the thing slouched closer. One of its arms was gone in a stump, and there were human faces—eyeless, gaping mouths and iron-flattened noses—sewn into its bare torso. Its blue-painted head looked from Marianne to the old woman, and it shuffled closer.

"Stop . . ." Marianne's legs wouldn't work. "Please . . ."

"Anne-Marie . . ."

"Not my name," Marianne murmured, and when the thing staggered close, she screamed, hands up to protect her face. It limped past, approaching the old woman.

Tony said, "Politics is hell, ain't it?"

"Anne-Marie, no—" The thing backed the old woman into the office—she screamed—muffled when the door slammed. But Marianne still heard her, and now there was a barking growl, a snarling, and the screams jolted and gasped in wet shudders. Marianne tasted bile.

"Please," she said. As the woman's shrieks became a wounded animal begging for mercy, a primitive part of Marianne prickled, and she blinked tears. "Please . . . stop."

Tony tapped her shoulder with his hacksaw. "Why did you call the Governor?"

"I heard a recording . . ." Marianne tried to slow her breathing. "A voice—my voice—talking to the Governor. Only he wasn't the Governor. He was just a Councilman. But that isn't my name. Why don't I remember?" The screaming stopped. "Who was that woman?"

When he leaned closer, Tony smelled of harsh disinfectant, as if he'd been coated with cheap soap. Marianne retched, covered her mouth—nothing came out.

"She's a friend of a friend," he said.

"I just want to go. Please let me go."

"No one ever won an election without stuffing a few ballot boxes, stuffing a few bodies. Am I right, Anne?"

She swallowed, stomach turning. "My name . . ."

He guided her toward the table. The grid game board was still there. It came into focus as she approached: rows of flesh were clustered in the center, surrounded on four sides by trios of severed fingers. Little knobs of meat, with pale, discolored fingers around the edges.

He noticed her staring. "Oh, do you play? No? The President loves his chess, but I always preferred *Fidchell*. The highwayman game. It's cleaner." A film of dark blood and yellowish fluid coagulated on the game board. "It's more true to life, I think. When pieces are cornered—like you and your mother—they just go away."

My mother. Again, the thought brought a frustrating hole where shapes and feelings should have been in her memory. Like a dream that had been scrubbed away.

"Do you want to remember? Would that be helpful?" He said it, as if she were a child who hadn't been paying attention.

Suddenly, she was a little girl standing in the July heat on Nan's stoop. Memories blotted back in emotional spurts, almost too fast to follow. Watching older kids race down the block with Independence Day sparklers, Anne had overheard her mother laugh off something Nan said. A snatch of conversation about family debts and the evil eye.

"Your people came all the way across the ocean to hide from me," he said. "Like all the others. But I promised Lorrie-Ann I would take her daughter. And your mother will burn ... after the polls close, of course. You are a lucky bonus."

Anne's Nan was named Lorrie-Ann, born in County Cork. And Mom ... Oh, Jesus.

"Now," he said, smiling, "let's see if we can't get that skin off of you."

The lights came on, and Anne heard herself scream.

***

"All in the merry month of May . . . When the green buds they were swellin' . . . Young William Green on his deathbed lay . . . For the love of Barbary Allen . . ."

Anne sipped her coffee, stared bleary-eyed at the modest Polling Station 38 sign taped outside Saint Andrew's First Church of God. It had been a rough week. When they found her mother—'Not anything you want to hear about,' the policeman said on the phone. 'We'll need you to come in.'—she went home. They'd lost her suitcase flying back, and in New Jersey, she'd signed papers, arranged for the funeral and called her aunt Sophia, her cousins in Pennsylvania and Detroit. Anne even emailed a few of Mom's more distant relatives back in Ireland—Nan's side of the family—but none of them came. It had been a small, cold funeral on Friday. Early November rain had chilled her through her heavy coat and scarf.

Now, Anne heard a woman sing a sad, high song out the open window of an idling car:

"He sent his servant to the town . . . To the place where she was dwellin' . . . Sayin', Master's sick and he sends for you . . . If your name be Barbary Allen . . ."

Still early, but a few voters were arriving—the polls had only just opened. Anne watched an Indian woman with a baby and a group of young businessmen.

After the funeral, Anne had insisted to Thomas that she was fine, that she needed to be alone. When he'd protested, they'd had an ugly fight. At home, Anne had made a bowl of popcorn and dumped it in the garbage. She'd sat on her living room couch and wept for her mother while rain throttled the windows.

"So slow-lie, slow-lie she got up . . . And slow-lie she came nigh him . . . And all she said when she got there . . . Young man, I believe you're dying . . ."

Anne had turned on the television, flipped channels and stopped: clips from political races across the country, and she'd watched the incumbent Governor of Kentucky falter and search for words, watched his polite, good-humored Councilman opponent smile and say, "I believe that God has given our people a choice. We are a proud nation, a *just* nation." And Anne had been convinced that he was smiling at her through the screen. "And we are strong enough to find our true path again. I am ready to lead you there." The screen had cut to the national broadcaster, who now declared the Kentucky Gubernatorial election a 'dead heat.' Over the weekend, Councilman Morris had gained even more ground, and now he was projected to win by eight percentage points. She'd told Thomas that she needed time. This time, he hadn't argued.

"Oh yes, I'm low, I'm very low . . . And death is on me dwellin' . . ."

Anne approached the idle sedan and waved to Tony, the Councilman's bald campaign manager. Somehow, she wasn't surprised to see him.

"No better, no better I'll never be . . ."

She called, "Would you mind turning that down?"

He cupped a hand to his ear. "What?"

She walked closer. "Turn it down."

"If I can't get Barbary Allen—"

He clicked off the stereo. "You've come back to the Bluegrass State, Ms. Mallory. Shouldn't you be in New Jersey?"

"Absentee ballot."

"What brings you here?"

She pointed to a Starbucks across the street. "Coffee."

"The Governor would like to speak with you. I'll drop you back here when you're done."

She sniffed her coffee. He was the reason she'd come back, after all. A compulsion to watch it end; *I have to see him again.* Anne hopped into the passenger seat.

"The election isn't over," Anne said. "You're not superstitious?"

Tony barked a laugh. "Superstitious?"

"You called him the 'Governor,' but the polls—"

"Oh sure it is. All we have to do now is count ballots." He turned onto a road that bordered a vast cemetery, slowed to squint through the gates: lots of people walked between the headstones, but that was strange, Anne thought, *where are all of the cars?* They drove on, and at the next red light, when Anne asked where they were going, he said, "Shelbyville polling place—the Governor is voting, having his picture taken." They approached an Interstate 64 highway ramp. "It's not far."

Anne watched Louisville diminish into cornfields and housing developments. A sign passed: *Shelbyville: 15 miles.*

"It was a shame about your mother."

Anne put her hands on the cardboard coffee cup, watched steam rise through the drinking hole. "Yes. It's been hard."

"Was she politically active?"

"I'd rather not talk about her." Anne burned her tongue on the coffee. *Shelbyville: 8 miles.* "How did you know I would be at that church?"

"Hey, come on now." He held up one hand, as if surrendering, and she smelled it again: industrial cleaner, bleach. "Where I grew up, we had a saying that you can't change the destination, only the route."

"Where was that?"

"Ah, it's all condos and hotels now. No one in Dublin even remembers my name."

"You're from—"

"I told you, I grew up there. Wasn't born there. America is much more fun— the people here have a sense of humor."

They turned onto the Shelbyville exit, past a clump of truck stop chain restaurants, and continued to a neighborhood of giant sequoias and antebellum mansions. They pulled into a handicapped parking space alongside a red-brick public school. *Polling Station 07.* People crowded the lawn, and there were at least three camera crews: there. Morris was smiling with a line of uniformed children. He shook hands with a teacher, then—when he saw Anne and Tony—called, "Thank you very much for your time everyone. I can't wait to have a beer." Laughter from the crowd. Morris met them on the school steps.

"No troubles?" Morris asked Tony.

"None."

"Excellent. Ms. Mallory, I am so happy you could join us again. I was sorry to hear about your mother."

Well-dressed people flowed around them on their way to the polls. Look at them, Anne thought. They're not . . . . The women, white-haired and thin, wore elegant dresses and pearls; the men came in full suits.

Morris smiled and nodded to the voters. "It was cancer, did you say? Terrible thing."

"No, not cancer." Anne watched the mob of silent, elderly couples approach the school, but no one—not the news cameras or the school children—seemed to notice anything odd. There were hundreds of people. "I don't understand. I've never seen anything like this."

"Tony is the miracle man," Morris said. "Get out the vote."

"Who are they?" Anne said. They smelled like fresh dirt and leaves. "They're almost ..." She felt dizzy. "They're dead."

Tony and Morris exchanged a look, and the Councilman clapped an old man on the shoulder in a cloud of dust. "Well. Yes."

They weren't all old: Anne saw bored twenty-somethings and a black woman with a pair of babies. "They can't be registered," Anne murmured. She wanted to laugh or hide. This was insane.

Tony said, "How do you think Kennedy won Illinois?"

"This is crazy, I don't—you're joking." But he wasn't, and she asked, "Who are you?"

The exhaustion of traveling, the bone-draining trauma of her mother's funeral arrangements—it was over with Thomas, wasn't it?—Anne felt it all suddenly, in her twitching left eye, in the pain at the front of her skull. She felt sick. The voters kept coming, in a surreal Sunday-mass procession to Grover Cleveland Elementary School.

"You're from Ireland," she said, "you weren't really born in —"

"There is a river of salt," he said. "Walls of human bone and cartilage. There are no names; there is no such thing as time." He smiled again. "Have you ever been to Las Vegas?"

"I don't believe you."

"Yes you do. On your eighth birthday, your mother took you to Florida to visit your grandmother's nursing home. It smelled like moldy flowers, remember? You didn't want to go. It had only been six months since your father moved out.

Remember what Lorrie-Ann said?"

Anne's mouth went dry. No one had called Nan by her first name. She was always just 'Nan.' Anne's right hand shook, until she clenched it tight. "Stop."

"Her brain was poisoned from the liver cancer, but she told your mother that a bad man wanted to eat her. Eat all of you. Remember that? Lorrie-Ann said she came to America before your mother was even born, so that bad man would never find her. The nurses called it dementia."

Anne pressed a fist to her forehead, closed her eyes, and tried to pace her breathing. Walk away. Go. Don't listen to this.

"Well, I never wanted to *eat* her," Tony said, laughing, as if this were all a joke. "After that visit, your mother stayed in the hotel room, let you play on the beach alone, and that night, the phone rang—"

"Shut up."

"Your mother is mine now, just like I told Lorrie-Ann she would be. And it's because of you, Anne. Because I found *you*—a lucky little pawn."

"I said shut the fuck up."

Morris approached. "Is something wrong?" he asked.

"I have to go," Anne said. "Take me back to my car."

"I hoped we could talk," Morris said.

Her arms trembling, she might collapse or lunge at him. "Why?" She gestured to Tony. "Why is he here?"

"Why not?" Morris said. "This is a political alliance, Anne. Honestly. Tony simply represents a special interest with a different currency."

Anne said, "Let me go."

"Go?" Tony repeated and shook his head, smiling, as if that were a terrible joke. "Oh my, no. Your pieces belong to me."

"No, Tony, not this one," Morris said simply. He squinted into the sun, as if impatient to wrap this up. "The mother—that's fine. Old world obligations. I don't want to know about that. But we have enough bodies on our hands, as-is."

"Sir—"

"I said 'no.'"

Anne felt hollow, her arms stiff and legs numb. Would she fall if she tried to run? This wasn't real.

Tony nodded, smile tighter. "Fine." And to Anne, "Until this is done, then. Take a different place on the board."

Watching the crowd, Morris rocked on his heels, still listening. "I like that. Pawn to F-2. Good idea."

"And after?" Tony asked.

"Yes," Morris said. "After is fine. If she comes back on her own. But not now."

Tony leaned in close, and Anne winced, her nose pinching with a sudden, bleach-sting smell. "If you ever come back—*when* you come back—I will own you, too," he whispered, and then, loud enough for Morris to hear, "But for now, go back to your newspaper. No one will notice the difference. Anne-Marie, Mary-Anne: change places, lucky pawn. Who knows? This may even improve your relationship with that skinny man from Connecticut. Think of it as an early Christmas present." Tony gave her a First Class plane ticket to Newark. The name was wrong. "You leave in the morning," he said.

"I ... who is Marianne Ellis?"

Six years later, Thomas called to Marianne from the front door: a suitcase had been delivered, misplaced in-transit years earlier. Inside, under the clothes and toiletries, Marianne found a digital recorder and heard herself speaking with the Governor of Kentucky, the man who would almost certainly be the next President of the United States. But who was Anne Mallory?

***

"Am I really going to skin you alive? You have to understand, just as you can't help but laugh if a cartoon rabbit whaps a fat hunter on the head with a mallet, it amuses me to hear you scream. I can't help it."

Anne sat on the basement couch, breathing hard. Tony stood over her with a hacksaw, but she wasn't bound. There were knives, pointy instruments, and bolt cutters on the table where the lop-headed thing had been. I have to run, Anne thought, but Tony would certainly stop her. He'd deliberately left her un-restrained so that she would try to escape, as if she were a mouse or an insect. I have to *try*, she told herself again, but she didn't move. Tony had said that she should understand, and the memories had returned in shadowy bursts, as if she'd dreamt her life as Marianne. Moments ago, the old woman screaming in the back office had been crazy and anonymous; now, she was Anne's mother. Which was impossible. 'And that,' Tony had said, 'is much funnier.' The carpet squished and oozed like bloody topsoil when he shifted his weight.

"I won't tell anyone," she said.

"Tell anyone?" Tony set down the hacksaw and picked up a shiny cheese grater. The blade was narrow and sharp. "What would you say? That a handsome man from Leinster kept his promise?" He stepped closer. "Give me your left arm."

"Who are you?"

"I am your destination." He pressed the cheese grater to the back of her arm. "Hold still . . ."

The door at the top of the stairs opened, and Morris called down, "Tony, you haven't seen Angela's red jacket, have you?"

"Cleaners," Tony said.

Morris came down two steps, smiled. "I'm sorry?"

"It's at the cleaners, sir."

"Thank you," Morris said. "Carry on."

When he turned to go, Anne said, "In New Hampshire—what happened in New Hampshire, sir?"

Morris hesitated. "New Hampshire?"

"How did you lose the primary?"

Tony jammed the grater into her flesh, and the skin broke in a line of blood that made Anne jump and cry out. "Oh please, by all means," Tony said, "keep talking."

"No, it's all right." Morris came down, oblivious to the weapons and the blood. "New Hampshire was tough, no question."

Morris helped Anne during the first campaign. He was the reason she escaped to live those years as Marianne, without remembering any of this.

"Was it funny?" she asked.

Morris stopped. He looked from Anne to Tony as Tony prepared to peel the skin off the back of her arm. "Was it funny?" Morris repeated. "Wait, Tony—I want to hear her speak in words, not vowels."

"He must have thought it was funny," Anne said. "Why else would he let it happen?"

"Oh, you are clever," Tony said. "And we're so dumb, we'll turn on each other. Please."

"You're not dumb, you're crazy," Anne said. "In New Hampshire, you let Morris lose—"

When Tony leaned close, his scent became sweet, like a rotten apple. "I cut two holes in your great-great-great uncle Michael's back and pulled out his lungs. I wore his skin and his face, as I nailed him to a tree at Kilcrea." Tony was sweating. "Your family belongs to me, just like always. Here or on the green hills, doesn't matter."

"He isn't all-powerful," Morris said, though he didn't look as certain. "Well. It's been nice speaking to you again."

"You're a dog, Governor," Anne said. "He's tightening your leash, and you know it. You finished third in New Hampshire—"

Tony dragged the peeler down her arm, and she screamed, grabbed his hand.

"Wait," Morris said. "Tony, stop."

Tony's grip loosened, the blade paused. Anne was shaking with pain. There was blood all over her arm, flowing out of the meaty wound and dripping onto her legs.

"I am going to win by fifteen, maybe twenty, percentage points tomorrow," Morris said. "What difference does New Hampshire make?"

"You can't control him," she said, gasping. "Your children, your wife—someday he won't care. Look at him."

Tony smelled like old sewage. "Liam and Meg begged me," he told Anne. "In their funny little voices by the River Bride, they forgot everything before the pain."

Anne watched Morris. "What if he does this to someone you love?"

"Your cousin, Sara, was smart too. But she cried and cried because she couldn't reach the food, because she didn't have any hands . . ."

"Stop, Tony." Morris nodded. "Let go of her arm."

Tony looked up. "After I cut it off, certainly."

But Morris was serious. "Stop."

Tony said, "Mr. President, we are not children." When Morris stared back, Tony stopped smiling. "You don't *need me*? Victory is so certain you don't even need to count the votes? We need each other, Mr. President. *Casat un meit*—"

"I don't like that language," Morris said. "I told you that. We're not in your home."

Tony released Anne, and she staggered away, cradling her wounded arm. "What do you want?" he said. "You want to give her another plane ticket? Her name belongs to me."

"You're right." Morris thought about it. "She makes me uncomfortable. She has to die."

"Thank you."

"But I want you to go."

Tony placed the bloody cheese grater on the table. "The election is tomorrow."

"Once I'm President, I'll call you. You need a break."

"You'll call me." Tony nodded to Anne. "Bravo, well done. A little life-or-death desperation can be inspirational, can't it?"

"Tony," Morris said. "I'll call you."

Anne edged along the wall, closer to the stairs.

Tony ran his hand over the knives, stopped at the hacksaw. "You said that already."

"I need you to leave now."

The back office opened: Anne saw shadows, and something growled.

"No," Tony said, and he picked up the hacksaw. "I don't think I'll be going just yet."

Anne ran. At the top of the stairs, she heard Morris scream, and she shouted, "The Governor is hurt! He's hurt!" Secret Servicemen rushed to the basement stairs, pistols ready. Anne heard them curse, and as she banged out the front door, there was gunfire and a woman's voice singing, *"And all she said when she got there . . ."*—Men screaming, "Jesus Christ!" "Stop, stop!"—*"Young man, I believe you're dying . . ."* Her rental car had plenty of gas.

***

It was still raining in New Jersey. Anne and Thomas watched the aftermath at the office. The Governor of Kentucky, along with his anonymous assassin, and five Secret Service agents had been killed. In the chaos, a new President was elected, and Anne worked into the night. The clock read 3:04 am when she finally arrived home—Thomas would be another few hours—and the phone was ringing. Though Anne would forget the details of the conversation, at the end of the call, her voice weak over a static wind, Anne's mother said, "Thank you."

Objective 3
KN Gould

KN Gould lives in Oregon with his wife, children, and dog. He is a lifelong fan of the Chicago Bears and Van Halen (with Sammy Hagar).
His work has been included in more than a dozen anthologies, including Stories of the Dead: A Tribute to George Romero, Weirdbook #36, Krampus Tales, and Grey Matter Monsters. His debut novel, Path of Totality, will be available in 2024 from Wicked House Publishing.

~

Mom + Dad,

I know you guys worry about me over here but you shouldn't. The real fighting is hundreds of miles away. I've heard it's pretty brutal up there but my job can be boring at times. Remember, I'm driving a truck through vast stretches of desert where my only company is the vehicle in front of me and the vehicle behind me.

The going is slow. Wrecks and craters litter the highway. Detours are common and time consuming. We get yelled at by the mid-level commanders for delays but there's not a lot we can do about it. Sometimes the blockages are bad enough we have to stop and wait for the heavy equipment to come up and clear the way for us. It's nice, but rare, when we get a good, long portion of open road where we can really make good time.

I think I'm getting good at converting kilometers to miles (and vice versa) in my head. It's a pain in the ass but not too difficult, a kilometer is just shorter. Why can't everyone measure distances like we do?

I'll admit I'm a bit uncomfortable being so far away from home. You were right about that, Mom. Being half the world away was bad enough but crossing the border into unfriendly territory was a whole different experience. I could practically feel the shift in atmosphere. It's in my mind, I'm sure. We haven't run into any trouble but I sure am glad when the allied troops or armor are close by.

Those troops are some of the coolest guys I've ever met. This is truly a global effort. I've met soldiers from five countries since I crossed the border. There's a language barrier at times but we usually work it out. There's a friendly rivalry between the nations, they basically smack talk each other like Dad does with Uncle Lou. All of them band together to tease us civilian contractors though. We're not "real fighters" according to them, just glorified delivery drivers. They don't mean it, not really. We not only transport humanitarian aid to civilians (food, water, etc) who have been caught up in the crossfire, we also get much needed supplies to the front for our side. They do appreciate us (I think).

This one guy from France, Gabe, gave me a pistol to carry. His offer was nice but I told him no at first. Us drivers are technically classified as noncombatants as we aren't supposed to be armed. Plus, we are so far removed from the actual shooting I didn't feel it was necessary. Gabe laughed at me. He told me he'd taken the gun off of an old man not far from here after a squad stopped him for creeping around near a checkpoint in the dark. He was about eighty and alone so they thought he got lost or something. Turns out he had a full magazine and some spares. He was looking to kill as many "invaders" as he could before he got taken out himself.

"Screw the rules," Gabe said. "If you need to use it, you'll be glad you have it. Everyone has them around here, even the great-grandpas. You should, too. Just in case."

So, I have it secured in a holster on my ankle. Just in case.

I'd better go get some sleep. Moving out early tomorrow.

Your son,
Leo

***

Mom + Dad,

We haven't made it very far since my last email. The roads are getting worse as we approach the city. Detours add time and sometimes they're just as impassable as the main highway. Usually, we can get a real roof over our heads but every once in a while, I have to sleep in the truck.

Yesterday, we were driving on one of those back roads and came to a wooden bridge. The thing looked to be a hundred years old and was barely wide enough for me to get through. IED's are always on our minds (they drill that into us in orientation). This would have been a great place to ambush us with a few small explosives and send our cargo into the shallow creek below.

I swear I held my breath the whole way over the bridge. I had to drive real slow because my rig is so heavy. Each groan of the wood made me think it was going to give out.

At the other end of the bridge was this woman and child. He looked to be about eleven or so, with dark hair like yours used to be, Dad. The woman could've been my age, maybe a little older. Too young to be his mother but you never know. She had a worn-out look to her, like she hadn't given up just yet, but she was close.

The boy held a fishing rod over his shoulder. The woman stood in front of him, as if shielding him from a threat. I was confused, surely she wasn't threatened by us. It wasn't until I drove past them and I could get a better look, she didn't look afraid. The hate in her eyes could've burned a hole right through me. I swear, if she could have killed us all, right then and there, she would have without a second thought.

We were told we'd be welcomed as liberators here, not by everyone, but by the vast majority. This wasn't a land grab - we weren't burning crops or seizing oil fields — we were here to try and stop the insanity that has been going on for too long. This woman reminded me we are the invaders, whatever our motivations are. I wonder about her, what her story is, who she's lost, and what happened to make her hate us so.

I do think the history books will paint us as the good guys, I believe in what we're doing here, that's why I volunteered. I know you think it was a knee-jerk reaction to what happened with me and Alice. If I'm honest, I'd have to admit our break up was the kick in the butt I needed to make such a big decision but what's been going on in this corner of the world has been weighing on my mind for a long time.

A lot of the people I'm with feel the same way. At some point you have to stand up and do something instead of impotently shout into the void. There are others here for the paycheck or those who just happened to be enlisted when the fateful decision was made to fight. Nothing against those guys at all, we all have the same goal. I'm here to make a difference, even if I'm not a fighting man.

I'll talk to you later. Love you both.

Leo

***

Dear Alice,

I wanted to wait to write to you. Things were too fresh and I was hurt. Truth is, I am still hurt, I'm just dealing with it better than before. I'm glad you wrote me first; I wasn't expecting that after the way we left things.

No, I didn't travel all this way to a war zone just to get away from you. I will admit it was tough to go anywhere back home without having some memory of you attached. I needed to change that or I would be constantly wallowing. Signing up to come here, that was simply good timing. It's a good job, good pay, and my resume will be that much better when I get back. The change of scenery is a plus. Getting away from home and out of my comfort zone has already given me memories to last a lifetime.

The desert can be boring but the sunsets are magical. It's the kind of thing I wouldn't have necessarily noticed before. I mean, there's a sunset every damn day, you know. Why is this one special? Maybe it's being around the soldiers. Even though we're far from the hardest fighting, there's an atmosphere of dread, like each sunset could be the last.

Like today, my rig broke down by the side of the road. Something I couldn't fix by myself. Me and my buddy Luka waited with our two trucks for Command to send help while the others moved north. A car from the local police force pulled up to "see if we needed any assistance."

Luka's been over here longer than me so he warned me to be wary around these guys. "Heads up," he said as they parked behind us. Their emergency lights were flashing even though there was no traffic.

The two policemen spoke so fast I couldn't keep up with what they were saying. Luka told me later they were asking a bunch of questions about what we were hauling, where we were going, etc. Their eyes were hidden by sunglasses and their hands were resting on their guns. Even with the gun I had in my ankle holster I was very nervous. Anything could happen in the middle of nowhere with no witnesses.

Local police, at least the ones who still have their jobs here, are supposed to be on our side. That's what HQ told us. Reality wasn't quite so black and white. With the upheaval and violence, many of them had a mercenary attitude. They would make deals with anyone as long as it was in their best interest.

Things were getting tense but Luka stepped up. I saw him shake hands with one of them, slipping a few bills into his hand at the same time. Two minutes later they were in their car and on their way.

"How much did you give them?" I asked.

"Do what you gotta do," he said, avoiding my question. "Better to pay up voluntarily than get our shit taken the hard way."

I didn't need to ask what the hard way was. I never felt so far from home.

I will try to write you more if that is what you want.

Leo

***

Hi Dad,

I hope you are well. I sent this email to your personal account since the last one made Mom worry so much. You can decide what you should share with her.

The deeper we go north the more problems we run into. I'm still far from the main "contested territory" but I've learned that doesn't mean I'm far from the enemy.

I really don't consider these people my enemy. What's happened here is not their fault. Most of them are just trying to make ends meet and live their lives. I'm sure they would prefer that we turned around and went back to where we came from but, as you know, too much has happened. We're not going anywhere.

No matter that I don't consider them an enemy, I seem to be theirs. Guns are everywhere here; you have to get used to that. It's not the ones with a rifle slung over a shoulder you need to worry about. It's the ones who hide their stash until the time is right to shoot at us. Gabe tells me about how he and his guys uncover hidden arsenals once or twice a week. Then, just days ago, I had a sniper take a potshot at me as I was rolling down the highway. Don't worry, I'm fine. The round went through the hood of my truck but didn't hit anything vital. They taught us to just keep going, don't stop unless you absolutely have to. I radioed in the approximate location and HQ sent a squad but I bet they found nothing but sand.

It happened again today. Thankfully, the shooter had the same poor accuracy as before. I do wonder of he's aiming at me or my rig. Is killing me the goal or is it slowing the supply chain for the war effort. Either way, my convoy has extra support now (that means more soldiers with big guns and armored vehicles) so we'll see if this keeps up.

The burned-out homes and businesses become more common as we approach the big city. I've seen the name of the city on so many of the road signs but I can't even begin to try and pronounce it. On our maps it is listed as Objective 3. These recent shots taken at us have made me more nervous with each passing hour. A city like Objective 3, with a half-million people (before the fighting started) means a half-million potential guns pointed in my direction.

I don't think I was naïve when I signed up for this job. It's just now that I'm confronted with the realities of war and seeing the remnants of once-peaceful communities, my own mortality seems more tenuous than ever before.

There are no atheists in foxholes, or so I've heard. I never considered myself atheist but I know I've been pretty lapse in my faith (Mom reminds me of this all the time). Recently, I've started praying for the first time in years. I'd like to think this is all God's plan and I'm here to play my small part in it. At the very least, coming here has done that for me.

If you share any of this with Mom you should share that last part. She'd be happy to hear it.

I hope to hear from you soon.

Your son,
Leo

***

Dear Alice,

It was great to hear from you again. You're like a little reminder of home to keep from getting too lonely. The only thing I hate is how long it takes for emails to make it through the censors. I understand, I guess. They need to make sure I'm not giving away any vital information like classified troop movements or something. I'm just too used to the ease of pressing a button and having my words instantly received on the other end.

I made it into the city. Or, should I say, I'm inside the city limits. The part I'm in is mostly suburbs: residential houses, schools and such. We're using a parking lot belonging to one of those vacant schools for our main base of operations. First thing we did was hand out canned food and bottled water to the locals. A lot of them haven't had power or running water since the invasion started. I think the higher-ups look at these goodwill efforts only in terms of how it benefits them. "People are more likely to help us if we give them necessities. At least they'll be less likely to try and kill us," I heard one of them say.

Turns out he was right. An older woman, maybe fifty-five or so, asked to speak to an officer. Luka told me she gave up solid information on guerrilla fighters operating in the area in exchange for extra rations. These guys are "enemy combatants" and not exactly soldiers. They're also a giant pain in our asses. She's got grandkids she's taking care of so she decided to tell us where those guys were holed up. Luka said, "If you ask me, our side made out like bandits on that deal, just as long as we catch some of them."

I never heard what happened or if we did "catch some of them." One morning, a few days later, Luka came in and woke me up.

"Leo," he said, "get up. You should see this." He sounded serious, somber even. I rubbed the sleep out of my eyes and slipped my boots on. This was new, he'd never woke me in the middle of the night.

I followed him around to the back of the school. People had gathered. It was dark except for a couple of flashlights. Luka gestured to a second-floor window. I couldn't see what he was pointing to at first. When one of the beams lit up the figure I gasped.

He told me later it was the same woman who had given information days before. I didn't know that at the time. Her head was covered with a dark hood and her hands were tied behind her back. They had tied a rope around her neck and threw her out the window. Pinned to her chest was a cardboard sign with one word written on it. COLLABORATOR.

I'm shook, Alice. Seeing her up there like that, killed to make a statement to others, I mean, what kind of person could do something like that? I'm sorry if this is too much for you but I guess old habits are hard to break. You always were the one I spilled my guts to. I hope that never changes.

Please keep writing me.

Leo

***

Dad,

I got your email yesterday, couldn't believe how long it was. You've always been so stoic and reserved. I'm not complaining, I was just surprised.

What you asked is something I have found myself wondering during my time here. How did this happen? How do any wars happen for that matter? It wasn't that long ago (relatively) that anyone suggesting we would have gotten to this point would have been laughed at and ridiculed. When I was a kid things had begun to deteriorate but we had no idea this was coming.

A contested election, age-old grudges, sides being drawn, us vs them mentalities, those coordinated bombings, and the economy, such as it was. It was all a recipe for disaster. I know who I blame for the majority of the carnage but I guess it will be the historians who will dig through the rubble and assign their own.

When I get philosophical, I think about the difference between here and home. People are the same – fundamentally, I mean – all around the world, right? We're all cut from the same cloth, only separated by circumstances. How far away are we – am I – from the people living here? I can't imagine how it would feel to see foreign troops marching down our street or occupying our town. What would I do in such a situation?

Having said that, I do not believe I could bring myself to do the things I've seen others do in my short time here. Desperate times can change people, I guess, but you raised me better than that. One after another, I see instances of ruthlessness. There are those who will take advantage of any situation and this is no different.

Tales of Sley House 2023

We had a problem with this one small gang of opportunists. They would wait down the road leading away from our aid dispersal station. Needy people – which is most everyone still living here – would wait in line all day in the hot sun. Afterwards they would leave, a lucky few in cars, most on foot. The gang – backed up by guns, knives, and clubs – would meet them on the road and take their "toll." Modern day bandits like something from medieval times.

Tough as they thought they were, those pieces of crap folded quickly when Gabe and his crew found them and rooted them out. Locked up in the city jail is too good for them if you ask me.

The nights are getting cold. Objective 3 is at a higher altitude compared to what I saw driving in from the border, snow could even be possible but not for a couple of months. I'm glad it's not Summer anymore. I would rather deal with cold and snow than unrelenting desert heat. That's me being selfish. The current residents will have a tough time if the temps continue to get lower. The ones that were able to leave have left. The rest are stuck.

I'd better get some rest. I will take your advice and try to see the good in others, even when that good is hard to find. Right now, it's very hard.

Your son,
Leo

***

Alice,

I'm sorry it's been so long since I last wrote. I am spent, emotionally and physically. Your last three emails are all sitting here in my inbox, staring at me accusingly. These last two weeks have been like walking in a fog, doing my job the best I can but being on autopilot the whole time. If I think about it too much, if I dwell on it, I think I'll lose my mind.

Luka found me early one morning while I was eating breakfast. "We're moving out. Command says double-time it. Something's up."

The trailers were already being loaded by the time I got to my truck. The usual supplies: food, bottled water, emergency blankets, medicine. I asked where we were going but got brushed off. As long as I could follow the guy in front of me I would get to the right place.

We headed out of the city as the sun was rising. I will always remember that as the last sunrise before everything changed for me. The view from the driver's seat was soothing, the soft pink coming up over the horizon as we made our way southeast, away from Objective 3.

Our crews had already been this way, I could tell from the road repairs and the fairly smooth trip. The buildings and houses slowly gave way to empty desert and sporadic foliage. We turned off the main road and I still didn't know where we were going. Three turns later and I wasn't sure if the road we were on even had a name.

The chain link fence with razor wire on top extended as far as I could see to the east and west. Tall, wooden towers were evenly spaced along the fence. I assumed they were guard towers, erected to keep people out of whatever this place was. I drove through the open gate, now manned by our guys, and followed the single gravel lane to a group of buildings at the top of a short rise.

Two of the structures dominated the scene. They were virtually identical; large, imposing, gunmetal gray, two story warehouses – weathered from the sun but looking fairly new – built close together. One was perpendicular to the other, creating a L-shape. I parked in the empty area behind one of them. There was ten or so other trucks just like mine doing the same thing. Soldiers came over and began to unload my trailer. I spotted Gabe there and gave him a wave.

"What is this place? You been here long?" I asked.

"Brother," he said, his sunken eyes looked tired, "this place is the end of the line. Hell on Earth shit."

As I soon found out, Gabe wasn't wrong.

Following him past the flurry of activity the arrival of my supply convoy created, I saw what he was talking about. Row upon row of neatly lined, open tents, filled the space in front of the warehouses. Cots, ten to each tent, sat on the bare ground underneath the meager shelters. The people – mostly sitting or lying down – looked so haggard and weary they were practically dead.

"Detention Center is what they called it," Gabe said. "Most of the fuckers running it got outta here when they saw we were coming. Arrogant pricks never thought we'd actually invade." His grip on his rifle tightened as he spoke.

More than half the beds were empty. I tried to estimate how many there were but stopped when I hit fifty tents. It was a sea of green canvas with only narrow breaks in between.

The men and women we walked past were filthy, soiled clothes hanging off their bodies. They barely looked up at the medics assisting them. The smell was overwhelming and I was glad to be outside. Many were beyond help, at least to my untrained eye. One man was on his back on the ground. His arms were bent at the elbows, his hands twisted into claws. Flies had gathered around his face and skittered across his eyes.

"Why doesn't someone cover him up?" I asked, fighting the urge throw up.

It was only my second time seeing a dead body.

"Too many, Leo. They'll get to him."

Turns out, most of the dead were out of sight, still in the buildings I'd first seen when I drove up. I looked at them differently then, now that I knew what they held. Men in one, women in the other, the ones who were deemed beyond help were put there to die, away from the others.

I'm shaken and shocked but am I being naïve? This has happened before. The details are always different but the results are the same. It started as laws were passed to protect against "those people." Restrictive laws morph into detention centers and those centers are filled with people who need to be secured behind fences and gun towers "for the greater good." Dehumanizing and rationalizing go hand-in-hand. "They aren't like us," and "They're dangerous," is how they not-so-subtly get the average citizen to buy into it. Greater tragedy follows soon after.

I thought I knew the extent of the violations here, it's a big reason why I signed up in the first place. I had no idea the scope.

Then I saw the mass graves. They were way out past the fences in the opposite direction from where we drove in. Standing over the open pit, you could barely see the gray warehouses in the distance.

Two of the graves were uncovered, bodies tossed in haphazardly in a rough line. Sand and dirt had blown in, giving them a dry, mummified look. Each pit held at least a hundred people. I didn't want to count them.

Gabe told me this was where they took those that had taken ill and died. In such close quarters, with a poor diet, sickness spread quickly in the camp. Later, as the invasion kicked off, they began to expedite the process. I stood there, looking at the land stretching to the horizon, and imagined a gun to the back of my head. This view was the last thing the bodies below me saw before they were thrown away like trash.

Did they think they could hide what had gone on here?

Beyond the open graves, arranged in neat rows like the tents, were long mounds of disturbed earth. A bulldozer sat silently between two of them, its grim task done. So many, too many. If each one held a hundred victims, I was looking at the final resting place of thousands.

I felt woozy and sat down right before I threw up. I wasn't embarrassed in the least.

I'll write more later. I just can't anymore.

Leo

***

Mom + Dad,

By now I'm sure you've heard about the camps. I wouldn't be surprised if you know more about them than I do, what with the news reporters all over the place. Where I'm at, I'm lucky to get a thin trickle of information. The rest of the time I'm relying on word of mouth from incoming troops and support personnel.

What infuriates me even more are these war criminals and their supporters (I can't believe they still have supporters) who vehemently deny these camps exist. Those of them that do acknowledge the camps claim the conditions here were "not as bad as the opposition media propaganda would have you believe." Makes me want to strangle someone.

I'm telling you, the scene here is beyond description. Words wouldn't do it justice. What I've seen is the tip of the iceberg; I'm told our guys have liberated five other death camps ran much like this one. Their lies won't hide the blood on their hands forever. That day, when I first arrived here, I stood over a pit full of the dead. To me, they blended together in a faceless mass of horror, too much to fully comprehend. One of the victims caught my eye. A young man, I think. It was hard to tell. Even in death he held on to a rough piece of wood across his chest. Looking closer I saw the piece of wood was hung around his neck with a thin rope. It was a sign. On it he'd written I AM AMERICAN in English, using roofing tar for ink. His fingers were still covered with the stuff. I don't know his name but I'll never forget him.

I desperately want to come home but my time here is not done. There is much to do. We must end this. The only way to do that is to keep pushing the war effort forward.

Since our discovery of the camp outside Objective 3, my assignment has been shuttling back and forth between the camp and the city. Sick, injured people, supplies, or soldiers mostly. The worst is transporting the bodies. I can't help but think of them in the back of my truck as I drive, each one formerly a living, breathing person with a soul. Knowing they're riding along with me makes my imagination run wild. Sometimes I swear I hear them faintly crying out, like from a great distance.

A few nights ago, it got to be too much for me. I started hyperventilating and had to pull over to the side of the road. I jumped down from my rig and tried to get myself under control. The brisk night air helped some. Bending over with my hands on my knees, I focused on slowing my breathing and heart rate.

Tales of Sley House 2023

Standing there, in the glow of the headlights, I looked up and saw the sign telling me I was almost all the way back to Objective 3. I took the time to jot down the name so I could tell you in my next email.

Albuquerque.

I wanted to make sure I got the spelling right. This really is a beautiful land. It makes my heart hurt to think of the evil committed here, forever staining my view of the place.

Sorry I have to cut this short but I'd best be getting back to work. Don't worry about me, I'll be okay. Write when you can.

Your son,
Leo

***

SUBMITTED AS EVIDENCE

I hereby swear or affirm the above as true and accurate testimony regarding events in the Coalition Southwest Sector during the specified time frame. This should not be considered the entirety of my testimony as audio/video recordings of interviews have also been conducted and submitted (see attached appendix). It should also be noted that several emails from the same approximate time period are currently missing or otherwise unaccounted for.

Translated to English from the original Italian correspondence, the above has been provided by Leonardo Bianchi, an adult citizen of Italy, as well as his family members, as corroboration of previous, now disputed, testimony in the ongoing war crimes trials in Philadelphia, Pennsylvania, USA. Mr. Bianchi worked as a civilian contractor in the aforementioned territory immediately following the Coalition invasion. His observations were first-hand and relevant to the accusations (specifically articles 2, 5, 10, and 12).

By signing below, you are stating that you have not been coerced or threatened in any way. You have also not been promised any sort of compensation in exchange for your cooperation in this matter.

Signed,
Leonardo Bianchi

Skin Deep
Curtis Harrell

Curtis Harrell has a recurring dream where an invisible entity lurks in the back room of a house he hasn't lived in for forty years. His poetry, short fiction, and one-act plays have all been attempts to hold a conversation with whatever that thing is. Curtis has also recently had some of those works collected and published by Sley House Publishing under the title MEL-POMENE'S GARDEN.

~

Nosmo King could conjure almost every detail from any day in his life with a disconcerting ease, a suspicious card trick of the mind that, if he rubbed it in their faces, made his friends and family view Nosmo as either a shady Superman or a mediocre freak. Unlike some other people with this curious power, he wasn't particularly troubled or prone to letting the past walk him like a dog, mainly because his mother, once she recognized his unnatural recall the summer before he entered third grade, responded with *whatever* each time Nosmo complained that they had eaten liver and onions only *last Tuesday* or that she had promised on the Thursday afternoon after Easter to buy him a new pair of PF Flyers. Nosmo had overheard her confiding in their next-door neighbor, a doe-eyed Italian widow whose horny teenage daughter had stolen his bicycle the past April 27th and then his sled January 16th, that "his memory is too much, I say. It's like living with a small, pooting history book. Why couldn't one of his arms have just withered a bit." So Nosmo learned to keep it all in, to "swallow it like a man," as his father often mysteriously advised.

So *handy* is how he rationalized the flood of images that colored the long line of days leading to now, though he kept them private. For example, early on February 27th, exactly a month after his 67th birthday, after a breakfast where he had burned his toast and smelled himself needing a shower, Nosmo was sitting on the throne, pants around his porcelain shins, and he discovered a dime-sized bruise on the top of his right knee, a bruise that had completely faded by February 20th but now mysteriously reappeared. Nosmo recalled that on Valentine's Day his grandson, with the murderous tow-headed glee of a two-and-a-half-year-old, had hammered him with a xylophone mallet as he napped on the living room couch. Now the bruise was back, and Nosmo didn't know why. He knew it was the same bruise because it was the same veiny green circle surrounding a red mole, like a miniature bullseye just north of his patella. With his liver-spotted middle finger, Nosmo poked it. He entertained the idea that his skin was giving out on him.

Other disturbances of the normal had visited Nosmo recently, things he was having trouble swallowing. In addition to the crow that claimed residence in the cedar outside his bedroom window, croaking as Nosmo labored through his buttock squeezes to mollify his sciatic nerve, the pressure of his tap water had dwindled to a trickle. The crow was particularly troubling because his presence there outside the window queered Nosmo's thinking on squatters. People despise sidewalk bums, but no one thinks twice about these feathery vagabonds hustling in the trees. It seemed okay to tolerate their squawking belligerence if they were up off the ground in that airy realm where you couldn't give them a sideways kick when no one was looking. But this bruise business undid him in a way that exceeded the avian invaders; the bruise seemed to deepen instead of fade. The reappearance rattled around in his mind like a flatpick stuck in a guitar. The faucet dribbled on his foamy toothbrush.

Two weeks later Nosmo discovered a swarm of bites on the top of his right foot. Seed ticks, but this was also an old wound resurrected. First, there were no ticks this early in March lying in wait in the tall grass like tiny haters, and Nosmo recognized the uncanny arrangement of red specks in the shape of the constellation Orion, complete with his itchy belt. Nosmo recalled the previous August 28th when he had very hesitantly, almost hadn't, waded the field beside his house with his 9 year old granddaughter, butterfly net in hand, futilely swiping at fluttering bugs who made him look like some kind of entomological sissy. In a whole afternoon, his granddaughter, a future Wimbledon star he was sure, had captured one Monarch only to lose it in the panicky space between the net and the insect cage. She had consoled him that she was glad that they hadn't had to use the killing jar because she would have let the butterfly go first. Nosmo, upon hearing her talk about the jar, had sobbed like a little boy and blamed it on the itchiness in his socks and his terribly tired legs. Embarrassed by his gulping spasms and grief, she had apologized for making him sad, and they hugged there in the green hay and forgave each other.

Eight puncture marks resurfaced next, five in the crook of his right elbow and three in his left, one haloed with a sunken black bruise. Nosmo could see the exotic eyes of the nurse who had graduated from the college he used to teach at as she fumbled with the needles and apologized profusely from behind her surgical mask, using his flabby old arms as jabbing practice. It was the second Friday the 13th of two years before. Her English, like her eyes, was compelling in its halting foreign urgency and pathos, and Nosmo forgave the pain as only an old idiot could. He wanted to console her like he would any inept beauty, wrap his arms around her and stain the back of her scrubs with his shaky embrace and leaky veins. But she finally found the mark, and his thick corpuscles rose in the vial like mercury on spring's stingiest day. Only halfway to a hundred degrees she slipped the needle out and declared the test successful, bowing like a geisha backwards into the sanctuary of the medical warren.

His wife wakened him with a surprised hoot a few weeks later and gesticulated at him with her long painted nail. Nosmo lay on his back, beard pointed skyward, and could feel the pinch of a scab running from his forehead back across his bald scalp.

"What the hell?" she said. "It looks like one of the kids peeled out on your head."

Nosmo rose and shuffled to the bathroom mirror to once again encounter the abrasive result of a tow strap snapping and whiplashing over his skull. His best friend Nar had apologized for the mishap profusely, bringing him a lukewarm Bud Light to press to the burn, and that was the Friday evening before the fourth of July five years ago.

"You need to see the doctor, old man," she said and, dressing, captured her huge bosoms in her brassiere, lightly jumping up and down in a way that made her Chihuahua bark at the window, "I remember that scob, don't I?"

Nosmo nodded.

"Well what the hell?"

The doctor was booked up, and in the week and a half it took Nosmo to get in, a scar unstitched on the inside of his right forearm and was in need of medical sewing.

"We paid for that once already," his wife fussed at him. "Those ER sons of bitches better make it right."

He'd mishandled some sheet metal building a shed for a pig that had appeared in his front yard six summers ago and wouldn't go away. Now he picked at the super glue he had closed the gash with and pondered the décor of his doctor's waiting room. An impatient old vulture in a white coat, his doctor had let his trophy wife hang inspirational sayings on all of the walls of the waiting room and the examination rooms too. A handsome woman she was, as well as the receptionist, and proud of the "Health Makes Wealth" banner she sat under at the front window through seasons of flu and mucousy colds and that one STD which presented a smell like dirty feet.

"You're next, Mr. King," she cooed at him from behind the sliding glass.

Once into the labyrinth of halls, designed, Nosmo was sure, by a licentious doodler who fell back on architecture after washing out of Johns Hopkins or the Mayo for his derisive bedside manners, so that the patient was unsure whether an exit was reward or failure, he followed the taut white back of a nurse to a station where she took his vitals and eyeballed his head wound which had now begun to weep.

"When did this happen," she asked, dabbing the pad of her pinky finger on his scalp.

"About five years ago," Nosmo replied, and she recoiled in a way that made another nurse walking past shatter a urine specimen on the checkerboard linoleum.

"Wait here," she commanded.

Nosmo, resigned to the docility of the doctor's office where he hoped for deliverance from this string of old bodily insults, sat and waited.

"Room 3," his nurse barked, now wearing a unicorn band aid on her little finger.

Nosmo avoided the examination table and sat on one of the chairs against the wall. To his left, high up, was an arrangement of terra cotta letters that spelled out "Getting Better Means Getting Better!" Underneath it was a large clock face fashioned as a sun, and it had stopped. Through the thin walls, Nosmo could hear Dr. Plinky curtly overviewing the machinations of the large bowel to explain the patient's sudden and embarrassing flatulence, particularly during church services and waiting in line at the DMV. The pants fabric over Nosmo's left knee wetted with blood, the revisitation of a nasty scrape he had received from slipping on the icy sidewalk outside an adult bookstore seven Christmases ago.

"Well, it's old Dore Gray! What in the hell is happening to you?" Dr. Plinky demanded as he barged into the room.

"My skin," Nosmo stammered, "is getting old hurts again. This seeping welt on my head first occurred five years ago, the blood staining my knee seven. The wounds are showing up like Scrooge's ghosts and refusing to heal."

Dr. Plinky flipped through Nosmo's chart and then tilted back his head and considered Nosmo through his bifocals. He ordered Nosmo to strip and examined the bruise, the tick bites, the needle punctures, the scab, and the bleeding scar and knee.

"My nurse entreated me to send you to the shrink, but I seem to recollect the blood drawing incident—I think your wife insisted we give you a discount on that procedure—and these records confirm the head scab and the stitchery on your forearm."

After a long reflection, the doctor sat on the squeaking wheeled stool and said, "I have been a deacon in my church for fifty years, and I am not certain what that means to me now. People like you make appointments to confuse my thinking on the simple physiology of our corporeal machines, and you leave me gasping in my beliefs. Medicine is as far away from a science as decent poetry or a satisfying bowel movement."

Nosmo took the proffered paper towels and absently wiped at blood in several places.

"My comely parasitic wife has transformed these walls," he said, sweeping his thin, white sleeved arm over Nosmo's head, "into mottos for morons, and no one complains. That proves that two good boobs are worth more than a middling brain. What do you want me to tell you about your cryptic malfunctions of the skin?"

"A diagnosis," Nosmo shot back, aggravated by Dr. Plinky's harangue, "My old lady is herself abundantly hootered, and that has never crippled my critical faculties. I'm paying you money for relief and not your gripes about your wife's shortcomings as an interior decorator. Dig deep in your med school learning and tell me something that will let me sleep tonight."

Dr. Plinky scowled and absently pulled at the hem of his lab coat. He massaged his temples with his thumbs and exhaled loudly. He abruptly rose and stretched his arms over his head.

Dr. Plinky circled the room three times and then eased back down on the squeaky stool.

He said, "Epidermal hyperthymesia is the description of it, and Plinky Syndrome should be the name for it."

"Should be? What the hell?"

"In all my perusals of the journals describing abnormal maladies, I have never been entertained by something so odd and inconvenient as what you present. You may very well be the first ever instance, and I just coined the term in case it gets named after me although that honor is dubious at best. The name will probably just become the answer to a tricky question on midterm exams meant to screw with the GPAs of med students. We both know you have hyperthymestic syndrome, that is, the ability to remember far beyond the capacity of we of average memory function. Somehow, your skin has exhibited this freakishness as well, old abrasions and conditions showing up helter skelter. I have absolutely no idea why you have become a sideshow marvel nor any idea why it is exhibiting backward through time. At this rate I give you less than a year."

The doctor slipped his prescription pad out and scrawled along the bottom.

Then he ripped the page free and pushed it into Nosmo's bloody hand.

"This is for the stronger Tylenol. Don't overdo it, and remember that righteousness without tears is but arrogance, and your skin may be trying to talk to some other part of you that isn't retarded at listening."

Nosmo renegotiated the maze of hallways to the receptionist's station, and, from this vantage point, at the window where he coughed up his co-pay, a sign overhead proclaimed "Give Your Body Credit!"

Over the next few weeks, suddenly, and at inopportune times, Nosmo's dilapidating body embarrassed him, and each time he was haunted by the sawbone's diagnosis about whom his skin was trying to talk to. When he accompanied an old friend to church for communion, he knelt at the rail while both his palms burst forth fresh blood, the result of an barbed wire fiasco a decade ago, and the priest had fainted. Pulled over for a burnt out taillight, Nosmo horrified the lady trooper when his face broke out in large running pox so that his cheeks resembled a chicken's plucked ass. A young woman sitting behind him at the theater ran screaming from the werewolf movie when, in the course of fifteen minutes, he regrew a full head of hair. Waiting for his wife in the produce aisle, he got a boner by the banana display, a priapism relapse 20 years ago, and store security cautiously approached him for shoplifting.

***

When the scrapes and skinnings of his twenties and teens began parading all over his body, Nosmo's wife took a keener interest. Here surfaced injuries she had never seen, and, instead of the ailments being reruns she had tended to once already, these new depredations were novel and interesting to her in a morbid maternal way. She spent most of each day flipping through the doctor shows on cable—the 800 pound women who had to have their cheating husbands hose them off on the patio, the poor Home Depot clerks with cantaloupe size lumps hanging off the back of their heads. She had a soft spot for people with extra toes or fingers and often googled stores where they could find gloves and EEE shoes.

Nosmo sat in his recliner which his wife had shrouded in gauze and watched her peel eggs in the kitchen sink.

"You know," she said, flicking an eggshell from her index finger, "the first hurts that started creeping back on you—I remembered most of them. I'd have to study them a bit, but I could mostly see the day that they happened."

Nosmo had a roll of toilet paper impaled on a sawed-off broom handle and used it to swaddle a fresh wound on his left foot.

"But," she continued, "these later ones are spooking me. It's like I get to see you before we got hitched. There," she pointed with the small end of an egg, "for example. What cut your foot?"

"Never mind, hon. I'm not sure it means a thing."

"It does," she insisted. "I mean it. I'm getting a tour back through the accidents of your youth. I'm waiting for something to really gross me out, intrigue me, something that will make me feel all thick with pity. I bet we could get you on one of these medicine shows. There might be dwarves or hermaphrodites in the green room."

"Why in the world do you watch that crap? No one wants to be a freak. My mama said people didn't want to be bored with yesterday things. She said that people wouldn't trust my memory any more than their own, so I should just keep it to myself."

"Your mama was a mean woman, Nosmo. Now tell me what cut your foot."

Nosmo sighed heavily and surrendered.

"This cut was from a broken bottle I stepped on when my family went to that lake in Oklahoma where the bath house was crawling with tarantulas. When you went to take a shower, the spiders would swarm up out of the drains, and I ran out onto the sand and cut my foot."

"How old were you, ten or so?"

"It was on August the 3rd, 1964. I was eleven."

"And there," she gesticulated with her eyebrows as she held the bowl full of eggs, "that shiner that just welled up on your right eye."

"On Saturday, May 11th, 1963, I was batting in the bottom of the ninth, two out and the bases loaded, scored tied. It was the Tris Speaker League championship. I sucked at hitting. I sucked so bad my own dad was stuffing a first baseman's mitt he had swiped from the other team into a duffel bag so we could go home. The count went to full, and the pitcher sailed in a fastball that hit me right in the eye. I blacked out, and when I came to the runner on third stomped on my fingers as he crossed the plate. The beanball gave us the win."

"That's a good one, hon! What about those bruises all up your shins there?"

"Those are where a girl named Deanna Groce showed me that she had a crush on me by kicking me under our desks. It was in fourth grade, the day of the spring equinox when our teacher made us put sheets over our heads and hold onto a rope as he led us around the playground for some reason. Deanna flirted with me until I cried."

"That's sweet—her crushing on you like that. Do you ever wonder what I was doing back before we met, if we'd have been boy and girl friends?"

The question caught Nosmo off guard despite the fact he thought about it every day.

"Yes."

"You have? What is it you're thinking—that I might have been playing a love song on your shin bones?"

She smiled and gave him goo goo eyes over her horn-rimmed reading glasses.

Nosmo's gut hollowed now. His mind thrashed about for a way to explain the one thing he had never revealed to his wife in the whole of their nearly forty years together. The thing sat below his diaphragm like a watermelon ready to roll off the counter. It was an overripe secret that was going to smell up the room.

"You have?" she repeated.

In a phlegmy rush, Nosmo burbled, "You know when we look over your old picture albums? Those photos are like little windows looking back to when you were a girl. Below each photo your mom used a silver pen to date them. When I see that date, it opens a window in my head showing exactly what I was doing when you posed for the snapshot."

Nosmo's wife turned a cold eye on him from the sink.

"You know that photo of you in the cheerleading outfit from May 2, 1966? While you were going through your cheers for the camera, your hair up in that beehive, I was hiding in the bushes with a boy who was visiting my grandma's next door neighbor, and he kept vomiting blood. I thought it was tomato soup, but he was real pale and said he couldn't help it."

"Nosmo!"

"And that one where you're sitting in your brother's lap on the glider from June 22nd, 1969? I was playing with my dog in the backyard of my house in Cleveland, the air all smoky from the river burning. We had to take him back to the pound the next day because he had ripped a neighbor girl's shirt. She looked enough like you to be your sister, and I used to think about her when I was waiting to go to sleep at night. My dog snagged his tooth in her collar as she tried to climb up on our back porch, and he tore her shirt off. I tried to hand it back to her, but she was crying and covering up her nipples with her grubby hands."

"So you're telling me that you can see our lives together in the past, when we were living in different places, in different states even?"

Nosmo had to say something really true. His desire to make her understand what he knew made tears cramp in his jaw.

"I see our childhoods like rails on a train track. We went along our separate ways, side by side. And then, somehow, like that trick of perspective when you look down the tracks, the two rails came together."

"What's with all the semaphores and tricks of speech, you old fool? What're you trying to tell me?"

"Something I don't expect you to believe," Nosmo said as he glanced sideways at his wife, her arm churning the eggs into salad, "but the memory that makes me believe in fate, the one that makes me feel like there is some giant celestial finger prodding us toward our meager destinies, is that picture of you with Mickey Mouse on Main Street in Disneyland, June 27th, 1961. You can't see me in that photo, but I was somewhere behind you in the crowd with my Pappy, close enough to brush against you, maybe. Maybe we both stood in the same line for ice cream. I think I might have held the door open for you to the Magic Kingdom."

Nosmo's wife planted the wooden spoon in the bowl of egg salad like a battle flag.

"We've spent many evenings rocking together out there on the porch in the evening gloam, just two people being together. You made me think we knew each other. I thought we had no secrets, and now you throw this peeping Tom stuff on me? Isn't this part of that whole sickness and health vow you recited in front of the preacher?"

"Sometimes I wish I could do one simple thing," Nosmo said, "and that is just forget. To tell you the truth, I get tired of carrying these memories around like a suitcase full of home movies. I get tired, hon. You know that photo of you walking with your grandpa down that street in Colorado?"

"Outside his house in Craig—you know—where he walked his poodle every afternoon."

"On that day my sister and I were hunting butterflies out in the field behind our house. She didn't catch anything, but I caught a spicebush swallowtail. I watched it batter against the folds of the net, its wings like a velvet painting in the sun. I was going to let it go, but my sister held the killing jar up to me and told me I had to put it in. She said I had to. This butterfly would make us the keepers of all that flew around our house, she told me. This butterfly crucified on the cardboard square would save us from ignorance and the slack-jawed stares of the smelly-pants boys on the bus. She said we could keep it forever and look at it whenever we wanted. It would become ours. We would own its beauty is what she said. She didn't understand that time would gnaw the colorful scales into dust in the bottom of a drawer. I already owned it, in my memory, and I could see it and all its colors anytime I wanted. She didn't understand that I wanted to keep it alive in my mind. She grabbed it by its powdery wing and stuffed it in the killing jar. I threw my net in the weeds and ran home. I swore I would never catch another butterfly."

"You know, hon, that sometimes if you find your arms all full of treasures you just need to find a place to set 'em down. Your sister is a mean woman, too."

***

Curiously, Nosmo's wounds ceased in the coming days and weeks. Though scarred and healing, no new epidermal atrocities visited his person. He was thankful though purposely indifferent. He tried to make no mention, but his wife broached the topic one afternoon as she finally began unshrouding his recliner of its bloody gauze.

"You know, old man, I think the doc had something when he told you about listening. I think you had that thing he described, what was it, 'epidermis retardo'?"

"He said—," Nosmo started.

"I like to call it Rumpled Smart Skin," his wife snorted as she bagged the bloody bandages.

"Listen—,"

'Everybody needs somebody that they can talk to. John Prine said that, and he was right."

"For heav—"

"And, by the way, that nurse from Dr. Plinky's called and said that they still need to do the surgery even though you passed that kidney stone, just to see if it all came through. I told her that no one is taking a scenic pecker cruise on my dime, darlin'."

O'Shaughnessy's Cryptid & Spirit Removal, LLC
M.C. St. John

M.C. St. John is the author of the short story collection Other Music. *His stories have appeared, as if by luck or magic, in* Cosmorama, Flame Tree Publishing, Nightscript, Thirteen Podcast, *and* Wyldblood Press. *He is also a member of the Great Lakes Association of Horror Writers, serving as co-editor for the horror anthology* Recurring Nightmares. *See what he's writing next at* <u>www.mcstjohn.com</u>.

~

After Frank had fumigated the old woman's attic for fairies, he smoked a cigarette, waited for the poison to do its job, and went back up the ladder to collect the bodies.

On him he carried a silver hook attached to his belt by way of a retractable wire, a version that janitors use for their many custodial keys. When Frank came thumping down the rungs, his hook held a dozen dead fairies. The tip pierced through the fairies' diaphanous wings, which were as limp as the bodies belonging to them.

"I got 'em all," he said. "They're tough little buggers without the gas. They bite when they know you're on to 'em."

"Oh, what *awful* things," the old woman said, reaching for her purse. "Just last week, they enchanted my fur coats to dance in the halls, broke my china plates, and ate my antimacassars like spaghetti." She shuddered. "I don't want to imagine what they would have done to *me*."

She handed a bank envelope to Frank.

"I can't thank you enough," she said.

"It's my job, ma'am. And I've been doing it for a long time."

From the porch, Frank waved goodbye to the old woman and walked down the crushed gravel driveway to his van. The fairies on his hook bumped together and made sad, jangled music, like windchimes on an autumn night. Frank paid no mind. He was busy figuring out how much gas and diner food the old woman's money would provide.

He went to the back of the van and opened the rear doors.

Inside, meticulously arranged on pegboard lining the walls, was his essential gear. There were steel traps, lures, fumigation tanks, powders and pellets of various poisons. There were also scimitars, silver daggers, talismans, vials of nightshade, cans of graveyard dirt, and canopic jars of gods-knew-what. What's more, there were ropes of dried garlic, rabbits' feet, rabbits' blood, ponchos made from the pelts of werewolves, a battered Ouija board, and several plastic milk jugs filled with holy water.

Finally, there was Frank's daughter.

Norah sat cross-legged on a burlap sack of sylvan oats, which Frank used as bait for wild unicorns, much to his daughter's chagrin. As usual, Norah had a large leatherbound book opened in her lap, and was taking notes in a moleskin journal. She had begun a chapter in the large book titled *Caring For Your Chimera*. In her journal were anatomical sketches of the creatures, alongside doodles of hearts and rainbows.

"Take these," Frank said, and handed her the hook.

Norah wrinkled her nose. "Dad, *no*. I refuse to be complicit in your immoral actions."

"Did I commit a crime?"

"Uh, yeah. *Murder.*"

"Norah, really. We're not gonna have this argument again."

"Because you already know my position." She pointed at the hook. "The only thing those fairies did was fly into that woman's attic to build a nest. They didn't do anything wrong."

"It was only a matter of time before they would do something *very* wrong," Frank said. "Fairies start with mischief and end with mayhem. Rearranging books leads to enchanting dentures and, before you know it, that old woman is gnawing through her own arm. Is that right to let happen? To know that something bad is coming and step aside?"

"Fairies can't help that they're mischievous. It's in their nature."

"You're right, fairies can't," he said, "which is why people like us take care of them before they get out of hand."

"People like you, Dad. Not *us*, but *you*."

Frank opened his mouth to respond, but closed it. He found himself still holding out the hook as if his daughter was going to help him. His fist trembled. The dead fairies clanged together in a maddening chorus.

With a grunt, Frank dumped hook and all into a steel box and locked the lid. Stenciled on the side of the box were the words *Biohazardous Magic*. He had shucked off his coveralls and sat heavily on the van's back bumper when he said, "Your mother wasn't an enchanted tree-hugger. She knew when vermin needed putting down."

"And look what happened to her when she followed your lead," she said. "You didn't *need* to kill the troll in Seattle, did you? You had already caught it in one of your awful traps. You could have tranked the poor thing and moved it to a more secluded bridge, away from the joggers and bikers. But you didn't. You told Mom to grab the UV flashlight so you could turn the troll to stone and smash it for good…"

Frank stared at the crushed gravel between his boots.

The driveway gravel was the color of the stones beneath the Aurora Avenue bridge. He was pretty sure at least. Details had a way of warping with each act of remembrance. Memory was malleable and oftentimes dangerous because of that power. No matter what small details changed, though, what happened in the end remained the same.

Always the same.

That night in Seattle, Wren climbed those gray stones, slick with rain. She was heading back up to the street and the van. Under the bridge, mingled with the relentless rain, the captured troll wailed and wailed. Its leg was caught in a trap of Frank's making, one with tight springs and sharp teeth. His traps had bagged cryptids and lycans and once a lagoon creature the size of a linebacker. When Frank's traps were sprung, the caught thing never made it out alive.

The troll was wailing in pain and fear. Because it knew what Wren was going to the van to get. The death light. It knew that when she came back it would be its last night under the Aurora Avenue bridge—or any bridge, for that matter. So the troll did something that Frank had never seen before or since from a creature in his years of the extermination business.

Still wailing, not so much now in fear but rage, the troll leaped from the ground. Frank heard the clack of the trap's teeth again, which was odd to his ears. He had only set one trap, not two. Then he understood. The same trap snapped twice. He watched the troll's leg tumble down the rocky slope, foot over stump, gaining speed toward the river.

But only the leg.

The rest of the troll had wrenched itself free.

It was a desperate creature, bent on survival. Better to be a one-legged troll that could hobble than a two-legged corpse in a steel box. In that moment, the troll could have gone the way of its rogue leg down to the river. There, it could have risked swimming to escape. Alone and bleeding, but laced with adrenaline, it would have a decent chance of fording the river.

Instead, the troll grabbed Wren's arm, and the two went down together.

There was no time to move, no time to change what was happening. What *did* happen.

Frank scraped at the mess of driveway gravel with his workboots.

"That thing deserved to die," he said.

"When, Dad? At what point did that troll deserve it? I watched from the guardrail that night. I saw it all." Norah slammed the leatherbound book shut. She wiped at her eyes. "You know what? I don't care. I don't want to talk anymore."

"Finally something we can agree on," Frank said.

He threw his coveralls in the back, slammed the doors shut, and stalked around the van. He twisted the ignition and the motor roared to life.

He drove away.

To a certain stubborn degree, Frank had to commend his daughter. When Norah said she didn't want to talk, she meant it. Across the entire state of Kansas she remained silent. During a gas-up in Iowa, where even Frank had to stretch and check his cell messages, Norah marched in and out of the bathroom with ruthless efficiency. Then she sequestered herself to the back of the van without a word, writing and sketching broodingly in her moleskin journal.

Once or twice Frank peered into the rearview mirror, tilting his head to catch the page Norah was working on. He knew that she wrote entries for each of their—*his*—jobs. She noted the genus and species of creature Frank had been called on to exterminate. Afterward, with a grim and sullen satisfaction reserved for the likes of thirteen-year-olds, she tallied the number of dead for that job. She then added the number to a running grand total of all creatures their "charnel wagon" (her words) had carted off this mortal earth. It was a pretty big number. Frank didn't know whether to be proud or ashamed of it. Sometimes it was both.

But in between the scathing entries for her dad, Norah also wrote notes to her mom. When times were good, Norah would divulge to Frank a few tidbits of what she had written.

A female hydra lays a number of eggs equal to the number of heads she has at ovulation. Cool, huh?...

What do you call the ghost of a chicken? A poultry-geist...

Got Dad to try tofu. Baby steps...

I want you to show me how to French braid my hair...

For Frank, it was nice to hear Norah addressing her mom in the present tense. It felt as if Norah was writing a postcard to Wren, as if her mother would return next week from some long trip. When Wren returned, everything would be as it was before the job in Seattle.

Norah's words conjured the image of Wren in Frank's mind. He would suddenly remember the vivid hazel of her eyes, her loving, sardonic voice, the crinkle of her nose after he cracked a bad joke—the same move he saw in Norah's face, now that she was growing up. That brief bit of recognition, of life, warmed Frank and defined the good times on the road.

The long drive across the plains states was not one of those good times.

The few surreptitious glances Frank had made in the rearview mirror were met with Norah's baleful glare, a violent flip of the journal to a blank page, an angry sigh. For miles, the only consistent sound came from the muffled chiming of the dead fairies in their steel box.

By dusk, they had crossed into southern Illinois. Frank pulled off the highway onto a dirt road that ran between acres of tall corn. Soon the road opened up to a dooryard. A graying farmhouse stood on the hill before them, its porch lights attracting iridescent clouds of gnats. Frank parked the van, cut the engine, and leaned back against the headrest. From the quiet came the fitful lowing of cows in a nearby barn.

"It's likely a crank call," Frank said, "but the farmer offered cash up front for me to assess. I didn't know what to make of the details he gave in the voicemail." He chanced checking the rearview mirror, but only saw a clenched hand. He looked away. "To be honest, I could use some help on this one, Nor. Those booksmarts of yours."

Silence.

Frank cleared his throat. "We can do things your way this time. No traps or poisons, unless we absolutely need to."

A soft rustling of the sylvan oats, of Norah shifting. Frank went on. "We need the money to make it to Chicago. We haven't had a break in a while. You still want to go to the Field Museum and see all of those crazy extinct animals. I want to see if those mothman sightings along Lake Michigan are true." Frank listened to the restless cattle. "Also, if we're stuck in this part of Illinois, I doubt there'll be vegetarian options."

An amused snort came from that last comment. Just a small one, but it was something.

Encouraged, Frank said, "You don't have to say anything. Séance rules. If you're willing to help with this one, just knock. Once for no, twice for yes."

Frank closed his eyes and waited.

The moleskin journal shut. Knuckles softly hit the journal's cover once… then twice.

"Okay," he said. "Let's see what other animals are on this farm."

Outside, while Frank fixed up the snaps of his coveralls, he heard Norah climbing out of the van. He glanced back to find she was already dressed in a pair of coveralls, which were big on her. Norah had cuffed the long pant legs above her sneakers and rolled the sagging sleeves halfway up her forearms. Her belt hung loose, the device with the retractable hookwire dangling.

When she caught him looking, Norah said, "I found these coveralls in a storage box. They're Mom's."

"I know," he said.

"I'll grow into them."

"I know that too."

Norah cast her eyes to the farmhouse. "Looks like the whole family's here," she said.

Seeming to materialize like the gnats beneath the lights, five figures gathered on the porch, shifting restlessly and watching them. A stout man, the farmer, adjusted the bill of his baseball cap as if he were conducting a strange variant of semaphore. Not to be outdone, his tall, thin wife crossed and recrossed her arms. And weaving in between them were three young children, who traded spots peeking above the porch railing or between the balustrade slats. The stout man came first, scrambling down the porch steps to shake hands.

"Thank you all for coming out." He took off his cap and rubbed his forehead. Sweat glistened in his buzzcut. "I rightly didn't know who to call, I was so rattled. Only person I thought to turn to was our preacher."

"Because you thought you needed an exorcism?"

Frank wasn't joking. The farmer goggled at him.

"Mister, I don't know *what* we need. What I do know is that whatever's on this property ain't of the human variety. I opened up to Pastor Clausen, seeing as how he is knowledgeable in these sorts of things. Instead of a Bible verse or a blessing, he gave me a phone number. Your number." He blinked at Frank. "Said you helped a friend of his with his church in Hannibal?"

Frank turned to Norah, who already had her journal in hand, flipping pages. "Hannibal, Hannibal… here it is," she said, pointing to an entry. "Reverend Kellerman, By The River Salvation United Methodist, March twenty-twenty. The hungry one, remember?"

"I do now," Frank said. He exchanged a knowing look with Norah before turning back to the farmer. "Reverend Kellerman had something digging up fresh graves in his churchyard. He called to have it trapped and boxed. Turned out it to be a ghoul, a nasty one too."

"A *what?*"

"Never mind. It's not important for you, but good to know for me."

Norah closed her journal and raised an eyebrow. "For *us*," she said.

"Right. Us," Frank said, returning the smile. He turned to the farmer. "Your pastor was right to have you call us. We took care of the problem in Hannibal, and we can take care of the one you have out here. The question then is, what *is* the problem?"

"I'll tell you what," the farmer said. "*A werewolf.*"

He pointed above the dooryard to the purpling sky. A full moon was slowly rising above the cornfields.

"My granddad used to say the turning for werewolves happened in late summer. He said the better for them to move from the woods and hide in the high corn. I thought that was all Dust Bowl talk and superstition. But then I heard the howling… and then one of our cows got dragged out into the field… and I saw the claw marks on the barn door…" He shivered. "…and I started thinking Granddad knew what he was talking about all along."

The farmer made to talk more, but his wife beat him to it. After having seen her husband point to the moon, the thin woman had beelined it across the yard, her arms crossed so tightly around herself she looked to be in a straightjacket.

"No, Paul, *no*," she said. "Enough with that moon talk, and your granddaddy's tall tales. I know what *I* saw, and it wasn't no wolf. Not unless a wolf's got wings."

"Lorrie, we've been over this—"

"Then you should know that what *I* saw perching on *our* roof was no wolf."

Frank cut in. "What was?"

"*A pterodactyl.*"

"A pterodactyl," Frank said.

Norah leaned into her dad. "I don't need to go to the Field Museum for extinct animals," she said. "The Field Museum came to us."

"You see, Lorrie?" Paul the farmer said. He wrenched the bill of his baseball cap from side to side, scowling at his wife. "You see what that kind of talk makes us sound like?"

"My talk? And your jabbering over werewolves makes us sensible?"

"It makes *some* sense."

As if a hidden trigger had gone off inside of her, Lorrie cried out and flung apart her crossed arms. Her right hand flapped back to the house. "You look at our eave then. *Look at it.* I did. The same claw marks on the barn door are dug into the porch shingles. That means the same thing that made both those marks got a hold of Gertie and drug her out of the barn."

"Yes, Lorrie. *Drug* her out, as in using feet. I saw the tracks in the dirt, near the parts of Gertie that were left. Feet with claws that walk on the ground."

"But you didn't find where the tracks led off after," Lorrie countered. "Does a wolf… a *were*wolf… suddenly disappear after eating? No. Because it wasn't no werewolf. It was something with wings that took off with the rest of Gertie."

"And you suspect it's a pterodactyl," Frank said. It wasn't a question, but it sure as hell wasn't a statement either.

"Something like one," Lorrie said. She scrunched her eyes shut, reliving a memory.

"I saw it out the kitchen window while I was washing dishes after dinner. It flew over the cornfields, circling like a crow. Except it got bigger as it came toward the house. Crow, hawk, buzzard, *vulture*… I thought it was a trick of my eyes. It was the biggest, ugliest flying thing I ever did see. It swooped around the house all of a sudden, and the kitchen got dark, like I'd drawn the shades. Except it wasn't no shade. It was a *wing*. A wide, leathery wing, there and gone with a flap like an angel of death. When I heard it roost onto the porch, I dropped the plate I had been cleaning. It smashed like a shot. So did my nerves."

She popped open her eyes. Her face was pale and stricken. "The kids' room is on the second floor, above the porch. I couldn't imagine, didn't *want* to imagine—"

"Lorrie—"

"That *thing* was eyeing our babies, Paul. If the window had been open, it would have plucked them out easier than it did Gertie from the barn. Then it would have flown them off to its nest and… and…"

She turned away, her shoulders hitching. Paul went to comfort her.

"It's all right," he said. "We don't know what it is, but we want it gone, and we found the people to do it. Isn't that right?"

"We'll do what we can," Frank said. "Setting lures will be the first thing to do."

Lorrie whirled back and grabbed her husband to steady herself. "You're going to draw that thing *to the house* to trap it?"

"Ma'am, I don't know how else to exterminate it if it's not close."

"Then you can't expect us to stay here tonight." Lorrie looked to Paul. "You can't expect the kids to be here when that thing comes back around."

Paul nodded, patting her arm. "We'll leave, okay? We'll stay at the Lincoln Lodge in town tonight. Eat some barbecue, let the kids share a pig trough sundae at Porky's Creamery, and get some good sleep. How about that?"

"O-okay, yes," Lorrie said. She took a deep breath and relaxed her grip. "It'll be like a short vacation, where we don't have to think about monsters."

"Right," Paul said. "That'll be these people's job." He cast a nervous glance into the cornfields and then another into the sky. Then he reached into the back pocket of his jeans, where the denim had been worn into the shape of the wallet it held. "How soon can you start?"

"Now," Frank said.

As stars prickled the sky around the rising moon, Paul and Lorrie packed up a faded blue truck with overnight bags and their kids. While the adults talked and fretted with Frank, Norah had gone over to the children in the backseat and shown each of them sketches from her moleskin journal. She had hoped that two out of the three children would agree on the creature they saw peering into their bedroom window. On that count Norah was disappointed.

"I seent *that*," the oldest girl said, pointing at a page.

"A bog witch?" Norah asked. "Normally, they live around, well, bogs. Are you sure that's what you saw?"

"Uh-huh. She lookt like the one who givet the bad apple to the pretty lady in the cartoon." The girl solemnly shook her head. "I don't like that witch."

"That ain't what it was," the middle boy said. He nearly tore the page out of Norah's journal to make his point. "It was a vampire, like this one here. It had glowing eyes and sharp fangs and it stuck out its claws and did this to the window…" With a devilish grin, the boy crooked his fingers and tapped the glass of the backseat window. *Tck, tck, tck.*

"Stop it, Sam. You just like showing off. That wasn't what it was."

"Yes, it was."

"I seent it and it *wasn't*…"

As for the youngest sibling, she wasn't much help either. With her thumb in her mouth, the girl sat in her carseat and stared wide-eyed at every strange illustration Norah showed her. Only when the little girl caught sight of a banshee did she start to keen like one, and Norah quickly closed the journal to placate her.

"Any luck?" Frank asked. He and Norah stood on the porch and watched taillights flit through the cornstalks. The family's truck was headed to the highway.

"Well," Norah said, "I have it narrowed down to a prehistoric furry flying thing that eats cows and maybe children by the light of the moon. Oh, and it sucks blood, casts spells, and likely comes from Ireland."

"Right, *that* old thing." Frank leaned on the railing. "This sounds like a bust."

"What about Gertie the cow? And the claw marks?"

"I'm not saying that there isn't something out here, Nor." He glanced at the sky. Dark, pewter-colored clouds were gathering in the west. "It just may not be *our* kind of something."

"You think a regular wolf or coyote took Gertie? And a big, but not extinct, turkey buzzard went by the kitchen window and scared Lorrie?"

"Stranger things," Frank said. "We should know."

"Then what do you think we should do?"

"Stay and watch and see if something does come," he said. "Where you going?"

"To lay down lures," she said, "like we were paid to do."

"Lures for what, exactly?"

"Every furry, flying, bloodsucking thing that they thought it was." Norah nodded to the van as she walked toward it. "We have herbs and bait and lures that'll do the trick. I've studied up on most of the creatures, or things like them."

"It's a lot of work for potentially nothing. Now if I set some of *my* traps…"

"You said we could do it my way, Dad. Remember?"

"Okay, okay," Frank said. "Show me the ropes."

For the next hour, they plundered the pegboard walls in the back of the van. Frank set trip lures around the farmhouse. In certain lures, Norah drizzled rabbits' blood laced with an herbal tincture to attract werewolves and vampires; in others, she poured graveyard dirt and whispered culling spells to coax banshees and bog witches; and in a large lure on the porch roof, she dumped the contents of several canopic jars—the oldest entrails they had in stock—and mixed in dried corn from the Farmer Paul's feed supply to tempt a prehistoric bird of prey.

When all was set, they went inside the farmhouse. With the blessing of the family before they drove off, Norah pulled ingredients from the pantry and fridge for dinner. She and Frank mixed up corncake batter. Frank fried them up, topping them with blueberries and syrup. With their plates and mugs of coffee in hand, they sat at one end of the large family table to eat.

"These are way better than diner flapjacks," Norah said. "Good work."

"If we gave up the family business, at least I have a future as a fry cook."

"Just don't ask me to be a waitress."

"You, take orders? Don't think so." Frank sipped his coffee and gazed at an empty kitchen chair. "I can't remember the last time we had a proper meal in a house. Can you?"

Norah swallowed her bite of corncake. "Not since Seattle."

"Three years."

"It feels like forever."

"Yeah," Frank said, "it does."

The lace curtains stirred around the window above the sink. From outside came the sound of rain pattering in the dooryard. The alkali smell of petrichor, so much like the salt of the ocean, wafted in and surrounded them, tingeing the warm, cozy air of the kitchen with a bitter chill.

"Did you write anything on the drive?"

Norah knew what her dad was asking. She nodded.

"Did you want to read it?"

"You won't like it," she said. "I'm complaining to her about you."

"I can take it. In fact, it might be good to hear," he said. "How else am I gonna change?"

Norah pulled out her journal and flipped through the pages. She landed on the page from today and creased down the spine to read it better. But before she started in, they both heard the snap and hiss of a tripped lure.

Frank cocked his head toward the open window, listening for more than the pelting rain.

Norah turned to him. "Where——?"

He put a finger to his lips. "The front of the house," he whispered, "near the van. Something smelled us."

On the table, set out next to the bottle of maple syrup like another place setting, lay a pair of UV flashlights and a silver dagger. Frank and Norah each took a flashlight. Frank took the dagger and slid it into a holster hanging from his waist.

"Upstairs," he said.

"Why?"

"You've got a better vantage point. And you're safe."

"But I want to be with you."

Frank stared at Norah. The coveralls suddenly looked far too big for her. "I'm not having you take my lead." He turned off the kitchen lights. "Get ready with that flashlight in case I need it up top from you."

"Okay," she said. "Dad?"

"Yeah?"

"Be careful."

"That's the plan."

Frank crept onto the porch. Above him, rain drummed on the eave, echoing with dull thunder. He saw the ghostly gray outline of the van in the dooryard. The lure there—one that had been slathered in herbs and rabbits' blood—had been sprung. Something bulky wriggled in the lasso. Frank could tell it was no werewolf; at best it was a fox.

With his hand on the dagger hilt, he went out into the rain.

Frank watched the wet, writhing animal, still thinking it was a fox or maybe a coyote pup. But that changed as he got closer. The thing in the lure was pale and hairless, its muscles flexing in the mud. It didn't have a head, or legs for that matter. Only that wasn't quite right…

Frank froze, staring down.

In the lure was only a leg.

A troll's leg.

And as Frank stared, the leg started to melt like cotton candy in the rain. One moment it was the stout, muscular leg Frank had watched tumble down a slope of gray stones into a Seattle river. But the next moment, the leg turned gooey and insubstantial. The lure tightened, slipping through the flesh, catching nothing.

The thing did it on purpose, Frank thought. It tripped the lure as a decoy to—

Behind him, glass shattered.

He whirled back to the farmhouse.

There, on the porch eave, where it had waited for Frank take its bait, loomed the troll. The last and only time Frank had seen it—in the flesh and not in his sleep terrors—had been under the Aurora Avenue Bridge. He had hoped it had been his final time. But now the one-legged troll was here of all places, clawing at the window frame.

But how?

A flashlight beam stuttered to life and shot through the broken glass. The troll, pinned in the light, roared and lunged at the window.

When he heard Norah scream, Frank ran.

He heard another snap of a lure just in time to high step away. It was the lure they had set on the porch roof, which the troll had thrown off while hiding. Clever, too clever for a troll. With his mind reeling, Frank scrambled inside the house and up the stairs. No time to think, no time to go back to the van, no time to change things, never any time.

He flew into the children's bedroom and stared. Like Lorrie's worst maternal nightmare come to life, the monster had crawled through the window and now crouched next to a pile of the children's cheerful but wet stuffed animals. But it wasn't the three farm kids who were in danger; it was his daughter.

Norah had been knocked to the ground. She rolled over and crawled to the UV flashlight she had dropped. With a lunge, she retrieved it and trained the high-intensity beam back on her target. Roaring, the troll brought up one arm to cover its eyes. It swung its other arm wildly, knocking down a shelf of knickknacks. The light burned its rough, scabby skin to a chalky white. Sensing it was under real attack, it began to spasm.

It was then Frank knew for certain the thing wasn't a troll, let alone the troll from Seattle.

While in its throes, the creature sprouted scraggly hair, its nose stretching and crooking at the end. In the shifting light, it now looked like a trembling bog witch. Then it screeched like a banshee and its fangs grew long past its leathery lips. It lowered its arm, revealing eyes like burning phosphorous—a vampire or a werewolf, depending on the angle. A dry, rustling *thwick* in the shadows suddenly brought forth a pair of terrible wings that filled the room, shuddered, and closed again. Then back to the troll, or something like it, the traits swirling in the light…

And something else that glittered. A line, straight and taut, in the flashlight beam.

The retractable wire.

Frank saw the device, like his own, on Norah's coveralls. Somehow in the struggle the silver hook had caught onto the creature and stretched the wire.

But this thing was no bundle of attic fairies. It was *heavy*, growing heavier as the troll parts of it were turning to stone, as it leaned back on its one leg toward the open window…

"Norah," Frank said, *"don't kill it."*

She threw back her head, wet hair flying. "*What?* Why not?"

Before Frank could answer, the monster hit the window ledge. It bent half-way out the window, its forepaws—it was now a good percentage werewolf—flailing in the rain. The hook dug in, and it yelped. The wire had reached the end of its loop. Norah was the anchor keeping the thing from falling out.

Until she wasn't.

"Dad, I—"

She slid along the rain-slicked floor, the heels of her sneakers squeaking. Her scream mingled with the monster's cries. And still the wire held. It was Frank's design. It wouldn't break. Norah and the monster were going out the window together.

Frank grabbed Norah's shoulders. She stuttered to a stop, but a brief one.

"Lean back," he said.

Norah did, and Frank got a better hold of her. He wrapped his arms around her, hugging her close. He felt her slipping and dug in his heels harder.

"I can't let go," Norah said.

"Hold still, I've got it." Frank reached down for the dagger. "Just a little more…"

They both jerked forward.

The creature, still yowling from the UV burns and the hook, thrashed its paws, which turned to talons, which then turned to hands. The thing was scared, desperate. Then it faced Frank and Norah, locking its wide, frightened eyes onto them one last time.

Suddenly its skin smoothed out, and its cries took on a human tone.

A young woman now hung from the end of the wire.

"Mom?"

Frank slipped the point of the dagger into Norah's coveralls. He worked it around the clip of the wire device. "We have to let it go, Nor."

"But it's *her*, Dad. You see her too, don't you? *Don't you?*"

"It's not her," he said, and stared, and blinked, and looked away.

"…but she's right there… she's so close… *Mom…*"

"She's gone, the real her," he said. "It's just you and me now. It's what we have. Do you trust me?"

"…Y-yes."

"Then hold on to me."

And she did.

Norah held him as Frank cut away the last of the coverall fabric. Norah kept holding him as the device and its wire shot off, and even when the shadow of her mother fell out of the window. And Frank and Norah held each other while they went to the ledge and peered out together. They spotted the creature—by then it had turned into a dark and shapeless thing with glowing eyes—at the edge of the cornfield. It stared back at them, holding its hurt arm. Then it ran into the cornfields, heading west, away from the highway and toward unknown country.

Afterward, Norah asked, "Do you think it will come back?"

Frank shook his head. "It knows we let it go. It'll take its chances somewhere else." He watched the falling rain. "Any idea *what* it was?" he asked.

Norah reached down and picked up her moleskin journal. Its pages were warped with rain. She tried flipping through the pages, but they stuck together and turned to mush. The ink ran, her sketches and notes blurring together. The past records were gone.

"No," she said. "Looks like I have more research to do."

"And a new record to start for the business," Frank said, looking back out into the night. "Zero kills. One relocation."

95

The Tales of Genevieve Sley

THE TALES OF GENEVIEVE SLEY

*P*oisoned thoughts, poison tongue, poison pen.

Nature is funny, isn't it? In equal measures able to heal and to destroy. My greenhouse is a continual source of delight; the rare blooms and specimens that shouldn't grow for me, do; they respond to my ministrations—subtle shifts in moisture and feeding resulting in almost instant, often infinitesimal results. But they all grow for me.

The humid air, which Charles curls up his lip at, calls clammy, feels fresh to me, as alive as my plants. Invigorating. I can't get enough of watching my babies thrive on different mixtures of compost, marvelling at the cycling transformation of death into life—and some of my more exotic individuals, which require a more gruesome feeding—into death again.

I store their extracts near the door, in a cabinet. RG comes in to gaze at them now and then, peruse the contents, request new formulations. Intermingled with vials of fluid that can soothe blistered skin, are those that will cause blisters to raise, or vessels to constrict. Seeds to be ground into powders, mixed into tinctures, sometimes ordered. No wonder Charles only comes in here when he has to.

These stories speak of healing, of revenge. Of nature's way of making things right again.

Love Always, Bomb City
Michael Rook

Michael Rook is not cursed. Sure, he was named after a ghost, doesn't sleep, and writes to release the thing in his head, but he definitely doesn't blame his parents. Find his newest stories in Penumbric Speculative Fiction Magazine, The Last Girls Club, *and the anthology* Dark Corners of the Old Dominion, *for which he also served as an editor. More tales are coming soon. In the meantime, check out his Instagram (@michaelrook10) and website* www. michaelrookwrites.com, *home to his occasionally interesting blog.*

~

Caitlin almost missed it, the *click* from under the Lincoln's driver's seat. Benji was bouncing around the car's mammoth front chairs, his toddler-sized Nikes probably scuffing the white leather. Meanwhile, she sat in the back with Todd, listening to him as the Cuyahoga River weaved quietly through Cleveland alongside the otherwise empty parking lot. Todd kept delivering his pitch for them to stay together, not deterred by the presence of Caitlin's kid by another guy. No, of course not. He did seem to like Benji—he'd even agreed, without coaxing, to bring the boy along for this all-important date. Seconds ago, it had been impossible not to let that influence her as she listened to his pleas…

But that was all before the *click*. Caitlin caught it exactly when Benji, giggling, leaped from the front passenger's chair and landed on the driver's.

Her heart convulsed.

She thrust her arms over the headrest and fixed Benji to the chair, not allowing a pound of his pressure to release. Her blouse ripped with the effort and his questioning blue eyes started to water.

But she had to do it—because the Lincoln Continental didn't belong to Todd. He'd borrowed it from Caitlin's Uncle Ciro, Uncle Ciro, who spent his days sipping gin & tonics with the other suit-clad brutes in the garlic-haze of *Bella Fortuna's*, occasionally erupting about the labor troubles with Allied Waste and the Irish Prick. Uncle Ciro who liked to call himself "traditional" and who'd surely have supported this final attempt of Todd's to win her back.

Uncle Ciro, who'd also become paranoid that someone might "get him."

Because it was the Summer of the Car Bomb.

The national press had dubbed Cleveland "Bomb City, USA" just a few months ago. There had been that many car bombs during the ongoing mob war.

Solid marketing, though, right, Baby? Todd had once teased before she'd punched his shoulder for not being as funny as he thought.

He was oblivious now. "It's like there's two of me," he said, elbow of his corduroy jacket on the door. "One side with you and one that wants, I don't know, more… But I can kill that side. I *did*, because I really just want you and—"

"*Stop!*" Caitlin cried, but cringed, as if her voice might set off the explosives. Still holding Benji, she shivered, bracelets rattling.

Todd recoiled, chunky glasses catching a glare.

Caitlin searched for help, but Lot D of GE's Nela Park campus had emptied long before their walk back from dinner. Her co-workers, including the other commuter-college girls, had already escaped. The Bulb Building, like all the Georgian Revival structures of the massive campus—as described in the "Christmas Light Festival" brochures she'd sweated to copy-edit—stood dark. Everyone had fled to the Fish Fry at Holy Rosary's or Little Italy's restaurants. No one was left.

Suddenly she caught sight of some never-more-loved branding: a silver and blue AT&T phone booth at the building's north end, lit and vacant.

"Hang on," Todd said, hands raising. "Baby, I thought not knowing the truth, all the truth, was the—"

"*Stop!*" she unloaded again. Benji would cry out, he would, but she still didn't release her pressure. Wouldn't one slip trigger the dynamite?

"Didn't you hear it?" she said. "Under the *seat?*"

Todd's face expanded. He shot a look at the floorboards.

"Your Unc— The garbage strike?"

Caitlin locked eyes with her son. "No, Benji Boy. Quiet time now. Quiet."

Without asking, Todd opened his door. Caitlin swung that way, brown wave of her hair following. "Don't!" she hissed, but he plunged out.

Outside, Todd opened the fat steel passenger front door and then began to slide back into the car, doing so carefully, like the activists/troubadours/soldiers/lovers of his poems. It was immediately clear what he was going to do: replace Benji's weight with his own on the pressure-triggered explosives. In seconds, he'd gotten one Levi's butt cheek next to Benji's sneaker. Caitlin nearly screamed as he uprooted the boy's foot and laid it on his thigh. Then he slid further, replacing Benji's weight totally. The three of them froze like that, Benji shivering as he stood atop Todd, Caitlin in the seat behind them, arms over her ex's shoulders and still holding the boy.

"Let go," Todd whispered.

"I'm not moving."

"You've got to come get him. Benji-Boy, ready for a ride? Ready for a ride with Mom?"

Mom got her to exit into the warm September night, into industrial aromas dueling with something more natural, if not totally clean, coming off the river. Her fingers slipped on the driver's door and she thought she might blow an artery, but on the second try she popped it wide and reached for Benji.

"Momma. I don't like…"

"Blue Bear, it's okay."

Todd, still sitting, passed Benji into her arms. She quickly retreated. Benji blubbered while she whispered a grateful Hail Mary.

Todd stayed put, hands at ten and two, as if simply about to joyride the Lincoln around the campus. He nodded to the phone booth. "Get help," he said. "I'll stay."

"No. No, no."

"We don't even know. It'll be nothing. A gas, a gag when the cops get here. Maybe we'll make Channel 3. The weekly bloopers."

He smiled. And sweat.

"You don't move," she whispered. "Not an *inch*."

"Not an inch. Whatever you say, my love."

She rounded the car, gearing into a jog, Benji's weight pulling at her shoulders. A breeze kicked up.

"*Love you!*" Todd shouted.

"*Always!*" she shouted back, not really thinking about it, but meaning it, it being true.

She sprinted then. At the phone booth, she lowered Benji into the space between the phone cubby and the ground, her legs shielding him. She hauled at the door, though it didn't fully close. As she grabbed the phone, her breath eased a notch and the wind off Lake Erie, so warm and hefty, grazed her like a hug.

But the heat grew like a radio knob spun off its axis. It shoved her, the explosion. The phone's printing and buttons enlarged way too quickly, becoming blurs. Her forehead hit painted steel just as she heard the blast, heard it for a quarter second, as she'd tell the cops, heard it for a heartbeat's worth, before all went dark.

***

They started dating again at his funeral. What else could she say? *It's not "free love," alright, but we weren't actually <u>together</u> anymore. Just seeing each other. It's complicated…*

"Almost three years," she said to the Schmidts, the German couple from the two-story Tudor next door. "It'd have been three years around Christmas."

Tales of Sley House 2023

So many names: the Berns, Bianchis, Rolnicks, Lees, Gordons. The Wakefields, who tearfully swore that Todd would have sidelined the poetry and singing soon, gotten a Union job as a teacher, maybe even at Heights High, with great benefits for her and Benji. Caitlin curled her lips but stayed quiet, it not the right time to get indignant: *After graduation I'm going after a marketing job in sports. They're doing lots more marketing now, not just advertising. The Browns, okay, the Cavs, better. My dream? The Indians. They'll have good benefits too, don't you think?*

The Gordons, Rosebaums, Eichlers, Scates, Fiozzos.

A young, out-of-uniform cop, Panzero, whispered that the car bomb had had a timer in addition to the pressure trigger, so, no matter what they'd done, it was going off. Goombas had started setting them that way, Panzero said, trying to get capos on streets like Euclid or Carnegie for better press and less chance of blowing up bystanders. This bomb had been shitty though, fired fast, but what did ya expect with half-brained Micks… He'd hurried away.

The Guzauskas, Quinns, Raspisardas, Taliaferros. They talked of Todd like a prince, not as a slam, but a matter of potential. What he *would've* become. Such a striking man. Such a *passionate* one. A principal for sure. And he'd have proposed real soon, not like Caitlin's mom warned: *He's the kind of disease you'll have to cut away.* The mourners were sure Todd held no intention of being a dirty swinger. And they didn't even know about the nights with his weird Ceremonial Magick friends—which he'd swore was all a joking hoot. *I'm never rolling over for some bullshit tradition,* he'd scoffed once in earshot, before adding, *Just kidding, Baby! I'll be Catholic for you!*

The sadness, the awe—from so many.

Caitlin swiped at her skirt, a navy number not as long as she'd maybe have wanted. What was appropriate for the widow—yes, that's how it felt—of a college senior blown to paste? Sure, he wasn't perfect, but he was so young, and now just collateral damage of a local mob war. Speaking of, Uncle Ciro had already skipped town, to Key Largo or Key Biscayne, leaving Caitlin and the family to offer answers, though they had none.

She pulled Benji to her knee, stilling him and his Evil Knievel chopper. Todd's mom's oil paints flitted up. How often had she smelled that late at night, eased and listening to Todd breathe after hushed sex? It'd never felt that way with Benji's father, the teenage boy she'd fucked just once to not be a virgin anymore, but he also not Catholic enough to stick it out like her. Todd, at least for the first year or so, had been so *devoted.*

"Caitlin?" someone called. "Done yours yet?"

She maneuvered Benji into the chair and weaved toward the scrapbook.

Rather than messages, Todd's parents had asked for poems. A goose-looking woman spun the book Caitlin's way. The pen had run off, so she dug in her bag, upending detectives' cards, keys, and the pocketknife she'd carried since Dad had run her girl scout troop. Eventually she found a chewed Bic.

Roses are…

Her shittiness stung. They'd gotten together because of words, hadn't they? Marketing and poetry? Changing the world with words? She scratched out her start and slashed new lines:

Your heart burned red.
You left me blue.
Always, I'll love you.
Caitlin

She hurried back to Benji, her heart writing lines her mind wasn't ready to hear.

A light-pole of a woman wrapped in sequins waded through the crowd, book in hand.

"There are no appropriate words," the woman said, quick and well-enunciated. She laid the book in Caitlin's lap. The spiral binding and plastic cover registered before she found the guts for the title: *Love Always, Bomb City,* by Todd Galveston.

"He'd almost finished," the woman said. "Deborah Rochelle, his thesis advisor. I thought…" She paused. "I hope it brings you comfort, eventually. Much of it's beautiful."

"Was he good?" Caitlin asked, suddenly needing to know. "Really good, I mean?"

"It's hard." The professor glanced away. "You hope for all of them, you do. He… I don't take them on if I don't hope for them a little more than the others. And he should have had so much more time to keep working… Excuse me."

Rochelle broke away, butting into the crowd. Other mourners found Caitlin. Their looks, that special look, the one reserved for the steady girlfriend of a boy they'd *all* hoped for—she'd loved it when it'd first been granted to her and realized she loved it again, couldn't remember when she hadn't. *Widow.* Yes, she'd always be Todd Galveston's widow now, even without a ring. Who knew, maybe they'd find one blown into the river?

She bowed forward, crunching the book.

***

She saw him again for the first time later that night. She woke long after

Benji had drifted off in his own room, her head buzzing from too much wine.

The buzz weakened when she noticed Todd, standing by the window overlooking Little Italy.

He wore the same outfit as the night of the car bomb, corduroy jacket and all, and when he walked to the bed and kissed her, she kissed him back, the sensation so real she popped away and held him.

"How?" she said, maybe still drunk, feeling light.

Todd smirked. "You said *always*."

They kissed and shed clothes and came together naked, her head buoyant the whole way. When they fucked, some still-rational part of her mind screamed she had to be fucking herself, *her* hands his on her breasts, her fingers his cock inside her. But then he came and she felt it inside of her, the wet and the warmth. Her rational mind cracked a little. But her emotions, her heart, loved it and stopped her from asking questions. It felt so much better than the sorrow. That was enough.

In the morning, he'd gone, but the bottom of her class notes now included a poem, written in his hand:

My heart burns red.
I can burn away your blue.
Always, I'll love you.
Todd

She should have broken into sweat at the physical evidence. But she didn't. She kissed the paper and drifted back to sleep.

***

What rapture, what a blessing: to be so loved that your lover returned from the dead? Todd appeared every night. Benji asleep, they screwed and talked and watched horror movies on *The Hoolihan and Big Chuck Show*.

"Chuck is solid," Caitlin said deep into the second week, curled into Todd's arms. "Hoolihan is bogue, though. They need a better contrast."

Todd grunted. "*Contrast?* That from class?"

"Just an opinion." She rolled over.

"The little guy is funny." He pulled the sheet from her chest. "Do you want to keep watching?"

In daylight, she analyzed it—class lessons indeed, psychology more and more the rage in marketing. Her situation almost felt Shakespearean. She'd dumped a guy she'd once loved, only to have him… after death… return? Who wouldn't feel guilt and want a second shot? Beyond that, Todd was *different*. She'd seen him differently, yes, after his funeral, after the parking lot, but it was more than that. *Devotion.* His commitment to her had cranked up to a level she'd only ever dreamed of, desired, especially as graduation neared. Now it finally all belonged to her.

But late into the fourth week, as October gave way, they screwed on their sides and she felt him probe her ass with his cock. She bolted upright. Ass-play might be en vogue for some, but she'd never been so excited by it that she'd allow a poke up there, ghost-lover or no.

Todd—not a delusion, but something else, something *real*, something physical—tossed the sheets from all but his shins, ghost cock at attention. "Just thought we'd try. My bad, my bad. Come here."

She stared at him, then her bed, where he dented the sheets and cast shadows. She found his brown eyes glinting in the TV.

It was all crazy.

And scary.

"Go," she said. "Wherever you go, go."

"Baby?"

"I need… I need some time. Please."

He seemed to want to say something, but he climbed out of bed, assembled his clothes, and walked toward the darkest corner, vanishing.

Big Chuck cracked a laugh and she shut off the set. Knees in the carpet, she flattened her palms to her face and breathed until her shaking stopped.

A few nights later, her having asked impossible questions since the Big Chuck night—*What the fuck are you, Todd? What's going on here?*—and him having given unsatisfactory answers, she told him to go for good. They'd not even undressed.

"Baby, I'm here for you. We can have *always*."

"I can't do this. I'm cracking up."

"It's real. For me, it's like—"

"Todd, leave! Please!"

Her lamp couldn't quite reveal it, but she thought his expression darkened. Without a word, he made for the bedroom door. After he exited, the door remaining open—really open, not in her head—she rushed to follow, thinking of Benji. But the short hall lay empty. She woke Benji and hugged him close, ignoring his questions.

She kept to herself for over a month, barely talking to anyone but Benji. Mom worried and Dad tried to get her to see someone. Friends at the Bulb Factory first showed concern but then seemed a little creeped out. Each night she looked for Todd. Sometimes she thought she saw him, but if he stood in the shadows, he never emerged.

His letters made it clear that he hadn't truly left. A new one arrived each week in the mail, scratched in his handwriting, each long, covering many sheets of paper. And each read like a multi-part cocktail: one part apology, two parts expressions of everlasting love, one part nostalgia, one part request for her to say *come back*. Her words were all that was needed; he could do the rest.

She refused to read the letters anywhere but in a corner of the bright lunchroom at work, but she read every one.

Finally, Thanksgiving Eve, unable to turn down holiday wine at the end of her shift and with Benji already dropped off at her parents to spend some time with relatives, she agreed to go to Shooters. There, tall PBRs and some weed surely acting as lubricants, she didn't even think about Todd. She laughed, joked about regular things like Jimmy Carter's peanuts. She even accepted one beer more than planned, from a friend from class, a sharp-jawed, older guy on the G.I. bill. Harold had been in Vietnam and had scars on his wrists.

"Torture?" she asked.

"That was from after," he said, looking away. "I did it."

She ran a slow finger over the scars, then pulled his chin in her direction.

By the time they fell into her bed, she only felt and smelled and looked at the nearby: lightened places in the night; his body longer and taller than any she'd been underneath; the sharp, rubberized smell of the condom as he crept open its package and she encouraged him; the expanse of his gaze as he entered her.

But later, Harold's screech, high but masculine, yanked her awake.

"*Holy Christ, Holy God!*

She clicked on the light, bolstering the early morning.

"No, *no!*" Harold shouted. "They found us! Somebody's hit, oh shit, bug out, bug out!" He jittered from the bed in ugly hops, his gaze on the floor.

"Chill, chill!" Caitlin shouted. "You're here, you're with—"

But Harold continued to screech, and she followed his stare.

What she found made his jungle-flashbacks seem righteous.

Bright blood, organ bits, and bones stained the room in all directions, some even sprayed to the ceiling.

"Fuck *you!*" Harold hollered at her, barely stopping to grab his Army coat and boots, not bothering with socks. "Witch! You let 'em in! Charley! Fuck *you!*"

His heavy body slammed down the stairs and out the front door. He didn't even bother to close the entrance to the street. Early winter chill crept up.

In her room, the gore remained.

Blood ran like streams from her bed, splitting into tributaries. Throat clenched, she began to hyperventilate as she noticed the flesh chunks on the comforter, a finger caught in a lampshade. She swallowed vomit when she looked at the chair and the bloody fabric snagged on its back.

The same corduroy pattern as Todd's jacket.

And Todd wouldn't take away any of it until she wept and all but begged. Afterwards, she collapsed, exhausted, and he left without a word.

But he hadn't really gone, had he? She prayed the Hail Mary.

What would make him go away for good?

Anything?

***

Todd's letters increased to daily. And though he didn't show himself, Caitlin suffered worsening nightmares.

In his letters, Todd remained lyrical and devoted, but now and again, things rawer, odder, and more desperate surfaced:

I've had offers on the other side. There are lots of pretty girls here. Even when I say I'm taken, they ask. But I always say no. I'll wait for you. Always.

And once in a dozen letters something else slipped through. *Changing the world with words* came to mind, though now paired with nausea:

I can't wait to show you the red river, Baby. That's how you get back. You just follow the red river.

Winter settled, snow turning gray and black behind rusting DoT plows. She lingered in the Bulb Building after shifts. She hung around the college library 'til it closed. She even slept at her parents', Benji already there, until Mom and Dad said they needed a break from babysitting before the relatives arrived for Christmas.

All that time she'd obsessed over a single question:

What would make Todd go away, finally and forever?

One morning before sunrise, she locked Benji, hard asleep, in the apartment. Exhaustion had finally dragged her into rest, but a dream of Todd had forced her into the cold that sliced up Mayfield Ave. In the dream, Todd had held her hand as they wandered a darkened festival with horrific magical attractions. It just broke something.

Little Italy, from streetlights to restaurant doors, wore holiday adornments. A bakery, *Mia Bella Vita*, leaked warmth and confectioner's sugar from its rear doors. Other restaurants began to wake up too, including some owned by Uncle Ciro's friends. They'd serve her hot coffee, but instead she headed toward the great Gothic church looming over the corner of Mayfield and Coltman, its turrets and sculptures of saints prodding the sky like gargoyles.

Holy Rosary's doors, never locked, let her slip into the main candle-lit hall. A homeless woman slept in a rear pew. Caitlin crept toward the altar, not sure where the priest's chambers might be. She needn't have worried. A young priest, Father Marty—she'd known him in high school—showed surprise as he carried candle oil. He helped her into a pew as she faltered.

After hours of talking—she'd *known* Father Marty might be there, if she was honest, even gone looking for him specifically—they transitioned to *Mia Bella* and drank hot tea. She unburdened herself, confessing it all. Father Marty questioned her gently, asking if she'd seen "someone." The Church now embraced psychiatry after all, it, like all human things, guided by the hand of God. But he never, in any of their talks, offered disbelief. Eventually, he sat still while she made her unsettling request. The one she'd certainly intended all along, hadn't she? For those whispered words of *exorcism*, they returned to the private rectory.

"It wouldn't work," Father Marty said.

"Why?"

"There's nothing to exorcise. No one's possessed."

Caitlin sighed and glanced at his bookshelf, spying the blue and white of their yearbook. He'd had a quiet crush on her, hadn't he? And she *knew* that. What was she doing? Was she so desperate…

"Marty—Father, no. I shouldn't have come. It's me, I'm just—"

"Besides, it's more symbolic than anything. You dig that, right? It's about what *you* think and feel."

She rose. "Benji… I need to get back."

"A cleansing ritual," he said quickly.

"What?"

"An exorcism isn't right, but a cleansing ritual might be. I know it sounds pagan, but we have those too. Maybe that would convince… him… how serious you are about wanting him to leave."

Caitlin hesitated.

Father Marty gave her a shy smile. "Do you want me to try?"

That night, Benji dropped with angry grandparents, their silent gazes like rocks hurled in a village yard, Father Marty and Caitlin spread out his instruments in her bedroom. With rapidness, he led them through the cleansing ritual, pausing often and stammering in Latin.

After, and with nothing having happened, they doused the candles and Father Marty collected his things. At her door, he lingered, but Caitlin urged him away, queasiness coming on.

But, *but*… she slept. No nightmares. No screams.

No Todd.

She woke early, refreshed, excited even. She gathered all of Todd's letters into a trash bag. She opened the kitchen bin, but then pictured the dumpster behind *Mia Bella*. She grabbed her coat.

Outside, for some reason, a hodgepodge crowd, from uniformed men to slipper-clad women, gathered outside Holy Rosary's.

"Lord God, I *denounce* you!" someone shouted. "Lord, I've spoken with the *Devil!* I've laid down with the profane. Fuck you, Jesus!"

Caitlin wiggled through the crowd in time to see the head priest and an attendant rush down the steps. They yanked at Father Marty, shirtless, his thin chest and arms ripened red by the sub-freezing temperature. She shouted his name. but rather than respond, he fought at the hands pulling at him, keeping his gaze angled toward the concrete saints high above.

"Lord Father, I screwed with the dirty and I *loved* it!" Father Marty yelled—

—but sounded like Todd.

Suit-clad men hustled by and helped the older priest and the attendant.

"I swam in it, Lord!" Marty/Todd screamed just before they dragged him inside, face darkening with the effort. "I swam in the red river, God. I *drank* it and it tasted better than you! I liked its answers better than yours!"

Todd's voice from Marty's possessed mouth. Caitlin's grip loosened, and the trash bag hit the pavement, canting, its top opening. Letters, like oversized, awkward snowflakes, spun into the breeze.

At her parents' house, she opened the door hard enough to dislodge icicles. Mom commanded her to stop, but she dashed to Benji's room. She locked them in before vacuuming up the toddler in a massive hug.

"What, Mommy, what?" Benji said.

She just hushed him, and she didn't ease until his breath began to labor. Without words, they fell asleep.

When she woke, dull early-afternoon light oozing through the windows, lake-effect clouds promising another storm, Benji sat up.

"Blue Bear," she said. "Mommy's been crazy, but it's going to stop—"

Clear as fresh typewriter ink, Benji responded in a voice not his own.

"The priest deserved it," Todd said from the toddler's lips. "He didn't under-stand. The red river doesn't belong to a side."

Caitlin grasped Benji, but Todd just kept talking from the boy's mouth. *Todd.*

"I understand it," Todd said. "I think I can go anywhere now, by the river or the paths. There are paths too, Baby. We can see where they go. I'm learning so many things, I can do so many things."

"*Benji!*" Caitlin shouted. Something snapped in her throat. Mom and Dad keyed open the door and pulled the two of them apart. While Dad pried away Benji, who fell terribly quiet, Mom slapped her.

Caitlin curled into a corner and sobbed as they took away Benji. Her father's effort to wrench free the boy had left scratches on her inner wrists.

It made her think of Harold.

That was from after. I did it.

Suddenly she had an idea for how to make Todd go away for good.

A final plan.

A terrible one.

She scrambled to grab her coat and bag and then burst out the door, her mind on nothing but Benji and keeping him safe.

Whatever that took.

***

Caitlin steered her Vega like a nervous teen. Snow fell, the roads a nasty stew of slush, road salt, and ice that forced her to crunch slow tracks to the closed Nela Park and its thousands of Christmas lights, which gleamed like Broadway buried by thunderous squalls of lake-effect snow.

As she went, she whispered prayers for her plan.

She arrived at the replica National Christmas Tree, the same as stood in D.C., and skittered the Vega to a halt. The wind grated her cheeks, worst on the one that still stung. Thoughts howled, rotating around Benji, and him speaking with Todd's voice.

And her plan…

When something all-powerful consumed you, fixated on you, how did you beat it?

By convincing it to beat itself.

That was your only hope.

Or destroy yourself.

She sloshed through un-shoveled snow to a bench facing the Tree.

A shadow emerged from behind it.

Todd still wore his corduroy jacket.

She started to cry a little.

Todd's expression immediately showed concern, significant and honest as he'd always been when she'd wept.

"Baby, I'm here," he said, hurrying to a knee. "I thought you wanted to

110

meet? I could hear you calling while you drove."

Caitlin's breath caught. What couldn't he do now, or *know?* Maybe he already knew her plan. But she swatted away her tears, trying to play the part.

"When I first brought you here," she said, "you said it would make a good poem. Ever write one?"

Todd smirked. "Not yet. I will, though. For you."

Caitlin bit her tongue. "Todd, I—"

He shook his head sharply. He also lightly gripped her arm, the sensation still shocking. "First," he said. "About Benji. I'm sorry, but I had to get your attention. I can do that now, go into people. With the priest… I had to. He *wanted* you, you know that? I saw that when I was inside him. But I'm sorry. Okay?"

I can do that now, go into people. It replayed like crushing waves. She pulled her purse close.

"Todd," she whispered. "I can't do this. We can't… I loved you, so much."

She met his gaze. His intensity, his anger—its power—it nearly made her give up.

"Is it money?" he said, almost in a growl. "Is that why, really why, you left in the first place? Or looks? I can change both, you know. I can do so much now. Actually, I don't know what I *can't* do. I keep learning. The paths… Baby, you've got to see the paths—"

"And the river," she said, the words just finding the air.

Todd nodded. "And the river. For sure."

Actually, I don't know what I can't do.

Another wave, heavy as a collapsing roof. The same feeling for weeks.

No more.

She burst from the bench, trudging lines in the drifts. She pawed through her purse, dropping it altogether when she found what she needed. She pictured Benji in his room—only to have the image morph into Benji speaking with Todd's voice. *Please God*, she prayed.

"I've figured out something," she said. "Something deeply true about us, Todd."

She held the pocketknife over her left wrist and spun towards him.

"Baby," Todd half-shouted. "No!"

"Neither of us can move on if both of us are still… " She paused, afraid to say it out loud. "*Around.* Not after what we had. It ran too true, like your river."

Todd's eyes narrowed while his fists curled.

She continued. "You've said you've had offers on the other side. Lots of pretty girls. But you always say no. For me. That's how much you love me, right?"

He stared at her without breath to make steam.

"That a far-out idea," she said. "Dating in Heaven? They don't mention that in mass, though maybe they should. Might be better marketing to lots of the congregation. How many people, when they're alone, would admit that they'd love to leave their spouse once they'd done *'til to death do us part*? Like us. Of another chance to fall in love. Lots of chances even, minus the guilt?"

"But I haven't done it. I want you, more than anything. Doesn't that show?"

Caitlin quivered.

It wasn't going to work.

Benji.

She brought the knife closer.

"Stop," Todd said, reaching out.

"That's the problem for us," she shouted as the wind picked up. "We're too in love. We can never move on. So, I have to go. Otherwise Benji won't grow up right. We can't be together and be around him. He needs a normal life, and he can't have that with us."

"Benji…" Todd said, eyes growing with some realization. "Your parents, they'll take care of him? Yeah, they'll take care of him for us. And we can visit him—when you think it's right. I'll show you how."

Caitlin shook her head violently. He thought she was going to kill herself to *be* with him, in Heaven? She wanted to vomit.

Benji.

"No," she said.

Todd seemed to bristle. "What do you mean, 'no'?"

"We won't be together, Todd. We won't. We'll just both be gone. Maybe we'll be friends up there, out there, eventually. Do you think?"

Now Todd's gaze lit aflame. He rushed forward, almost grabbing her shoulders, but he backed off when she moved the knife closer to her wrist.

"Are you serious!" he roared. "After what I did for Benji? For you? I *died*. And then I came *back*? I came back and you're still saying *no*?"

Caitlin nodded, tears warm in the cold. "You won't hurt Benji, though, will you? I loved you, I really did, but it's all just too much. I just want to go away. But don't hurt him, please?"

She pressed the blade into her skin—not breaking it, but achingly close.

Something shifted in Todd's expression, but this time not into something darker. She couldn't see as well suddenly, but she just made out the change.

Todd's lips hung loose under his mustache. "You think I'd hurt…" he whispered. "Benji. And, and…" He nodded toward her wrists. "You'd rather *this* than be together."

Caitlin nodded.

Todd started to shake his head, the way you did not in acceptance, but denial. The *always* kind of denial.

"Baby, I can't let you do that. We belong together."

Caitlin felt as if the bones inside her body wanted to collapse. Her mouth wavered.

"Then *you* do it," she said, the words cracking. "You do it." Silly as it was, she offered him the knife. "End yourself."

He looked with incredulousness at the offering. "*What?*"

"It isn't your fault, any of it," Caitlin said, clinging to the final appeals she'd thought up, the last-ditch words to push him over the edge. "Sometimes our love and words just can't keep our promises. It's not our fault. We tried. So, you do it. End yourself. For me."

Todd stepped away, his gaze wild.

She'd failed. Which meant she had to go through with her own bluff. She brought the knife back to her wrist.

"For Benji," she said, and pressed the blade the last bit needed.

Blood found the airborne snow as if that's what it had wanted all along.

Todd threw up his arms.

Suddenly, lights started to blink, the National Tree going on and off—though it didn't have blinking strands, which she knew. A new wave ran over her as the blinking intensified.

Suddenly *all* the decorations flashed, everywhere, the whole of Nela Park rioting in frenzy.

Todd squeezed his fists.

Bulbs began to burst, not on the National Tree, but also not far off. Seconds later she smelled fire. Lights within some of the buildings began to spasm.

Todd, star-intense eyes locked on her, pulled his arms to his chest. Something exploded. Further off, a new sound pierced the crackle of burning pines and cables.

Sirens.

More explosions rocked Caitlin while the lights continued their fits. The sirens got closer, near enough that their red and white lights cut into the other ones blinking and glowing—

Except for Todd.

Todd burned, burned like a thousand lights set on fire, burning a hole in the night itself.

The illumination grew so bright Caitlin had to shield her eyes, blood smearing her face.

And suddenly, all the lights, all hundreds of thousands of them, extinguished.

Except for one set.

The National Tree blinked in a pattern. Several times on, several off, sometimes quick, sometimes slow as a pulse.

S.O.S.

Caitlin fell into the snow, holding her wrist, vision dampening. And she didn't open her eyes again until she heard a medic shouting.

"Here! Over here! We've got one!"

Arms bore her up and something was wrapped around her bleeding wrist.

"Miss, can you hear me? Can you? You're going to be okay. You know that? You're going to be fine."

To which she nodded, once again crying.

But not minding this time.

Not at all.

The Wasps Are Coming for All of Us
Phil Keeling

Phil Keeling is a writer and playwright. His work has been featured in periodicals, anthologies, and theatres all over the US. His first novella, Juice, *will be released November 2023 from Psychotoxin Press.*

~

He was seventy or seven hundred years old. Absolutely somewhere in that range. He'd lived in the house for as long as anyone could remember: a creaking wooden shack of a home that sagged and swelled with the changing weather.

A house with a bad back.

The house felt like it had sprouted into existence around the same time as the Old Man. The same way that you have to accept that the Civil War or wireless telegraphy existed in a time before you were around. Some people have an easier time accepting the world before their birth than others. I think that's why so many people were afraid of him at first. Afraid of him in the same way that they're afraid of all old people: dust-covered relics of times that perhaps we'd like to forget about. They refuse to let us pretend these uglier times didn't exist. So we accept them in silence, neither confirming nor denying their existence.

We don't talk about what they say about their new Mexican neighbors. We don't talk about the incontinence or the complaining or the constant stories about death. And we most certainly don't talk about when the Old Man starts getting swallowed by his own house.

I was never sure why I went. The Old Man frightened me. He frightened everyone. He had been old since I was born, the sort of porchbound neighborhood centerpiece that your mother waves at on the way to church and then bleakly mutters to no one in particular, "Any day now. Any day."

The Old Man had been a pretty reliable sight around town or on his porch, where he'd smoke cheap black cigars that smelled of vanilla and whiskey. And then one day he just disappeared, though weeks went by before anyone really noticed. Everyone assumed the worst and talked the Methodist preacher into checking on him. Not because the Old Man was a Methodist, but because they knew the Baptist preacher would make a big production of the whole thing with himself in some sort of starring role. No one even considered the Presbyterian minister.

After ten minutes, the Methodist preacher stepped back out onto the porch and marched straight to his car, dabbing his forehead with a handkerchief as he went. The Old Man, he said, was sticking to the walls of his house.

"Damnedest thing I ever saw," he'd said, somewhere between laughing and having a conniption. "Sweet Jesus, but I need a drink."

And it was true. At some point early in the year, the Old Man had sat in his favorite chair, and the boards of the nearest wall had reached out and taken hold of him. I had been away at college when it all began, but my mother had described in great detail the way that the wooden planks had somehow split open the paper-thin skin of the Old Man's back and driven themselves into the meat and bone inside, fusing together as if they had always been one.

The sensation appeared to have little effect on the Old Man beyond his annoyed grunting at anyone who came too close to inspect him. At some point, the doctor in Toccoa had come out to assist, but had given up after the Old Man screamed to be left alone.

"If the old bastard wants to get eaten by his house, I won't stop him," the doctor said.

At first, people brought him dishes filled with noodle- and cream cheese-based casseroles, even offering to spoon the food into the Old Man's mouth when the slowly creeping wood of the house claimed his arms and legs. The Old Man ignored them, though, and after enough muttered commentary calling him "obstinate" or "ungrateful," the visits began to stop.

By the time I'd come home for the holidays, a damp cold had settled into the mountains, and the air in our neighborhood smelled perpetually of smoldering cordwood. No ambulance had come or gone from the Old Man's house since I'd left, my mother informed me. So everyone was left to believe that he was still somewhere inside that decomposing shack.

When Mom noticed me folding one of her old quilts and asked what I was doing, I told her that I was heading down the street to check on the Old Man. It was cold, and I couldn't see any smoke coming from his chimney.

"Well, I can't imagine *how* he'd build a fire, the state that he's in," my mom said before reaching out to touch my face. Her hand was soft and warm.

"Oh baby," she said with a small smile, "You'll go to heaven for this."

I often wonder how she'd react if she knew that I just wanted an excuse to have a cigarette without her knowing.

The Old Man's door was unlocked, and I was struck by the silence of the home as I entered. There was no buzzing of fans, no gentle crash of an icemaker, no hum of central air. It was still, and getting darker as the sun made its way down. I made no effort to silence my footsteps as I stepped inside, but I didn't call out either. I think that's because I'd never learned his name.

The air in the house was damp and stagnant, like a cold malarial jungle. It smelled faintly of sweat and something sweeter that I couldn't put my finger on. Not unpleasant, but unnerving all the same.

I found him in the living room, wedged so far into a mass of papery wood so that only his drooping head protruded. If the original anchor to his house had been made of wooden planks, they had long ago been covered up with thin layers that make up a paper wasp's nest. The layers came in frozen waves that flowed over his hidden body and crept up his neck like a mudslide. I wondered how long it would be before his entire head was encased.

His eyes were closed, and I assumed that he was asleep, though I wasn't sure why. For all I knew, he could have died days ago. What little furniture remained had been arranged to surround the Old Man, as if he had been giving a performance and the chairs and threadbare couch were meant to be theatrical seating. There was no television or radio, and I wondered if he'd ever had electricity. I was ready to light a cigarette when he started to scream.

It was a wild, gasping shriek, like a gale forcing its way through a crack in the window. He blinked at me with his wet, foggy eyes, his mouth hanging open. Even in the waning light I could see that his teeth were brown and lined like pieces of wood, like the planks in the house had forced their way into his back and up through his gums. He shook at the sight of me, and light flakes of the papery wood that held him in place scaled away and gently showered the floor beneath him.

And just as suddenly as the shrieking began, it stopped. The two of us stared at each other for what felt like minutes until the Old Man's lips squeezed and wrenched forward with a *thoop* sound as he spat a loogie of some sort of sweet-smelling sap against my shirt. I yelped in disgust, and the old man seemed to lean forward, babbling in an old Confederate dialect that I'd never heard outside of old movies.

"You don't just let yourself in," he croaked. "You don't just come inside and make yourself at home—Chrissakes, boy!"

I wanted to shout at the Old Man, or least give him a little swat, but he had a point. Something in his reaction to my rudeness shamed me, though I wasn't sure why. I wiped the sappy spittle from my shirt and rubbed it into my jeans; somehow that was better. I apologized and held my mother's old quilt in front of me, using it as both a peace offering and a shield against further projectiles.

"It's cold," I said. "I thought I'd bring you a blanket. If you need one."

He stared at the blanket as if he'd never seen such a thing in his entire life. His eyebrows knitted together and he made a hacking sound from deep in his throat so horrible that I was certain he was ready to spit on me again. Instead, he let his jaw hang slack, the disgusting fluid dribbling out of his mouth and onto several little crystalline stalagmites of what I assumed was more of his tarry drool, now dried and frozen.

"What's your name, boy?" he asked, a thin string of saliva connecting his face and floor.

I told him, and he nodded as if he'd suspected this all along.

"Well, now you're my guest," he said. "So why don't you do an old man a favor and gimme one of those smokes?"

He smiled wide and I could see that my guess was correct: his teeth were made out of wood.

***

We didn't talk about much, those first couple of nights. I just lit his cigarettes and listened to him jabber on about whatever was passing between his ears. He told me how to properly can meat so that it didn't spoil or explode in the jars. About siphoning gas from strangers' cars and using it to fill his own tank. When the weekend came, I read the college football scores to him and he mumbled the names of quarterbacks and receivers that were true sportsmen but had never set foot in a professional stadium their entire lives.

Part of me thinks I stayed to listen to his accent. The way syllables were lengthened and multiplied, like bees passing through smoke: it was intoxicating and exotic, despite the fact that we were both from the same neighborhood in the same town. As he spoke, gobbets of his treacly spittle would build up and fall from his jaw onto the worn wooden floor of the living room. I made a move to clean this up once, but he scolded me harshly for this.

"A man should be allowed to make a mess in his own house," he said glumly, though I think he just didn't like that I noticed the drool in the first place. So for his sake, I learned to ignore it.

My mother did her best to ignore the smell of smoke on me when I returned from these visits. In a southern household, the only thing ruder than a bad habit is pointing it out to someone's face. So instead she wondered out loud if the Old Man had ever been treated for emphysema before he started turning into a tree.

When I came back on the fifth day, the couch in the Old Man's living room had disappeared. When I asked him if it had been stolen or sold, he only looked at me blankly.

"What are you talking about, boy?" he asked, and I could see that he was genuinely perplexed. "What couch?"

***

After a week, I'd spent most of my afternoons and evenings visiting the Old Man, a fact that left my mother sore and dramatic.

"If you wanted to spend some time with a lonely old person, you've already got one at home."

Still, she never protested loudly when I'd leave, and even sent me with cellophane-wrapped paper plates of leftover food from time to time. The Old Man was always quick to deny these gifts, telling me that he didn't really need to eat anymore. And besides, he'd be gone soon anyway, and my mother's cooking would just be wasted on him. There was one evening, however, that the Old Man stopped mid-sentence when he noticed something on my plate: a devilled egg, the sight of which made him drool like a rabid dog, increasing the already considerable height of the pillar of dried sputum that had been growing rapidly since we'd met.

"I thought that you didn't have to eat," I said, bringing the egg closer for his inspection.

"Devilled eggs," the Old Man said, "Aren't about nourishment, boy. They're about something else."

And without another word, I brought the little egg to his lips. The old man sucked the thing into his mouth with such force that his lips were stained with paprika. He chewed once, twice, and then swallowed, his fogged eyes rolling up into his wood-lined skull with a look akin to religious ecstasy.

As the food made its way down his gullet, a humming emitted from deep inside the folds of his delicate paper coffin. Not the burble of a satisfied stomach, but something more active and edged.

"Don't mind that," the Old Man said, with an uncomfortable smile.

"Do you have stomach issues?" I asked.

He shook his head.

"Those are the wasps inside. They eat meat, but an egg will do."

***

I spent Christmas Eve with my mother in her calm, dull Methodist Church. The service ended with the traditional candlelit singing of "Silent Night," and the white wax of my taper dribbled down its length almost in time with the music, an arch of cooling wax growing exponentially against the paper hand-guard.

Christmas Day was spent in Mom's house with distant relatives that neither of us remembered all that well or were particularly close to. After her third glass of Chardonnay, her face looked drawn and exhausted, and I helped her lay down on top of her neatly made bed, the duvet barely registering her presence.

I'd wrapped a carton of cigarettes as a Christmas gift for the Old Man, and snuck out before sundown, leaving the house to the mercy of second cousins and great uncles. I knocked on his door, but didn't hear the Old Man shout for me to come inside. Like my first visit, I let myself inside, calling out a Merry Christmas and already beginning the process of opening the present for him.

The living room didn't have any furniture in it now. Even the broken tea-cup we'd used as a makeshift ashtray was nowhere to be found. The stalagmite of dried sap and spit had built up to the height of the Old Man's face by now, though there was no face to be found. Instead, a dull mask of new wood had encased what little he'd had exposed the last time I saw him. The crystalline mass reaching from the floor almost looked like it was supporting the grim death mask of wood, a strut in a bizarre architecture of wood, paper, and sap.

I came as close as I dared to the mass that encased the Old Man's head, wondering if I would hear him breathing somewhere inside of the shell. There was nothing but silence at first, just like the first day I'd visited this house. Then, as if responding to my proximity, a juddering hum started up inside of the Old Man, a terrible invertebrate drone that rattled inside of his cocoon.

I unwrapped the carton of cigarettes and leaned them against the foot of the wooden mass that had once been the Old Man. As an afterthought, I left my disposable lighter there as well. I wished him a Merry Christmas and left the house for the last time. The sound of wasps followed me all the way to my mother's front door.

***

Classes for the spring semester had just begun when my mother called to tell me about the Old Man. The wooden mass hadn't stopped growing after it had engulfed his face; it kept on spreading to fill half of the living room, like a gargantuan termite mound. The doctor from Toccoa had returned, and in an impromptu autopsy, had carved into the mass with a handsaw. My mother had watched from a nearby window with several other members of the community, each of them speculating on what the doctor would carve out of the growth.

"Was it wasps?" I asked.

There was a brief pause, as if she didn't know what to make of this question.

"Wasps?" she asked. "No, it wasn't wasps."

"Well then what was it?"

"Nothing," she said simply. "The doctor sawed up that mound into all kinds of pieces and didn't find anything. It was just wood and paper and sap in there. It was like that poor man never existed at all. Why would you ask if it had *wasps* inside?"

I didn't answer, instead telling my mother that I loved her and that yes, I would be home for Easter.

That night I offered my roommate a slug of some contraband schnapps that I'd snuck past the RA and into our dorm room. I normally wanted nothing to do with him, an overanxious business major, but something about the memory of the Old Man made me feel extra courteous. At least for now.

The ingredients were something like peach syrup and doom, but he thanked me and enthusiastically took an extra-large swallow of the stuff. His breath came up like the sound of a pressure cooker releasing trapped steam, and he squinted through watery eyes, asking me who on earth would willingly drink that stuff.

"Schnapps isn't about nourishment," I said to him, elongating the vowels and adding extra syllables. "It's about something *else*."

And the two of us laughed and drank from the bottle until our ears were filled with a dull roar and our eyes spun sideways. That night in the dark, I stared at the ceiling of my dorm room and thought of my mother, wondering what she had expected to see when they'd carved open the Old Man's papier-mâché coffin.

By the time I'd graduated, they'd torn down the Old Man's house. If I'm being honest, I don't think of him that often. But in the summer of my graduation, I politely asked a grist of hornets not to make a hive on the wooden slats of my mother's porch, and they haven't troubled her since.

Curtain Call
Trevor Williamson

Trevor Williamson holds a B.A. in Modern Languages and an M.A. in Spanish Literature. Trevor is the co-host of the Sley House Presents *podcast, which features book reviews, audio fiction, and author interviews from across genre publishing. He co-edited two previous anthologies with Sley House Publishing, and this is his first fiction publication. Along with his brother, Collin, Trevor co-hosts the* Books & Badgers *podcast distributed by Sley House's network of podcasts. Every weekend, you can find him curled up with a good book in his home in Northwest Arkansas. You can follow his adventures online on most major social media platforms as* Sley House Presents.*

~

I arrived early and was shown to the banquet hall, where a statuary silence hung in the air. The tables had been set with glittering sets of crystal, expensive plates that probably cost more than I made in a week, white tablecloths with gold trim that sparkled in the low light. Even without anyone around, I felt underdressed. No matter that I'd bought my jacket just for this occasion or that it had set me back more money than I felt this event was worth to me.

I was about to sit at one of the tables when I heard a door open and close somewhere behind me. Turning around, I caught a tall, well-dressed fellow in a tux begin to make his way to the stage facing the tables. He stopped when he saw me and frowned before making his way over.

"Sorry, but I'm not sure I recognize you. You are…?" he asked, rubbing his hands together in a nervous fashion. The puzzlement was plain on his face, but as he drew nearer, I recognized him from the television.

I stuck out my hand to him and nodded politely. "No need to apologize, I definitely feel out of place, Mr. Wilhelm. My name is Glenn Mosely, I, er, well…"

Wilhelm cut me off as he seized my hand. "Right, the contest winner," he said, flashing me a practiced smile. "Glad you could join us. Have a seat."

He gestured to a table near the rear of the room, pulling out a chair for me. I sat and he grabbed the chair next to mine and leaned into it. "So, I owe you a congratulations on winning the contest. You must be a pretty big fan to have won the quiz to enter." His smile didn't quite meet his eyes.

I shook my head and waved a hand at him. "Oh, I don't have much of a mind for that trivia stuff. Honestly, it was my son who won the contest, but he came down with a terrible flu and he couldn't make it, so he insisted that I come instead."

Wilhelm paused for a moment, as if really seeing me for the first time. "You'll have to forgive me, I didn't realize the prize was transferable."

"Neither did I, to be honest, but my son's a pretty clever kid, and he found some loophole or other in the prize terms and insisted that I go in his place and tell him all about it. I don't mind telling you that he is a very big fan of yours. I thought it wouldn't be too bad an idea if I could score some points with him by coming."

"How kind of you both," he replied, and his shoulders fell back. His eyes softened and he crossed his legs. "Tell me more about your son."

"Oh, he's a big fan of yours. I bet he's seen every one of your programs. He's so excited about this new film, and we got our tickets already." Wilhelm's smile drooped slightly, and his eyes wandered to his watch. I don't know why, but I felt a brief feeling of shame, as if I had somehow let him down. "His name is Carter. He's a very bright boy, very clever, mind like a sponge. You should see him when he gets excited, he manages so much energy!"

Wilhelm laughed along with me softly. "How old is Carter?"

"Twelve. Oh, you should see the look he gets when he watches your program. He hangs on every dramatic pause, gets these wild ideas for stories after every episode." Wilhelm continued to smile at me, so I went on. "He goes off to his room and draws pictures of scenes he liked from the program, makes up whole new combinations and stories all his own. He and his friends will work up little scripts with all the different characters from the show, and he puts on a little theater in the back of the house for me."

"It's just you and Carter at home, then?"

I nodded silently for a moment. "Oh, yes, well, since his mother died some three years ago. He took it very hard."

Wilhelm and I enjoyed the silence for a little while longer, the room hanging over us. "I think that's why he wanted me to come so very badly. After his mother… we had a difficult time adjusting to one another. Your programs, well, especially some of your older ones, helped us find each other again. He came out of his shell a bit with me when we talked about it."

"So you're a fan of my work as well?" Wilhelm wore a smirk even better than he wore his tie.

"Oh, don't get me wrong, Mr. Wilhelm, I like your shows plenty, but it's all a little too manic for me. You know, all the running around and shouting and flashing lights. It's a bit sensationalized, isn't it?"

I drew a deep chuckle out of Wilhelm, and for a moment his face took on that boyish appearance he sometimes had. "Fair point, Mr. Mosely. You can call me Jon, by the way."

"Er, thank you, Jon. I hope you don't take any offense to me saying what I did, I just never did develop much of a critical eye for television. Not like my Carter, anyway."

"And what is it you do, Mr. Mosely?"

"Oh, I just repair washing machines. It's not any glamorous life or anything, not like you have here," I said, patting the table.

Wilhelm grew quiet again while something seemed to rattle around in his head. I wasn't sure what to say. "Do you have any children, Mr.... er, Jon?"

He blew out a lungful through his nose, long and slow. "No, I can't say I ever had the chance, Mr. Mosely."

I didn't respond to him for a heartbeat or two while he studied my face. I didn't quite know what to say, so I didn't say anything.

"You're a good man, Mr. Mosely. You let a man think.

"I suppose there's a bit of justice in the fact I never had a child. There's really no way I could ever have been a decent father." He turned his eyes to the table for a bit. "I spend so much time traveling around on a shoot, so much time in interviews or hosting galas or these sorts of idiotic publicity events," he said, waving his hand in the air around us, "that I don't think I'd ever be able to devote my time to a child. There's no *Impossible Horizons* for me to bond over like you do for your son. There's just work."

We let the idea hang between us before he took another breath and asked another question. "What was Mrs. Mosely like?"

It was my turn to let my lungs out. "Oh, she was a right hell of a woman. Beautiful as... well, maybe not as beautiful as the people on your programs, but she was beautiful enough for me. More beautiful than I half deserved, I'm sure of it," I said, conscious of the tight bulge in my stomach. "She was a happy woman, right up to the end. Never let a sun set on her anger, always found a way to forgive and let go. It was a terrible thing to watch her waste away the way she did, to see all her energy gobbled up and spit out. It's like... it's like the sun couldn't give off any more heat after she was gone. Like you were just cold all the time.

"You ever have a love like that, Mr. Wilhelm?"

Again, he tapped the table with his fingers and exhaled. "No, nothing like that. I think you're a rather lucky man." His voice rose a little more, like a practiced orator, though his face didn't have that manic energy he had when he performed. "I've had this or that girlfriend, a fling or something to throw over to the papers.

"Let me tell you a little industry secret, Mr. Mosely: none of these relationships are built to last. It's all a little marketing scheme. The paparazzi sure love getting a photograph or two out of me with this or that date, but most of my 'relationships,' if you can call them that, are just publicity stunts."

He paused for breath, looking over his shoulder as if expecting company. "I don't mean to say that I've never felt something for a woman, just that my image is too valuable. People don't… *see* me for who I am. They see me every day, but they only see what they want to see."

I nodded along, like I understood. "My marketability rests a lot on my seeming eligibility as a bachelor. I score a few points when I have a new date or a new girlfriend, but I get bigger opportunities, better roles when the media thinks I'm hot. And, for better or for worse, I'm hotter on the backswing of a relationship than I am in one."

"It sounds complicated," I said. He nodded his own silent agreement. "And lonely."

"How could that be?" he grinned, and again it didn't reach his eyes. His smile was bright and wide, but his voice sounded angry, his eyes tired. "I have all my fans to keep me company."

"I suppose I never knew how hard your work could be."

He waved a hand at me, and his grin was gone. "I don't know I've ever known anything different. Even when I was a child, all they wanted from me was anything but authenticity. Haven't you heard that old saying about all the world being a stage?"

"Is that what this is for you? A stage?"

He regarded me solemnly for a moment. "I've played so many parts I've forgotten which one I am. Did you know I started acting when I was only fifteen? It wasn't much of a role, but my father shoved me out the door to make money, and I wasn't sure how. I followed some posting for a stagehand, someone who could lug around props and equipment backstage for a little production company. When one of the young leads got wasted in his dressing room, I was the only one who knew any of his lines, so I subbed in for him.

"That show was not my best performance, but it was enough of one that I started as an understudy then took over the role full-time. I was seen by a television producer around that time and that's when I started getting calls from talent agents wanting to sign me so I could be their next rising star."

He looked at me curiously. "Do you know how many production assistants I've worked with, how many directors, how many cinematographers have wanted a piece of my success?"

"I don't," I replied. I'm not sure he caught the insecurity in my voice.

"I remember all of them. I remember how many people I have had to suck up to over the years, how many people I've worked with who only saw what I could do for them instead of what we could do together. I've only ever been looked at one way since I was fifteen years old, and I'm…" His voice trailed off.

His thought hung in the air and he stared after it, as if he could will it to come back if only he hung onto it with his eyes long enough. Eventually, though, his gaze returned to me.

"You sound tired, Mr. Wilhelm."

He nodded, straightened his tie. He reached forward and picked up the crystal champagne flute in front of me, toyed with it in his fingers. "Maybe I am tired, Mr. Mosely."

The door behind us creaked and he turned his head back to see a few richly-dressed men and women begin making their way into the banquet hall. He cleared his throat and stood up, straightened his tie, and ruffled out his wrinkles. He was about to walk away when I cleared my throat. "Oh, er, before you go, sir, my son wanted you to have this."

I pulled out a folded piece of paper from my jacket pocket and handed it to Wilhelm. He took it and unfolded it and for a moment something washed over his face. He started laughing after that. "Goodness, this is a real treasure, Mr. Mosely. Do you know what this is?"

I had packed it for the drive over to the hall, so I had seen it. It was a picture of a man in a mask standing in a hall of what looked like sleeping people. I didn't quite understand it, but it was bright and colorful, with plenty of blues and reds and blacks. "It's a picture he drew for you."

"Not any picture," he responded, still studying the drawing. "It's a scene from one of my older performances. Do you read much, Mr. Mosely?"

"Just the papers every morning."

He shook his head. "Of course. This one is from an adaptation of an old American author, very famous." He folded up the picture and handed it back to me. I put up a hand to reject it.

"No, no, he was adamant that you have it."

He smiled and put it in his own jacket pocket. "Tell your son thank you. And tell him that we have the same taste in literature." He sighed and patted me on the shoulder. "I'm glad you're here, Mr. Mosely. I know you don't think yourself much of a critic, but I do think this will be one of my finest performances yet."

"I have heard from the publicists that the film is quite good."

He laughed and leaned over the table to pour some water into the champagne flute he had taken up. "Sure," he muttered, then wandered off toward incoming guests.

I sat alone while the new arrivals mingled, and soon the hall was filled with the chatter of voices. Some laughed, others mumbled in low tones where they wouldn't be overheard, and gradually they began making their way to various tables around the room. I was given a studious berth by most of the newcomers, and I began to think in spite of the cost that I hadn't spent nearly enough on my jacket for the evening.

Finally, I was joined by a few others. A man and a woman sat down on the far side of the table from me, neither of them so much as paying a look in my direction. An older woman, hard-packed and squat, sat down next to me with a waft of souring perfume. It smelled like the old, cheap sprays my grandmother wore back in the day. Based on alcohol, the floral notes would break down after so much time or so much heat into a stringent-smelling cloud.

The woman regarded me with one blurry yellow eye, fake lashes clumped with bad mascara, her other eye swollen shut and weeping. She had three hairs sticking out from her chin, and her hair was greasy on one side. Still, her clothing was likely the most expensive of her ancient day, with heavy fabrics well-sewn to keep the sagging flesh of her body in the familiar shape of her former womanhood. She regarded me suspiciously before finally barking at me through a snarl of jumbled teeth. "Who are you? Never seen you 'round before."

The other two at the table took notice of me as if for the first time. The woman, slender and long-nosed, lifted a hand protectively to her neck. I sank my shoulders instinctively.

"Sorry, Glenn Mosely," I said, offering a hand. The fat woman sneered at it. "I'm, er, a contest guest."

"*Contest* guest?" the woman exclaimed, and her one good eye scowled at me. "Who ever heard of such a thing?"

I admit she had me there, since I had never heard of such a thing, either, before entering. "Yes, there was a, er, sort of sweepstakes and my boy Carter won it, although he–"

She cut me off with a guffaw, looking over at the man and woman across the table. "These dreadful publicists, whatever will they come up with next? Can you *imagine?*"

I wasn't sure what she was asking the couple to imagine, but they both chuckled and nodded at her. The man, who had a rather weak chin and the eyes of an owl behind spectacled glasses, his widow's peak less a peak than a great plain, sneered in my direction. "I suppose you're here for the banquet and the film?"

I nodded along. "Yes, that's correct. Oh, and some time with Mr. Wilhelm, although I suppose I've already done that."

The three looked at me as if I had grown a second head. The long woman leaned over the table to speak to me in hushed, conspiratorial tones. "Did you just suggest that you've had a private conversation with Jon Wilhelm?"

"Er, yes, I suppose I did."

"You suppose you suggested it, or you suppose you had an actual conversation with the man?" The old woman's lips flicked spittle onto the tablecloth.

"Oh, I mean that I've already spoken to him. We talked quite a bit, actually."

The woman across the table scoffed. "Imagine being so casual about speaking with one of the finest thespians of the age. He's only gone and had a conversation with *the* Jon Wilhelm!"

"And I can't get him to join me for a round of golf," the man intoned to the laughter of the two others at the table.

"So you know him?" I asked. From the looks they gave me, you'd think I'd've swallowed a live fish in front of them.

"*Know* him?" the man retorted. "Why, we've only financed the first several series of his latest program!" They looked at me as if I should have understood their wealth and their relation to this event.

"Oh, yes, of course, how silly of me." They turned toward each other and carried on their hushed conversations with each other, and I lost any interest in trying to keep up with it.

All around me, similar conversations were happening at various tables, the guests all getting seated while Wilhelm danced around the room making this or that greeting. As he drew closer to us, I could see the strain near his eyes, the many people around him treating him with this or that reverence, fawning after him like some golden god. When he stopped at my table, I noticed a tightness in his voice that wasn't there when he had first spoken with me.

"Ah, Mr. and Mrs. St. James, so kind of you to join me for this celebratory event. And Helene, you look as healthy as ever." I had to stifle a chuckle at that line, and was pleased when Wilhelm snuck me a little wink. They made small chat for a brief moment before Wilhelm rushed off again.

He swooped up to the stage as the wait staff began to file in from some side doors, each laden with a bottle of champagne. The lights dimmed and a spotlight lit up the small stage in front of the banquet hall, where Wilhelm stood behind a small podium with a microphone. "Ladies and Gentlemen, thank you so much for coming to this event with me tonight. It is my genuine pleasure to be your host." A small round of applause sounded through the hall.

Wilhelm bowed politely, though shallowly. "Please, please, we can save our applause for the film's encore. I wanted to say a few words to you all before we begin tonight's main course. As you are all by now aware, tonight's guest list was no accident.

"Indeed, I worked hard with my agent to arrange tonight's little banquet in lieu of a more traditional red-carpet event, and with the exception of one individual," he said, gesturing in my direction, "you were all hand-selected to receive an invitation. That is because each and every one of you had a hand in making me the man I am today." A few soft claps recurred, though Wilhelm ignored them this time.

"Yes, without all of you, I could not be here. I would never have found so much success. Whether it be because of your tireless direction, your committed financing, or your endless promotion, I find myself in this unique instance. I never could have dreamed that I could make it this far when I was only a boy, but here we all are. I'm sure many of you would call it fate. I might call it a run of bad luck." A chuckle rose out of the crowd, and his smile could be seen across the room.

All around us, the wait staff began pouring champagne into crystal flutes, and each patron picked one up. Wilhelm also leaned over with the flute he had carried off with him, and a staff member poured him a sparkling glass.

Helene and the St. Jameses had received their glasses, though when I reached for mine, I realized I didn't have one. I raised my hand to flag one of the wait staff down to tell them I had no glass, but they didn't even seem to see me.

On the stage, Wilhelm continued. "Please, if you will, I would like to celebrate this moment with you all." He raised his glass up toward the light, and I watched the hall mirror him. "I hope you'll accept this first glass as my heartfelt compensation for all you've done to bring me here. To your health!"

A resounding cheer rang out, and each of the guests raised their glass to their lips in unison. I watched as Helene beside me guzzled down her drink and the St. Jameses eagerly sipped long from their flutes. When I turned my attention back to Wilhelm, his attention had turned back to me.

I saw him in that moment. The real Wilhelm. The veneer of boyish charm had faded away like the sheen in his hair. His eyes were dead cold, pinched near his nose. His hair looked mussed, gray in a halo about his head. The suit he wore seemed to hang on him, and his smile had too many teeth, like a shark's open mouth.

Next to me, Helene coughed, setting her glass down on the table. She reached a hand to her lumpy, whiskered neck, and sputtered again. Her weeping eye turned to me, open just a sliver, all red and milky underneath. Her other eye stared at me in a blind horror, and she opened her mouth in time to spew out bloody vomit in my direction. I had enough good sense to scoot my chair back in time to avoid the geyser from her mouth and watched as she collapsed onto the ground in a senseless heap.

Across from me, the St. Jameses each clutched at their throats, too. Mr. St. James tried to loosen his tie before a bloody foam ejaculated from his mouth, and he crumpled face-first into his soup bowl. Mrs. St. James got halfway out of her chair before she fell to the floor, splitting her head open.

All around me, the well-dressed men and women were clutching at their throats, gagging on the contents of their intestines as a putrid poison tore them viscerally apart. I watched in horror until every last one of them had collapsed, insensate. The statuary silence hung over the room again.

Only Wilhelm and I were left alive, and he still bore that maniacal grin, the manic fever in his eyes that made him so dazzling to watch on screen. He stepped down from his stage with his champagne still in his hand. Picking his way back to my table, stepping over the bodies stretched out in places over the floor, he reached into his jacket and returned Carter's portrait to me. I unfolded it silently and saw that Wilhelm had signed it.

"It's a real shame I never got to meet Carter, Mr. Mosely," he said. His voice sounded normal again, and the maniacal grimace had left his face. He seemed all the more tired now. "I really think he and I could have had a time of it."

He returned to the spotlight with his glass raised high, his back turned to me. "Alas," he said, lifting the glass to his lips. "The show must go on."

Don't Drink the Water
K. A. Hough

K.A. Hough is a Canadian writer, author of Ground Control *and editor who balances her passion for exercise and science with her love of cookies and nonsense. She has a voracious appetite for reading, especially for rediscovering the classics: everything from Austen to du Maurier and Atwood to Wilde, as well as modern humorists like Douglas Adams and David Sedaris. Her guilty pleasures are Mammy Walsh and Inspector Poirot.*

In her spare time, she follows her husband around the world, wrangling three energetic kids and a codependent dog, runs, and drinks tea.

~

Their flight had been delayed but what's an hour… or two… when you're heading to the beach to do nothing for a week?

So, they'd arrived after midnight, stretching out legs that had cramped from the four-hour flight, the muggy blast of warm air not as welcomed as it should have been after leaving the cold and snow behind. Lizzie, especially, was cranky, her excitement for a beach vacation much tempered by hunger and fatigue.

"Come on, kiddo. We're here! Paradise!" Michelle could hear Don's voice in a pretense of jollity, that he too, was struggling to stay positive. He reached for the back of their daughter's neck and gave it a squeeze, but she shrugged it off with an irritated scowl and climbed the steps of the last bus waiting in the airport parking lot, idling under a streetlight, spewing diesel fumes that heated the thickened air even more. Unlike her, but she was clearly exhausted, purple circles under her brown eyes, her caramel-brown skin looking pale and sickly in the cool LED light of the coach.

"Rest against my shoulder. I'll wake you up when we arrive." Don sat across the aisle from them and was caged in by a large man whose brick-red skin showed he hadn't arrived on the same flight from Toronto, and whose breath held more than a few airplane-sized bottles of rum.

As the coach started to move, Michelle strained to hear the driver's welcome over Don's companion—"Name's Gary"—who had apparently tried to change his flight, but the airline had somehow routed them out of Cuba—"…and we're not *in* Cuba, right, babe?"

'Babe' sat another row or two back, Michelle figured, as she could hear a voice slurring the same story to another hapless victim. "I mean, *Cuba*, right, babe?" Gary was 'babe' too, it seemed.

Spanish. Michelle's vacation Spanish consisted of *por favor, gracias, cerveza,* and *baño*. All the essentials. She let the driver's words wash over her, musical and smooth, punctuated by Gary and Babe's louder conversation, as she looked out the coach windows. Palm trees, yes, and paved roads, but squat, run-down buildings, broken-down old cars, and fences reinforced with wooden pallets streamed by, briefly illuminated by the coach's headlights. The bus moved slowly, trundling through definitely-not-tourist regions, and in the reflection of the window, she could see Lizzie's eyes wide open and staring. Anxious.

"Don't worry," she whispered. "The resort will be nice."

It had better be nice. They couldn't afford it, not at all, but Don had insisted they go away. "It's been years," he had said. "We need this."

They *needed* money. She needed a job, hadn't worked since the layoffs, had been overqualified or underqualified for everything else—and even before that, she hadn't made enough. But, Don was employed, so he got to make the financial decisions. And, a week in the sun… it *would* be lovely. No cares, no cooking, no cleaning. They could pretend to be that kind of family, the kind who deserved luxury.

"We slept on the beach last night. Wasn't the first time, was it, babe?" Already, she'd had enough of Gary, whose voice stabbed overtop of the driver's now accented English, something about the golden sands of the Playa, the golf. They were still driving through decidedly non-golf communities. A few mercados lit by neon lights, multicoloured strings of LEDs lining their windows. 'Best Bar.' 'Best BBQ and Ribs.' *A lot of bests*, Michelle thought, watching Lizzie's glance flick warily from one to the next.

"Don't drink the water," the driver was saying. "Bottled water is ok, but you don't drink from the tap." A pause. "No ice cubes," evidently in response to a question from the front row. "Don't drink from the tap. We want you to get back home safely. Use bottled water to brush your teeth, unless…"

Whatever he said next was shouted out by a burst of Gary. "Only drink from the bottle. The *rum* bottle."

"You said it, babe."

Michelle's reflection caught her by surprise. The lighting was unflattering, sure, but it couldn't have been just the shadows that made her look so… *old*. Deep creases framed her mouth, frown lines carved between her eyes: a gaunt, dour-looking old woman, old before her time from stress and worry. *Not poverty, but close enough*. She sighed, and smoothed her brow, tried to arrange her expression into one of calm and youth. The last thing she needed was for Don to decide he was tired of her. They were both 43, but she looked two decades older… at that instant anyway. She saw herself flinch at another bark of laughter—"Right, babe?"—and caught Lizzie looking back at her. She tried her best to grin, but it felt unfamiliar.

"You just wait. It'll be great."

***

They pulled their bags into an open-air lobby; she had hoped that leaving the bus's dank, blowing air would be more of a relief. Michelle could feel her hair well on its way to frizziness. The coach pulled away with Gary and Babe still inside. "Thank god."

Don smiled, easy-going and cheerful, somehow in vacation mode at two am, in a line of other exhausted people waiting to check in. "He wasn't that bad," he said, but then, he always could talk to anyone. He reached his hand out, and waited. "Come on. Hands in." Lizzie, a mature eleven-year-old, rolled her eyes, making him wait before thrusting hers out, then Michelle added hers to the pinwheel. Dark-lighter-lightest: the Thompson family colour wheel. "3…2…1… Thompson!" His voice boomed in the breezy lobby, and they all wriggled their fingers.

His enthusiasm brought a wan smile to the girls' faces. When it was their turn at the counter, they accepted bracelets—orange for the adults, yellow for Lizzie—though the desk clerk had pretended to be surprised that she wasn't eighteen, winking discreetly at Don when she blushed and turned away.

"Rafael will show you to your room," said the clerk with a friendly smile, somehow not showing a trace of fatigue despite the hour, his grey and yellow uniform looking fresh and uncreased. An elderly man, his skin pale and seemingly paper-thin, a few strands of white hair swept over his otherwise bald head, stepped forward to grab their luggage. *Help him*, Michelle tried to telegraph to Don, but Rafael straightened up, and strode ahead of them, his shoulders square and confident. They followed behind him: out of the lobby, past a darkened pool deck, down dimly-lit pathways, and between large blocks of apartments, their windows and balconies silent and dark. *I'm sure I'll appreciate this in the morning*, Michelle thought. A shaky elevator brought them up to the second floor, and Rafael swiped the card to open their door.

The large room was almost *too* air-conditioned, but beautifully clean. The tile felt smooth and cold under her bare feet, the two queen-sized bed impeccably made. "Cocktail?" Don's teeth flashed, and Michelle slumped.

"Tomorrow, I promise."

"Mañana, mañana," he teased. He handed a bill to Rafael, whose grin broadened.

"Gracias, señor." And he was gone.

Lizzie headed to the closest bed, but Michelle stopped her. "Teeth first, *then* bed." She opened a cupboard to find the minifridge, and pulled out a bottle. "Use this."

A peek into the small bathroom, where Lizzie had just turned the water on to rinse her toothbrush—

"Hey! Bottled water!"

Lizzie started. "Sorry," she mumbled, through her toothpaste.

"No problem, hon. We just want to stay healthy. We can't drink the tap water here like we can at home."

"I don't think it's as bad as all that," said Don, joining them, dwarfing the space with his size. "Mike and Marie were here two months ago, and he said they weren't super careful. Came back raving about this place." His eyes clouded and dropped for a moment, then brightened. "Said a week here changed his life. He left all his problems behind."

Her alarm went off at eight. They needed to eat breakfast before meeting the concierge at ten.

"Whassat for?" Don mumbled, pulling the sheet over his face.

"They announced it on the bus. It's for the tours, the… I don't know what else. You probably didn't hear him over Gary. But ten, in the theatre, and that buffet's not going to eat itself." It might not be a great buffet, but this vacation meant a break from cooking, and Michelle was eager to eat as much food as possible that she hadn't prepared, off dishes that she wouldn't have to wash and put away. *Manage your expectations*, she reminded herself.

The warm wind hit them first, wafting sweet and salt as they stepped out onto the stone pathways towards the main building. Under the bright sun, the dazzling blue of the sky—everything was transformed. Michelle watched Lizzie's tired face and posture lift as they passed between palm trees and tropical flowers. They were greeted by uniformed staff here and there, men and women aged young to old sweeping and pruning, always smiling. Lizzie gasped audibly when they turned the corner and the pool came into sight. In the daylight, it sparkled aqua, chaises grouped in sets of two under oversized umbrellas.

A red-haired, warm-eyed hostess greeted them in the dining room. "Hola. Tres?" She held up three fingers.

"Sí," Michelle responded. "Tres." She mimicked the hand motion, and read the woman's name tag. "Gracias, Rosa." The hostess beamed back, and Michelle felt a flush of pleasure. *Maybe I can learn Spanish while I'm here. In a week. But I can continue when I get back home.* There must be a free app she could use, between cooking, cleaning, applying for jobs… worrying about Lizzie needing braces and new shoes, not to mention summer camp… She followed Don to the table. They'd need more help; he hated asking his parents for money, but what else could they do? He worked so much already.

The buffet stretched over four aisles, though Lizzie turned up her nose at most of the dishes, unfamiliar and thus unwelcome. But everything was so clean, staff bustling about smiling, sweeping, and wiping, clearing plates… Michelle couldn't keep the smile of delight from her own lips. *How lucky are we?* she thought.

She carried her plate, heaped with plantains, ham, and passionfruit, over to their table, meeting Don as he returned from the omelette station, a perked-up Lizzie holding a plate of pancakes and pineapple trotting behind him.

"I could get used to this," he said, waving his hand at another smiling server. "Coffee, black."

"Por favor," added Michelle, and the man grinned back, braces twinkling. Their uniforms, long sleeves and long pants of light grey with yellow details and trim were all so neat and clean, every face pleasant. The only frowns she saw were those of the clientele, sour-faced couples and families glumly texting and scrolling, ignoring the riches around them. "Who *are* these people, spoiled enough to be so miserable in paradise?" Not her, that was certain. She was going to enjoy every second. There was no reason not to be dazzled.

Salvatore 'but call me Sal' was waiting for them in the theatre. He worked for the hotel, he explained, and could answer all of their questions. Booking à la carte restaurants via the app or guest services. Towel cards. Departure tax, $50 each, to be paid in cash at the airport when they left. At that, Michelle's stomach twisted. Another $150, US, no less. More money that they didn't have. She looked at Don and saw his expression—he was clearly upset, but he patted her hand. "It'll be ok," he whispered. "I promise."

Sal walked them through the available excursions, and Michelle again tried to paste a neutral expression on her face. She'd never been on a catamaran… and there was a waterfall tour and horseback riding on the beach… no, this wasn't about *her*, but she wished she could offer it to Lizzie. It wasn't Lizzie's fault that they were poor, that she'd lost the small paycheque from her job pre-pandemic. She was a good kid, but more and more, she saw her little face, so much like hers—but with Don's colouring—harden at a 'no' or a 'too expensive.' Tough lessons to learn at eleven, but maybe better now, better than those blonde girls over there, the ones with sparkly green resort bracelets, obviously a higher-tier experience than they'd bought, who were plainly not impressed by anything around them: not the blue skies and palm trees, not the beautiful pools, not the sliver of ocean they saw from the path. They didn't even smile in their selfies, the tenth ones they'd taken since they'd sat down in the theatre.

"The water?" Sal was saying. He spread his hands wide. "It won't be what you're used to. Look around this place. Look how happy all our hardworking staff are, here in paradise. There's clearly something in the water." He winked, and Don gave a little grin in return. "But, we offer bottled water, all included, of course. You can use it, if you'd like, to brush your teeth." He gave an exaggerated eye roll, then winked again. "And our ice cubes are very safe. We recommend soaking them in alcohol, just in case." Everyone laughed politely. Well, not the selfie-takers, but the rest did.

"What do you think? To the beach? Or the pool?"

"Beach," Lizzie declared. "Let's go."

"Sunscreen," Michelle said, reaching into her bag, and both her daughter and her husband groaned. "Listen, you have half my genes, so sunscreen." Don grabbed it from her hand.

"SPF 85? Is this even real?" She swatted his arm and reclaimed it, shooting him a glare as she squirted a thick white puddle into her palm. "Toothpaste would have been cheaper. Probably even more effective," he muttered.

Lizzie grimaced as Michelle started to slather her arms. "Mom, stop. I'll do it."

"Ok, but I need to make sure you haven't missed any spots." *Oh, the look.*

Don walked on ahead, calling back over his shoulder, "I'll get us a drink, ok?" By the time Michelle had sunscreened her own exposed skin and spot-checked her now-sullen daughter's work, the chalky residue looking like they'd both glow in the dark, Don was at the front of the line for the tiki bar by the pool. *I can't blame Lizzie for complaining.* She hated the greasy feel herself, but her fair skin and freckles would quickly turn to bright red and peeling, or as had happened once in high school, blistered and seeping. No daughter of hers would resemble bacon, not on her watch. Even if she had to fight through her newfound tween attitude.

"Meet Luis. He's going to take good care of us this week." Don held out a folded bill, which the already-smiling bartender took with a nod.

"Thank you, amigo. Dos cócteles del día—" He slid two cups full of unnaturally pink liquid across the bar, then turned to Lizzie. "Y tú—princesa. What can I make for you?" Lizzie dropped her attitude and affected shyness again, her smile all sunshine.

"Do you have pineapple juice?"

"Jugo de piña? Sí, señorita. For you." He added ice cubes to a plastic cup, poured in the juice, and, using small tongs, dropped in a cocktail cherry, then topped it all with a drizzle of grenadine. Lizzie squealed, the sunscreen forgotten and her mom forgiven for the moment.

"Thank y—I mean, gracias." Don raised his eyebrows at Michelle, and she made a face back.

"Shall we?" He slid his sunglasses onto his face and extended an elbow; Michelle took it, holding her drink in the other, the beach bag over her shoulder.

"This place is beautiful," she breathed, as they followed the wide pathways, swept clean by smiling gardeners here and there, 'Keep off the grass' signs dotting the manicured lawns. A short walk, less than three minutes, and they stepped from smooth stone onto hot sand. "There!" she pointed. "Three chairs under an umbrella." *Perfect*. She held Don's drink as he spread out the towels, and they both sat down with an ahhhh.

Lizzie was prancing on the hot sand. "Can we go in the water now?"

"Let your mom and I finish our drinks first, ok?" Don raised his in a toast, he slid his sunglasses down as their cups bumped, so their eyes could meet.

"I can't believe we're here," Michelle said. "Thank you. I mean it—thank you." She knew she was welling up, but was surprised to see tears in Don's eyes, too. He'd been working so hard, the poor man, and she'd been feeling down for years, it seemed.

"Nothing's too good for my girls," he said.

"Braids for la princesa?" The spell was broken by a woman's voice. Don jumped, startled into a frown. 'María'—according to the nametag pinned to the front of her uniform—stood in front of them with an eager smile, holding a blue plastic stool in one hand and a sheath of laminated pages in the other. She thrust the sheets towards Lizzie, and Michelle saw that each showed a variation of braids. *It might be a good idea*—Lizzie's curls were prone to tangles… add in some salt water and wind, and—

"No. Thank you." Don's response was short, too sharp. *Too expensive*. María's smile didn't fade. She continued to hold them out for another moment, a small tattoo of a daisy visible on her bony wrist, with an old scar twisting up from it like a stem. She shrugged, then retracted the sheets, her long grey sleeve falling back down over her skinny arm. Her large eyes, a warm hazel, twinkled, and Michelle thought for an instant that she looked familiar.

"I come back another time." She looked directly at Michelle—*Of course I don't know her, but*—and walked over to another couple seated a few chairs down. "Braids?"

Don pushed his glasses back up over his eyes, his brow creased. His breathing, shallow.

"It's a living, I suppose," Michelle said, lightly. "And she gets to do it in such a beautiful place. And the cost of living is so low, off the resort…" She knew she was babbling, and she took a sip to stop herself, the ice cubes bouncing off her lip. She turned to watch María walk away. There was something about her…

"How 'bout *now?*" Lizzie had chugged the rest of her juice and placed the empty cup on a little table. Don shrugged, and got to his feet, setting his own beside it; he'd only had the one sip. The ice cubes had already melted. He flexed his hands into fists a few times, then shook them out.

Taking a long swig of her own drink, Michelle crunched a small piece of ice as she swung her legs off the chaise, plunging her feet into the sand, cool in the shade, and lifting her hips, slipped her skirt down to her ankles.

"You're really going to leave that on?" Even behind his sunglasses, Michelle could read Don's look.

She shrugged, tugging the sleeves of her sunshirt back down to overlap where the sunscreen ended. Covered from her chin to her waist, its long sleeves coming down to the back of her hands, she felt a little silly—nobody else on the beach wore anything like it. Lizzie had refused to pack the one she'd bought for her, even going so far as to sneak it out of her suitcase at the last minute—after Michelle had sneaked it in. Her colouring would give her some protection, but… "When I'm fifty, and only look forty-nine, you'll thank me." She rubbed a splotch of thick cream more evenly into her thighs.

He snorted. "I'll thank you for smothering our daughter with toothpaste and wearing a turtleneck on our beach vacation. Fine, let's go." He stuck out his hand, and Lizzie grabbed it with one hand and Michelle's with the other, the way she had when she was small enough to be swung up between them. Together, they ran to the water, slipping and sliding on the hot sand and laughing as they went. Behind them, María went from umbrella to umbrella, slim and angular in her neat uniform, her smile never dimming.

"…Braids?"

***

Their week was flying by. *One week, that's all we get*, Michelle kept reminding herself, Lizzie, Don. She felt a pressure to enjoy herself completely, a stress to relax as much as possible, and Don seemed to feel it too.

140

When she awoke, their room was still dark—not blackout-blinds dark, but still-middle-of-the-night dark, faint light from the grounds sneaking in through the edges of the curtains. She was alone. Her thighs burned where the sheet brushed against them. Her mouth was parched, either from the innumerable beach bar drinks, blue and delicious, or from the sun and heat—just dehydrated, not dehydrated and hungover, she told herself. After all, she didn't have a headache. In the next bed, she could barely make out Lizzie's slumbering form, but she could hear her breathing, deep, wavelike. She propped herself up on her elbows to look around; lit up by his tiny screen, Don sat on the couch in the corner of the room, his headphones on.

Michelle lifted the sheet gingerly and padded across the still-too-cold tile, reaching for the bottle of water he held in his hand. He jumped in surprise, nearly dropping his phone. He pulled the headphones from his ears, and shifted the screen so it lay face down on his lap. Taking a long drink—*Ok, there was definitely a* small *hangover brewing*—she sat down beside him.

"You okay?" she whispered, licking her lips. They felt dry, tasted salty. "Come to bed."

Don cocked his head to one side and stretched. "Maybe in a bit. Just want to finish my show." She drained the bottle, feeling it crinkle in her hand as she put its cap back on. She eased herself back to her feet, tossed the empty bottle into the recycling bin, and grabbed him another bottle from the minifridge. He didn't look up.

"Don't stay up too late, ok? Another big day tomorrow." He grabbed her hand and kissed her palm, then held it to his cheek.

"I love you."

She yawned. "I love you too."

She didn't feel him come to bed, but he was back beside her when she woke in grey light, his regular breathing showing that he had finally fallen asleep. Michelle eased out from under the covers and tiptoed over to the curtains. Her fingertips had barely brushed the thick fabric before the burst of light flooded the room, acknowledged by twin groans emanating from the two beds. *Whoops*. She shrugged. "Wake up sleepyheads, we're burning daylight!" The buffet awaited.

Their table had somehow taken on a tinge of the same pall she had noticed at breakfast on their first morning: slouching, dead-eyed expressions. "Straighten up," she hissed. "We're the lucky ones." ...or were they? She watched Don's gaze flash between the clientele and the staff, other sullen couples and families experiencing such unappreciated luxury amid the smiling servers, their 'Holas' musical and sincere as they cleared tables of half-eaten food and filled glasses in a fluid dance. *They should all be happier*, she thought, taking in the contrast. We *should be happier.*

She watched Rosa step out from behind her hostess desk just as a man, similarly attired, his pants clean and pressed, backed into her with a dining cart. They laughed, and both returned to their duties smiling. Always smiling.

"Pool today?"

"Ok." *We should smile more*, thought Michelle.

***

The day flew by, like the day before and the day before that, despite her barely moving from underneath their umbrella. Lizzie contented herself with a set of diving rings for a while, and just as she was losing interest, asking for a third time if Michelle would play with her, or Don, two girls, their blonde hair now braided back from their sunburned faces in intricate designs, asked if they could play too. They looked about the same age, plus or minus, as Lizzie, and just as bored. *Probably too many selfies*, Michelle thought. Across the pool, a heavyset couple of the same colour pink raised their hands in a weary wave. *Perfect.* She settled back and returned to her book. Once in a while, Luis paused in front of her umbrella, removing her empty cup and replacing it with a bottle of water or a fresh drink—today's cocktail was orange—sweating condensation on the cold plastic outside, ice cubes rattling inside. It was a good thing that they weren't *too* alcoholic, these drinks.

The pool, the beach. The fruity drinks interspersed with bottles of water. The easy routine of each day. *Hola, Rosa. Hola, mama. Hola, Luis. Hola, mama.*

She even joined the aquafit class: fifteen minutes of bobbing around, waving her arms just enough to embarrass her tween, enough to justify lying still for the rest of the day, sipping drinks that warmed in her hand. She'd finished her book... but the lobby had a lending library of vacation reads: crime, thrillers, romance... this place had thought of everything; it truly was paradise.

"Stop calling it that," Don said after dinner, his bowl of ice cream slowly dissolving into soup. He looked tired, less like someone in the middle of a holiday than someone who desperately needed a holiday. Wary, terse. Like the people they had been *four? no, five?* days ago. *Don't get used to this*, Michelle tried to tell herself. *Keep feeling lucky. Remember how special this is.*

"But it *is*. We'll have to thank Mike for this recommendation. This place *is* life-changing." He grunted.

Lizzie had gone to bed. Don was inside, in the cool, on his phone. Michelle sat on their balcony, the warm breeze rustling through the palm trees, lulled yet excited by their whispering fronds. *Come baaaack,* they seemed to say. *Or better yet, ssssstaaay.*

She'd found an old notebook at the bottom of her purse, and held a pen over it now.

What had she done in high school? Or in any job? Maybe if she made a list of her skills, she'd see it in front of her, find the key to a job or even a career. She knew they couldn't stay, but she wanted—needed—to be able to come back here, to be among these serene, cheerful people. To not be a burden on Don.

He was tenser yet at breakfast, and barely lifted his eyes from his phone. Lizzie might have been happy, but she was picking up on the mood. *We're no better than the others.* "We should be grateful—" Michelle started to say.

"Just… stop, ok?"

She did.

"Maybe we shouldn't have come," she murmured to him on the beach. Lizzie was far enough away, digging for coconuts under a palm tree. Her blonde friends must have gone home—no, there were their parents, strolling pinkly towards one of the massage cabanas. Michelle watched María approach a family down by the water, her blue stool held under one sticklike arm, her refrain of 'Braids' floating back to her on the wind.

"You're too stressed out about being here. It's too much money, and—"

"It's fine," he snapped. "Just stop it. All you do…" He covered his face with his hands for a moment. "I'm sorry. We just… we just need to enjoy every second of being here, and I want it to be perfect. Forever memories, you know, and if you're going to be worried…" With visible effort, he relaxed his shoulders and put on a smile, unconvincing even with his sunglasses. "I'm sorry. I'm present. I'll do better."

"Just remember, you can leave all your problems behind," she teased. "Mike said." She looked over to where Lizzie kneeled, her feet splayed out to each side. "What did Marie think? Did she have as wonderful a life-changing time as he did? As I am?" She couldn't picture Marie enjoying anything. She had never seen her face shift out of a frown, any of the times they'd had to make small talk at Don's company events; Mike and Don had worked together for ten years now? Fifteen? That's a long time to never see someone smile.

She'd been at the Christmas party, held in late November because it was the only time the restaurant had had left, but they'd tried to make it festive, even if the weather hadn't cooperated. Mike and Don had talked to each other intently, not including their wives in their conversation. They'd stood with the men anyway, a step away. Marie was short—shorter than Michelle by a few inches, and slouching brought her down a few more. She'd worn a shapeless black dress over her too-skinny body, her hazel eyes huge and unhappy in her thin face. Just below her three-quarter sleeves, an old scar, paler than the rest of her skin, squiggled into a square of gauze on her wrist She picked at this, listlessly, with fingernails bitten to the quick. Michelle scanned the room for a topic of conversation. She'd already talked about the unseasonable warm spell, and was out of ideas.

"I got a tattoo for my fortieth," Marie said, suddenly, her thin lips barely opening. *I'd guessed fifty. Or more.* Her forehead was heavily lined, her elevens pronounced. "Haven't even taken the bandage off yet, and I regret it already." *Help,* Michelle tried to say with her eyes, but Don wasn't looking.

"Oh," she responded. "What did you get?" It seemed like the polite thing to ask. That, and 'Did it hurt?' and they'd be back to silence.

"My father used to call me 'Daisy May,' so I got a daisy. Don't know what I was thinking. It's stupid." She tucked the tattooed arm under the other, her shoulders hunching inward.

Michelle had nothing else to offer. "Did it hurt?"

"I'm thirsty," Don said, and her attention was back on the beach. "Want some water?" She squinted up at him. He smoothed his palms down the front of his shorts.

"That would be nice," she said. "Would you get one for Lizzie too?"

He smiled, tightly. "Of course."

"Please," she said. *Was that it? He needed me to say please?*

He walked away, towards the beach bar. She felt the breeze flow across her legs, through her hair, as she watched him stride in the sun, tall and brown, his hands flexing in and out of fists. She hoped that returning home would somehow make him feel less stressed. *One day left to leave his worries behind,* she realized. One more day till they'd return to their little apartment, where she couldn't pretend to be wealthy enough to deserve this level of luxury, where she'd search out the church camps and the best payment plan for Lizzie's braces. Where Don would have to call his mom and ask for money. Where she'd fall back into her role, but this time, she wouldn't complain about it. This time, she'd reach out, get a good job, help Don move them into a nicer place…

Winding through the chaises longues, their arms full of beaded necklaces, two blonde girls in the resort grey and yellow—surely not old enough to be working—offered their souvenirs to the tourists, their tanned faces maintaining bright smiles even when rejected. Michelle's brow furrowed. *Weren't those*— Without their braids, it was hard to tell… By the massage cabanas, the wife of the sunburned couple had stopped to watch them. The husband grabbed the woman by the shoulders and steered her in; the curtain swung shut, removing them from Michelle's sight. The girls, still grinning from ear to ear, separated, advanced on the next umbrellas.

Back at the palm tree, Don walked up to Lizzie and crouched down beside her. He handed her a cup of water, and she took a sip, then another, looking at him with big eyes. Don placed a hand on her shoulder, then under her chin, and Michelle watched Lizzie's expression transform into a bigger smile than she'd seen on her daughter's face for months. He dropped his head for a moment, then stood up again and crossed the sand to where Michelle sat.

"What was that about?" she said, reaching out her hand for the cup he held in his other hand. His sunglasses were on, and he smiled, framed against the underside of the umbrella, handsome, tense. "She looks like a completely different kid."

"This place is truly life-changing," he said. Behind him, María approached Lizzie. She set her blue stool down in the sand for a moment, and as she dropped her head, the hunch of her spine called to mind Steve's Marie. Lizzie reached out for one of the laminated sheets, continuing to beam, her smile altering her face to making her look like a stranger. María's sleeve had pulled up again, revealing the scar on her forearm. And her tattoo, a blue daisy.

And the girls with the jewelry…

"Those girls," Michelle said absently. She brought the cup up to her lips, and let the cool liquid flow into her throat. *Nice, but strange.* "Do you see Li—" She stopped speaking, as Don gently placed his hand under the cup, tipping it so that more of the water streamed into her. A tingling sensation began in her stomach and twinkled through her body, and she continued to drink, even as she realized, fleetingly, that she wasn't drinking from a water bottle, that this was resort water. Luis appeared over his shoulder.

"Señor," he said softly, "the uniforms are ready for them. We'll take good care."

Under his sunglasses, a tear streaked Don's face. "I'm sorry," he whispered.

Michelle broke out into a great big smile. She didn't care. This place was paradise.

Foraging
Allie Marini

Allie Marini (she/her) is a Florida Woman, cross-genre writer, visual artist, maker, and tarot reader. She is also a member of Horror Writers of America, American Literary Translation, and National Tarosophy Associations. Find her online: @kiddeternity www.alliemarini.com *or* www.creepygirltrap.com

~

The Widow lives way out in the woods, just past the edge of Whisper's Walk, and everybody from town says she's a witch. They say it right out in the open, because she hasn't been to town since way before I was born, not even for church. So, there was no chance that the men standing outside the general store could get caught gossiping about her like old biddies. That's how I knew how to find her, those bigmouth men from town. Cause Momma always sent me out on Saturdays with the weekly list. Never Marjorie, who's too weak to pull the wagon full of feed and flour. The men sat on the corner bench and paid me no mind. I'm just Scoggins the pig farmer's ugly daughter. I might as well have been a ghost in front of Islet's General Store, tucking Momma's list into the pocket of my pinafore.

They shoulda listened to their wives, who always say *Little pitchers have big ears,* but lucky for me, they just keep shooting into the breeze. That's how I know all what I know. Like not just that I'm even uglier than what Marjorie says, but all the things in town that really matter. Like how Vanzant is gonna lose his land to the bank if his peanut crop doesn't turn out, or how Savannah Bowdon got in a family way and that's why she had to marry pimple-faced Gladdis Laverty, instead of Lucien Sloan, what did it to her. Lucien ran off to Jacksonville the night Savannah's daddy came knocking to get Lucien to do right by his hussy daughter. I got not one bit of pity for her, stupid heifer. She's only a little prettier than me, and dumb as a bag of bricks, thinking a boy like Lucien Sloan was ever sneaking into her daddy's barn for anything more than just the fun of rolling in her haystack. She can't even boil a stupid peanut right, and all the know-how that takes is putting peanuts, salt and water into a damn kettle.

When I heard the men talking about Savannah's unfortunate predicament, that's when George Staney said that Savannah's momma shoulda marched her dumb ass up The Widow's front steps and dropped a tooth and a fingernail and money into the coffee can and got some moon tea the second she found out

Savannah's blood had stopped. *That way*, George said, *Even though they'da been in debt to that old woods witch, at least they coulda got her a better husband than Gladdis Laverty.* Besides having a face full of craters, Gladdis was well on his way to being as big a brute as his good-for-nothing daddy. Their only skill was dressing the meat from hunters better than them. Jack Spellman laughed—*George, you still believe that old malarkey?* I could hardly believe my fortune hearing them, so I took my time. George shot Jack a dark look, dark as the sky before an August storm, and said, *I know she buried them husbands of hers out in the vegetable patch, all three of them, and I know she put scarecrows up over the bones. And I know that lots of folks put all kind of things in that Folgers can of hers, for all kind of reasons.* Shame I couldn't take any longer, but I was pushing it because there's a fine line between dumpy girl hitching her wagon and nosy brat eavesdropping. So I made sure to jangle the door good and hard so the bell sounded all the way out to the street.

Sugar, coffee, flour, cracked corn, grits, molasses, pinto beans, rice, cornmeal, kerosene. Same list every week. Daddy trades fatback for eggs with the Beals from the next house over, and he trades ham hocks for milk and butter with dumb old Savannah Bowdon's daddy. Momma keeps a vegetable garden out back, but even so, when I came back and unloaded the groceries, I knew she was gonna hand me the basket and tell me to go find something for supper. Never Marjorie. She's out on the porch steps she swept, watching a quart of sun tea brew. Momma says she's already helped with her chores. She always helps Momma make dinner, too. Marjorie's a looker. She'll get married sooner than me because of it, so I'll have more time to practice after she's gone. The shame of it is that I'm the older one, and I also know there's no use saying anything. Momma's favorite thing to say is life ain't fair, and I need to get used to it.

***

Dandelion greens, swamp cabbage, blackberries, pokeweed, mustard greens—anything we can eat goes in the basket. When we don't have enough meat to trade and sell and eat, Daddy sends me out after squirrel, snakes, frogs, thrashers—whatever I could move quicker than. Once I got a possum and it was the proudest he'd ever been of me. Marjorie could never do that part. She'd come home with an empty basket, and she wouldn't even get in trouble for it. But if I ever came home with an empty basket, I'd catch it. So, I make sure I never do.

I can always find something to forage, even if it's just stinky old wild onions. I spend hot, sweaty hours looking for anything safe to eat and come home smelling like the hogs. Marjorie didn't even say thanks whenever I handed her the basket. She just wrinkled her nose at me and said, *You stank.* Momma said, *Go wash up*

Marion, and help your sister get supper ready. Daddy's gonna be hungry when he gets back in. While I was washing up, I found a tick, so fat all his legs were splayed out, buried down deep in the fat right above my knee. I used the dirty tip of my fingernail to dig his head out and then popped him between my thumbnails and pinched him between my pointer and thumb. I could feel him, not yet dead, squirming to escape. While Momma and Marjorie chirped at each other in the kitchen, I held him over the tip of a candle and waited for the sizzle and satisfying pop as what was left of his body crackled into the flame. Only singed my fingertip a little. *That'll show you, tick.*

When Momma noticed me standing by the screen door, she said, *Marion, get your fanny in here and help us, it's almost time for Daddy to come in, and supper better be ready when he's done washing up. Go fill the pail and then get in here.* She kept her huge back turned to me while she talked, the spread of her hips filling up the whole space in front of the sink as she cut lard into a mixing bowl of cornmeal for supper, cheeks pinched in concentration. Her plain brown hair—*Chestnut,* she would correct, remembering her beauty queen years— was scraped back into a bun so tight that the skin on her forehead was almost pulled smooth, except for one deep crease as she frowned and turned the cornbread batter into the cast-iron skillet. It only took me three good pumps to fill the bucket, because my back is as broad as Momma's. I made sure to skip over the loose step on the back porch when I came back up. I edged in next to her at the stove, and when I gave the water, I spilled a little over the side. She gave the fat above my elbow a good hard pinch, and said, *Quit being so clumsy, girl.*

Momma always pinched me hard because she knew my fat genes came from her side. When she was my age, she won a sash and tiara and spent a glorious year as Miss Possum County. Then she got with me. She reminds me all the time it was me that ruined her figure. A year later, Marjorie came and Momma's hips never were the same, spread all wide and lumpy. But because Marjorie is pretty like Momma was, I'm the one that gets the blame. Marjorie can get herself a better husband than a pig farmer. The kind of husband Momma thinks she deserved. The kind she hates me for spoiling her chance at. I know I didn't have any part in *that* except the fact that I was born, so I don't spare it a second thought. I get pinched for Momma's bad choice and worse luck, and I know it ain't right. But I know better than to say so, because like I said, Momma's favorite saying is, *Life's not fair,* and I'd do well to get used to that. She ignored me every time they were in the kitchen while she watched over Marjorie's cooking, making sure she was ready for a husband's kitchen. Even though it was always me who paid attention to every word she said.

Most days, when I helped Daddy with the chores outside, I wore breeches and waders and got dirty like a man. Marjorie would be on the porch with Momma, studying scripture, or sewing all the little frilly things that went into her hope chest. Things we weren't supposed to have the money for, but that Momma always managed to find somewhere, somehow, for Marjorie. She would load up the wagon with vegetables from the garden and send me out to the neighbors' doors, once my face was scrubbed pink and my scraggly hair combed into two presentable pigtails. Money for Marjorie's doss came from the work of my broad back.

While they cooked, I sat down at the table to shell a basket of field peas, just listening like a little pitcher with big ears to Momma and Marjorie. They clucked and *tsked* and sighed over stupid old Savannah Bowdon and her bad luck having to marry Gladdis Laverty, who everyone assumed would have to marry a girl like me, ugly as we both were. They said it like I wasn't even there at the table listening, because, well, I should know it by now anyway, so it didn't really matter if I agreed or not. It's just how things are. *Like I'd want a foul-breathed bruiser like Gladdis Laverty anyway.* Good for me Savannah needed someone willing to be a daddy, and fast, so Gladdis saw his chance.

A piece of pea shell jabbed under my thumbnail like a splinter. When I tweezed it out, it left a little dot of blood under the nail. I stuck it in my mouth and sucked a little, till I tasted iron. *Gracious sakes, Marion! Go wash your hands again, we don't need to be eating your mouth germs with supper!* Momma yelled at me, back turned, like those eyes she says she's got in back of her head saw me with my thumb in my mouth, even if it was just for a second. When I came back to the basket again, they were whispering about The Widow and her tea—Momma said, *Well, guess that depends on how far gone Savannah is. I tried it when I got with your sister, and it didn't take. Hadta get married anyways, so maybe it's best Savannah's momma kept her money. At least married to Gladdis Laverty, they'll never want for meat.* Marjorie tittered. I just acted like I didn't hear it. I figured I've more than paid her back by now.

When I finished shucking the peas, Momma took the bowl and handed it off to Marjorie, and told me to take the shells to Daddy for the hogs' slop. *Tell him it's about time to come in and get washed up for supper.* I heaved the basket up over my shoulder and steadied myself to go down the rickety back steps and into the muck of the back, out near the hog pens. Daddy just grunted as he took it from my hands, emptied it, and handed it back to me. I made sure to wipe all the mud off my shoes before I came back in and gave the basket back to Momma. I didn't wait for her to tell me, I went to fetch the pitcher and basin to fill so Daddy could wash up before we ate. Then I went back and waited for Momma and Marjorie to hand me the plates and forks to set the table. Supper's quiet. Daddy's what you'd call a man of few words, and Momma and Marjorie don't talk at the table like they do in the kitchen. I twirled dandelion greens on my fork and sopped up the juice with the burnt edge of cornbread. Their bitterness and char were a taste I'd grown accustomed to.

After supper, I put on my nightgown and filled the lamp to read my scriptures before bed. My favorite passage, where I've worn the pages thin as an onion skin, Matthew 5:6—*Blessed are those who hunger and thirst for righteousness, for they shall be satisfied.* It gave me a certain satisfaction to read, especially because under my mattress, I had a stub of a pencil no bigger than the first joint of my thumb that I stole from school. I knew that Edwin Mayo got blamed for stealing it. But the way I figured it, he'd prolly stolen something that he didn't get caught for, because Edwin Mayo is a known thief. So, I'm not especially concerned that he took the blame for it. I needed that pencil more than he needed to not get paddled. There was just no way Momma would ever give me money for a pencil she didn't think I needed. I use it to write things in the empty spaces in the margins of my bible, because Momma doesn't look there. I'm a dutiful daughter. I don't misbehave. It's the same reason it never occurred to Miss Belvedere to check my pocket for that pencil. I wrote down what I knew. What I heard downtown. I drew a map to where I thought The Widow might live. I wondered how much it cost to fix a problem. What The Widow might take let me trade for what she knew. What I might have to drop in that Folger's can besides a fingernail or a tooth.

***

By the time I had something worth taking to The Widow, Savannah Laverty was already showing, with a belly as fat as a Daddy Longlegs. She rubbed it all the time, like she was reminding everyone she was gonna be a mother, as if anyone could forget. *Stupid heifer.* When Momma sent me out with the basket, I acted normal like I always did. Momma never looked after me going out to the woods. There was no reason for her to worry; that was mostly true. There was no chance of a boy waiting back there to try and get me with my skirts up, and she knew I always came back with a full basket. I headed out into the woods, towards the fork in the road near Whisper's Walk.

I made sure to fill the basket with more than what I needed to bring back. Hopefully enough to trade for whatever The Widow needed to fix a person like me's problems. Her house wasn't as hard to find as I'd figured. It was just there, at the end of a dirt road, like any other house in the county. Except there were no other houses nearby. There was a vegetable patch in the side yard with three scarecrows, just like George Staney said there was. Up the front steps on the

151

porch, right near the front door, there was a swing and a rocker. On top of the railing, there was a Folger's can and a bell. I dropped my thumbnail, the one with the spot of blood from the field pea shell, into the can. It was too small to make a sound, so I rang the bell and waited, quiet as a mouse at night. Like a mouse, I knew somewhere out there in the dark where I couldn't see it, there was an owl that could see me, and that its wings made no sound when it hunted.

The shuffling of her feet came from inside the house. I'm not sure what I expected when she opened the door. A face like a crabapple? A pointy black hat? But she didn't look all that much older than Momma. *She must have those good genes.* Or maybe she was just one of those women who took to being a widow, like black dresses were made for them. She looked me up and down. *You the older Scoggins girl,* she asked. *Marion, right?* I nodded my head. She motioned to the porch swing, and said, *Set yourself down, I'll get us some tea.* When she came back to the porch, she had a mason jar of tea for both of us, nice and cool. We sat all quiet for a spell. I had to admit, it was nice to just sit down for a minute. I didn't ever get to sit on our porch swing, Momma and Marjorie always hogged it. I got the feeling The Widow was sizing me up to figure out what it was I needed from her. Rocking back in her chair, she said, *I know you don't need no moon tea. You're too clever for that. What are you here for, girl?* Now, no one ever asked me to speak my mind. Not anywhere. At school, it didn't matter what I knew. In the kitchen, Momma only ever talked to Marjorie. I've had no friends to speak of since dumb old Savannah learned how to make boys like her, and nothing to look forward to but a lifetime of small defeats and disappointment.

What I *wanted* to tell her was that it's not fair. Not fair that Marjorie was so pretty but mostly useless and I was clever, but got all Momma's fat genes. Not fair that I followed all the rules and I was a dependable daughter, but Momma scowled every time she looked at me. It wasn't fair that to Daddy I was just a mouth to feed that wouldn't fetch anything of value, even though I was capable. Not fair that I envied Savannah Laverty for a man that wouldn't be good to her and wouldn't have deserved me, but since we were both ugly, he'd the best I could be allowed to hope for. It wasn't fair that I worked hard and listened well, and had no one to love me, would never have anyone to love back. While I looked for a way to say all that and not sound like I was ungrateful, The Widow's face softened into a little smile. *Life ain't fair,* she said, and my heart sank, like a flat rock that skipped once, then went underwater. She leaned forward in her rocker, and patted the top of my hands, folded politely in my lap. *But* fair *and* even *aren't really the same thing, now are they?* Just like that. Who knew that shale could float back up to the top of the lake? *Even,* I thought, looking out to the side yard, and the three scarecrows that kept away deer and thrashers. *I can live with even.*

The Widow told me that people in town called her a witch because after her last husband died, she owned her land and her house and she wasn't beholden to anyone anymore, and they didn't like that. She said she was just clever, like me. And when a woman was clever, everyone thought that had to be some kind of magic trick, or that she had to be cheating somehow. *They like to say Witch because that's a person you can burn. But the thing is, being clever makes them need me. And they hate that even more. They need me, and they can't make me bend to their will. So of course, to them, that means I'm a witch. Freedom to do, and knowledge to use — that's a better kind of magic, Marion. That's power, and it tends to bring this back to even. After all, the world loves symmetry. As above, so below,* she explained.

But the coffee can? I asked. She covered the gap in her smile with her hand. *The fingernails and teeth… well you just never know what you might need to fix something, now do you?* she said with a wink. *Who's to say I'm not just using that stuff to fill the scarecrows and keep the deer and rabbits out of my lettuce?* She said that clever magic is like the men's Saturday night poker games, but with different stakes. *Somebody's always cheating,* she said. *But that balances out because somebody else is always playing a bad hand.* All of them depend on a stroke of luck. Lucky if they don't get caught. Lucky if the man with a better hand folds first. One man's good luck is another man's misfortune, and like anything else, that ain't always fair. *But,* she said, *you can make it even, when you're clever.* There are only 52 cards in a deck. If you're patient, you'll know where they all are. You won't have to say who's holding one they weren't dealt, because you'll know. Then you can just look after what's good for you and what you're holding. *That's the thing about luck,* she told me. *You can't really change the cards you been dealt. You just got to find a way to make those cards work to your favor, by figuring out what everybody else is holding and keeping your face still. Can you keep your face still, Marion?* I nodded my head, *Yes.* She said, *I thought you could. Now then, let's figure out how to change that luck for you.*

I stayed as long as I could before going back. When I gave Momma the basket, it brimmed with muscadines, swamp cabbage, and purslane. She took a look in it and said, *You sure done all right this afternoon. Go wash up and get to helping Marjorie.* And I did as she said, just like any other day. And tomorrow I'd do the same. Not fair, but it didn't have to be. *Even* takes patience. But now I had something to look forward to. Saturdays after I came home from market, I went foraging, like always. Except now, I went out to help The Widow in the kitchen. She taught me which herbs will bring back a woman's blood when you make moon tea, what to grind up to give a wife peace from her husband for the night, how to pull the poison out of a spider bite, and what kind of things I'd need for a new moon.

Tales of Sley House 2023

***

One wet August night, Doctor Pearl went out to the Laverty's. Savannah's goat-faced little sister Sierra pounded up to our porch before bedtime, breathless and excited to be an auntie. She said it was a little girl, Daisy Lou. Beautiful and blonde as the daddy that ran out on her, and fat as a butterball. All I could think was, *Another little girl, what a damn shame*, but I held my tongue and helped Momma wrap up a side of bacon to send over. Once the house was quiet and dark, I eased open the screen door and slipped over the squeaky third step. Before I got to the edge of the woods, there was a horde of mosquitoes swarming my face. I crushed their bodies against my cheeks with both hands, pushing sweat and blood and my own indignant tears into the little fan of frizz at my hairline.

In my nightgown, eaten alive by mosquitoes and my own jealous heart, the woods were dark and alive in front of me, unfolding and shuffling in the moonlight like a deck of cards. The roots of swaying trees, glowing under ruffles of fungi. Dead logs, covered white as ash, each stem and cap pointing up towards the sky, like arrowheads. *Blessed are those who hunger and thirst for righteousness, for they shall be satisfied.* I took my basket and ran until my blood hummed like the mosquitoes chasing me. *I'm so hungry,* my heart screamed. *I need something to satisfy this emptiness, this want.*

***

Savannah Laverty's little girl, Daisy Lou, was hollering her fool head off. When Savannah came over just before noontime, she handed Daisy Lou off to me to put down in the dresser drawer—we didn't have a bassinette. Never did. Marjorie and me both slept in the dresser drawer till we were big enough not to fall out the bed. When Daisy Lou woke up, she wailed for the better part of an hour while I hung up the wash. Savannah and Marjorie just kept swinging on the front porch, like they didn't hear a thing. Savannah was hoping I'd do it for her, and of course, what else could I do? Turns out, being a mother wasn't as fun for Savannah as it was to be expecting.

By the time I got to her, Daisy Lou's little face was the color of a beet and wrinkled like a raisin. I could smell her dirty diaper before I picked her up and felt the heavy dampness against the palm of my hand, seeping through her wool pants. *You don't deserve this, you deserve to be wanted.* I spread an old sackcloth on the floor and put Daisy Lou down gentle on top and peeled off her dirty diaper. I patted her round little belly, tickled under her chin, until she shoved her fist in her mouth and stopped crying. After I made sure her rump was clean and dry, I

154

gave her a dusting of cornstarch so she wouldn't get a rash. I swaddled her like a little cigar and she made this sound, like a little bird playing in the yard, halfway between a coo and a laugh and a hiccup. I felt a hot wave of jealousy again, for the love of this living thing that Savannah didn't care one lick about. And for poor Daisy Lou, because that was the only person in the world she had to depend on, and *ain't that a damn shame*. I jiggled her on my hip until her big gray eyes closed and her breaths turned into sleep again. I put her back down in the dresser drawer. *You deserve to be wanted, someone needs to teach you how to be clever*, I whispered to her, and she grabbed her chubby little fingers toward my face. Because to her, small as she is, I am beautiful, because I love her. When I came out of the room, Momma handed me the basket and said, *Whenever you get back, you can make supper on your own. I'm going to sit with Marjorie and Savannah and have a little visit*. I didn't argue or complain. I never did. I took the basket to go foraging.

August had been thick and wet—perfect weather for chanterelles and wild greens. There was dandelions, sorrel and purslane everywhere. I collected them into fat hanks of green, nestling them in the basket next to a mound of deep yellow chanterelles, the color of egg yolks. I found fat, sweet blackberries for dessert. I hurried to fill the basket, worried that Daisy Lou might wake up again before I got back to the house. On the sideboard, I saw that Momma had pulled a hamhock from the smokehouse. That meant Savannah was staying for supper, so I went and got Daisy Lou out of the dresser drawer and put her in a sling so I could jiggle her up and down while I cooked. I made a pie crust and got the blackberries ready to fill it. I cut lard into a bowl of meal for cornbread. I got the stewpot filled with the mushrooms, greens and hamhocks. While it simmered, I cut a bunch of crookneck squash from the side garden to go into the skillet last, just before we sat down to supper.

On the front porch, I heard the rhythmic squeaking of the swing chains straining against the heft of Momma and Savannah Laverty's enormous bottoms. After she popped out Daisy Lou, Savannah's fat genes kicked in, which I must admit, pleased me to no end. Marjorie's rocking kept the time with the clack of her knitting needles. She never took to knitting well enough to learn how to increase or follow a pattern—all she could do was knit row after row in garter stitch. While supper cooked away on the stovetop, I bounced Daisy Lou on my knee, one ear pricked up to hear the bubbling of the pot in the kitchen. Before I knew it, nearly an hour had passed, and it was time to take out the cornbread and set the table. I went to tell Daddy it was time to wash up.

Momma, Marjorie and Savannah were already at the table by the time I got back to the kitchen. I served myself a big piece of cornbread and a glass of milk.

Tales of Sley House 2023

When Daisy Lou started to cry, I excused myself to take care of her for Savannah, who gave me a big dumb cow smile with her fork halfway to her mouth. As she chewed, I could see a slash of pink ham hock caught in-between her front teeth, as she smacked her lips on strips of bright orange mushroom and grease-slicked greens.

***

The summer rains had started back in June—you could almost set a clock by them. Somewhere around three o'clock, they came in hard and fast and then cleared up just as quick as they rolled in, leaving behind a curtain of humid mist. Perfect weather for blackberries and wild mushrooms to flourish. In June, I'd just started to learn my clever magic. One afternoon, The Widow emptied a basket onto her kitchen table and spread mushrooms out in front of me like a fan. *What do you see, Marion?* she asked, rolling little yellow trumpets out in an arc like a butter-colored rainbow, bending across the length of the pine tabletop. I looked at each of the caps and stems and gills spread out like cards in front of us. I picked one of them up—fleshy and pale at the stem, rippling up like a flame into the deep yellow curl of its edge. *This one's a chanterelle,* I said, holding it between two fingers, picking up one of its neighbors with my other hand. *And this one looks like a chanterelle, but it's not.* I held the two mushrooms side by side in front of her, then laid the chanterelle down. *And this one's different, too,* I said, nudging a smaller one from the center of the yellow rainbow. *Clever girl,* she said. *You've got an eagle eye. Tell me how you know that those there're different from the others.* I held up the first mushroom to the sunshine coming in through the window and ran my fingernail up the side of its stem. *It's too woody here,* I said, *chanterelles got more meaty stems than woody. This one's got true gills, they go down all the way to the stem. Chanterelles got wrinkles and ridges, but no real gills. This one's also a little more orange than yellow.* She smiled at me, a gap peeking beneath the edge of her lip, from where her second husband, the mean drunk one, knocked her tooth out one night after he lost at poker. It was second nature now, the way she tucked in her smile to hide the space where the tooth used to be, her pretty smile ruined by a lick of bad luck. *Now the other one.* I rolled it over the tabletop, tallying up all the ways it was different. *It's smaller and got a skinnier stem than the other two. Tough, too. It doesn't ruffle along the edges. And the middle of the cap is tan, not really that yellow or orange.* The Widow smiled her gap-toothed smile at me again. *Wash your hands, now,* she said, gliding her hand up to cover the pale pink gum peeking between the good teeth. *See,* she said, *That's why your Momma sends you out with the basket and not Marjorie. You can tell the difference between a chanterelle, a jack-o-lantern, and a sulphur tuft. Those there, the jack-o-lanterns, they're poisonous, if you eat enough of them. They grow on the stumps and roots. At night, they glow a little bit. It's real easy to spot 'em at night, if you know what you're looking for. I've heard it said that they even taste good, like you wouldn't even know they're poison, especially if they're cooked up in a mess of greens and ham hock. The sulphur tufts, they grow on dead wood. Them, they're bitter, but not if you cook 'em. And all you'd need of them is a taste and you'd be done for. Now, how unlucky do you think a person would be, if someone were to cook up them mushrooms for supper, instead of chanterelles, Marion?*

The Marchand Sisters
Emily Ruth Verona

Emily Ruth Verona is a Pinch Literary Award winner and a Bram Stoker Awards® nominee with work featured in Under Her Skin, Lamplight Magazine, Mystery Tribune, The Ghastling, Coffin Bell, The Jewish Book of Horror, *and* Nightmare Magazine. *Her debut thriller,* Midnight On Beacon Street, *is expected from Harper Perennial in 2024. She lives in New Jersey with a small dog.*

~

I.

There were footsteps on the stairs again. Light, clumsy footfalls which mimicked the sound of toppling doll furniture. Bridget. It had to be. No one else made their way up to the attic with such brash determination, as if she were scaling a mountainside. Or pillaging a village.

Vivian Marchand set her paintbrush down and stared into the canvas stretched out before her. She was losing daylight, but she was certain she hadn't quite gotten the trees the way she wanted them. They looked like dark, brooding clumps of wet color instead of the light, airy forest which had unfolded in her mind. Sophie once said that that Vivian painted fairy dreams, to which Liesel replied very plainly that there were never any fairies in them. Bridget insisted that this meant they were nightmares, not dreams. At the moment, Vivian felt inclined to agree.

"They are taking Bosey!" Bridget announced in a breathless, scandalized voice as she reached the top of the steps. Vivian did not need to see her sister to be sure that she was standing with her hands on her hips, hair ever-frizzy and dress already wrinkled from having been skirmishing about the house in it all day long.

"And what do you propose I do about it?" asked Vivian, still staring critically at her canvas. "Bosey" was what Vivian's younger sisters, and Vivian too when she was a girl, called the Bösendorfer piano. Their father had acquired the piano from Vienna as a wedding present to their mother when they'd first moved into the Muinkkaai house in Ghent by the river, the one the girls occupied with their aunt to this day. They were Belgian through and through, but Vienna, their father said, was the best place to acquire such an instrument. Their father had passed in 1903, shortly after Liesel was born, their mother two years later. Only Vivian knew how to play, but she never practiced, and Aunt Alice insisted that they could do far more with the money it would fetch than the instrument itself. Of course, Bridget—who never so much as sat on the piano bench—was devastated at the decision. Change of any kind, big or small, was simply inexcusable to her.

"You must act!" Bridget ordered. "Go down there, lay in the doorway, and tell them they shall not take it! On your life!"

Vivian smirked. "And what about your life?"

Bridget shrugged her bony shoulders. "I'm not big enough. When I tried to keep them from coming in, they just stepped over me."

At this Vivian laughed outright and finally looked to see the proud, ripe pout on her sister's stern face. "Did you say goodbye to Bosey?"

Bridget shook her head.

"Say your goodbyes," Vivian counseled. "You'll regret it if you don't."

Clearly dissatisfied with this course of action, Bridget turned staunchly on her heels and stomped back down the attic stairs; Vivian was certain she even heard her sister walk up and down those steps a few extra times, for added effect. She dropped into the chair by the window. Exhausted. The Bösendorfer wasn't the first piece of the house to depart, and it wouldn't be the last either. Aunt Alice was doing her best, no one could fault her for that, but she was an unmarried woman with four girls to support—four girls who were not even her own. Vivian tried to imagine what it might be like to go your whole life without children and then to one day find yourself responsible for so many of them. She had no desire for motherhood, though she'd never shared the sentiment with anyone—not even Aunt Alice. Vivian wanted to be a painter and at sixteen she knew well that one could be one or the other but not both. "When a woman does something, she must do it whole," her mother used to say. Vivian would do this—give painting her whole, even if it left her with nothing else to show for it. Bridget was considered the stubborn one in the family, but Vivian had her own resolve, buried deep beneath layers of pleasantries and formality and familial duty. She was the sort of girl who would smile and nod and not once agree with what was being said.

More footsteps. Vivian closed her eyes and groaned. This time they produced a short, hard *tap tap tap* against the stairs. Liesel, she was certain. Bridget's steps were louder, Sophie's starker. She said nothing as Liesel's small, blonde form reached the attic.

"Bridget has fainted," announced the child.

"She has not fainted."

"She says she's fainted."

Vivian looked up and saw the quiet, knowing look that smudged the corner of her sister's mischievous smile. Vivian smiled back, rising and moving towards the big desk in the corner of the room. "Bridget always finds a way to make a stage for herself." She lit the lamp which sat, soot-covered and overworked, on the left-hand side of the desk above one of the drawers.

"You're going to be up all night," said Liesel, eyes twinkling.

Vivian pulled the chair to the desk, floorboards creaking beneath the weight, and opened her sketchbook. "What makes you say that?"

"You're always up all night when you draw."

"The only way to get better at something is to practice."

"You practice a lot."

Vivian looked up. The mischief had gone from the little girl's face. "I won't be up all night," she said before returning to the pencil sketch portrait of their aunt that she'd begun only a few days before. Painting by lamplight was out of the question—not in such a confined space—and so sketching had become Vivian's evening ritual. Twenty minutes passed. Maybe more. Vivian was so immersed in in the high, curved line of Aunt Alice's cheekbone that by the time her sister took her leave she didn't even hear her descend the stairs.

One hour melted into two, which melted into three, and Vivian's eyes grew strained. She'd be scolded in the morning for forgoing dinner and using up so much oil, but she could not help it. She had yet to get the face just right and until it was to her satisfaction, she could not be lured from her seat.

Leaning back to examine her work, the artist rubbed the back of her neck until it produced a quiet *crack* like that of firewood kindling and then yawned into the back of her charcoal-covered palm. She'd gotten everything but the eyes, which still could not quite convey the soft yet stern nature Aunt Alice tried so carefully to hide with practicality. She was a gentle soul—a bleeding heart even, not that she would ever let such slander be said of her.

Vivian's eyes grew heavy and as she leaned back in her chair to yawn again, she closed them for a moment, just to regain her senses. There was a gentle *tap tap tap* on the stairs, gentler than footfalls, which served as a metronome to her tired brain. *Tap tap tap.*

The sound hummed, at first distantly, then louder and thick as if someone was softly rapping directly against the inside of her temple. Lulling her to sleep. *Tap tap tap.* She wondered dreamily which of her sisters was up so late fooling around at the foot of the stairs. Though before her mind could conjure up a culprit, tiredness overtook her, and she drifted off into the safety of whatever dreams her brain had to offer her.

II.

"You're in trouble…"

Vivian awoke with a terrible pain in her shoulders. She slumped up in the chair to locate the origin of the sing-song-voice that had awoken her but when she went to speak, she found herself yawning instead.

"Aunt Alice says you are to go down and have some breakfast, then she wants you to go straight to bed," said Bridget, running her forefinger in half circles around the base of the long-dead lamp on the desk. A tactile girl, all movement and shape, she was wearing the peach-colored dress Aunt Alice preferred be saved for special occasions, but to Bridget every day was a day to look her best.

"What?" Vivian finally replied in a haze. "Why?"

"She knows you were with your sketches last night"—those keen eyes narrowed— "and she is *not* pleased."

Vivian sighed. "Tell her I shall be down soon."

A haughty upward tilt of the chin. "I'm not to return without you."

Moody, Vivian prepared to pull herself from the warm, worn comfort of her chair and another yawn escaped her as she steadily but unevenly rose to the soles of her feet. "I smell eggs," she said after a moment. "Sausage too."

"Aunt Alice said it was to be kept hot for you. 'Senseless girls need hot meals' she said."

Vivian smiled. Bridget's imitation of Aunt Alice was theatrical, more caricature than portraiture. She arched her chin, furrowed her brow suspiciously. "All the more reason to remain senseless then, wouldn't you say?"

"Only if you can bear the bore of it!" said Bridget brashly.

Vivian stretched her arms back as far as they could go and blinked the bleariness from her eyes. "Well, no time to lose," she declared. "A little bird told me there's sausage to be had."

An eager light flashed across Bridget eye's, one which betrayed the sophistication she so often played at and showed her true years. "Can I sit at your desk while you're gone?" she asked, falling into Vivian's chair with a careless creak which made the older girl wince.

"Absolutely not."

"But Vivi!"

"You'll make a mess of things."

"Oh, no—but I *promise* I'll be good!" Bridget argued.

Vivian shook her head. "You can hardly keep yourself still as it is," she noted, eyeing the jittering of Bridget's left knee. The younger girl stood up and pouted.

"The oppression in this household is unbearable," she said with a rich, forlorn sigh.

"It shall make you strong," Vivian told her teasingly, bending and kissing the top of Bridget's fair head before the girl could stop her.

Bridget listened to the steady thump of Vivian's sock-clad feet as the elder girl descended the stairs in search of the breakfast she'd been ordered to take. As all fell quiet in the attic, she sighed. It was such a terrible bore to be a second daughter. She had none of Vivian's authority and none of the allowances made for Sophie or Liesel. And so she was shuffled about the household, forever in the way no matter what she did or where she went.

Raising her arms, Bridget assumed a ballerina stance and tipped onto her toes, taking a practiced turn about the room. If there was money for it, she'd take dance lessons, but as there wasn't, she had to settle for her own self-imposed tutelage. Aunt Alice had a friend who worked at the ballet and could sometimes get them in for rehearsals. From these scarce performances Bridget had absorbed everything she could, studying each tilt of the shoulders and curve of the feet. After each trip to the theatre, she'd go home and practice, imitating what she had seen as best she could.

Bridget stopped by the window to examine her reflection in the glass. Their mother would have liked the notion of there being a dancer in the family—she was sure of it. When she closed her eyes, she could feel her mother's long, delicate fingers on her shoulders—encouraging her to stand up straight. Soft palms adjusting the position of Bridget's head. She could almost smell their mother— almost. She'd discovered a bottle of their mother's perfume in this very attic not a year before and though there was little scent left she had breathed it in deeply, desirous to inhale all she could. It had smelled of lilies and lilacs or what Bridget believed to be lilies and lilacs. She could catch a taste of that very scent in the air now. So smooth—so elegant—but wild too. Exactly how she imagined their mother to be.

III.

"What are you doing?" came a voice suddenly, a pinprick through the lily silence which had just a second ago engulfed the entire room.

Bridget turned to see the thin, dark-haired figure of Sophie standing behind her, hair aglow from what little morning sunlight streaked across the room through the window, like an angel descended from the heavens. Angelic, almighty, and looking a little irritated. "Nothing," said Bridget. The floral scent was now gone.

Sophie arched an eyebrow but said nothing. She had a quiet, dignified authority about her. Of the four of them, she was the most like Aunt Alice.

"Well?" Bridget urged. "What do you want?"

Sophie stood with her shoulders still and arched like that of a soldier reporting in the field. Her hands hung flat against the stark grey fabric of her dress. "I want my book."

"What book?"

"The misfortunate book!"

Bridget looked away, uninterested. "Perhaps Liesel has it."

A thin frown had formed a deep-set line on Sophie's face. "I've already asked her. She says she hasn't got it."

Their mother had given them what they all called "the misfortunate book"—or, rather, she'd given it to Vivian who had given it to Sophie once she'd outgrown it. *Les Malheurs de Sophie—Sophie's Misfortunes*—by the Countess of Ségur. It had been their mother's favorite, so much so that Sophie herself had been named for the title character. At least, that's what Vivian said and she would be the person to know. After all, she was the only one of the four who could remember their mother reading to them. Bridget had been too young at the time to remember, and Sophie had been just a baby, but Vivian remembered. And sometimes, if the girls were very good and stayed out of her way as she painted, Vivian would sit and read to them as their mother had. Use all the character voices, as their mother had. It was the closest any of them were ever going to get to veritably remembering her.

"You are always doing this," Sophie lamented. "Taking things and losing them!"

"I haven't lost anything," said Bridget, raising her chin defiantly. She marched across the room and Sophie spun in something of a half circle after her. "Where are you going?"

"To prove that Liesel has it."

Sophie didn't believe her in the slightest, but Bridget took off anyway, skipping down the stairs and humming to herself in that low, soft voice which Aunt Alice swore would one day drive her mad.

Sophie sighed, looking around the attic helplessly. Having sisters meant things were always being borrowed and never given back. Bridget would lose anything that belonged to anyone so long as it wasn't her own. Sophie knew it well and it made the poor girl's cheeks flush with anger to think of all the beautiful things Bridget had invariably ruined for them all. Every dress she'd ever worn had been passed from Vivian to Bridget to herself. Vivian always took great care with her things, despite the occasional paint stain or charcoal smudge, but Bridget—Bridget found ways to put holes through everything. Aunt Alice was forever darning misshapen clothes that Sophie would be forced to wear in a year or two.

Suddenly, something fell to the ground with a soft but sturdy *thud*. Sophie jumped—whirling around to see that it had been nothing more than a pencil which had gone and rolled off the desk. She bent down on one knee to pick it up and, as she did, noticed the corner of something peeking out from beneath the desk.

She pulled the book out with both hands, wiped the dust from the cover and smiled satisfactorily. The misfortunate book. But how had it gotten all the way down there? Bridget had probably hidden it on purpose, Sophie determined, as she hugged the book to her chest. Bridget was always doing things like that.

She cradled the book tenderly in the crook of her arm. *"Thank you, Maman,"* she whispered, not knowing even as the words parted with her lips why she'd felt compelled to say it. Somehow, in that very moment, it felt as if their mother was there—had helped her to locate the book. Their mother, who had named her little girl Sophie before bestowing upon her the misfortunes of a motherless life. She frowned then, her expression souring. *Les Malheurs de Sophie.* Sophie's misfortunes, indeed. She nuzzled her cheek against the book's worn cover, murmured her thanks once more, and headed downstairs to find a safe and proper hiding place for the book.

IV.

Dawn was stretching sleepily across the sky. Slowly. Reluctantly, like a child rolling in their bed to escape the burgeoning light. Liesel pressed her forehead to the windowpane, looking out across the waking world with quiet, pensive wonder. She was Sophie's mirror image—eyes, nose, mouth. All of it. Save for her hair, which was as fair as Sophie's was dark.

The pair might have been mistaken for twins if Sophie did not stand over a foot above Liesel, who was the family baby in every way. Small. Curious. Withdrawn. Her sisters were always so busy painting and dancing and reading, but Liesel—Liesel had taken more and more to sitting in the attic of late, gazing out at the village as it moved into different stages of long, weary days. Watching the light shift slowly across the calm of the river.

A thought crossed her mind and the line of her mouth pursed pensively. "Does the sun rise where you are?" she asked, her breath fogging the glass. Liesel wiped a palm across it to restore her view, leaving a wet smudge across the windowpane.

A *tap, tap, tap* trilled out from somewhere deep in the attic.

Liesel's expression darkened and she shook her head ardently. "No! I didn't!"

Tap, tap, tap…

Liesel conceded guiltily, chin tucked into her chest. "It wasn't meant to make them fight," she said. "I just thought Sophie should come see you! She never comes up here anymore, not like she used to."

Thinking she'd spotted a glimpse of their mother out of the corner of her eye, Liesel whirled around only to be met with the emptiness of the attic.

Tap, tap, tap…

"I didn't mean to make her mad at Bridget…" Liesel continued. She looked around the room as if she might see their mother standing in some corner of the room, but she never did. There was no one there. There was never anybody there. "I just thought if I brought the book up to the attic then maybe Sophie would read it up here and then maybe she'd hear you like I—" her voice caught in her throat. Her sisters did not recognize their mother, at least not in the way that she did. They felt little moments here and there—a touch on the shoulder or a whisp of perfume—but they never talked to their mother the way Liesel talked to her. And they never heard the words worked into the groves of those gentle *tap, tap, tap*s…

Sometimes Liesel brought their mother's photograph up to the attic so she could look at it while she listened. The *tap, tap, tapping* was so light and airy it almost sounded like music. It would ring out from one end of the room and then suddenly from the other like the calls of an orchestra. Their mother had loved to sing. Loved the piano.

Whenever Liesel examined the photograph closely, she noted how very much like her they all looked, in their own ways. Vivian had her hair, Bridget her lips. Sophie had their mother's eyes no doubt, and Liesel—Liesel was certain she recognized something of herself in their mother's perfect nose. Only, there was something sad in their mother's expression. She couldn't quite explain what it was, but she saw it distinctly. Vivian looked that way sometimes when she was annoyed at something. Sophie too. Never Bridget. Bridget didn't know the meaning of sadness or was good enough at pretending not to know it which might as well have been the same thing to Liesel.

Suddenly a gentle *tap, tap, tap* rang out from the windowpane in front of her, startling the girl as it gently shook the glass.

At this, a vein of worry etched itself across Liesel's small brow. "Will I still hear you when I'm grown like them?"

She already knew the answer. Even before their mother spoke. *Tap... tap, tap...*

Liesel frowned. "But you'll still love us the same—even when I don't hear you?"

A warm, firm series of *tap, tap, tap*s sounded from the frame of the window.

"Might I tell them one day, Maman? When they are older?"

Tap, tap, tap...

Liesel grinned, gazing out at the burgeoning daylight. One day she'd tell her sisters. She'd wait and she'd watch and she'd look after them and one day, even if they didn't believe her, she would tell them.

Nonfiction Horror
Robert Nazar Arjoyan

Robert Nazar Arjoyan was born into the Armenian diaspora of Los Angeles. Aside from an arguably ill-advised foray into rock n roll bandery during his late teens, literature and movies were the vying forces of his life. Naz graduated from USC's School of Cinematic Arts and now works as an author and filmmaker. Find him at www.arjoyan.com.

~

That asshole massacred eleven kids before putting the AR-15 in his eyeball.

I was one of those eleven.

Son of a bitch plugged me behind my left ear. And I just had it freshly pierced the week before. Talk about a waste of money, huh? The mortician sewed it back on, though, earring and all. I actually felt my own red mist stick to me as I hit the cracked tile.

Me and ten other unlucky motherfuckers.

But let me tell you something, yeah? Death is a lot easier than life. Don't get me wrong and just wait a minute before you piss yourself with outrage. Do I wish I didn't get fuckin shot?

Yes, duh, of course.

But being a teenager in the United States of America these days sucks dick. And being dead doesn't. Being dead is a breeze. From where I'm standing—and I use that word fluidly—I can see a sort of sense in dying. You'll understand one day.

What? You will. You *do* know you're gonna die, right? Anyway!

My name? My name…

Maybe it was something like Santos or Livvie or Nshan or Mike or LeVar or Daria or Oscar or Arav. You don't really need a name where we're at. You're just… known?

Yeah.

See, here's the reason why being dead ain't necessarily the worst: I'm not scared. Well, I'm scared in a healthy sorta way. There's a lot of weird stuff that goes on here and it takes getting used to. What I mean to say is, I'm not afraid of the old things. You had your irreversible climate change, your fundamentalist fascism, your erosion of choice, your shooter drills (didn't really work, did it, ha ha ha), your crippling debt, your soul-slurping social media, your forced pregnancies, your lack of decency, your decline of democracy, your hatred of critical thinking, your book burnings, your systemic racism.

I don't have to deal with any of that bullshit nonsense anymore.

But my friends still do. The unlucky motherfuckers who grazed by with their skins and their souls. My mains: Carrie, Timo, Duffy, and Jodi.

They cope as best they can with the ever-truncating lifespan of childhood.

And I want to see how they're doing.

You come too, yeah?

The timing of this slaughter was just sloppy. I guess it would've sucked whenever, but mere weeks before the best time of the year, before everyone's supposed to get spooky and have fun and shit? It's just been funeral after funeral after funeral. Pisses me off, man. If I could sigh, I would.

I might be dead but I'm still human.

We were all at the funerals too. You could see our bodies, but not us. I was in a pretty cool casket, I must say. My parents did it right. Anime stuff, you wouldn't know. Most of us got something customized.

Remember: we were children. We had just started eighth grade.

Bastard.

Incidentally, my time in the new digs so far has been spent looking into the cocksucker and finding his bitch ass. Me and the ten, in fact. Think we're closing in.

But that's for later.

Jeez, I hope they're OK, my folks. I was their only one.

My friends that made it out alive feel like shit because they made it out alive. Do you understand me? Run through that sentence again then jump down to the next paragraph.

I remember Carrie from our group. Carrie had long, long braids and she introduced meditation to us. It was called Vipasomething, I don't know. We tried it and sometimes it worked but mostly it didn't. How could we take nice, mindful breaths when we were suffocating? My/their generation was/is being conveyed on a charred belt into a stinking abattoir, the disinclined inheritors of a world gone wro— Vipassana! There it is! Yes, it was Vipassana meditation. Vipassana. That was gonna bother me, wow. I called it Lickassana. Get it? Lick, ass. Carrie would get so pissed! She rolled around in my blood for camouflage, the seeping blood from my bullet-broken head. She kept apologizing to me as she did it. Her braids were mucky. The last experience in-body for me was watching my gentle friend who wanted us to meditate writhing in my spilt gore.

This is the execution of innocence.

Whatever, here's my pal Jodi's place. We can go right in, just follow me and keep close.

But before we enter: look around and you can see kids coming out to trick or treat. What a sight! Halloween is my favorite holiday. The candy, the films, the monsters. My friends, I bless them, condoned my obsession but never went hard like me. Alright, alright, after you, there we are. I'll get the door.

Ah, Jodi's dad. I always felt that he had the prettiest eyes I'd ever seen. They still look nice—just a little more muted, like the green of them leaked out a bit.

Hi, Alan! Pfft, like he can hear.

OK, so, I think the way this is going to work is by me, like, beaming my perception into your brain. It might feel pokey. Ready? Aaaaaaaaand…

***

I'm fucking kidding, dude, just read.

"Jodi, are you guys gonna go out?" asks Alan.

"Maybe, Dad. Not sure yet," replies Jodi, flashing him an everything-is-fine braceface smile. Her voice sounds tired. It says fatigue.

"Me and your uncles and our old gang, we'd go door to door on Halloween until the grown-ups thought *we* were too grown-up. They told us we had to start handing them out instead of guzzling them down."

"And when was that?" asks Jodi, her left eyebrow arching up, reminding Alan of his grandmother, dead these many years and in fine fettle.

"Nineteen," replies Alan. "Maybe they were right," his tone dipping into a furtive valley. Jodi is thinking that her dad is wrong, that those adult bodies were wrong.

"To be honest," and Jodi is *always* honest—one of the things that drove me nuts about her— "I think Timo's parents don't want him going out."

"Well…" Alan pauses, and I know what's kicking around in his head and he's wondering if he should say it and I hope he does because that would make me fall for him some more.

"…I won't tell."

Good for you, man! This is just what to do. Let us be, let us be, let us be, to paraphrase Sir Paul. *You* might have misplaced your fortitude on a stop along the way, but we're forced to summon it daily. So, on a rare moment, close your eyes and unlock the door.

We always try to come home.

But as much as Alan can attempt to fiddle with the exterior machinations of Jodi's life, excursions into her interior murk get confusing and swimmy and lost in the spelunking dark. The parental prerequisites have changed violently during these past couple of generations. The gap is too wide, the life experiences from either side out of reach, leaving between parent and child a gaping, yawning, greedy pit.

He loves her so much, has so many wishes for her.

"I think we're just gonna watch a scary movie or something."

Now, now, now, horror movies are my jam, not theirs. They never let me show them the dope shit in full. Like I said before: Jodi doesn't lie. Something is up, something is afoot.

And it… wait…

I think it has to do… with me—

A scream, in the street!

Jodi jerks her head toward the sound, and while I'm not corporeal, the same ripples of instinctive memory rock through me. I feel it most where my tailbone would be, for whatever reason. In the dimming light of a setting sun, we source the screech and both relax. Running towards us at a light clip, and apparently assing about, are my old friends: Duffy, Timo, and Carrie. Alan quakes under the threshold of the front door, also easing up. Fuck, man, they shouldn't call it *post*-traumatic. Nothing *post* about it, is there?

"Jo?"

The hot orange shine of light bouncing off dense cloud brings back the minty green of Alan's eyes. There lives a blind animal where I'm staying—close enough to an animal, I guess—who has eyes just like that, which do the same thing when licked by illumination: they resurrect.

"I'm gonna go inside and get ready for the night and, um, if you're not here when I come back out with the goods then just—"

"No, Dad, like I said, we're just gonna watch a movie."

Lie. And he knows it.

"Only… be careful."

She searches his face, the luster of his eyes taking their leave, trailing behind the embanking star, and settling into their newer, older home.

I hope he lives forever, she's thinking.

"OK."

"Kiss?"

She nods. He steps toward her and plants a heavy one on the crown of her head, welling all of his stored cosmic goodwill into his daughter. She feels it drip and pool around the soles of her feet, the rise of it levitating her off the hardwood deck and into safe haven. A benediction, a shelter. Wrongly secure in the knowledge that she is unwatched—you are watched by something at all times,

FYI, even now—Jodi melts a bit, letting the weight of everything fall to the wayside, and enjoying the affection in a simple way, a child's way.

"Jooooooodiiiiiiii!" Duffy calls out, and oh God, his voice cracked!

Damn, his voice cracked…

When did that happen?

They get closer and I suddenly feel how out of place I am, how broken time has become. I think myself further, and further I go, to the other side of the porch, my back against a storm of bounding steps and breathless voices, my mind shambling between past and present.

They're talking to each other like I didn't get murdered.

Like I never even lived.

What's Alan doing now? He's opening the screen door. No one seems to notice him. But we do, don't we?

Ugh, what a good dad.

"Come on, then, let's go, already." It's Timo, anxious to get the deliberate disobeying of his parents over and done. His voice hasn't dropped, not yet.

"We could just… stay here, guys," offers Carrie. Her braids are gone. That's a fucking shame. "A movie's a movie, right?"

She's scared. They all are.

"I wanna go," declares Jodi. "I think we should."

Count me in, I say from formless lips, words aborted from the jump, heard by none but you.

Duffy puts a hand on Carrie's shoulder. Tall, handsomer than before. Cheeky shit wants to do stuff to her.

"We'll be fine, Care," he assures.

How does he know that?

"How do you know that?" Carrie asks and I can't help but feel like chuckling. And also wondering: did she pick up on that from me or was it just a thing?

"Four is a good number and we're tough," states Duffy. Carrie lets that settle, like she settled and played dead next to the open shell of my head.

"Fine," spitting the word out like a piece of muscly meat.

"Do we need to grab anything?" inquires Timo as they all set forth, down the porch steps two at a time and straight for a glowing horizon. Duffy slaps his backpack as an answer.

I look back at the chair next to the door. Alan's talisman. Jodi shouldn't forget a thing like that and I can't take it to her. *You* certainly can't.

Goddamnit, they're on the sidewalk now.

"Wait," demands Timo.

"What is it?" Duffy, impatient.

Timo doesn't speak, not immediately.

"I gotta poop."

"Oh, jeez, that's twenty minutes gone, bro, come on!" Duff again. Always antsy.

"What do you want me to do? I gotta poop! Jodi, can I?" Timo indicates to the house with his head. If I didn't know better, I'd say he was indicating to me.

"Of course. If anyone else has to go, now's the time." Still mama of the group.

"You know, I think I'll go too, just in case. Where we're headed… I'd just hold it in and I don't like doing that," says Carrie.

They look to Duffy. His eyebrows shoot up.

"I went already!" He watches them rush up the stairs with a crooked grin across his heart-shaped face. Let's you and I move aside. If they walked through us, their night would be ruined. I've been told that such a happening leaves one feeling boggled and churned.

Better.

Jodi lets them in and her eyes fall on the weathered wicker chair beside the door. The plastic jack-o-lantern left by Alan is filled to the brim with candy and chocolate. Her teeth flash in a metallic beam. Kit-Kat, Skittles, Snickers, Reese's, Candy Corn, Milky Way, Baby Ruth! Jodi hooks her fingers around the pumpkin's handle as Carrie and Timo reenter society.

"You babies ready? Did your doodoos and weewees?" Fuckin Duffy.

"I hear if you pee in a graveyard, something will come out of the ground and rip your dick right off."

Timo's brash fantasy releases a hail of laughter from Carrie and Jodi. Even Duffy is giggling, forgetting his cool dude impression for a second. You see, this is something the other three—and me, frankly—would never have expected to exit from the little man's mind or mouth. Timo is… Timo. You have a Timo, I'm sure.

But Timo's different now.

A part of me wants to just linger here, watch them walk west into the ascending night, maybe try and spook the older kids without costumes daring to grab the spoils of Halloween from those who made efforts true blue. You see, I'm also different. Just as the gulf between parents and their children ruptures wider and longer, so too does the rope untwine between the living and their dead.

Yet, as I watch them dwindle in size, another part of me, the still *me* of me, the me that belonged to my friends, nudges me down the stairs.

You better hurry if you wanna catch up! I see them up ahead, past that gaggle of Ninja Turtles. Come on! We don't have to say *excuse me* or anything. See, being dead is simpler.

Duffy reaches for a goodie from the scalped pumpkin, but Jodi swats his probing hand away in time. "Hey!" he calls out.

She says nothing, just bumps up that eyebrow. Oof!

OK, nearly there. Let's hustle.

"Guys!" Timo, hollering. His voice tinged with terror, the tendons wrapped around his throat threatening to tear. His thin arm points, stiff and maybe never coming down again.

It's the hair which flattens their hearts, that crushes the breath in their lungs.

I first caught sight of it down the hallway from my Algebra class. It was an ugly shock of orange mingled with a waxy white. And here I see it again, on the street, its wearer back from whatever grave held him. Scented us to this very spot with an aim to conclude his carnage.

The fright steaming off my friends' skins is too much. Extreme, unanticipated, pungent. They don't speak. They can't. Any expression of their synced, unnameable panic would dry in the boiling cauldron of their chests, never reaching the parched desert of their mouths only to evaporate on scalded, swollen tongues. All four gripped in the teeth of a terror.

Maybe I can do something. Maybe I can send hi—

The crowd backs away from this piece of dog shit, and it becomes clear.

It's a costume.

Motherfucker has a cardboard cutout of an assault rifle. And he's smiling, the mean-minded whore-son. He's even smeared red across his cheeks and forehead.

My friends curl into themselves.

Why is no one doing anything? Literally not one person is confronting this filth. Maybe they're sending thoughts and prayers. Everyone's just giving him a wide berth.

And… I am too. I notice it now. As much as I'd like to give him a cold ride down to Hell, I know I can't. Not because I'm still nascent in my continued version of being, but because I'm terrified. I thought the thing that killed me was back.

I turn myself toward Duffy and Carrie and Timo and Jodi. Their faces contorted and taut, their muscles rictal and mortified. What bile courses through their systems? How much of their insides will it corrode and flood with sleeping cancers? I wish I could hug them as they hug one another now, equalizing together, breathing in unison.

Vipassana.

In time, they stand up straight and walk, unglued from each other but still a finger's flick away. The line they've formed is the line they tread, unbreaking. The fact that they're still bound on their private walkabout and not running back home stuns me. How? Well, Duffy said it best.

They're tough.

Little is spoken, choosing instead to keep their own respective counsel. This allows me a moment to rest. You won't mind, right?

Let's, for now, purely drift in their wake and see where they lead us. I'll tell you that the bustling streets are being forsaken for the quieter, out of the way roads. The inlets which once were trafficked by kids at all times - where deals went down, sex was mishandled, jokes were dirtied, games played, toys lost, and memories found. Now, these gulleys and rivulets, peopled by our own parents not long ago, are strictly off limits, and have become home to pedophiles and junkies and kidnappers and the Devil himself. These channels are off limits, kiddies, go play somewhere else, they say. OK, fine. Where? Fucking where?

"Man, it's hot, ain't it?"

I'm not sure how much time has eked away, friend. The white stars turning on from behind the upstairs curtain tell me it's been about twenty minutes? But Duffy's right. I can see the sweat prickling his bulbous nose. He wipes it away with the crook of his inner elbow, a scar rippling up ivory on his tanned sinews.

"Only getting hotter, Duff," proffers Timo. Of the gang, Timo has grown to be the wariest of the world and its woes. He knows too much information about all the bad things, that whatever good there is to find gets shoved beyond the back of his interests. It's not the good stuff that's gonna get them, he reasons. It's the bad. Problems waiting on flexed and fidgety haunches.

"How's the chocolate, by the way? Do they still have some shape or are we dealing with goop?" Carrie, asking the important questions.

Jodi immerses a hand into the pumpkin and feels. "We're good."

"Gimme a Skittles, Jo," demands Duffy.

"Not with that kinda talk."

Stubborn as a pack mule, he waves a dismissive hand, suddenly above his sugar craving. Jodi, the saint, gives him what he wants anyway.

"Thanks," he says, back to being an only child of thirteen.

"Guys?" she asks, holding the pumpkin up at arm's length.

Timo takes a Snickers, Carrie pincers out a packet of M&Ms, and Jodi goes for the Reese's cups. They rip their parcels open and indulge. My parents took me to church in the past and I didn't really buy into much of it. But, when they passed out communion, there was a weird tinge of I-don't-know-what in the air as the congregation quietly accepted stale bread which they believed to be flesh reborn. It always left me with questions and curiosity.

As I watch them munch on their sweets, I feel the same way as I did in the pews of my interred childhood. From the deep silence, pocked only by wet chewing, Jodi speaks.

"Nobody take the Almond Joy." They nod. I guess she's calling dibs. Though… I can't remember her ever caring for that particular bar. Oh, well.

"Anyway, we're here now," pipes up Timo. He sounds a lot chunkier thanks to the thick Snickery goodness cycling in his mouth.

"Thank God we're not alone," says Carrie, running a hand across the perfect circle of her head and creating a sound like sandpaper.

And I know why she's thankful. Finally, we see where these rascals have brought us. A cemetery. On Halloween! When I'm dead, they do this. Very uncool.

We cross the gates and pass the smattering of fellow visitors who are on their way out. I see a small hill, the grass overgrown and billowing in the whistle of a breeze. The four of them hike up the incline, Duffy bringing up the rear. The last bits of sunlight halo them. It's pretty to watch. Because in spite of the decay on which they trod, which will one day claim them for its silent ranks, my friends gambol.

Timo grabs a blanket out of Duffy's pack and spreads it on the ground. Jodi upturns the pumpkin and sends candies cascading to Earth, their spill drumming a jazzy beat for the deceased. Carrie sits down next to the holiday bounty and pats something on the ground. Maybe she's leveling the blanket, we'll know in a minute. No, it's a stone. A marker, I mean.

"Liya'd be hella mad if she knew we were here."

Who is this *Liya?*

"No doubt. But I think she'd also be kinda stoked." Duffy whips out his iPad and after a few swipes and taps, I see a classic begin to unspool.

Halloween, John Carpenter, 1978. Unoriginal, maybe, but fitting nonetheless. I don't blame them one wit—like I said before, these guys aren't aficionados.

"How long is this movie?" asks Carrie.

"It's short, like ninety minutes or something," answers Duffy. Ninety-one minutes, to be exact, Duffy! I love this movie, obviously.

Something snaps in the surrounding blackness. An animal looking for a meal, probably, but it gives them all a good jump. You'd never do that in a movie, the timing is too convenient. But then, this isn't a movie. Movies have rules, certain markers that help signal change and issue warning. There are none of those in real life. Can you imagine Michael Myers killing people with a fucking M-16 instead of a butcher knife?

"Someone hand me that Almond Joy," says Jodi. Carrie finds one and presents it to Jodi. As the movie rolls, Jodi rips open the plastic wrapping of the candy bar.

"We love you, Liya, and we miss you. Happy Halloween." They all chorus that last bit.

Happy Halloween in stereo.

Jodi sets the Almond Joy down on the marker.

Liya Wai

2009-2022

Our daughter, your friend

Oh.

Liya. Wai. *I'm* Liya Wai. This was my name.

And I fucking loved Almond Joy.

I told you at the start that being dead doesn't suck. I changed my mind. I want nothing more than to sit with my friends and watch movies and make mistakes and get in fights and fall in love and grow up and do high school and go to college and maybe get married and save the fucked up world or just have kids who end up getting exploded in a movie theatre or a playground or a mall but I can't and I won't because Liya Wai languishes under the dirt as dusty and useless bone.

"What the fuck is that?" Jodi asks, her voice a tremor.

I went off a bit, didn't I? My bad. Let me dial us back in here.

"People in costumes," Duffy dismisses with a wave of his hand.

"I don't know what they are, but those are *not* people, Duff," answers Carrie.

She's right. They're my countrymen. And they're here for their own take on trick or treat, raring to get off on what the greatest country in the world has to offer.

"Looks like they're coming our way," observes Timo.

"Eh, just ignore them," advises Duffy. "The movie's getting good."

They all sort of move their butts away from the slugging monsters and face the screen, watching as a little boy in a clown mask stabs his sister to death.

The incoming horde look at me and nod, acknowledging one of their own kind. They glisten in barbaric opulence, their insides wrapped around their outsides, teeth where teeth should never be glinting like needles in the yellowing moonlight. One stands over ten feet tall, eyes popping out of its inverted knees. Another swivels its seven heads as it speaks in seven tongues, cursing the foul earth upon which it skips. A third jellies through the grass, its glomming trail burning an acidic path and spewing forth hissing clouds of new disease.

But my friends pay them no mind.

The Hell trio lurches closer, smelling the broiling pain from this young group. So seasoned are they, so ready for feasting. One of the monsters snarls something most inhuman, making its intentions unambiguous.

"Shh!" spits out Timo and my airy jaw drops. The three things cluster together, frozen for an instant by the unanticipated gall. The denizens from another place look to me for help or explanation, maybe. I shrug.

"Here," says Jodi in a curt way. "Take these and go." She assaults the grotesqueries with the remaining candy. Duffy, Carrie, and Timo enter the attack. It's nonchalant, their barrage, but it sends the clearest message: you don't scare us.

And why should they? *How* should they? These renderings of unspeakable dimensions are far past the scope of humanity, so unreasonable that despite their very real physical presence, the freaks might as well be horrors of fiction—trifles for my friends who battle the scourges of nonfiction horror. Michael Myers can't scare them, nor can a rotting hag from room 237 (217 if you're a purist—STEPHEN KING RULES, an old shirt of mine shouted). Jason Voorhees is a nothing and so is the lame-o with the Scream mask. Freddy Krueger is just a dream, fuck's sake. And these guys over here? They're being pelted with sugary goods by children.

You yourself, however, would be food by now.

They were tricked, these ghouls, and so tricked they take their leave, hoping against hope to find a treat somewhere else. I don't have the heart to tell them they're gonna starve tonight.

"Fuck off!" yells Duffy and simmers down as the film rolls onward.

"Guys, this movie is kinda boring," Timo proclaims.

I am shocked and appalled at this heresy—but I get it. I really do.

"Yeah. Should we go back to my place?" asks Jodi.

They all agree and get to packing up.

"Too bad Liya missed that," one of them says.

"What are you talking about? She was right there," says another.

And for a second, I'm part of the group.

"Yup. With her the whole time."

"Should we have brought flowers?"

Then I remember myself.

The four of them wave goodbye with their still-growing hands. They walk and we list behind them, back through the same routes and forks. We find ourselves back in the relative safety of Jodi's street. The trick or treaters have thinned out, their baskets full, the night heavy. The few pods that remain kinda linger, chatting and soliciting houses for more tooth-rotting loot.

"Motherfucker," growls Duff under his heated breath and through his bared teeth.

It's the asshole, the one dressed as the shooter. Standing down the block.

"Oh, hell no," cries Carrie and sets off for him. Timo, Jodi, and Duffy pursue, their feet barely touching the pavement.

The smell of victory wafts from them; they are not to be stopped.

Jodi dips the pumpkin low, and with a swing powered by Fury, brings it up under the pretender's jaw. Somehow, that plastic acts as rock, and a cracking snap is heard.

The jackass falls to the ground and it takes all three of them to pull Timo away, his blitzkrieg of kicks watched by the whole street. Like before, no one does a thing.

Carrie grips a handful of his dyed orange hair and rips a hunk from the scalp.

Duffy spits on him.

Fuck me, I just remembered:

His sister was killed too. She was one of the eleven.

Let's give them a minute to recoup while we do a bit of our own surgery, yes? I want to give this virus nightmares that won't quit. I want to curdle his mind into a maggoty soup.

Boo, bitch.

The screams rip the air and fill me with glee.

Down some houses, Duffy, Timo, and Carrie follow Jodi up her porch steps. Alan meets them at the door and moves aside as they enter in single file. I hope to see them again but, if there's any rightness in the world, it won't be for a long goddamned time. I'll miss them all.

Alan looks out once more to survey the street. Does he see me? He's still looking at us. Or through us. We won't know, will we? And there he goes, closing the door behind him and locking it.

The kids came back home.

Well, I think that wraps up our night. You've got things to do, no doubt, and so do I. Remember this: some of us are shitheads, for sure. But most of us—well, *them*—they're gonna make the world livable again for your grandkids.

They're tougher than you'll ever know, tougher than you'll ever be.

I've got a piece of good news: the real killer, the actual fuckface, has been located. He's being held as we say our goodbyes. The ten have already started getting to work on him. Me? I think I'll hack off his ear with the tab from a can of Sprite. Someone comes, sews it back on, I do it again. It'll pass the time.

Be seeing you.

What nature won't allow for is the spiritual, the universal, the deep, dark, dank horrors that slink through what appears empty darkness. We are steeped in ritual, in the word, the motion of the hand as we consider the spirit.

What balms soothe your soul cannot be found in nature or in the alchemist's lab. These are but hollow treatments for the angst of the spirit. The acidic smell of dirt, the fragrance of the plant, tricks the senses into thinking this is all there is, ignoring the miasma of horrors that rush to us, even now, from the richest penumbras of the cosmos. Silent. Haunting, they steal for us, ready to either bend to our will or snuff us out completely.

The stories we've chosen to end this anthology play with the senses, for sure, but they also trick and cajole the unimaginative into thinking this is all there was. Meanwhile the great slumbering eldritch beasts wriggle their way to our world to rob our sanity and subjugate our souls.

The Dark House of Dr. Friday
Matthew Chabin

Matthew Chabin hails from Portland, Oregon. He worked as a journalist in the Navy, as a teacher in the Czech Republic, and in several volunteer capacities with the Tibetan community in Dharamsala, India. He currently lives with his family in Japan, where he teaches full-time. He holds a Master's in creative writing, and his work has appeared in a number of journals and anthologies.

~

I'd heard of these places, old houses in the Japanese interior—thousands, supposedly—left vacant by the rural exodus and declining population. Only this one wasn't vacant. It felt like it should have been. It was way back in the crook of a little-used road, crouched in the shade of towering bamboo thickets, mired in drifting summer dander and the metallic scream of cicadas. One of those old *kanawatsugi* classics—no nails, no glue, timbres fit together by the most exacting joinery. And a man lived in it, a retired doctor who paid me double my usual rate to climb the hill and call on him every Friday afternoon. Dr. Sado.

Dr. Friday, in my calendar.

"Is your power out?" I asked, that first time he led me down the hall, under the shadows of the staircase, past the old photographs I couldn't make out.

"I prefer to conserve energy," he said. His English was good, a little stilted. I suspected he didn't need English lessons so much as he wanted someone to talk to. Well, I needed money, and these side-gigs paid out under the table. If he wanted to talk, I'd listen.

We sat in the living room. Sunlight came from the windows in milky beams, swimming with dust, and fell on polished wood, jade, and lacquer. Spoils from the boom years when everyone had money. The bookshelf was full to bursting and papers covered every surface, esoteric doctor stuff I could only guess at. Whatever his interest in saving power, he kept the TV on at a low volume the whole time I was there, as if he didn't entirely trust the silence. That first time, I remember, it was showing a Kurasawa film.

"That's 'High and Low,'" I said.

"Tengoku to Jigoku," he said, seating himself across from me. A bar of amber light crossed his lower face, revealing a notch of scar in his chin, while his eyes glistened in the dimness like watered stones. "Heaven and Hell."

"Right. The translation loses something, doesn't it?"

A slight breeze from the open window did little to alleviate the heat. The cicada song droned through the walls and something in the old house creaked. I imagined the joints straining against each other with each seasonal infusion of heat and damp, eternally wed, locked in mutual suffering. I wondered if some fault in the carpentry, some mis-fit joining or patch of rot, could cause the whole thing to collapse. I imagined a sound like thunder and a sudden box the size of a washing machine, oozing blood. Nasty thought—I shoved it aside.

"I wrote a paper on Kurasawa," I said. "On his noir pictures."

"No-ah, yes. It is an American-style cinema?"

I wagged an equivocal hand. "European by way of America. Noir…like no-'r,'…is a French word. We just called them thrillers."

"And yet, Kurasawa did well with the form, would you say?"

"Oh, incredibly well. This one's up there with the best of Wilder and Welles."

"How do you think he did it? What I mean, if it wasn't his culture, how did he master…no-'r'?"

We were charging right into delicate subjects. "Well…they all take place during the American occupation. Japan and America…share that postwar malaise that everyone says is at the heart of noir."

"Malaise?"

"Depression? Anxiety?"

"Ah, yes. So between America, Europe, and Japan, war makes a common language."

"Um…maybe? I didn't go quite that far in my paper, but…."

He laughed, a sound like cracking wood that caught me off guard. "Maybe you didn't go far enough, then!"

"Maybe," I said, grinning uneasily, and took a drink of my tea. Something harsh in his tone, as if he'd really meant the criticism.

"May I ask," he said, sounding mild again, "how does your family call you, Richard-san?"

"Oh, friends call me Dick."

"Dick Spalding," he said. "A good name for a noir hero."

I laughed. "Yeah, I guess."

On the screen, the killer had just slipped his police tail.

***

He was an odd duck, Friday—I felt comfortable making that judgment even across cultures. He was stately and well preserved in years, narrow framed with lustrous black hair and a touch of silver at the temples. He dressed in pressed shirts and linen trousers. The old Renault he kept under the leaning porch cover was polished to a passable showroom shine. Viewed straight on, both house and man made an impression of quality holding its own against time.

He always met me at the door and offered me a cup of cold tea and a moist washcloth to wipe the sweat from my face. There was a small garden beyond a low, stone fence (about the only outward sign of upkeep), and sometimes we'd sit out on the porch and discuss his bonsai shrubs, or the habits of boars and foxes. More often we talked inside, in the gloom of the unlit house. Our sessions, as I'd suspected, weren't English lessons so much as paid conversations, and the whole exercise left me feeling vaguely whorish.

I gathered he was a cultured guy. I dug out a couple of my old school papers, 'Psychological Space in Basho's Interior' and 'Destructive Huantology in Mishima's Golden Temple.' Figured I could mine them for conversation, keep him happy. I just had to be careful to not sound like a dilettante, as odds were good he knew more on the subjects than I did.

On my second visit we ate grapes and kiwi wedges with our tea. The TV was showing tennis: Naomi Osaka was beating Serena Williams. He watched me watching it. "Quite a rivalry," he said. I confessed that I didn't follow tennis much, and he seemed to scowl without actually changing his expression. Faux pas or no, I sensed he was in a bad mood today, and for a long time we just sat there.

"Would you say she is Japanese?" he said after a while.

"Osaka? How do you mean?"

"She was born in Japan, but lived her life in America, yes?"

I shrugged. "She's Japanese by birth, right?"

"By birthright. This is a term from the west, I think. In Japan, the obligation goes the other way."

"I'm not sure—"

I stopped because he'd reached into a drawer in the desk and taken out a big, black, semi-automatic pistol. He laid it with a *clink* on the table, then produced a kit with oil and brush tools. I watched as he dumped the magazine, stripped the gun, and started cleaning it. "I thought guns were illegal over here."

"Very illegal," he said. "Rare as dragons' teeth."

The cicadas droned furiously. He worked the slide—*clck-clck, clck-clck*. "This one's from the war. My uncle, Toshihiro, took it from a man he killed. It's a Colt. Like in Stray Dog, you know? Have you seen the metal cages with the doors that drop?"

"Sorry, which?"

"You'll see them in the woods. They are boar traps. Sometimes this farmer I know catches a boar, and he calls me. Saves him the fee a licensed hunter would charge to come up and shoot them." He took a brush tool and reamed the barrel.

"You do it for free?"

"Why not. It gives me a chance to fire this old gun. Very powerful weapon. So, I put out my own boar trap. I caught one a few weeks ago." I watched him pop the bullets out of the magazine and line them up, like taking inventory. "Tell me, Dick-san, how is your relationship with your father?"

The old fox was changing up his serves today.

"Not good. We don't talk much."

"Sho ga nai," he said, and started feeding the bullets back into the mag. On the television, the New York crowd was booing Osaka's victory, and I wanted to be somewhere else.

***

I told myself I needed the money, and I did. That wasn't all though. Something about the house…pulled me. And there was the dream.

I'm walking up the hill, past the last view of rice fields and apple orchards, that last stretch where the bamboo closes off the world. The air is hot and still. I come to the house. It's dark, as always. I start to go in through the garden, then I hear something from the back. I step over the stone wall and go around, between the side of the house and the crowding bamboo. Something is screaming back there. I can't see yet. From out of the buzzing, midday sky comes a crack of thunder.

I snapped awake, the echo of the shot like an iron taste in my mouth. For some reason I was aroused, hard as a brass bolt. I got up and paced the room. Nothing doing. *Cherchez la femme.* I dropped into my chair, turned on the computer, and searched 'Japanese milfs.' *Sho ga nai.*

***

On my third visit Dr. Friday was conciliatory. "I apologize if I offended you, Dick-san. I should not have asked such a personal question."

"It's fine."

We sat in the afternoon shadows, eating strawberries and sipping beer. The TV was showing *I Wake up Screaming*, Laird Cregar ghoulishly sweating Victor Mature, his guilty heart charging him like an unstable reactor.

"Can I ask, Sado-san, if you have any family?"

"I have a wife and son."

"I see. Where do they live?"

"They live here." I looked around the silent walls. I'd passed the unlit stair-way five times now, and it had never occurred to me that someone might be up there. "My wife is a retiring woman. She stays out of sight. And my son…."

He spoke elliptically, but more freely as he drank, and the picture came to-gether. His first wife had left him for another man, 'a foreigner,' leaving him with the care of their son. The son had shown some academic promise. He'd wanted to go to America, but the old man was determined that he should be a doctor, like him. Three times the boy had tried and failed to pass the medical school's en-trance exam. In his shame, he'd grown despondent, and retreated into his room. Now he never left.

He leaned forward conspiratorially, his eyes going to the roof. "You may hear him scratching and moving around up there. It's like living with an over-grown rodent."

"I'm sorry," I said, hoping he'd snap to the impropriety of what he was saying. I was beginning to suspect he used our little sessions not just to alleviate his loneliness, but to air that famous *honne*, that inner face the Japanese subject hides from the world. Perhaps it was exactly because I wasn't Japanese that he felt he could unmask himself, not because I mattered so much to him, but because I mattered so little. I tried talking to him about Basho, but he seemed to have gotten into the movie. He sat there holding the gun, his face gone stony, eyes flickering with the boxed images. After a while I got up and let myself out.

***

I'm walking around the side of the house, and that squealing-screaming slips through the blanketing shrill of cicadas like a signal tuned through static. I come around the corner and stop. The back of the house is torn open, as if some enormous animal had been penned inside and broken out. Vines overrun the collapsed porch, the broken beams. The rock garden has been almost entirely reclaimed by the jungle-like underbrush, and I can make out a little naya shed at the back, the thatched roof caved-in and festooned with flowering creepers. The desolation gives me an uneasy feeling. I want to back out, retrace my steps and be away before something terrible happens. Then a woman stumbles from the tall grass.

I see right away that she's a looker, despite her disheveled state. Her long black hair is tangled, her lipstick smeared across her lips, and it looks like she's been crying. One naked breast hangs out of her half-open blouse, and something in me stirs. Her skirt is snagged on a thorn bush. She bends to yank it free, but

189

it won't come loose. I watch her struggle. Maybe she feels my gaze, because she looks up and our eyes meet.

She straightens and covers herself, a dignified sort of beauty. She's older than me, late thirties or early forties. "Mr. Spalding," she says, and her voice shocks me, this Japanese woman speaking in aristocratic American English (Mid-Atlantic, I think they call it). "I inquired at the hotel for the name of a reliable private detective, they mentioned yours."

I hesitate. This is no time to fall in love. "Why don't you tell me about it from the very beginning."

Her smile is coy and serpent-wise. Her fingers pluck at the edge of her blouse, and my body stirs. Cherchez la femme, for she is death. I've never wanted anything so much. A rumble in the clear blue sky. She looks up. "There's no time," she says, fear in her voice. "He's coming."

"Who's coming, Mrs. Friday?"

That screaming again.

I woke up swaddled in damp sheets. I sat back against the wall, the blood pounding in my ears. Certain things were becoming clear. I knew what I had to do.

***

Clouds were massing over the mountains. The cicadas, perhaps addled by the changing air pressure, screamed their layered antiphons ever louder, shredding the silence to a pulp of shrill white noise. The air moved in sluggish, blundering gusts, sultry as dogs' breath; the bamboo hissed and whispered. The path resolved into a warped, earthly perspective, all eyes to the vanishing point: the house of Dr. Friday.

I'd noted the freshness of the fruits he'd served, the absence of refrigerated chill, the crumbled store receipt on the table: Friday did his shopping on the days I visited him, a little before my arrival. I estimated the trip would take him an hour, give or take, the nearest grocery being twenty minutes' drive. If I was wrong, I'd be stuck out in the weeds (like that time in Mexico), but for a guy like me that was any given Friday.

I kept to the side of the road as I approached the house, staying out of view of the windows. At ten meters I hopped the ditch and entered the bamboo. The Jorou spiders spun their webs here, and the silk clung to my sweat. I clawed my face as I made my way through the pale, serried masts, and barely stifled a cry as a fat green body scuttled down my arm and parasailed to the ground. I'd been worried he might have left already and denied me a fix on his return, but the Renault was still there. I leaned against a bamboo stalk and waited.

I hadn't been there more than twenty minutes when he came out. I slid down the stalk and rested on my haunches, watching as he came around the side and got in the car. He wore a white linen jacket today, a matching fedora and dark shades. Old-style class, damn the heat—you had to admire the sonofabitch. He pulled out, and I waited until I couldn't hear the car before I moved. Time to meet this family of his.

I rang the doorbell and heard a faint chime within. I counted thirty seconds and rang again. Nothing stirring, nothing "scratching around up there." I made a fist and banged hard on the frame. Listened—zippo. Okay, so she was a retiring woman, and the son was one of those *hikikomori*, grown kids who live in their rooms like hermits—some kind of Japanese culture complex. Stands to reason people like that would rabbit when the meter-man came around.

Or maybe you're a liar, Friday.

I tried the door. Locked. Unusual for rural Japan. I went to the window and thumped the bottom sash with my palms until it opened a crack. I dropped down and put my ear to the gap. Nothing. I worked the window up until I could put my head and shoulders through, and walked on my hands until I was in. Dark and quiet. I went into the living room, to the desk, and took out the gun. Jesus, it was heavy, a deadly weapon even without the bullets, 'MODEL OF 1911 U.S. ARMY' stamped on the side. Feeling a little queasy, I stuck it in my belt at the small of my back.

Armed, now I climbed the stairs. I tried the first door on the left, a hinged job with a handle. Bathroom, none-too clean. I tried the sliding *shoji* door across from it.

Well, this was the kid's room alright, more like a nest, stuffy and full of stale odors. The floor was covered with quilts, the walls with old movie posters—*Les Diaboliques, The Killing, Castle of Sand*. Trash bags in the corner overflowed with plastic bottles and wrappers; a chair, bench, and a low table made a command consul around the computer, cigarettes stubbed in the ashtray, jerk-tissues over-flowing the wastebasket. *Living the high-life, weren't you kid.* I picked a pornographic manga off the shelf—*My Immoral Auntie*—and let it slip from my fingers. My hands were shaking. I set my teeth against the weird stir of nerves and went out.

Last door, another bedroom. A woman's room, much neater, the stuffiness more aromatic. Pressed roses in a frame, and a toe of nylon hanging out of the bureau. I breathed in and felt a rush of logy arousal, like breathing sexual ether in here—*Jesus, get it together man*. They'd been here, he hadn't made them up. But where were they now?

I went downstairs, down the hall, and through the living room. A sliding door opened into the kitchen, where I'd seen him go from time to time. The buzzsaw hum of cicadas got louder when I opened the door. I'd thought this part would stay in the dreamworld, but it was real. The wall, porch timbers, and part of the roof were blown out into the overgrown yard in a wide cone of destruction. Bees sailed in and out, and forking rivers of ants streamed over the linoleum. An explosion. Gas? No, the stove was still intact, nothing scorched. It looked like someone had driven a car through it a hundred miles an hour, or a bull had broken out of its pen. *Shouldn't be here,* I thought, even as my feet carried me forward. I walked through the shattered wall, into the screaming daylight, and stopped.

She stood at the edge of the tall grass, her head cocked to the side, looking at me. Her blouse was half undone, her hair tied back in a simple ponytail. Sweat glowed along the line of her neck, the swell of her breasts. She held my gaze as she unfastened her skirt and let it fall about her legs. She turned and walked back into the bushes, her white panties winking from under the hem of her blouse.

I reached behind me and touched the gun. The hard steel was reassuring. I picked my way through the verdure and debris, stepping over a toppled stone lantern, following the path she'd taken. The grass was flattened by multiple passages. I saw the ruined shed, her clothes dropped beside the door. I saw the bloodstained cot inside. Behind the shed I found the freshly turned earth where he'd buried them.

The car was back in the driveway when I came out. He hadn't been gone twenty minutes. I came in through the back and found him sitting in his chair watching a movie, David Lynch's *Lost Highway*. "I can't make sense of this crap," he said.

"Helps to watch it a couple times," I said. "It's all there." He did that subtle scowl of his, wearing his face a bit harder without deigning to move his mouth. I walked across the room and shut off the box. "Cut the shit, Friday, you're guilty as Caiaphas. Your son was screwing your wife and you wouldn't have it. You pretended to go to town, but you doubled back, just like you did today. You found them together and shot them both."

He lifted his hands and gave three slow claps. "Not bad…Mr. Spalding."

I didn't like how he said my name. I took the gun out and let it hang at my side. "I want to know how a man can murder his own family like that. Maybe I want to know bad enough to do something out of character."

He took his hat off and dropped it on the table. Real cool customer, no rattle, maybe he figured he had nothing to lose. "When Akira, my son, was ten years old, he wanted to be a policeman. When he was fourteen, he wanted to be a movie star. Hollywood. I tried to steer him away from such nonsense, but I was unsuccessful."

"He was your son," I said. "He was going to be a doctor, like you. Isn't that right?"

"Why not? He was intelligent enough. I believe he deliberately failed his exams, or else he was too lazy to succeed. Either way, how could I reward him?"

"What did he want, exactly?"

"He wanted to run off to America and be a character in one of those movies! It told him, go, if you can pay for it. He couldn't, of course. He shut himself in his room to spite me, and lived like a parasite."

I had him now, but the buzzing of the damn bugs was making my head hurt. I felt sick, dirty, physically tainted by this place. My loathing for the old man was a lump in my throat, and sweat oozed down my body. "So," I said, stuffing the queasiness, "you got yourself a pretty, young bride to replace his mother. What was that about? Maybe show him up? Give him something to chew on while you were fucking her in the next room? Serves you right, she took a liking to him."

His scowl was real this time, his nose flaring with contempt. "She felt sorry for him! He was pathetic! They both were weak, both degenerate!"

"Both after your money?"

He sucked in his breath, and I thought he was going to explode again. Then an ugly smile twisted his lips. "Are you done with this charade, yet? Mr. *Spalding*?"

We stared at each other. Something pattered at my feet. God, I was so dirty. Dirt between my fingers and my toes, dirt covering my skin. What was that running down my body? Sweat? Why was it so thick? Why was it…so red. The gun slipped from my hand and hit the floor.

"Oh…god."

"Seeing clearly now?"

"No…"

The kitchen door slid open. I didn't want to look, didn't want to see her like that. She came and stood beside me. Her body was filthy like mine, caked in blood and dirt. At least she was with me and not with him. I sank to my knees beside her and she put her hand on my head. "Akira," she said.

"Wakarimasen."

I swallowed dirt, tried to think. If this was it, well… Might as well face it like the man he had never let me be in life. What would Dick Spalding say?

"I'll give you this Friday, you make a pretty good noir villain. Good chance you'll get caught, though. Most killers do. Only one thing I haven't figured out. How'd the back of the house get blown out?"

His smile turned tight and rueful. "You're right, Mr. Spalding. Most killers get caught. This thought occurred to me as well." As he said it, a wisp of smoke issued from his mouth. In the shadows of the unlit house, the scatter on the wall behind him might have been water stains or a rash of mold, but now I knew what it was. I looked down at the smoking gun. "Because maybe you two are my Hell, and maybe I am yours," he said. "But this has always been my house."

"Akira," she said. "Come with me."

I stood and took her hand, with only the dirt of the grave between us. We'd go out back again, and this time maybe we'd go farther, find some quiet grove deep in the forest and make love in the company of foxes and boars. I don't know if he watched us go, or if he just stared ahead. But the wind blew through the bamboo, and the cicadas screamed through walls. And no one heard.

Shambling Gary
Joel McKay

Joel McKay is an economics nerd by day and fiction writer by night. His fiction includes the shorts "Number Hunnerd" (Tyche Books), "Hands" (Brigids Gate Press), "Don't Rock the Boat" (Eerie River Publishing) and others, as well as the award-winning horror comedy novella Wolf at the Door *(Birchwood Press). He calls Prince George, B.C. home, where he lives with his wife and two daughters.*

~

I first killed Shambling Gary in the winter of 1933. We were working a claim in the Cassiar district, and I found out the sumbitch was pocketing some of the proceeds, wrapping them in an oilcloth he didn't know I knew about. Each night he stuffed it behind his cot in the cabin's log posts, a dark hollow that held the faint sticky sweet scent of pine resin. That smell ... a smell that harkened back to the summer before when we, full of hope, felled those trees together, a time when things weren't so desperate. The same smell that fills my nostrils each time he comes back. I *hate* that smell, hate it like I used to hate Gary.

I might not have reacted the way I did had it not been for his other misdeeds. He'd been nicking extra bacon for weeks when he thought I wasn't looking. A corner here, a slice there. One time I went for an unopened bottle of rye and found it watered down. He'd helped himself to a healthy portion and refilled it with creek water. He also started slacking off at work as soon as the weather turned. When it was warm and sunny, Gary wasn't a bad worker, but when the chill arrived, he lazed in his cot while I was out chipping away at the adit.

And then there were Alice's letters, my girl back in Boise. They were neatly folded and bundled in twine. I read them all. There were twelve, but by Thanksgiving four had gone missing. I found one with shit stains on it in the outhouse. I confronted him but we didn't talk about it beyond a few choice words. I didn't want to hear the truth from Gary, that something had happened between Gary and Alice before we left home.

You see, Gary had a thing for Alice since we were kids. She would play and wrestle with Gary, but I felt I won her heart. I encouraged him to find someone else, but he wouldn't budge. And his eyes were always on her when the three of us were together back home. When we left home, I watched angrily while they shared a long hug goodbye. I knew he read those letters in the shithouse by lamplight while I slept.

A locket with her picture in it had come with us to the Cassiar. When it disappeared from my things, I asked him about it, but he just shrugged, even spent half a day pretending to look for it alongside me. I woke up one night to rustling in the cot beside me. I didn't move, just opening my eyes far enough to see his scrawny face bathed in the pale moonlight, a half-crazed lust in his eyes, lips peeled back against his crooked yellow teeth. He held up the missing picture in one hand while he tugged on himself with the other. There was no sound except the gentle creaking of the bed springs.

A stronger man would've lost it then and there, but I'm not that man. I just pinched my eyes shut and tried to forget.

You see, working a claim is hard. The hope and excitement fades quickly and it isn't long before you start feeling like a prisoner splitting rocks in a work yard. Gary and I were best friends when we set out from home, decent companions by the time we crossed into Canada, and partners, at least civil, by the time we picked our spot in the Cassiar.

The rest of that summer was hard but mostly okay. We talked a lot more at the start, but that devolved to grunts and short words by the first frost. Winter is hard up there. There's a harshness to it that makes you feel trapped, confined. You start thinking differently about friendships and who you can trust. I began to consider my future beyond the Cassiar, not just what I wanted but what I needed. Gary wasn't one of those things. I was jealous about things he had back home. I reformed them in my mind. It was freeing, my reimagining, it conjured ideas and possibilities I would never consider under normal circumstances.

We found gold but not a lot. I think that's what finally did it. It's one thing to skim from a guy when he's awash in wealth, and an entirely different thing when he's got but scraps. I was always good at making money, Gary not so much. By then, we had less than scraps and most days our stomachs were growling.

When I found the oilcloth full of gold nuggets he'd squirreled away, I'd had enough.

I did it in the morning a few days before Christmas.

We needed water for the kettle and most mornings I went to get it, but I pretended to be asleep. Eventually he muttered a few curses, grabbed the pail, and tramped out the door. It slammed rudely behind him, but it didn't latch, clapping against the hard timber frames a few more times for good measure. I already had a headache, and that only made the dull, persistent ache worse. I remember thinking it felt like a beating heart in my skull, and that if I could just take a corkscrew and bore a small hole in my head to release the pressure, I'd feel better. But that was a mad thought. I needed to focus on practical solutions.

As soon as he was gone, I swung my feet onto the cold plank floor and grabbed the axe. The fact the door hung loose probably helped as he couldn't hear it open behind him while he knelt at the creek, chipping away at the ice to get to the water. I peered through the narrow opening in the door and grinned. I knew he had no idea. He didn't think I had it in me, did he?

I strode toward him to within swinging distance, not stopping until my shadow fell over him. He turned halfway but the axe was already coming down before he could get a good look at me. I don't think that first blow killed him, but it cracked his skull pretty good and spilled a lot of red in that icy pail. The second swing did it. I gave him a third and a fourth for good measure and then just stood there awhile looking down at him, watching that fleshy bag of meat and bone – those rotten dirty teeth he planned to kiss Alice with – shine in the early morning light; the only sound was the gentle icy sloshing of the creek. After a bit I dipped the bloody pail in the creek, filled it with water and went in to make coffee.

I left him there. You can't dig in the ground that time of year, and frankly, even if I could've, I probably wouldn't have. I liked the idea that I'd get to see his rotting corpse there each morning when I went to fill the pail. He had it coming. I even thought I might like to piss on him regularly for good measure, though I never got the chance.

You see, Gary came back the next night. I was playing a game of solitaire by lamp on his cot, that picture of *my* Alice set out in front of me, the oilcloth with its little treasures too. My treasures.

The night sky shuddered with a fierce snow that seemed to shift direction every few minutes, rattling the window that let the darkness pour in around me. I don't know for sure, but I think he stood and looked at me through that window for a long time before he came in, thinking about what to do with me, if he even could think. It's just a feeling I have.

He came through the door when I went to stoke the fire. He was slow and lurchy, his skin grey like worn out boot leather. The flesh where the axe had split his head open was still red and meaty, glistening in the firelight. But he didn't smell like anything yet. The only smell was the pine resin.

I panicked and raised the fire poker as he came at me. He impaled himself on it, seemed surprised by that, then kept coming at me, the poker driving deeper into his sternum as he scratched at my face with his dirty long nails. I panicked. Froze like the icy water in that creek outside, unable at first to shift my mind into the action necessary to deal with the ghoul. I still have the scars from that night, though I tell everyone they're the result of a run in with a mountain lion.

I left the poker in him and picked up a skillet, clubbing him again and again. There was no blood that time, just gore. He collapsed and everything went quiet except the loose cabin door as the winter wind battered it against the frame. A skiff of snow trailed out the door behind his booted feet.

I dragged him out and threw him in the creek that night. My fingers were blue by the time I got back in, and I sat next to the fire picking bits of brain from beneath my fingernails, my eyes darting between the unfinished game of solitaire and Alice and the doorway. The wind beat against it with a steady rhythm like a knock. I didn't sleep that night or much the next week.

Gary didn't come back for a while. I kept busy chiseling at the adit in the cold, taking regular breaks to warm my freezing hands by the stove. Spring was a long way off, but I wasn't so worried about food anymore now that Gary was gone.

Each day I went down to the creek to fill the pail and make sure Gary was where I left him. The ice had grown over him, forming a thick glassy coffin at the edge of the far side of the creek bed. I looked at that block of ice every day, some days for the better part of a morning, studying how the winter light formed shapes and shadows along the contours of the ice, tracing the blurry dark lines of his corpse, the position of his hands, the quiet deadness of his face. Each day it seemed the ice around him grew and I worried less about him coming back. Maybe I hadn't killed him that first time, only knocked him out. Still, I refrained from pissing on him, afraid that it might melt the ice and allow him to escape.

What a crazy thought, right? Gary was dead. I'd killed him. Twice over. He wasn't coming back. But one morning I could've sworn I saw him grinning at me through the ice. Maybe it was in my mind, but I saw those same warped, yellow teeth and remembered how they danced hungrily beneath the glow of moonlight as he longed for Alice in the cot beside me.

It was spring when I noticed he'd disappeared. I'd come back from a hunt, rifle on my shoulder, to find the tomb in the shallow part of the creek half-melted and cracked open beneath the April sunlight, the cadaver vanished. Maybe he'd simply washed downstream in the freshet.

I waded through the stream and knelt next to the ice, the tips of my weathered fingers tracing deep grooves that looked like scratch marks on the inside of the frozen tomb. Had my old friend been trying to claw his way out of his icy grave all winter while I slept, played cards, drank coffee, and worked just a few dozen yards away?

His shadow fell over me at the edge of the creek. He was slow but he looked the same. Grey, mottled, fleshy, ripped and torn. The eyes were gone, leaving only gaping black holes that made me wonder what unearthly force had taken hold of him.

I shot him twice and burned the corpse that night. After, I combed feverishly through the ashes with the butt of the rifle to make certain none of Gary was left. Swigging watered-down rye, I danced madly around the fire in bare feet singing his name while the purple-green borealis throbbed in the fathomless black sky above me. I pissed the fire out and fell asleep next to the smoldering coals.

In the morning, I woke up to his cold, slippery hands wrapped around my neck. His skin was charred but it was almost as if he was impervious to the fire.

I wrestled him off and yelled at him. He shambled toward me. I turned and marched into the cabin, grabbed the axe, and did the job again. This time I severed his head, legs, and arms, shot each of them with the rifle, burned them and scattered the ashes in the thawing creek.

After, I realized I needed to leave. The ground was still too cold to dig in but the paths out of the god forsaken place had cleared for the coming season of warmth.

I hastily packed my things, careful to stow Alice's picture and her letters in my pack (even the shit stained one), and left for good. I didn't bother with the furniture or tools. Let the next poor bastard have them, and Gary too. I took what little gold I'd mined and started south, the cabin door banging open in the wind as I departed.

***

I was in Boise around the time the big trees next to the river let their cotton fly in the summer breeze. It was warm and dry. The days were long, and Alice was there waiting. There was a muted look on her face when she saw only me. I tried to ignore it. She asked about Gary while we sat on the front porch of her parent's home, a rambling white colonial a few miles out of town that capped a grassy hill like a minaret. There was a porch swing we sat in.

I told her he slipped down an embankment and disappeared into a nameless river. She cried a long time, and I wondered if she had been true to me. I pushed those questions deep down inside me, sealing them off in my mind like Gary's murder and inventing my own version of things. A version I thought I could live with.

I went back to work in town writing news for the *Telegraph*. It wasn't much but after my adventures in the north I felt it was more than something. I pursued Alice, and eventually she came around when she realized she needed a strong set

199

of shoulders around the farm to keep everything going. We got married the following year. Her parents were ailing so I moved into the big house to look after the fields, while still commuting to write and submit my articles.

I'll admit that I still hadn't really gotten over what happened in the Cassiar. There were dreams, bad ones. I dreamt that he had his hands wrapped around my neck. I dreamt of him and Alice sharing that long hug goodbye in the early summer light. Often I would wake up in a hot sweat and have to whisper to myself to push those thoughts out of my head, those truths I couldn't yet face.

Sometimes at night while I sat next to the window reading in the wingback chair, I thought I caught glimpses of him outside, the ruined crevices of his face where the axe had split his flesh shining angrily in the moonlight. When the wind battered the screen door at the back of the house I thought of the cabin and Gary. When I swirled ice in the tea pitcher on hot summer days, I could feel the cold scratch marks he'd left on the inside of his frozen tomb. One time, driving back from town, I could've sworn I spotted him on the railroad track in the heat of the day, his fire-ravaged flesh stumbling along between the ties to nowhere in particular, the August heat waves convincing me I'd seen a mirage.

I started drinking more than usual, smoking, and playing cards, usually with the boys from the *Telegraph* after we put the paper to bed. I stayed out late, lost money and pulled waitresses down onto my lap. Alice complained and I lied. Often, I'd drive home long after the sun had set, when the heat of the southern Idaho desert is just dissipating and there's only the steady rattle of the crickets in the tall grass.

I would roll up my sleeves, roll down the windows of my Ford, tilt my straw skimmer hat back and let the cool air wash over my oily, whisky-infused skin, hoping I'd clear enough of the stench off before I got home and flop into the bed for a deep, dreamless sleep.

One August night I came home to find the front door hanging ajar. There was a light breeze and the screen door rattled quietly against the frame. The back of my neck turned to gooseflesh, and I felt the bottom of my stomach fall out.

Inside I went to climb the stairs when I spotted a wrinkled foot peeking around the corner of the kitchen floor. I found my father-in-law there, face down, his head caved in like a pulverized melon, its contents spread out in a thick red mess across the white tile floor. I heaved on him, spilling sour rye and half chewed French fries onto his naked foot and pajama bottoms.

I was frozen there, my jaw agape at the massacre. And then I heard the quiet rustle of bedsprings upstairs. And moaning. A low, hot, whispery moaning. A mix of fear and desire pulsed through me. I scrambled to my feet and pulled my way up the stairs on all fours like an animal.

As I climbed the moaning grew louder. It was Alice's voice, but not like I'd ever heard it. My manhood thickened but there was a panic and fear inside me too. The scent of pine resin filled the air.

At the top of the stairs, I found my mother-in-law sprawled on her back, her nightgown ripped open, heavy breasts laid bare and flesh torn apart as if someone had grabbed her mid-section and opened it like a jacket. Her ribcage and organs exposed to the stuffy house air, her face contorted in violent anguish, the carpet reddish-brown and thick with fluid. And still there was moaning, louder now, from the master bedroom.

I pushed the door open slowly and found them on the bed. The room was suffused with heat, sweat and pine, as if the walls had been slathered in a coniferous honey. A low blue dark streamed in through the window, allowing just enough starlight for me to see Alice naked on top of another man. His hands gripped her breasts. Her head tilted back exposing the contours of her throat, her auburn hair bouncing in the darkness.

She moaned. Loud. Again. And again.

Beneath her was the ghoul. His flesh dark and desiccated like the bark of a long dead tree, his blackened cock sliding in and out of her. What was left of his lips were curled back against his moldering teeth as she rode him like an unbroken bronc.

On the far side of the bed next to the open window was a floor-length mirror. I caught sight of him in it, only he wasn't a ghoul. It was Gary. His flesh was whole and alabaster. I caught that blue glint of my old friend's eyes in the reflection as he stared passionately at her, his hand cupped gently at the back of her head, his fingers threaded through her thick hair. Alice was unaware that I was there. She never seemed to be aware of me, our marriage more like two roommates than lovers, and that filled me with a deep loneliness I couldn't push out of my mind.

They climaxed at the same time, Alice's high-pitched euphoric scream coupled with his low, hollow grunt.

I found my courage, or maybe just my rage, and tackled them. Alice spun off Gary onto the floor beneath the window. I grabbed the ghoul and threw him in the opposite direction. Alice cleared her head and clawed angrily at me from the floor.

"What? What are you doing?" she yelled at me, enraged that this too would be taken from her.

I ignored her and grabbed the lamp. I lit it, raising it above my head to cast a faint amber glow through the room. Gary was sprawled on the floor on the other side of the bed, still smiling. Alice shrieked, but not at him. Where I saw his true form, she saw Gary as he once was, clean, muscular, perfect. She screamed at me, a hinged, blood-curdling noise that pierced the hot August night like a train whistle.

I killed Gary again that night. I hacked his body to pieces and tossed the legs to the pigs, the arms to the crows and buried the head and the torso in two holes at opposite ends of the property.

We told the police there was an intruder that escaped toward the tracks before I could catch him. The cops grunted and said something about more hobos than usual coming through town and it was left at that. There was a funeral for Alice's parents, but I don't remember much of it. What I do remember is that Alice locked herself in our room for a week and wouldn't talk to anyone. She might as well have been a ghost for all the noise she made. When she eventually did come out, it was like none of it had ever happened. She was all smiles and her normal self, and she never gave me a hard time about my carousing or drinking again. We never talked about Gary.

I found out she was pregnant a few months later when she couldn't hide it anymore. She tried to convince me it was mine but we both knew differently. She carried it like a glowing new mother, excited, happy, and the women from our church surrounded her with affection and support while I fell deeper into gambling dens and found new skirts to chase around town.

The night she gave birth I wasn't there. I was told the midwife's screams were heard from the train station. Apparently, Alice was quiet as a lamb. The baby was stillborn, grey, and covered in inexplicable wounds. The type made by a dull blade like an axe.

She chose a spot at the back of the house beneath the lavender garden to bury the baby. She didn't want me there and, by that time, I had one or two places I could sleep in town. The next time I went home I found her alone in the front room, her feet pulled up under her while she sat in the dark-green wingback and read those old letters carried to the Cassiar. She twirled the locket in one hand, and I felt a pain in my gut when I looked at her. A truth I wanted to forget.

The next time I went home she was gone. A few days later a fisherman found her body, white and bloated, floating in the water where the Boise meets the Snake. She had the locket around her neck. It was all I kept.

She left the letters stacked in a bundle on the nightstand next to the bed. After I buried her, I stopped going into town, except to buy food and booze. I didn't look after the fields anymore either, letting them go fallow and the grass grow long and fill with little squirmy things.

I spent days and nights, months, wandering the house with a bottle in one hand and a revolver in the other. I was waiting for Gary, the shambler as I'd come to think of him.

Gary stitched himself back together late the next winter. I don't know how. I've never figured out how any of it works, only that it does. It's easy to kill him but he always comes back.

So, I shot him once through the head, pissed on him and laughed. I think I laughed for an hour, drunk, sprawled on the bare floor in the front room next to his corpse. I stayed there for a day or so until he started moving. And then I killed him again. We repeated this routine until I ran through all the ammunition in the revolver, and I was low on rye.

One time, in a haze of booze, guilt and self-loathing, I let him get his hands around my neck and squeeze. There was nothing left for me in this life, I felt. Alice was gone. As far back as I could remember she was the only thing that ever truly mattered to me. I would have forgiven her anything. But with her gone there was no forgiveness left in me, and any hope of happiness washed away as my own personal ghoul rose from the dead each night to stalk me, reminding me what was gone. So I decided I would let him finish it. Yet staring into his cold, hollow eyes, I learned I lacked the courage. Truth was, I still hated Gary then. I hated him enough to keep going. So, I wrenched free and killed him again. That was a turning point for me.

***

That summer I sold the house and moved to Baltimore. The economy was still in the tank, but Roosevelt's spend and build programs were having some effect, and the guys at the *Telegraph* felt bad for me so they helped me find a gig at a paper in that city.

I did well there and worked my way up to editor-in-chief, then publisher. Eventually I had enough saved to buy a small rag of a newspaper just before the war broke out. I turned it into a going concern, which was easy to do back in the days when a healthy classifieds section was a license to print money.

When the war broke out, we did even better. I acquired other depressed rags around the country and turned them around after the war when things were booming. I even bought the *Telegraph*. I was a wealthy man by the time Eisenhower moved into the White House. And even though I dated, and occasionally caroused, I never remarried. It was Alice I wanted. She was all I ever wanted.

Shambling Gary turned up every few years. Sometimes at one of my homes or at an office or hotel I was visiting. Occasionally other people became his victims, but he never got me. It became a sort of cat and mouse game with a rhythm to it. Based on when I killed him, I could figure out how fast he would be able to pull himself together and how long it would take for him to stumble across the landscape to wherever I might be next.

I thought of new and entertaining ways to kill him. Once I dug a pit and filled it with sharpened rebar for him to stumble into. Another time I dropped a piano on him. There was an acid bath too.

Each time, unfailingly, he came back, and with him that sweet pine scent and all the memories it conjured. Each time he rounded a corner, or I caught sight of his rotten face, I flashed back to him and Alice and I hanging out as kids on her parents' front porch. I saw him and Alice share that long embrace before we set off for the Cassiar. I saw him in his cot, in the moonlight, the springs creaking. I felt myself swing the axe. I watched Alice rock back and forth on top of him in our bed as their hearts thrummed in unison.

And each time I killed him and laughed. I had to get rid of the victims too. I had enough money to pay the right people to clean up the mess, though sometimes I did it myself. Occasionally, the cops got involved due to circumstances or timing, but they never linked anything to me–no wealthy, white man was going to jail in those days. Still aren't, in most places.

By the time Nixon resigned I grew tired of the whole affair and moved to a villa in Italy. I honestly thought it would take him a lifetime to shamble his way there, but it was only three years. I'm not sure how he did it, whether he found his way onto a ship and waited or if he just walked into the water and kept putting one foot in front of the other.

He found me at a lavish gala on the outskirts of Florence one spring evening. It was black-tie, ballgowns and cocktails, and I spotted him in a shadowed corner of that monstrous palace. This time he just stared at me, his lips curled back in a mock grin. No one else had seen him yet so I wandered over to find a way to deal with it quietly. I know I wasn't the only one to pick up on the sudden aroma of pine pitch as several guests sniffed and covered their noses.

Gary waited for me. I'm not sure if Gary can think, but over the years we'd seemed to find a way to communicate about our little game.

I came to him in a strange little marble-tiled alcove, a place where the walls of the house didn't seem to line up quite right and the builders had to improvise, a place like that hollow in our cabin where he'd stowed our gold. My gold.

"My Alice," I whispered to him, the words escaping my lips before I even had a chance to know what I was saying.

I saw his charred lips peel back angrily and he lunged for me. I ducked out of the way, reached for a marble bust of some Italian's head and dispatched him quietly. I dumped his corpse in the garden and moved on, selling the villa shortly thereafter.

It was Australia next, Canberra to be precise. That took him a year and a half. Then India, followed by Norway, Peru, Japan, the Bahamas. I began to pick places not because I knew he couldn't get to them but because I knew they would take the longest to reach, giving me the most time to enjoy life before the clock ran out and my familiar pine-scented phantasm would reappear.

I studied geography and ocean maps, choosing locations on the far side of ocean trenches or mountain ranges that I knew he would have to cross, that would slow him down. I even got in touch with NASA at one point, using my money and privilege to explore a life in space. The technology wasn't there, though; it's only recently become possible to do that and I'm too tired now.

Through all of it I eventually came to terms with the fact that there was no stopping Shambling Gary. Like a chronic illness that makes itself known every few years, or the slow march of time that breaks a body and its organs down, death was always coming.

Through the nineties I spent a lot of time living in airplanes. I had the money and the technology allowed me to live a relatively normal life in the air, watching the news, eating chef-prepared meals, and dropping in on my many businesses and homes. I managed eight years without running into Gary. I like to think he just turned around in circles as I skipped to-and-fro between continents.

But there was a pattern to everything and eventually he figured it out, finding me on the tarmac in Oklahoma one October evening. My security detail dealt with him. I didn't explain, just doubled their annual bonuses, and told them to get rid of the evidence.

I turned one hundred a few years ago. It made the news. A billionaire centenarian, perhaps one of the last surviving titans of the days when Ford and Rockefeller roamed the landscape and broke the mold.

My body is breaking down. I can hike still, but I can't run and I'm a lot weaker. I suppose I might die soon but I don't think so. I think this goes on forever. I think it's up to me to end it.

I still have the revolver from Boise. I've put it to my head a few times, but I've never had the courage to pull the trigger. You can get a doctor to help you with these things now but I'm afraid I'd just wake up like Gary, and shamble for eternity.

So, I decided to come back to the place it started. That's where I am now. I brought the letters with me, and the locket. I haven't read them in almost eighty years. In truth, I'm not sure I ever really read them, not entirely.

You see, I lied. I wanted those letters from Alice to be for me, but they weren't. They were Gary's letters. His locket too. He and Alice … well, she wasn't my girl as much as I tried to convince myself she was.

I was never good with women, but I was a hard worker. Gary was the opposite. The Cassiar was my idea. A get-rich scheme hatched during the Depression when our outlook was bleak. At least, that's how I convinced him. Just one summer, I told him, then we'll be back, and maybe you can get married.

"Hey, maybe then we'll find you a girl," Gary had told me, clapping my back, and laughing.

And Alice had laughed too. Not a friendly laugh, a mocking one. The kind that made me hate her, and him.

When we left Boise, she had tears in her eyes but not for me. I nicked the letters as we built the cabin. I ripped up a couple and stained another one. He had every right to hide them from me, but not the gold. The gold was mine. I convinced myself she was too.

But I found a way to win, didn't I, Gary? Maybe not in the end but for a long while I did. And I had Alice.

I was surprised to find our cabin intact eighty years on if a little rundown. I always knew how to build things, didn't I? I paid a guide handsomely to hike me up here. We went slow, slower than he recommended, but I wanted to make sure you could keep up. I saw you standing among the trees at the edge of our camp more than one night. I guess you are waiting too.

When I murdered the guide, I did it in the creek. I shot him when his back was turned so it would be only you and me at the end. His body is floating in the grey-green water now. Maybe he'll shamble like you. Maybe we all will.

It smells like pine now and I know you're with me, Gary, your shadow falling over my bent frame like mine fell over yours that day long ago next to the water. I hear your footsteps outside the cabin as I scribble out my last words by the orange firelight of an old, rusted kerosene lantern.

Just let me finish this sentence, Gary, then I'm all yours.

But Alice? She was *mine*.

The Gehenna of Saint Augustine
Joachim Glage

This story was previously published online through Sci Phi Journal, and is used here with permission from the author.
Joachim Glage lives in Colorado. His short stories, often about imaginary and fabulous books, have appeared in The Georgia Review, LitMag, Sci Phi Journal, The Vanishing Point Magazine, *and many other periodicals and anthologies. A collection of these stories,* The Devil's Library, *is forthcoming from JackLeg Press.* www.JoachimGlage.net

~

"The better a thing the worse its ruin," Augustine said, but tenderly, to Porphyro, his last pupil. "Angels and men, when they fall, become more wretched than monsters."

When Saint Augustine spoke these words he had less than an hour left to live. At the time—the year was 430, Visigoths and Burgundians hounded the empire on various fronts, and Vandals laid siege to Hippo—he was still but Aurelius Augustinus, not yet a saint; but his voice, though rattling from illness, sounded nobly in the still-proud Latin of Rome, and projected the special authority he'd gained during his life, as if his vocation (as bishop, as a statesman of Roman Africa) would not yet relinquish him, and as if he were somewhat more than a man dying.

Lifting his arms from his sides—he lay in his bed, almost still—and raising his cold fingers to lend emphasis to the words, he said to Porphyro: "Our natural goodness is a gift from God. There can be no worse evil than to squander it."

The church was quiet. Porphyro looked about Augustine's chambers and saw that psalms had been hung from the walls. Augustine, with a hand half-palsied, reached out and clenched Porphyro's wrist.

In that moment, nearly a thousand years still stood between Augustine and his sainthood. Neither he nor Porphyro, of course, could have any inkling about that. Nevertheless the student swore that he could feel his teacher's soul radiating all about him, and he knew that it had been specially touched by God, and his eyes filled up with tears.

At this, Augustine paused, suddenly aware of the shortness of his time. It may surprise you, my good and generous reader, but the man who wrote *City of God* and the *Confessions*, and who had long warned congregations in Hippo and Carthage of the corruptible body, had not given much thought to the subject of his own bodily demise. (It should be granted, at any rate, that the strictly *physical* fact of death, at least as a theological matter, could be of only minor interest to someone like Augustine.) What strange new thoughts now came to him?

One need not be a varlet to know the knight's armor clatters before a campaign; likewise, one needs no special wisdom to predict that a man of old age—even one as notable and pious as Augustine—will, when harried by death, feel consternation about it. It is one thing to talk about dying, or about long eternities; it is quite another when rot creeps upon you. When Augustine looked up at weeping Porphyro, and felt his own heart quicken, he knew, for the first time and truly, that he was going to die.

"I've written a book that I've kept secret," Augustine said abruptly. Porphyro wiped his eyes. "I'll tell you where I've hidden the manuscript. You must promise me you will find it and destroy it, and not show it to anyone."

Porphyro was taken aback, but nodded.

"You must promise me that you will not read the book, either, but will destroy it at once."

Augustine's student looked pained. Eventually he said: "My teacher, I must speak the truth. I fear I am too weak to keep such a promise. My curiosity will be too great, and it will overpower me."

Augustine closed his eyes and, with some difficulty, clasped his fingers together, as if he meant to pray. He wheezed softly.

"Perhaps," Porphyro blurted out, fearing he'd disappointed that great *magister*, "if you tell me the contents of the book, my curiosity will be diminished, and I will be able to discard it without reading it."

Augustine lay silent and still and with his hands clasped for a long time. At last he spoke:

"It was not long ago. I had recently finished writing Book XXI of *City of God*, where, among other things, I attempted to deduce the qualities of hell. As you well know, I wrote in that book that hell is a place of fire, and that the souls consigned to that domain have bodies which suffer burning. I wrote that these bodies do not perish in the flames, but are doomed to suffer them for all eternity. I theorized, too, that any repentance in hell is fruitless, not only because the source of such penitence would be *pain* as opposed to *goodness*, but also because the *evangelium* proclaims it to be so: *their worm does not die and the fire is not quenched*."

Augustine paused, coughed, and then adjusted himself in his bed.

"At that time, just as I was about to begin work on Book XXII, a man came to visit me. I knew straightaway that this man was an unnatural being, for he appeared in the exact form of my old acquaintance, Faustus from Mileve, whom

I knew to be long dead. Faustus, as you may recall, was a bishop of the Man-ichaean faith, that sect that had seduced me in my youth, and which promoted the spurious doctrine that all evil comes from without, that is, from a kingdom of darkness that assails the kingdom of light. The appearance of this man, a blas-phemer long since buried and for whom, I confess, I once felt affection, and just after I had been immersed in thoughts about the very infernal forces that should have been tormenting him, suggested to me that I was in the company of a great power. The man said to me, 'I came to speak with you about hell,' and then he grinned, and I knew it was the devil."

Augustine fell silent for a moment. Porphyro raised up slowly in his chair, and barely breathed.

Augustine continued: "Very well do I know of the devil's forked tongue, and how he uses flattery, and enjoys the fruits of his manipulations; so I paid him no mind when he told me he was a great admirer of my work. I ignored him, again, when he complimented me for the great spiritual good that I'd done for Rome and the world. Finally, he said to me: 'When it comes to the subject of hell, however, you're simply off the mark. May I offer you a glimpse?' He then took my hand and kissed it. And then, without ceremony, he left."

Augustine adjusted himself again, and took a moment to rub his eyes.

"That night I had a dream, a dream that was more than a dream. It was a vi-sion. A vision of hell. The hell that I saw, however—or rather, the hell that I now found myself *in*—was not a place of fire, but of *water*. 'The water of knowledge,' a voice whispered to me. 'It encompasses everything.' It was as if I'd been sent to the bottom of the sea, only, it was not dark; the water was limpid and bright, and it functioned somewhat like the sun, making all things visible. Moreover, I found that I could move through the water with ease, and I walked about on the ground normally. Nothing floated or swam. And though it was exceptionally light and fine, perhaps even of a celestial quality, I somehow could *feel* the water at every moment. It moved over me, and its vibrations were like something alive.

"This hell that I saw, the landscape of it, was much like our own world, with creatures and plant-life and mountains and stones and plains; indeed the whole of beautiful nature was there. Nearby me stood a tree; I approached it. At that moment I understood how the 'water of knowledge' had earned its name. For what flashed upon me, from many of the water's vibrations, was not just the sight of the tree in its current state, but the tree in every stage of its existence. I saw it through the seasons, and as a seedling, and then as an acorn; I saw the changing life of the soil which nourished its roots, and the spread of the tree's ancestors in distant woods; I saw the flattening of mountains to make room for the tree, and before that the receding of ice, and fire and explosions that were terrifying to behold—all things that took place over eons, and seemingly for the sole purpose that I might now gaze at these simple branches. As if I, like some cosseted prince, were the beneficiary of all that's ever happened in the universe.

"Just then a voice spoke from behind me: 'The water shows you everything.' I spun on my heels and saw that it was Faustus of Mileve once more. Whether this was the real Faustus, or the devil again, I could not say. He continued: 'The water makes sure that we see the absurdity of God's generosity wherever we look.' And then he smiled at me, and it was just the way he would smile many years ago, when we discussed theology.

"Without ado, he cheerfully began to criticize what I'd written in *City of God.* 'Your first mistake,' he said, 'was assuming the primary substance of hell should be fire. The very lightest of elements!' Faustus laughed, and I could not help but laugh too. 'Even the simplest of principles,' he continued, 'ought to have suggested to you the opposite: that here, in this lowest place, the heavier elements, earth and water, should predominate.' Again I was moved to laugh. He went on: 'Your second error was conceiving of hell under that most human of ideas, that of *retribution*, as if hell were but a dungeon for crude comeuppance, or for the paying up of debts. But no, there is no paying of debts here. In truth, if there is a single axiom of this place, it is that: *No debt is ever paid.* Even to try is foolishness.'

"I then asked Faustus if hell was not a place of punishment after all. His answer astonished me. 'But it's all there in Genesis already,' he said. 'Knowledge is its own punishment, and perfect knowledge is perfect punishment.' He paused to allow my confusion to settle somewhat. 'It is just the same as with riches: the more you're lavished with knowledge the more fruitless the abundance becomes.' Seeing that I needed a further analogy to understand this, he said: 'Just as there are solitudes that are accessible only in crowded cities, so does a general *blur* become possible when everything is thrown into relief equally. Where everything is luminous nothing is. It is not only in the dark of night that all cows are black, as the saying goes, but in the bright and full day, too. Or as we sometimes put it in one of our proverbs, *There is more nothingness in a clod of dirt than in the empty air, and even the buzzing richness of nature only talks over itself.* Call it the nothing of plenitude. There's just so, so much. It humiliates you. It reduces you and even itself to naught.'

"We both laughed. I don't know why we laughed so much. There was something preposterous about it all. And then, while laughing, Faustus suddenly cried out: 'Oh you charmed creatures still on the earth! If only you knew how much passes right through you! If only you knew how faintly you exist! Here in hell we are dense, we collide with everything.' Finally, Faustus encapsulated his lesson with the following words: 'In hell it is evident—the water of knowledge assures it—that nothing we could ever do, even given infinite lifetimes, could earn the abundance bestowed on us. Even gratitude feels like foolishness. Nay, more than that. Gratitude is impossible here. We have too much.'

"We continued to talk, though I don't recall for how long. Time seemed not to exist. Faustus recited for me some more of hell's proverbs, and he told me what society was like there, and he showed me a dark molten sea where people sometimes boiled themselves, if they burned with too much guilt (somehow they found this soothing). We discussed more theological concerns, too, such as whether one can sin in hell, or pray, or repent, and how vast a place it is, and what manner of demon resides there, and if hell be eternal or not, and how much the damned can recall from their lives on the earth, and so forth.

"When I awoke from this vision, I immediately set about to writing it all down. This labor took three days. On the fourth day I rested, but fitfully. On the fifth day I resolved to keep what I'd written secret. I reasoned as follows: Either my vision was a lie, or, if it contained some part of the truth, it was nonetheless that part that the devil was desirous for us to know. Either way, I figured, it must be suppressed. Why I did not destroy the text myself in that very moment, I cannot say. Pride, perhaps, or doubt. Sin, in either case!"

Augustine then told trembling Porphyro how to find the manuscript, and admonished him one last time not to read it, and then waved him away.

Later that day Augustine lay dead, while Porphyro stole into a hidden recess underneath the baptistry. He found his way down a dark stair and then through a low-arched hall, as instructed, and then moved aside the third stone to the left from a sign of the cross that had been carved on the wall. The only copy of *De Gehenna* lay revealed. He took the text into his hands. "I have a home for you," he said, "in a library in a low place;" and then he fled away through a secret door, and over the mosaics set so carefully in the floors of the basilica.

Last Rest
Clay Vermulm

Clay Vermulm is a full-time creative writer and editor from Everett, Washington. He is a member of several writing organizations, including the Horror Writers Association, Northwest Independent Writers Association, Writers Cooperative of the Pacific Northwest, Cascade Writers, and Authors of the Flathead. In 2022, his debut horror/adventure novella Crevasse, *was published by City Stone Publishing. He has work forthcoming in Jennifer Brozek's upcoming flash-anthology* 99 Fleeting Fantasies *and has been published in* Tales of Sleyhouse 2023 *anthology,* Simile, Writer's Forum, *and others. When not at his desk, he is a climber of mountains, surfer of waves, player of board games, and a loving husband and cat-dad.*

~

Thirty-seven.

God dammit. Pat was gonna have a fit.

Grady took a deep drag from his cigarette, his fingers fiddling absently in his pocket as if that would conjure up a little more tobacco—as it was, this one was already half pocket lint. He didn't want to think about how much of it was cow shit and dirt—that's what it tasted like. Course' near everything tasted like cow shit after two months on the trail. Another deep drag, the sweet burn down his throat, spreading through his lungs and tingling on the edges of his fingers as the simmering ember consumed his old, brown rolling paper.

One, two, three, four…

Something moved out in the hills beyond the cattle. One bull, the biggest one, perked up. The setting sun silhouetted his massive horns as he turned to look behind the herd, towards that flash of movement. Whatever it was, it had been big. A bear?

Thirty-seven.

He'd counted probably thirty-seven damn times; wasn't changing nothing.

Grady's horse nickered nervously beneath him. Running a hand along the coarse, brown mane of the animal, he mumbled, "It's alright girl. That's alright." He gave her a little nudge with his spurs and snapped the reins. She didn't budge.

Song was a stubborn old horse—too long on the trail with too few carrots in her life. She'd belonged to him for four years now, and maybe that hadn't been her finest stroke of fortune, but he'd never hit her or let her go hungry. Something his wife had taught him—treat your horse better than you treat yourself, or you don't deserve to ride her. Grady gave her a firmer kick. Instead of going forward, Song reared and turned to the side, back toward camp where the distant orange glow of a newly made fire was just now showing in the waning light.

"Hey now, who's in charge here?" He pulled the reins roughly, knuckles whitening beneath his grip, his brow sweating from the fading heat of the relentless prairie sun. Reluctantly, Song turned and slowly started forward. Grady could feel his heart beating a little faster, feel his breath rattling from his chest. What the hell was she so nervous about? Song had grown up around big grumpy bulls. She'd ridden cross-country with him through hostile Indian country and everywhere else. He'd hardly seen her snort, but now…

There it was again.

Some flash up on a rise that looked down towards the gathered cattle who had grouped together for safety as night fell. Grady and Pat had driven them down into this little coulee, where they could graze on the greener grass and drink from the small stream that trickled across the dry plains. He was sure the local tribes had some name for this little bowl, but Pat always called it Last Rest. Another benefit to Last Rest, they were also out of sight. Being out of sight was the chief business of Grady and Pat. They'd been running stolen cattle up this way for near five years and, in that time, had gotten away with over six hundred head. After tonight, it was going to be riding for hell or high water until they reached the train tracks up near the Dakota border.

Grady sighed. He'd have to be getting back and whether by ill luck or bad karma, Pat would throw his tantrums, and blame them missing cows on his hired hand. Least Grady could do was find out what was going on. He clicked his tongue and kicked in the spurs a couple more times. "Let's go girl. Come on now."

Reluctantly, Song obeyed, snorting and high-stepping all the way.

As they trotted through the midst of the cows, the horse's nervousness seemed to infect the herd, huddling them closer together. The watchful eyes of that big bull followed Grady, long ropes of saliva drooping from its jaws as it chewed and snorted. His fingers drifted to the handle of his sidearm, an old six-shooter he'd 'earned' when they'd gotten off with that very bull. A big prize he was, and hard-won. Grady had technically started the shooting—started with the man who went to his hip with that damned pistol—he'd done it to save himself, not knowing what was about to follow.

Pat had done the rest. He'd started with the kid—a young girl who'd run screaming for her mother. Pat had ridden her down and when the mother came out, shrieking, pointing a rifle, Pat had bent low over his horse and charged toward the house. Unfortunately for her, the woman hadn't been a good shot.

Grady looked down at that little girl the whole time. Barely registering the screams and cries of the woman—barely registering that final crack of a rifle before the dull, lethal collision of a bullet. The daughter had been holding a little stuffed bear and it was all he could see—its eyes black as a mineshaft, sightlessly staring to the sky from the small limp hand of its former owner.

He'd scarcely slept a night since, that stare following him like the rising of the moon, the smell of that burning farmhouse carried on the smoke of every campfire—the cracking of wood like bullets busting through skulls.

His wife, Song, had believed some crazy things, back when she was alive. Back when Grady was an honest miner. They'd been a cause for plenty of controversy around the little Montana mining town—a white man marrying a Native. It happened plenty, but people always had something to say. That was the reason he'd kept his own native blood to himself. It was far enough down the line that he hadn't inherited much of the looks. Thinking of Song now brought shame boiling up through his chest.

He'd come back home to an empty house after his third season rustling. She'd warned him not to go off with Pat no more—said he'd bring nothing but evil down on them—she'd known what kind of man he was, somehow. Like she could smell it on him.

He saw her eyes in his dreams too, watching shoulder-to-shoulder with that little girl. Grady had just stood by, unwilling to fight the atrocities he brought into the world, but Song had always stood by what she believed.

Grady spat into the dirt, as if he could spit the dark thoughts, the shame and regret from his mind.

Hell, maybe she'd been right. Maybe he was cursed with a damn Spirit Bear. That's what she'd always said to him when he woke screaming from the night terrors—that smell of rotting meat, that crunching of bone and rending of flesh, those black eyes—still sticking to his mind; as real as the sweat on his heaving chest.

"Be easy," she'd say in her thick Crow accent, rocking him gently. "Your Spirit Bear is hungry tonight."

He'd never known what to say to that. Never believed it. Dreams were just that; thoughts running wild like Pat in his bloodlust, no law to keep them in line. Still, the dreams had gotten worse since she left—since Pat had basically become his only companion.

I never should have left home. He thought to himself, not for the first time.

All the while, that bull watched him and Song trot through the herd, up toward the rise—the intensity of its gaze emitting a palpable fear that seemed to clog very air, like that cloying smoke from the farmhouse—a whole little world that family had built, burning away into the Montana sky on the acrid scent of scorched furniture and flesh. When they reached the other side of the bowl, he dismounted and knelt in the dirt. Up here, where the wind ruled the land, the grass was more sparse, brown from the heat of the sun and the lack of moisture, and separated by patches of trampled-down dust from the herd they'd driven through the day before. Over the last few years, Grady had picked up a fair amount of tracking knowledge, but no one can track in the dark, and he'd been a bit late on seeing the signs.

Still, he had seen *something.*

Next to him, Song kicked at the dirt and whinnied, reared up again, and pulled savagely on the reins.

"Alright, alright, let's get back to camp," he said, giving one more cursory look around before kicking into the stirrups and throwing a leg over the saddle. No sooner was he mounted, then his horse took off at an eager gallop back toward the flickering light of the campfire.

***

"How many?" Pat snarled. He spat a blackish glob into the fire with a heavy, hissing thump. "I thought you was keeping an eye on them?"

"I'll go out and scout around tomorrow, but I'm telling you something is going on. Might be another crew sneaking off with our take."

If you hadn't stolen that damn bull, killed that family, burned their house… we'd still be ghosts out here. Grady had always thought of them as ghosts, silent, unseen. Now, he felt they'd become demons—bad spirits, Song would have called them. Now they were making ghosts, stealing more than cows—stealing lives and virtue. He couldn't help but look at Pat—the man looked like the damn devil with that pointed goatee, yellow teeth, and dead black eyes. How had Grady not seen it before? How had he not listened to his wife?

"What you lookin' at so hard?"

"Nothin'."

"Yeah?" Pat smiled, his fingers twitching down by the holster at his belt. Grady wondered if he even knew he was doing it. "Kinda looks like you got something to say."

"Just answering your question." Grady looked down at his dusty boots.

"Well, that's right kind of ya."

"What do you want me to do here, Pat?" Grady snapped. "I ain't got a clue where these bastards are wandering off to, I saw some large critter following us, and you just want to sit here and pick a fight with me. So yeah, I ain't got much more to say."

The fire crackled. The wind blew—a chilly reminder of the frigid night to come. It always amazed Grady how hot it could be during the day and how cold at night in this god-forsaken country.

Shoulda stayed in Virginia City. Might not have enjoyed working the same old hole in the ground, but I'd had a roof. I'd had Song. He shifted his weight against the hard ground before his left cheek could fall asleep. Pat just stared at him, murder in his eyes. It weren't real murder though. He needed Grady, couldn't do this on his own. If he could, Grady woulda' been dead months back.

Eventually, the anger seemed to ebb—or maybe Pat just got bored.

"What kind of critter?" Pat asked.

"Something big."

"Like what? A bear?"

Grady shrugged. It had to be a bear, didn't it? Nothing else this big was trotting around the prairie. Not on this side of the world. Back when he was a boy, he'd seen picture books of cats the size of bears, orange with black stripes from the jungles of Africa, or Asia or some such place. He could never remember the damn names of them places, but he remembered the pictures of those giant snarling cats. That wasn't the American west. Here they had wolves, cougars, and bears.

And the people, of course. No animal was half so dangerous as the people.

"Your tongue stuck too?" Pat pulled a can of beans from the fire that he'd put in to roast, his hand wrapped in a handkerchief. He stabbed the tin top with his four-inch bowie knife and worked the blade forward and back, peeling the can open before shoveling a mouthful out on the back edge of the blade.

"Musta been a bear, I guess.'"

"No bears this far east, not no more." Pat took another bite, his eyes glinting orange in the firelight as if daring Grady to challenge that fact.

Grady pulled some hardtack from his pack and gnawed on the leathery meat, working it between his teeth before swallowing.

Pat sighed deeply.

"Guess I'll take first watch since you can't even keep track of fully grown heifers. Want something done right, they say…" He chuckled to himself, as if that had been the funniest joke.

Grady chewed his tasteless hardtack in silence as Pat finished their last can of beans.

***

Pat looked out over the sleeping pile of meat down in the bowl. It was too dark to count, but he had a bad feeling the kid had was right. They'd lost two more, just in the past three hours that he'd been asleep. What the hell had Grady been doing when he was on watch? Probably jerkin' his pecker—thinking about that savage woman he'd left in Montana and never shut up about. Even named his horse after the bitch. That, at least, was fitting; Pat thought.

Thirty-seven would make twelve head lost on this trip. There'd been times they'd lost two or three, but twelve… Might be they could hit another farm on the way up, get it down to six or seven. Six or seven was expected.

Looking over to the right, he saw their horses—both wide awake, pacing around. Even Pat had to admit that was weird. His horse, maybe. Steel was a goddamn killer—didn't take to being tied. But that old mare Grady trotted around on would be snoring by sunset if they let her.

Stalking back to the fire, he pulled his rifle from its case next to his sleeping roll, clicked down on the lever-action with a smooth, practiced motion, and turned back out toward the hills.

As he got closer, Pat realized the cows weren't sleeping either. They were quiet, but their big-white eyes tracked his movements with a cautious weariness rare to the big animals. They breathed, heavy and dumb—even that big grumpy bull was keeping his head low. Pat's fingers strummed up and down on the trigger guard, the feeling of the steel sent a warmth up his arm and down into his guts. The wind whispered through his hair as he reached the far end of the herd. His feet crunched in the dry grass and brush, shattering the silence with the scent of sage.

A flash of movement up the hill.

Fear tasted like metal. Pat hadn't been scared for a long time—still, he remembered it well from the war—remembered the tramping of boots over blood-soaked soil—gunpowder leaking into his lungs with every breath of battle-black air.

His rifle flew up. Barrel leveled at the top of the hill, that practiced finger flew to the trigger—

There was nothing there.

Pat slowly lowered his rifle, adjusted the lamp clipped to the chest of his jacket, and dropped his weight a bit. Slowly, he crept up the hill, head on the swivel, trigger finger relaxed, ready. Resisting the urge to tremble, Pat alternated focus on his feet—making sure to miss bushes, gopher holes, coiled rattlesnakes—and the crest of the hill where he'd just seen a massive black shape move off and onto the open plain.

Huffing receded into the distance as he reached the crest of the hill.

Sounded like a bear. Even Pat could admit that.

He'd heard stories of these beasts. Pat could hear them now, but they all seemed like tall tales to him. One man said he put eight bullets in a Silverback up toward Oregon, still didn't kill it, and came home one arm short in the bargain. He'd heard of an entire wagon train down near Utah that'd been eaten like a Thanksgiving dinner, splattered all over the dusty road, and chewed to hell. Well, them bears never met Pat O'Conner.

How the hell is this thing hungry after eating twelve of my cows?

Across the dark expanse of the Great Plains hung the bright full moon, allowing Pat to see for miles. There, about a hundred yards from him, was the large hulking figure, now standing up on two legs, its silhouette making it look like a giant weasel poking from a hen's carcass. It was looking right at him.

CRACK.

The gunshot cascaded out over the sea of grass. The animal dropped.

CRACK. CRACK.CRACK.

Pat's boots crunched and thudded toward where the beast had dropped. He'd killed it with that first shot. Hell yeah.

Three more, just in case them stories were true.

The bear grew bigger and bigger the closer he got. That potent scent of sage morphing into the sour, musty odor of damp fur. The beast's breathing, deep and guttural, got louder and thicker. Pat had been stealing cattle a long time, making his living that way. So he knew a thing or two about weighing an animal with the eye. That bull down in Last Rest was easily 900 pounds, but next to this thing…

The bear twitched, muscle rippling up the thick fur of its matted, gray coat. A silverback. One shot to bring down a silver back. Pat O'Conner don't miss.

The bear twitched again.

Pat froze.

The bear slowly rose to its feet and turned to face him.

CRACK.

Pat O'Conner missed. Must have, because the bear wasn't phased. In a flash of impossible speed, the massive animal dashed into him, crushing Pat to the ground and pinning him beneath 1,200 pounds of slavering, frothing rage, breaking his gun like a dry twig.

Pat felt his bones splinter and snap as pain exploded through his body, A scream tore from his throat as he tried to lift his arm, but before he could even move, the bear reared up and smashed down on his chest with its massive paws, splattering Pat O'Conner's guts across the grass. He was still alive somehow—still watching as the bear roared, hauled him from the ground in its massive jaws, and gave a vicious shake of its gargantuan head.

***

"Make peace with the Spirit Bear. It will come for you."

He knew that voice.

Song.

It came from inside.

He stood at the porch of a farmhouse, the door ajar, smacking rhythmically into the frame as the wind blew it forth and back, forth and back.

Something was wrong.

The table was still set for dinner and a fire burned from within the cooking stove in the corner of the room, but nobody was around to tend it.

"Hello?" a voice called, from the bedroom. "Grady is that you?"

It was Song. She'd come home. Elated, he ran to the bedroom door, but when he grasped the handle, the heat of the metal seared his palm.

There was a fire inside. Was Song trapped in there?

"Grady?" She said again, this time sounding panicked.

"Song, get back from the door!" he shouted before jerking his six-shooter free and firing three slugs through the lock.

Everything fell silent.

The door slowly opened to a room devoid of furniture, painted all in black.

No, charred black.

Standing there in a single file line, a bullet hole through each of their foreheads, were the man, woman, and little girl from the farmhouse.

He gasped, stumbling back. What had he done?

There was a loud metallic clatter behind him. Grady turned to see the cast-iron stove tipped on its side, flames bursting from within, snaking around his feet, up the walls and curtains, erupting with billowing black smoke that clogged his lungs like the dark dust of the mines. There, blocking doorway, was a massive silver bear. Flame dancing in its cold, black eyes as it let out a terrifying roar.

***

Grady's came awake, sucking in a deep breath. The heat of the campfire

220

stung his dry eyes as he wiped sweat from his brow and sat up. He'd broken the habit of waking screaming from the bear dreams, Pat would kick him in the ribs and spit at him whenever he did. Tonight though, Pat wasn't there and like in the dream, he could feel something eating at him, screaming at his sense to be alert—be ready. To his right, the horses reared and screamed. Pat's wily stallion, Steel, thrashed over and over against the stake that they'd hammered in to hold him. Muscles bulged and strained beneath the creature's black coat, his eyes rolled to white, and with one last powerful jerk of his thick neck, he ripped the stake from the ground and galloped off, the stake clanging and clattering against the hard ground as the horse vanished into the night.

Grady hurried over to Song. She was pacing around at the end of her line, but not jerking at it like Steel had. Her ears pricked up like horns as she kicked the dirt.

"That's alright girl, that's alright." He followed the horse's gaze, which seemed fixed East, toward the far edge Last Rest coulee. There was something there.

A person. No, three people—standing on the rise, silhouetted by the pale moonlight which gave the night a strangely bright, ghostly air. He looked closer, straining his eyes. The figures were watching him. Even across the distance, he could make out a man in overalls and a wide-brimmed hat and a woman with long hair falling over her shoulders and down her back like a dark curtain. Grady knew them. It was the couple from the farmhouse. Beside her parents stood the little girl, her hair shoulder length, twin white orbs glowing out from her skull, her stuffed bear hanging limply by her side.

"Hey, what are you doing out here? It isn't safe!" His voice boomed over the bowl, cutting through the otherwise silent night. He started toward them. "Are you alright?" They needed to leave. If Pat saw them…

They're already dead. Some part of him knew.

No, that's not possible.

Where is Pat anyway?

The man and woman walked out of his sight, over the top of the hill. The little girl trailed after them, holding her mother's hand, casting a final glowing gaze over her shoulder toward Grady. Giving Song one final pat, he took off into the coulee on foot. He couldn't just leave them out here. He'd left enough people behind to die.

The cattle were still, like they too were dead. Grady could barely even hear their quick, shallow breaths—they seemed to inhale as one organism, following him with one set of seventy-four eyes. The horns of the big, aggressive bull jutted up from near the front of the herd, but it was hunkered low, just like the others.

He stalked toward the top of the bowl, the eyes of the cattle following him—like the eyes of a crowd at a hanging, watching the doomed ascend toward the noose. That's when he found Pat. Grady's breath hitched in his throat, his stomach twisting up.

Pat looked like a train had hit him. His eyes stared glassily toward the stars, his nose strangely straight and ordinary above the utter wreckage just below it. From his lower jaw to his groin, Pat was splattered like a mosquito against a forearm. A dark pool of blood glistened all around him, spread out into the grass and still leaking from the ragged edges of limbs that were strewn around the area. Just near the corpse was the Remington lever-action rifle Pat always carried, broken clean in two.

"What the hell…" Grady's pistol snapped up. He tried to stabilize it with both hands but was still shaking plenty bad. Would he be able to the hit broad side of a wagon if it was bearing down on him? No less, whatever had done this to Pat—a man who, for all his shortcomings, had been a master marksman and nobody to trifle with in a close fight, either. Whatever had done this…

A deep, rasping breath huffed out of the darkness behind him—it sounded like it came from opposite where the cattle were grouped up. There, the shadow of the bowl obscured his eyes from the aid of the moonlight. His flesh pimpled like a plucked chicken. Slowly, he turned, leading with his gun, then his head, then the rest of his body, hoping to see nothing but the bull. Instead, his gaze met a monstrous ghostly-silver shape with glowing white eyes. Those eyes looked right through him. He could feel them watching, waiting, but for what, Grady didn't want to know.

The creature rose on massive, thick-furred legs and faced him from its full height of twelve feet. It was a bear—but it was so much larger than he'd imagined. The bruin must have weighed a thousand pounds, four-inch claws glinted red-stained ivory from frying-pan-sized paws. Its mouth hung slightly open as it panted, sending white clouds into the chill of the evening. The bear tilted its head down slightly, looking him straight in the eyes.

He raised his gun, levelling it at the massive animal, near dropping it from shaking. *Calm down, or you're going to be as dead as Pat.* But there was nothing he could tell himself that would stop the trembling. He could smell the man's blood and organs spewed over the dusty grass. It clung to his nostrils and throat, made thicker by the rampant nerves ricocheting through his gut like a bullet in a coal shaft.

Grady looked back toward his campfire, which had now flickered down to little more than a weak wisp of smoke trailing up into the sky.

Song. That was his only chance.

She always had been, hadn't she? Ever since he'd left home with that horse named after his wife—ever since that wife had been torn herself from his life, leaving him desolate and depraved—he'd named the horse after Song because she was a chance for a new beginning, a chance to escape that past which so dogged his steps.

His spirit bear—the manifestation of his darkest deeds, his denial of his own people, his desertion of his wife and home in hopes of a quick score.

Could that be what he was seeing now, in the flesh? Song had warned him during their last night together.

"You must make peace with your Spirit Bear, or it will come for you. You can't outrun a thing like this."

He'd kissed her hair, thanked her for hearing him out. But ultimately, he'd ignored her. Just as he'd ignored her words of caution, her trepidation about setting out with Pat. Her fear of being alone in that town of lustful eyes and hateful hearts. He'd left anyway, assured her that everything would be alright. Hadn't he said the same thing to his horse just moments ago?

The bear dropped to all fours and let out a primeval roar, snapping him back to the present.

Grady turned and ran, not even realizing he'd dropped his gun until he was splashing through the creek halfway across the coulee.

Song. He had to get to Song. Surely she could outrun this beast.

Not meaning to, but unable to stop himself, he threw a glance over his shoulder. The bear hadn't moved, it just watched him, snarling. He could not say the same for the cattle.

As the monster bellowed again, they all lurched to their feet—as a herd, as a single animal. The huge bull in the front led the stampede as all thirty-seven enormous creatures thundered up the coulee, straight towards Grady.

Shit, shit, shit, shit!

He faced forward, leaning into the hill and pumping his arms as hard as he could. His lungs burned, legs trembled with fatigue at every concussive strike against the rocky earth. The world became the pain of breathing—the ever-growing storm of the approaching stampede. He crested the rise, nearly tripped through the remnants of his campfire, scattering the ashes across the grass, and scrambled on all fours to Song's lead. She was rearing, screaming, pulling as hard as she could—making it impossible to untie the knot.

The panicked cattle bellowed, grunted, and trampled toward him.

Pulling the hunting knife from his belt, he slashed down as hard as he could, severing the rope. Song bolted. Grady gripped the rope with all his strength, threw one hand up to her back, and tried to heave himself on, but she was moving too fast. He'd only slow her down; he'd only kill her, too.

Grady let go of the rope and stumbled face-first into the dirt, putting his hands over the back of his head as the herd roared over him.

***

A soft kiss fell upon his brow.

Song? he wondered—prayed.

The scent of tepid meat filled his nostrils.

Grady opened his eyes slowly. Standing above him was the spirit bear, one massive paw on his chest, pinning him to the dirt with irrefutable strength.

The bear rose, its massive weight pressing him further into the ground as it positioned itself just above his chest cavity, the claws of both paws digging through his shirt and into his skin, sending warm trickles of blood tracing down his gasping torso.

"It will come for you," he heard Song say, as if her voice rode the passing wind in that split moment, suspended across time.

He tried to say her name one last time—just to taste the sweetness of it—but the bear roared, cutting him off as it crushed down with all its might.

The crunching of bone and rending of flesh, those black eyes…

All Grady's thoughts ceased—snapped like a neck at the gallows, or split logs spitting sap from the heat of a fire.

Right Where She Belongs
Madison McSweeney

Madison McSweeney is the author of the horror comedy The Doom That Came to Mellonville *(Filthy Loot) and the heavy metal/folk horror novelette* The Forest Dreams With Teeth *(Demain Publishing). Her gothic poetry chapbook* Fringewood *was released by Alien Buddha Press in 2022.*
She lives in Ottawa, Canada, tweets from @MMcSw13 and blogs at
www.madisonmcsweeney.com.

~

Greetings, earthlings!"

The astronaut flashed her best smile: a wince. She imagined a thousand schoolkids a hundred thousand lightyears away replying, *Greetings, Spacegirl!*

Dr. D. Abigail Hendrix – physicist, aerospace engineer, Canada's youngest cosmonaut – *Spacegirl*. Another idea from the comms department. *It humanizes you.*

"Ever wondered how astronauts brush their teeth?" She held a toothbrush to the camera. It was brand new, not the one she regularly used, and purple: a compromise between functional blue and *girls can be scientists too!* hot pink. They'd done polling on that. "Never leave the planet without one!"

Adrian's voice crackled in her ear: "Your camera's off."

Dr. Hendrix frowned, quickly correcting herself. Because the camera was on. The button was firmly in the ON position, and the broadcast light glowed red. Muting her mic just in case, she updated Adrian. "Must be an issue on your end. Everything's in place here."

"Are you sure? Me and about eight hundred kids are staring at a blank screen right now."

"I'm looking at an on-switch and a red lightbulb that says, 'Filming in Progress,' so yeah. How's the audio?"

Adrian's reply was a thunderclap of fuzz. "You're breaking up," she called, removing her headset. The feedback only grew louder, no longer coming from the earpiece but from the walls of the ship, descending upon her from all angles. Dropping the phone, which floated, she clapped her hands to her ears, her thighs rising to her chest. She cried out, but the sound was stolen from her, whisked away and recycled into the cacophony. Then there was a new clatter, the phone smashing on the cold tin floor. She collapsed with it as the shuttle shuddered to a stop, then went into freefall.

***

The shuttle crumpled like a soda can on impact. Dana's relief when she saw that the oxygen monitor was not blinking red faded when she realized it wasn't blinking *green* either. She held her breath, then exhaled and started to laugh. It was as good a way to die as any.

She laughed for a long time before she noticed she could still breathe.

The OPEN HATCH button was smashed to shards, so she pushed one of the ruined walls aside and ducked underneath. Scraps of metal snapped and fell. The ground she stepped out onto was black and hard, the way ahead obscured by mist. Dazed, she deemed the atmosphere noxious, before realizing that the stench and the smoke came from her own wreck. When the smog dissipated, she saw a long grey plain terminating in a building.

The structure was squat and ugly, scarlet slabs of stone giving way to two rows of oversized windows, closed off by beige curtains. The only door that she could see, brown and heavy like the entrance to a prison, was set to the side, above a set of chipped stone steps and beneath a wooden cross, yellow as an egg yolk. A sign across the building's face, navy blue writing on white chloroplast, read: Galilee Christian School.

***

The being who found her on the schoolhouse steps was dressed as an Evangelical pastor. He couldn't have been – she was two billion miles away from the closest church – but the imitation was uncanny.

It took no convincing for him to come with her to the crash site; he followed meekly, hands in his pockets, interrupting her manic chatter only to ask if she wouldn't rather go to a hospital. He didn't question her when she retraced her footsteps to ground zero to find nothing there: no smoke, no shattered glass or twisted metal, no ship.

"The other way," she muttered, after they'd done a loop without finding so much as a dent in the ground.

"The other way?" the pastor-thing echoed, sounding perturbed. "That's nothing but-"

But the astronaut's eyes were already fixed on the edge of the schoolyard. "Nothing."

He swung his head to see what she was seeing. "I was going to say, 'construction.'''"

"It's transparent," she said.

"I think you should come home with me," he said, his tone concerned. "My wife can take a look at your head, we can give you some dinner, a change of clothes…" He pointed a finger towards the nothingness. "I live right over there."

***

The five who greeted her, efficiently hustling to offer chairs and heat up leftovers and find first-aid kits, were also convincingly humanoid. Uniformly towheaded and attractive, their faces settled into lineless smiles and placid contortions of concern as they attacked her with questions: "Are you okay?" "What happened?" "Is there anyone you can call?" She instinctively accepted the offer of a phone, despite knowing that she was not – could not be – on her own planet.

She was dead or dying, she thought, suffocating in the void, her oxygen-starved brain sending her off with the comforting hallucination of a kindly Christian family, and then the mother placed the receiver of a cordless phone into her outstretched hand. The device looked alien to the astronaut, if only because it was dated. She hadn't used a landline in fifteen years, not since she'd moved out of her parents' house and got her own phone plan. Even her parents only maintained one out of habit.

It was their number she dialled first, from muscle memory rather than affection. When she put the phone to her ear, the line was dead.

She felt like a body laid out in an operating theatre as the family watched her dial every number she remembered, tuning in each time to the same screech of static. She tried her parents again, in case she'd dialled incorrectly. She tried her office, her roommate, Dr. Cuddy, even her gynecologist, all with no success. "Is there something wrong with your phone?" she finally asked.

"No," the mother said, but made no attempt to demonstrate.

She burst into tears after a second failed round of calls. A hand, dry and firm, clasped around hers. "You'll remember once you get a hot meal in you." The logic made no sense, but in the moment it felt good and true, and the woman's grey eyes were kind.

"I'm Darla Henderson," she said. "You've met my husband, Daniel." She extended a long, white arm, like the limb of a mantis. "And these are our children – Danielle, Darlene, Denny, and Dan Jr." The children smiled benevolently, Dan Jr. the tallest on the right, Denny grinning gap-toothed on the far left, the two girls in the middle, nearly identical save for what looked like a three or four-year age difference.

Dr. Hendrix winced. Pastel families like this had always unnerved her – through no fault of their own – but the alliterative, subtly similar names felt almost invasive. She was almost embarrassed to provide her own: "Dana."

Darla clapped her hands, and the astronaut flinched backward. "Oh, that's adorable! you'll fit right in!"

***

Dana begged off church on Sunday. Once the Hendersons had headed down the road in their oversized grey minivan, she set out to search the house. She was half convinced that its interior was a façade, that a peek at the underside would reveal exactly what show she was on. She started with the simplest tricks, pulling open cabinets and cupboards, expecting to find them blank. But every storage area was full to bursting with all the linens, canned foods, and cleaning products a family of six would need. They weren't even suspiciously well-organized; the towels and sheets were neatly folded, but the cupboard under the sink was a jungle of leaking tubes of dish soap and fallen canisters of ant killer. It could have been her kitchen.

Next, she checked the bedrooms. This step petrified Dana, as there would be no logical explanation if she were caught. Midway through sifting through Daniel and Darla's drawers, she was struck with the unaccountable feeling that there were cameras watching her. She closed the drawer and hastened out.

The girls' room was as one would expect, bright and feminine with signs of sisterly warfare. Two identical beds sat at opposite sides of the room, a line of masking tape dividing the carpet between them. Danielle's (or Darlene's; she hadn't asked who was who) lay on the left, haloed by haphazardly taped drawings and pictures of dolphins, a dollhouse at its foot overflowing with half-naked Barbies. Darlene's (or Danielle's) was on the right, lined with carefully hung photos and posters of tween idols. The photos appeared authentic, the older girl pictured at various field trips and church events, playing with dogs and riding horses. Dana didn't recognize anyone on the posters, but perhaps Christian media had different stars. A whisk of the closet door revealed a mismatched selection of school uniforms and street clothes, in two different sizes. She skipped Denny's room, concerned it may contain a nanny cam, and tread carefully in Dan Jr.'s, which was littered with books and half-completed school projects.

Next came the basement. Her hesitation on that threshold was irrational, grounded less in reason than in old horror movies. But the space, when she flicked on the light, was neat and homey. The white carpet was dingy but recently vacuumed, and years of greasy childish handprints marred the walls. Two IKEA bookshelves leaned against the back wall, next to a laundry basket full of toys on the right side and a cheap desk to the left. On top of the desk – pushed into the corner closest to the wall, as if the family found the item distasteful – was a computer.

Dana hadn't seen a model this old since she'd taken Intro to Business Fundamentals in a dimly lit high school computer lab. The tower was a mute grey monolith, surrounded by a tangle of wires like angry snakes, and the back of the monitor bulged outward like the translucent shell some ancient blood-gorged beetle. It looked just like the computers she had used in school, except the letters etched onto the keys weren't from any alphabet she had ever seen.

Dana ran her hand along the keyboard, her fingertips studying the upraised designs on each key.

"I'm afraid that won't work."

Darla was standing at the top of the stairs, smiling tolerantly. "We don't have internet here," she explained. "There's so many temptations nowadays, and so much scary stuff online. We thought it would be best."

"Then why do you keep a computer?" Dana asked, disoriented. The Hendersons were supposed to have been gone all morning.

"Oh, it belonged to a sweet old man from our church. He stayed with us for a bit when he fell on hard times."

"Was he also not allowed to use internet?"

Darla showed no sign of noticing the barb. "You know, I don't think we ever had it himself. I think he just used it to type letters to his family in Russia."

Russia. Dana glanced back down at the keyboard, recognizing the Cyrillic script for what it was. "I see."

"He had this dinky little printer, too, used to drive it around in his car, when he was…" She trailed off, as if mindful of the homeless man's privacy. "…Well, before he set up here. I don't know what happened to it…"

Dana stopped listening. She didn't want to know what had become of the old man, so far away from his remaining family, or why he would leave behind his only lifeline to them. "Is that an encyclopedia set?" she asked, blurting out the first thing she saw.

"Atlases," Darla replied, her tone souring. "Daniel hates turning down door-to-door salesmen."

"I wouldn't have thought that," Dana said. "Your house is so…free of clutter." *Especially for a family of six.*

Darla smiled knowingly. "It's a full-time job. Anyway–" she turned to face the stairs. "…if you're looking for reading material, I would consult one of the upstairs bookshelves – there's nothing really interesting down here, but I've got some nice romances – nothing too sultry, of course. And I think Dan Jr. has some old paperbacks. Science fiction, and that sort of thing. He wants to read horror, but we try to push him to more wholesome content…"

Dana imagined opening one of the atlases to find the twisted geography of some ersatz earth, or nothing but hundreds of blank pages. There must be *something* amiss, or else why would Darla discourage her from reading it?

"Are you coming?"

"For what?" She'd only just risked a tentative step towards the shelf, and her heel was still hovering above the carpet.

"For dinner, of course. I'm just about to pull it out of the oven."

"Oh. Of course."

Darla watched her for a moment, as if to make sure she wasn't taking any detours. Dana followed obediently, wondering how many hours could possibly have passed since the Hendersons had left for morning service. She hazarded a final glance at the computer.

If they'd never had internet, then what was that ethernet cable connected to?

***

"You know, the school needs a science teacher," Darla was saying, lifting heaps of cream-drenched salad into oversized white bowls. "And I was thinking, with your…background. Everything you know about physics…"

"That would be interesting," Dana said, waving away an offer of salad. She didn't trust any of the food here, and had been living off what remained of her freeze-dried meal packets. "Lactose intolerant," she lied. "I'll make myself something later."

Darla frowned, her face shifting like putty. "I can make you a garden salad."

"No, no," Dana insisted. "I don't want to impose. That said–" She paused. She hadn't meant to bring this up yet, but she wanted to distract from her not-eating. Darla looked up expectantly.

"I know you're both busy Tuesday mornings, but I was hoping Dan Jr. could drive me somewhere." She'd asked to borrow the car before, but Daniel had blanched and turned her down with some unreasonable excuse about their insurance policy.

"Oh?"

"Downtown," Dana continued. "I want to go to the police station – have them run my fingerprints." The Hendersons maintained a pleasant fiction that their houseguest had amnesia, even though she remembered her name, birth date, contact information, profession, and entire life history.

"But I'm sure you haven't been in any kind of trouble," Darla replied. "They won't have you in their system."

"I know." Dana forced a sad, tight smile. "But it would put my mind at ease, just knowing I've tried everything to get home."

She half expected the clan to say sinisterly, in unison, *But we're you're new home now.* Instead, Darla replied, "Dan Jr.'s grounded."

This was true, at least as far as Dana could ascertain; the eldest Henderson offspring had initiated a one-sided, screaming argument with his parents the evening before, deeming them liars and hypocrites. This was the real reason she wanted him to drive her: if there was a weak link in this family, he was it.

"Think of it as a chore," she said. "You don't get out of chores when you're grounded."

She expected Darla to throw up another roadblock, but she acquiesced almost immediately. "Sounds fine to me." She winked conspiratorially. "Just make sure he doesn't have any fun."

***

Dan Jr. was sullen as he pulled out of the driveway, dust flying as the ill-maintained asphalt crumbled. He waited until he was halfway down the road to adjust his mirrors, re-angling them with an exaggeratedly distracted air, and was well into a needlessly abrupt turn before he began to fasten his seatbelt. "How long will you be?" he asked, the school and house disappearing.

Dana smirked. "You got a date or something?"

He glared at her without taking his eyes off the road. "I just don't want to be stuck parked in front of a police station all day."

This was not how she'd wanted this to go at all. She trailed off: "Well, actually…"

The boy eyed her suspiciously.

"Can you keep a secret, Dan?" She'd hoped to develop some rapport over the course of the drive, but his attitude ruled that out. Her only hope now was that he was mad enough at his parents to betray them.

"What kind of secret?" he finally asked.

"I don't want to go to the police station," she said. "I want to go somewhere on the outskirts of the city. It's…a place I remember. I think the people there might know me."

"Why didn't you tell my parents that?"

231

The excuse she'd planned was along the lines of *I didn't want them to worry*. Recalibrating for her new strategy, she instead said: "I know they think I'm a bit unstable."

"Yeah." He didn't stop the car.

"And as much as I like your parents – as much as I like all of you, *you* especially – I don't want to live in their spare room for the rest of my life. I hate to keep imposing. The sooner I can find my people and get out of your way, the better."

He turned the corner twice without replying. Then: "Do you know how to get there?"

"Not from here," she said, resisting the urge to remind him that she didn't even know where *here* was. "But if you get downtown, I can navigate."

She expected the world to fade into nothingness as soon as they'd travelled sufficiently far from the house; each block felt like they were getting away with something.

Don't get your hopes up. This is just an experiment.

Not until they arrived at the non-descript building on Industrial Road did Dana remember that she had no identification. But all the guards knew her by sight; most barely bothered to check her pass at all.

She had Dan Jr. parallel park outside the wrought-iron gate. Her lack of ID would be rectified easily enough, but a strange car and an unauthorized teenager might complicate things. Straightening the grey dress she'd borrowed from Darla, Dana walked quickly to the rectangular security booth. She smiled as she approached the window, expecting a familiar face. But she'd never seen this guard before. "Hi," she said. "You must be new."

"Good morning," the man replied, his tone neutral. "This is a restricted area."

"I know. I work here."

"Ahhhhhhh," he said, and smiled. "Then I imagine you'll have some ID? I'm sorry, I don't know everyone yet."

"All good," she replied. "I actually lost my ID. I was in an accident."

"I'm sorry to hear. I can probably look you up in the system – can I get your name?"

"Dana Hendrix. Like Jimi."

"D-A-N-A?"

"Bingo."

He had her re-spell her name twice. "What department did you say you worked in?"

Dana's teeth clenched. "I work with Dr. Marvin Cuddy." She dreaded saying his name, lest she find out they'd wiped him from reality, too.

But the guard perked up at the mention. "Oh, okay!" he exclaimed. "I know Dr. Cuddy. He'd be able to identify you?"

"Yes, for sure."

"I'll page him. He'll be down soon."

Something felt off. Guards were not receptionists: she'd never heard of them paging anyone to announce a visitor. Legitimate guests were always provided parking passes and temporary IDs well before entering the grounds. And the idea of Dr. Cuddy coming outside to identify someone? Absurd, impractical, and a security risk.

This whole trip had been too easy. Darla letting Dan Jr. drive her even though he was grounded, they didn't trust anyone with their car, and Dana was an unstable stranger. Dan Jr. going along with this forty-five minute road trip to nowhere. Now this.

It was like everyone was only pretending to put up a fight.

Barely thirty seconds passed before Marvin Cuddy threw open the doors and crossed the parking lot. Like everything else that day, it was too fast; his office was on the highest floor of the building, and the elevator was slow. But she didn't question it. She couldn't bear to.

In his haste to greet her, he'd neglected to remove his lab coat, which was as rumpled as ever. His slacks still ended slightly too high on his ankle, revealing mismatched socks, and his salt-and-pepper beard was trimmed a tad thinner on his left side than his right. Every detail was absolutely correct. Dana felt tears forming. She hadn't cried since this nightmare began. "Dr. Cuddy!" she cried, restraining the urge to hug him.

The look on his face was one of surprise, and she realized her mentor had probably thought her dead. *There was probably a funeral,* she thought, with horror. *He probably had to give a eulogy for me.*

Speech failed the doctor as he stared at her. Dana smiled – her first genuine smile in what felt like months – and her voice quavered as she whispered, "I'm alive."

"That's very nice," Dr. Cuddy replied. "Do we know each other?"

***

The ride home had been a series of jump cuts: pulling away from the facility on Industrial Road; passing the downtown fire station; approaching the Galilee Christian School; parked in the Hendersons' driveway. Walking through the front door, she was welcomed by a soothing cookies-in-the-oven scent that contradict-ed the roast that had been thawing in the kitchen when they'd left. She recalled trudging up the stairs and throwing herself into bed, but didn't remember being called down to dinner.

Darla spooned beige chicken in Alfredo sauce onto her plate. The absence of the beef roast was not explained, nor were there any cookies. In a burst of perverse humour, Dana almost asked "Where's the beef?", but it occurred to her that if this planet-that-was-not-Earth even had Wendy's commercials (which it likely did, given how precisely everything else was recreated), the Hendersons were too fundamentalist to have ever owned a TV. Instead, she asked, "Is Dan Jr. not joining us?"

Darlene looked surprised. "Dan Jr.?"

Dana's stomach tightened. "What, does he get sent to bed without supper when he's grounded?"

Darla and Daniel looked at each other. "Dan Jr. left for college."

"When?"

"Two days ago," Daniel said. "Don't you remember?"

"We sent him off with great fanfare," Darla prodded. "We had sandwiches, and a banner."

"I painted the banner!" little Denny chimed in.

"Of course, I remember," Dana said. She remembered no such thing. Her eyes landed on the wall calendar above Darla's head, which displayed an early winter scene and red Sharpie marks indicating it was November 18th. *Who leaves for college in November?* And wasn't Dan Jr. only seventeen?

"What's he studying again?"

"He's going to start with a Bachelor of Science," said Daniel Sr., wiping his chin with a napkin, even though he had yet to take a bite. "Specializing in Engineering Physics. Then he'll transfer out-of-state for his Master's in Aviation Systems, and before seeking his Ph.D. in Physics, with a focus on Aerospace Engineering."

Dana tensed up one nerve at a time as the pastor mapped his son's educa-tional path, freezing muscle-by-muscle, fork suspended above her plate. Know-ingly or not, Daniel had just recited her own education history, line-by-line.

***

As a budding astronomer, teenaged Dana had read all the *Space Odyssey* nov-els over a single weekend. Her bedroom ceiling reminded her somehow of the way Arthur C. Clarke had described the Monolith: perfectly smooth and flat, with no visible bumps or brushstrokes. She lay on her back for hours trying to find a fault in the paint.

It was nights at the Hendersons' that Dana particularly disliked. Nowhere had ever been so silent on earth – even in the middle of the night, there had always been a car rushing by or a drunk shouting or wind rustling the branches against her window. Here, though, it was like nothing outside her borrowed room existed at all. She was convinced that if she opened her door at whatever passed for 3 am here, she'd find herself staring not at a hallway, but into the colourless void she'd seen beyond the school.

And that, in its way, would be more correct than there actually *being* a hallway. She'd been thinking of this ecosystem as "another planet," but that was as childish a fantasy as any of the lies the Hendersons had fed her. She knew where she'd been when the shuttle broke down, and that it was lightyears away from any known body. But even if that were not the case – even if she had somehow managed to crash land on some alien world, one that happened to be an almost exact replica of her own – she would not have lived to see any of it, because she would have burned up in the *fucking atmosphere* upon entry.

Something pinged against her window. Dana rose abruptly, wrenching her back, and hobbled over just in time to see another rock nick the glass.

Dan Jr. was standing on the lawn, looking up. The gloom was so total that she almost didn't recognize him – would not have, save for the ethereal halo of his blonde hair in the moonlight. He raised his arm to throw a third stone, dropping it when she opened the window.

She almost expected him to break into song. Instead, he called out (his voice a husky stage whisper): "Grab your stuff and come down!"

"Why?" She felt stupid even asking.

"Just hurry – before they wake up!"

She packed quickly, every scrape of a drawer or rustle of linen dousing her in sweat. The hallway was so dark she couldn't see more than a few inches in front of her feet; the floor seemed to unfurl in front of her as she walked. Things lightened up she reached the stairs, but she winced at every step. *Funny,* she thought, *I don't remember them squeaking like this before.*

She expected resistance – Darla popping out to ask where she was going, one of the kids spying from the cracks of their bedroom doors and reporting her movements, Daniel Sr. in the living room with a hitherto-unseen rifle in his lap – but there was none, and soon she was crossing the front porch in one bound and snaking along the side of the house. Dan Jr. was still parked around back, headlights off. Dana barely had time to shut the door behind her before he stepped on the gas.

"What's going on, Dan?" Dana demanded.

The boy's eyes were rivetted to the road, the glow of the gas gauge bouncing off his corneas. "They're liars," he said. There was something in those eyes that hadn't been there before. Something older. *College boy.*

"What do you mean?" she asked, though she knew exactly what he meant. The phones and computers that worked for everyone else but her. The dates and times and names and ages that changed by the minute. The way Daniel dropped his voice and whispered that Dana was delusional, but only when he knew she was in earshot.

"Do you need clothes or anything?" the boy asked. A non-sequitur – then again, his mind was likely whirling.

"I'll be good." She glanced in the rear-view mirror to note her suitcase in the backseat. Three of his were packed in beside it, like he'd emptied out his whole dorm. "I assume you have toiletries?"

"What?"

"Toothpaste, that sort of thing."

"I don't remember."

"It's alright. We can pick some up when we…where are we going?"

Instead of answering, he stomped on the brakes. Dana shrieked as her chest smashed against the seatbelt. Dan grabbed her hand, as if to reassure her, but placed his other on her inner thigh. She flinched. "It's okay," he hissed. "You don't have to be afraid anymore." Without asking, he leaned in to kiss her.

It was a messy, teenage motion, his lips moist and inept on hers. Dana froze and let it happen. It was meaningless, she knew, borne of rebellion and adrenaline and panic. She closed her eyes and thought of nothing.

***

Dana always imagined weathered travellers falling to their knees and seeking bedside scripture, but the Gideon Bible in the nightstand looked like it had never been opened. Running her fingers over the bonded leather cover, Dana flipped through the impossibly thin pages with their impractically small print. She wasn't religious, but had always envied those who seemed so effortlessly able to connect to the divine.

Dan Jr. had probably brought his own copy, she thought, unless he'd renounced his faith as well.

She was trying to convince herself that Dan Jr. hadn't been gone any longer than it would take to ask the front desk for a comb and a toothbrush, but the clock told her otherwise. Fifteen minutes had passed since she'd first thought, *he seems to have been gone a while*; Dana wished she'd made a note of his actual departure time.

A knock on the door startled her. It was too late to be a maid, and Dan Jr. had a key. She exhaled when her too-courteous roommate let himself in. "I got you a toothbrush," he said, extending his arm limply, staring at on the stains on the carpet.

Something in his tone alarmed her. "What's up?" He didn't reply. "Dan Jr.?" she said sharply, then corrected herself: "Dan?" As if omitting the suffix would remind him that he was his own man, free him from the legacy of his parents, whoever or whatever they were.

"I called my Dad," he admitted. "I had to. It's the fifth Commandment. There's this woman…"

Dana felt her entire nervous system collapse. "What did your father say?"

"Just listen to me! There's a woman, with the same name as you, and my Dad says she looks similar, who was…"

"Who was *what*, Dan?"

"Don't freak out, okay? I'm just telling you what I heard, and you can figure out how you want to take it – I'm not sure if I even believe it. Just listen to me and then you can leave if you want, or you can let us – err, me – help you, but you don't have to do anything you don't want – I mean, you can even have the car if you want – if you want to leave, my Dad'll come pick me up – not immediately! I'll let you get really far away before I tell him where I am – I mean, I told him where we are, if anything happens they'll know where to find me right now, and the guy at the front desk, but he won't come for me until you've had a chance to go wherever you want to–"

"Dan!" He winced, and she lowered her voice. "I'm calm, and I will stay calm," Dana whispered, making a show of raising her hands above her hips and sitting on the edge of the bed. "Say what you have to say and I will listen and we'll talk it out."

Dan Jr. took a breath so deep it must have been painful. "My dad called the police when he noticed you were missing. They told him that they've been looking for a woman named Dana Hendrix, who's been accused of stalking and uttering threats. Against an astronaut."

Dana suppressed a reaction. "Okay."

"That scientist guy you went to see –"

"Dr. Cuddy."

"Yeah. He's also been getting threatening letters from someone, and they think it's the same person."

Dan Jr. let the sentence hang. Dana didn't pick it up.

"My Dad said it was actually a relief to find out, because now we know how to help you."

Dana was trying to remember if she'd ever mailed a letter in her life.

"And you don't have to go to one of those places. I don't think you did anything that's really illegal. We have a counsellor who works with the church…"

Dana's face brightened; Dan Jr.'s fell. "Don't you see, Dan? That woman – if she's stalking astronauts, she's probably obsessed with me, too. She probably gave the police my name when they booked her. She might have even made herself over to look like me." She forced a comforting smile, hoping it looked relieved and not crazed. "And that explains why Dr. Cuddy pretended not to know me, he's probably…" She trailed off, unable to finish the sentence with anything that made sense.

"We can help you," he repeated, shifting back into the boy who'd been brought up to believe that everything would work out if he just had faith.

Dana looked to to the window. It was very dark. "There's nowhere we can go?"

"Home," Dan Jr. replied.

She closed her eyes. "Alright."

"You'll come?"

"Yes."

It wasn't like she really had a choice.

***

Having barely started unpacking, it didn't take Dana long to gather her things.

She knew the chances of returning to find a welcoming and relieved family of six without an equal-sized detachment of police officers were slim. She was being delivered into an ambush, whether Dan. Jr. knew it or not. Either way, she didn't blame him.

Dana thought longingly of Dr. Cuddy and found the only images of him in her head, other than that encounter in the parking lot, were like still photographs. The kind she would have seen in a newspaper. Dana wondered if she was the kind of sick that could be fixed by a counsellor at the church.

Dan Jr. was in the bathroom. In spite of herself, she listened carefully for the sounds of expulsion and flushing, still partly convinced there was nothing at all behind any closed door. But every noise was accounted for: a stream of urine hitting water; the bowl roaring as the whirlpool claimed it; a running tap. Dan Jr. emerged, looking relieved in more ways than one. *You'll never fight with your parents again after this*, she thought.

He was by the door now, his hand on the knob. "Ready?"

She nodded, voice eluding her, and rose, not looking behind her as she flicked off the light. Metal nicked her finger. She hissed, jerking her hand away.

"You okay?"

She held her hand in front of her face, watching as a blob of red bubbled and erupted. Everything else looked very blue in comparison. "Yeah," she replied. "Got a band-aid?"

"I think there's one in the suitcase," Dan said, immediately bending to unzip the front pocket. *Well-brought up*, she thought sadly. The Hendersons had done a good job with him. As he crouched to dig around the bottom of the bag, the tail of his shirt lifted. Dana gasped before she could restrain herself. The flesh beneath the fabric was a flat plain, greyish and devoid of detail. An effect not finished rendering.

Sensing her seeing him, he turned around, slowly but sharply. "You shouldn't have seen the back end," he said, his voice flat, his eyes losing their lustre.

She staggered backward, reaching out to catch herself as she stumbled towards the nightstand. But her hand hit empty air, and Dana was falling toward walls that no longer existed, no floor beneath her feet. Beyond was the void – not the blackness of space or a blinding white light, but a place transparent as glass, with nothing on the other side. The last corporeal thing she saw was Dan Jr. looming over her, but even he was pale and two-dimensional, a piece of origami shaped like a man.

Then he was gone, and she was floating in the ether. *I guess* this *is what the ethernet cord connects to*, she thought dumbly, and laughed. It was as good a way to die as any.

At the thought of death, her descent stopped. What little physicality still existed in this realm – Dana, and some stray particles of air – was extinguished and recycled into an explosion of sound, repurposed into pain as her body hit the ground.

The shuttle crumpled like a pop can. The oxygen light was not blinking red, but it wasn't blinking green either. Taking a breath of surprisingly hospitable air, Dana pushed aside a shattered wall and left the wreck behind.

The ground was black and hard, the way ahead obscured by mist.

Behemoths of Flesh and Glass
Michael Bettendorf

Michael Bettendorf (he/him) is a writer from the Midwest. His recent fiction has appeared/ is forthcoming at Drabblecast, The Colored Lens, and elsewhere. Michael works in a high school library in Lincoln, NE - a place he tries to convince the world is too strange to be flyover country. Find him on Twitter/Blue Sky @BeardedBetts and www.michaelbettendorfwrites.com.

~

The overhead lights glitch in and out, giving the lobby of the apartment building a jaundiced hue, strobing like a nightclub on life support. I punch at the elevator buttons, but like everything else around me, the doors remain unresponsive. No chime. No electric whirl. No groaning cables. I guess I'm the only one trying to do their job around here.

Then again, I have no choice. I do this job for T and he wipes my debt. I don't do this job for T and I remain in his pocket. In this city. Stuck with a bunch of cold, hopeless deadbeats, doing bad things for bad people. Complicit in their decay. Not me. I'm getting out of here before the rot sets in.

A defunct retinal scanner droops from fraying wires, pulled from the wall and gutted for parts. I adjust my watch, considering the time. I'm never late. That's why T hires me. Reliability and honesty don't breed here in the Flatlands, but I've got a bit of both and word gets around.

"Whatcha got there?" a voice like bile asks.

What hole did that crawl out of? It's some tech-junkie, one eye hollowed out and replaced by a series of lenses. The aperture spirals open and shut. Can't get a read on me, thanks to the neural blocker on my watch.

Open. Shut. Open. Shut.

"None of your goddamn business," I tell him. "Unless you can tell me how the elevator works."

He laughs like a series of hard drives rewriting themselves to death. I notice he's got wires shoved here and there around his neck, crusty with blood in spots, fresh and sticky in others. He's all loopy, burnt-out on all the alleyway-tech jobs he's had done.

"Show ya where the stairs are," he says. "But it'll cost ya."

He pulls a piece on me. Some 3D-printed piece of shit that'll likely blow up in his hand if he pulls the trigger. My fingerless, weighted gloves could knock him into next week, but what would be the point?

"Yeah, yeah," I say.

In his condition, a hit to the head would kill him. Last thing I need is that on my conscience. Can't blame a junkie for taking desperate measures when the scales are tipped in his privation. He walks me to the stairwell where he's been living and I make my way to the twentieth-floor, sans watch.

***

I don't bother counting steps. My knees already tell me there are too many of them. I bang at the door of Apartment 12, an end unit. A series of locks open in a frantic sequence and I'm pulled through the crack in the door.

"You must be Jay?" I ask.

"You're late."

"Lost my watch."

I'm ushered to a barstool at the kitchen island which hasn't been used for eating in years. An archipelago of tools is strewn about. Microchips and circuit boards lay in neat piles. Beads of solder are stuck to a towel. A hot soldering iron smokes like a weak cigarette next to a damp sponge.

"That, and the elevator," I say.

"Didn't ask for excuses," he says. "T says you're the guy for this sort of thing."

"Depends on the thing."

I can't say no to the job. No way for a guy like me to make money without being a monster anymore. It's a weight this city puts on those without a trust fund and I'm tired of heavy lifting. That, and I said I'd do it, so I'll do it, but I find that squeezing a guy's balls while he's already got his pants down usually results in a better paycheck.

"Fuckin' T," he says. "If I wanted someone to bust my balls, I'd go next door."

"Look," I say, fiddling with a microchip. I wonder what would happen if I implanted it in the open spot where my watch used to be. Would I tweak out like the junkie downstairs or would I instantly understand a dozen languages? I put the chip down. "I'm your guy. Just give me some specifics."

"You're looking at it," he says.

I inspect the chip, but it's just silicon to me.

"Not very specific," I say.

He pours me something golden-brown from an unlabeled bottle. I hesitate until he pours a three-finger pull into a glass of his own. I bring it to my nose.

It's a peated whisky, but doesn't smell like charcoal. It has more of an iodine and rubbery smell. An Islay whisky. I take a sip, paying full attention now, because anyone who can afford this is worth my time.

"Used to work in research and development at Bio-Tekk," he says. "Now I'm more of an under-the-table sort of guy."

"Tends to be how things go in the Flatlands," I say.

"It's the only way not to be owned. Anyway," he says. "Someone's spoofing my code, duplicating my chips. People are dying. I don't want people croaking off gear some asshole is duping off my source code. I'm not a monster."

He doesn't say it, but I see the look in his eye.

"I get it," I say. "People dying is bad for business."

The targets aren't on his back, just his name, i.e., his tech, i.e., his cash.

"So cynical," he says.

"It's not cynicism if it's the truth," I say. "Either way, I'm in, but I'm going to need some information."

He tinkers with the microchip and implants it into a band.

"I've got a list of names," he says. "It'll be a good place to start."

This part is always awkward, no matter how many times I've done it in the past.

"I'm going to need an advance," I say.

He's got that look in his eye again. The one that shouts greedy *prick*. *Asshole*. I've seen it so many times over the years. Maybe it's the whisky or maybe I've built up an immunity, but the truth doesn't hurt so much anymore.

I hold out my hand.

"Other one," he says.

I'm confused, but money's money no matter what hand it's in.

He slides the band he was working on over my wrist and adjusts it to fit. He then connects it to the open slot. "We'll call this your advance," he says.

I feel the familiar jolt as it connects to my bio-enhancer system. By the time it installs, my arm up to my shoulder has gone menthol-cold.

"Should help with neural static," he says. "I assume that's what your watch had installed, yeah?"

I didn't bother to ask how he knew. T gave me the watch. Jay probably sold it to T.

"Right on," I say. We're at the door now. "Thanks. I'll swing by when I find something out."

"Don't linger," he says, and I'm already down the hall.

Back in the lobby, the tech-junkie is passed out on a decrepit couch made from old crates and a stained mattress. I walk past and hear the electric sputter of his eye.

Open. Shut. Open. Shut.

***

The first name on the list is Roy Hauer, but there's a note to call him Riker unless I feel like getting a knife in the gut.

The spritz of rain from earlier has evaporated from the concrete, turning the air into heavy dog's breath. I wade through it until I reach The Dazzler. It's as high end as a skin-bar around here can be. Dancers of all kinds do their thing, working the poles for the classicists, or performing freestyle floor routines for anyone into surprises. Doesn't so much matter as long as they show some skin.

There are private booths for people with money and private rooms for people with too much money. They welcome people of all kinds, but more often than not, they attract one type. The Roy Hauer type. I enter The Dazzler twenty bucks poorer and wave away a few dancers. Jay's watch blocks all sorts of siren's calls to my mind—little tingling bursts trying to nudge me into indulgence. Loud, electronic music blares overhead. The lighting is harsh enough to hide tech-scars and cellulite and pox marks and hair, but gentle enough on the eyes to accentuate the forms of the bodies moving on stage.

The place is packed for a weeknight. I walk behind who I hope to be Roy and feel a touch justified by the initials he has tattooed down the back of his biceps, visible only because he's wearing a cut-off shirt. A leather jacket rests on the back of his chair.

The person sitting across from him spots me first, their face all decked out in tech. Ornamental more than functional. They've had skin work done too, by the looks of the unnatural sheen it emits. It's a top-dollar job and I'm assuming one of the benefits of being friends with Roy Hauer.

"Riker," I say, remembering my manners. His friend smiles a dumb digital smile. Their teeth flash a prism of colors. What a fucking waste of an implant.

"Who's asking?" his friend asks.

"Not talking to you," I say and watch their smile fade to red. "Love the mood ring thing you've got going on. Surprised they don't pulse in constant embarrassment."

Riker's friend scowls, but I see Riker's shoulders budge slightly. Amused, not offended, I hope, but I honestly don't care.

"What color is that?" I ask. "Embarrassment, that is."

Riker stands, all his height apparently in his legs, and I stare up at his chin—a boxy thing I didn't think could exist on the human face.

"Jay mentioned someone might come poking around."

Riker throws a handful of cash on the table without looking. He tells his friend he'll be back, but not to wait around.

"Let's take a walk," he says.

***

"So you deliver for Jay?" I ask. The crowded sidewalks are progressively thinning out as we walk away from The Dazzler. The overhead streetlamps swarm with mosquitoes. We've managed to rid ourselves from most trees and grass and parks—all this concrete and glass—and yet we can't rid ourselves from mosquitoes. Still, they're the least of our pest problems in the Flatlands.

"No," he says. "I don't deliver for Jay. I arrange deliveries for Jay."

"Care to enlighten me on the difference?"

We hook a right down an identical street.

"It's a matter of presence," Riker says. "I organize the drop-offs, but I'm long gone before anybody shows up."

Riker walks like he's guiding me and I let him believe he's the one in control as I ask him questions.

"So you've no idea who picks up Jay's tech?"

"Not entirely," he says. "I have contact info, specifics of the drop-offs. You know, the type of tech, names of the buyers, the amount. That sort of thing. Even then, they're all usernames anyway. No one gives their real names out anymore, especially buying this shit. Jay could be selling all his tech to the same person using a different name for each transaction. As long as they're paying, what's the difference?"

I think it over while Riker leads us to a food cart and orders a milk tea.

"Want anything?" he asks.

"Coffee," I say. "If they've got it."

We stand and wait while our drinks are poured. Nothing is crafted anymore. All processed junk from cans or vacuumed sealed containers. Riker hands me a small foam cup of coffee. It's bitter and burnt.

"How does the payment work?" I ask.

We backtrack towards The Dazzler. I notice Riker fidgeting with his wrist and wonder what kind of enhancer he's using. Could be anything. People get them for all sorts of reasons. Regulate blood sugar. Pain killers. Micro-dosing whatever. And unless you want to piss blood, don't ask.

"It's all pre-arranged. Drop-offs are usually in mailboxes. All of them are password protected."

Riker explains how it's some multi-step encryption process Jay set up, but to me it's simply a way to convolute the digital paper trail. He sucks wads of boba through his oversized straw.

"Simple as that," he says.

I laugh and burn my tongue on sludgy coffee.

"Yeah," I say. "Simple."

"Look, Jay's a paranoid weirdo, but he's still in business," Riker says. "So what does that tell you?"

"For a guy that doesn't trust anyone, he relies a lot on middle men," I say.

"Yeah," Riker says. "It's how he protects himself. The more people between him and whoever his mind thinks is out to get him, the better. He doesn't operate like most people. He doesn't care if people talk. It's how he moves his supply."

"Hold on," I say. "Whoever he thinks is out to get him?"

Riker sucks more tea.

"Sometimes our brains manufacture problems."

Riker messes with his wrist some more and now I'm the paranoid one. I fixate on Jay's neurotic dispositions and take another sip of shit coffee. I let my suspicions subside and dwell on something else. The word supply bounces around my head for a minute.

"Jay have a supplier? Where does he get his stuff?" I ask.

"He makes it," Riker says.

I take another swig of coffee, feel grounds between my teeth.

"No, I mean the raw materials."

"Fuck if I know," Riker says. "Probably boosts it."

"Seems unlikely," I say. "Jay doesn't seem to be the type who gets out much."

Riker tosses his half-drunk milk tea to the ground as we reach the entrance of The Dazzler. His tea leaves a runny white trail speckled with boba and ice at his feet.

"Look man," Riker says. "I've had enough of the questions. Are we done?"

I stare at the mess on the ground as the milk separates from the water.

"Any chance you can send me a list of Jay's buyers?" I ask.

Riker eyes the doorman who's busy taking cash from underage kids. He rubs his wrist and it's there that I see it. A glint in his eye. Paranoia.

What else does this guy need, a notarized letter? I can sense Riker's impatience, but I can't help myself, so I keep talking, "He's got people breathing down his neck and guess what? You're one of the people he's wedged between him and his problems. So look here, Roy—"

He decks me in the mouth as if to force his real name back down my throat. I stumble. He grabs me by the collar. The doorman minds his business while another line of teenagers gawks in our direction. Riker calls me an asshole and lets me drop to the ground. As soon as I catch my breath, he decks me in the gut. I puke. The best scotch I've ever had, sour with bile and stale coffee, drips from my chin. Still, I remember Jay's list—his warning—and think it's better than a knife.

I wipe my chin and stand.

"Look," I say and wave the wrinkled piece of paper at him. "Your name's here too."

"Don't let him back inside," Riker says to the doorman and is gone by the time my eyes quit watering.

***

I can't shake the thought that Riker's hiding something, so I walk toward the address listed under his name on Jay's list. I fold the paper into an uneven square and shove it in my pocket.

As I do so, my phone starts vibrating as if by some divine surveillance. Some holy message. But I know better. There is no god watching me. Only devils.

"Hey, T. What do you need?" I ask and regret the words.

"Excuse me. Am I bothering you?" he asks.

"C'mon, T," I say. "You know it wasn't like that. I meant no offense."

I'm walking and talking and ignoring everything around me like a dope.

"I'm sorry," I say.

"No, no," T says. "I'm sorry. I'm sorry to be bothering you."

"Look, T, I'm sorry, all right," I say. "I didn't mean anything by it."

I'm a few blocks from The Dazzler, but the scenery doesn't change. It's all brutalist architecture. Behemoths made of concrete and glass. Flowerbeds sit dead and empty on the occasional windowsill. The only signs of life are people getting loaded on their stoops, aperture-eyes snapping open and shut.

T's been talking, but I only catch the last word, "Understand?"

I nod yes as if T can see me. I mutter a pattern of yeah, sure, sorry into the phone until I end up where I need to be. I double check the address as I approach the condo. Some cookie-cutter, prefabricated thing without a soul. The garage door is dented in slightly and Riker's barred the windows. Wish I could say it was overkill, but I get it.

T keeps going on about something—something about loyalty and couth—but I'm distracted, looking for an easy way into Riker's place.

"What I meant to say is," I tell him. "How can I help you?"

"How nice of you to ask," T says, his inflections exaggerated. Patronizing prick.

I approach Riker's door and pull an old Mimicard from my wallet. It's essentially a proximity reader that scrambles door credentials to match the card. It's old RFID tech, but reliable enough. Why try to find the right key when you can make any lock fit yours?

"You're helping me plenty. See, Jay gave me a call and says he likes you. He wanted me to tell you. He says if you do a good job, he'll have plenty of work for you." His tone shifts from offended to predatory just as the tone of Riker's door chimes unlocked. T's saying all this as I slip through Riker's front door. I know he's only telling me this to ensure I understand that he'll get a cut for whatever work I do for Jay. That I'm still his guy—not Jay's. What he doesn't know is this is my last job. Fuck T. Fuck Jay. Fuck the Flatlands. I'm getting out of here. All debts paid. I'm going somewhere with a breeze. Somewhere with flowers and trees.

Of course, I don't tell him this. Partially because I'm still in his pocket, but mostly because in the darkness, I see a flashing red smile and it scares the piss out of me.

"Shit," I say, confusing T, and he starts going off again. I have enough time to hang up before someone pops me in the jaw. I stumble back into the door, the knob catching me in the hip. The red smile is closer now, only they've moved to my right. I plant my feet and wait for contact, but nothing comes. Their smile fades to yellow in a weak glow, like a billboard advertisement that reads: hit me.

I do.

My knuckles feel only the slightest impact as my weighted-gloves make contact with their nose. My ears tell me what I can't see—an explosion of cartilage, a busted septum, and the quick, dumb shuffle of their feet as they stumble to the ground. There's an unmistakable thud I've only heard once or twice in my life, but sweat slicks my forehead and I start to worry, because nothing good has ever come after it. I hold my breath and listen for theirs, but the only noise I hear is coming from the ceiling fan, slowly circulating dead air throughout the room.

***

For a moment, I almost lose myself and walk out the door, but I remember the bleak void I saw when I flatlined, the result of my violent indecision—the reason for my exorbitantly expensive, top-tier bio-enhancer system—for my debt. My chain to the city. To T.

I drop to the floor and feel for their mouth in the darkness. I cradle their head and breathe, my mouth sticky with their blood and snot. Soon, I start chest compressions. Their body, the way it lies cockeyed and clumsy on the floor, feels too big for the room. And yet I feel so small while I loom over them, compressing their chest to force life back into them.

I think about this city and what it takes from us. Is it worth it?

There's a crackling phlegmy cough. All sputters. Then a glint in their eyes and a weak aura of color emitting from their mouth. I imagine how they see me, a behemoth of flesh towering over them, a weak killer turned pathetic savior, barely holding it together. I tell them it's okay and like a fool, I believe it.

Their eyes open and shut. The tech in their mouth starts to fade until it dims to nothing, like it's sapping their strength. Their skin is soft, but cooling as they go into shock. They hold my hand while their eyes open and then remain shut.

***

I search them in the dark, unable to look at my mess—a coward.

I find some cash. A couple painkillers, which tells me their augments were likely all cosmetic. There's an interior pocket on their jacket. A thin, but noticeable lump inside. I take it for a vape pen at first and take it anyway. I find a credit card. Or their I.D. Or maybe a badge. I walk to the narrow beam of light coming in from the skylight. It'd be the only organic thing left in this place if I didn't know it wasn't moonlight. But I know it's just the fluorescents coming in from the billboards and streetlamps above me.

The card shows a professional-looking photo of Riker's friend from The Dazzler. Their smile uninhibited by tech. It's a security badge for Bio-Tekk.

I dry swallow the painkillers and leave.

***

"What do you mean you fucked up?"

It's T.

"I fucked up," I say. "What else is it supposed to mean?"

"I mean how did you fuck up?" he asks. "I'm talking severity. Tell me."

So I do and he keeps talking.

"Okay, so there was some collateral. Big deal," he says. "Nothing we haven't dealt with before. Did anyone see you?"

"No," I say.

"Of course, they didn't," he says. "Because you're you. That's why I hire you."

"They were Bio—"

249

"Nope," he says. "I'm going to stop you right there. Those are the kinds of details we don't need to discuss. The less I know, and the more you forget, the better. Do you understand?"

I'm walking aimlessly now, my stride dragging. The painkillers weren't a high dose, but they've left me in a haze. Just enough to keep the edge off. I must have mumbled something resembling a yeah because T says, "Good. I knew you would," and hangs up.

I sit on the curb and fiddle with the vape pen. My head's cloudy and I take the painkillers to be stronger than I'd thought. But there's an electric whirl and a presence, like someone's trying to tap into my thoughts. Let 'em. They won't want to stick around too long.

A twiggy thing hunches next to me and tells me I've been a bad boy.

I tell them to fuck off and try to smoke.

They laugh at me, because it's not a vape pen.

"That's a nice mod you've got there," they say. "Give it to me." And there's an echo as I'm surrounded by tech-junkies. I notice Jay's watch has disconnected at my wrist, probably from the fight with Riker. Or the fight in his condo. Or doing CPR. I let it slip off my wrist. It falls to the ground. The junkies swarm around it, ripping hair and wires and piercings from one another fighting for it, forgetting my existence.

Lucky them.

***

I find a quiet place to install the mod.

The interface is simple and streams to my eyes. It's a database. Jay's list of buyers, but so much more. Jay's got dirt on just about everyone in the city. Politicians. Bio-Tekk employees. Roy Hauer types. Even me. Even T.

I scan the files, skimming, barely understanding any of it. I dig and find video clips and sound bites. Private conversations and situations where no amount of surveillance could have captured it, unless it was given willingly—or unknowingly. I browse some of the footage. Most of it seems useless. Tech-junkies tweaked out in alleys and shithole apartments. The occasional politician cheating on their spouse.

I look for recent data and see myself being choked by Roy Hauer outside of The Dazzler. I see Roy in his condo, kneeling next to the body. It goes dark soon after.

Whatever this is, it backs up in real time, likely through some private server. I see a file called contagion and it's the last thing I read before I disconnect the mod from my wrist and shove it in my pocket.

***

The outside of the building seems grayer now. Concrete stained and weather-beaten. Lifeless. I enter the lobby. The tech-junkie is sprawled out on the makeshift couch, one eye glassy while the other spirals open and shut, open and shut. I smile at the camera and wave to Jay. I wonder if the junkie knows he's been turned into a surveillance system. I climb the stairs three at a time, ignoring my knees' protest.

I kick in the door of Apartment 12.

Jay is scrambling, scooping various microchips and mods into a bag. The bag hits the floor as he holds his hands up, "Wait a minute, wait a minute."

He mirrors my movement as I chase him around the kitchen island in slow-pursuit.

"It's not what it looks like," he says.

"Then clarify it for me," I say. "I saw the files. The blackmail material. Contagion."

We circle, neither of us gaining an advantage.

"What's contagion? A bio-virus? Tech-virus?" I ask.

"T was right," he says. "You're good at your job, but you are a bit slow."

I've been trying to piece it together in my mind, but the painkillers and neural static have kept me from seeing it clearly. We continue to move around the island and I notice Jay tapping away at a keyboard-mod attached to his bio-enhancer.

"Shit," he says. "Why isn't it working?"

He's frantic and losing concentration. He trips over his bag and falls to the ground. He skitters against the cracked plaster wall. I roll my sleeve up and show him the empty slot at my wrist. I wasn't a genius, but I'm a good listener.

"You said it yourself," I say. "Your tech was killing people. Failed to mention your finger was flipping the kill switch."

And for the second time tonight, I loom over a body with a decision to make. I consider what's left of me—left in me. He tells me I don't understand and he's probably right. I'm just a behemoth of flesh, standing over a broken man.

I pull my weighted-gloves off because I don't want to kill him. I won't have to. Not with all his secrets floating around the minds of a thousand tech-junkies, revealed when I walked here with no neural blockers to face my own fate. He's still blabbering at me. Telling me I don't understand. I lean to pick him up, because I can't hit a man while he's down, and then I feel the bullet bite me in the back.

I turn and see T standing in the open doorway holding the tech-junkie's gun. I have to give Jay some credit, because I didn't understand. T pulls the trigger again, but this time the 3D-printed piece of shit blows up in his hand, the cheap material splintering and cutting his hand to ribbons.

The last thing I see before my eyes turn woozy is a Roy Hauer type behind T and then it's dark.

***

I come to as Roy Hauer pulls bullet fragments from my back. I bite down on my jacket sleeve while he shoves a hot soldering iron into the wound to cauterize it. I pass out again.

And like the turn of a light switch, I'm up and Roy's installing something into my wrist, but I'm too weak for any sort of disagreement. Soon, tranquility flows throughout my body and I don't care anymore. Keep it coming. There's blood everywhere on account of T's ruined hand. Jay bailed, bag in hand, while Roy tended to me. No matter, the target on his back isn't metaphorical anymore. His mug is everywhere now, thanks to facial recognition. His real name, too. Any aliases. Fingerprints. Purchase receipts. Mountains of personal data that won't erode fast enough are out there now.

Roy tells me about a blackmail conspiracy. How Jay was selling shoddy tech. How T provided the contagion virus. How they've been blackmailing people and blaming it on Bio-Tekk.

Maybe it's the painkillers. Maybe it's the gunshot. Maybe I'm just slow, but I mumble until Roy speaks up, "Jay was taking advantage of tech-junkies. Turning them into an invasive species, essentially. Spying on everyone, giving him dirt. But they needed a way to control the population, which is where contagion comes in. Tricky little virus. Genius, really, but most viruses have a way of getting out of control."

Roy is messing around with the mod at my wrist. My heart produces a skyline on the EKG. He's still talking. Something about how Roy and his partner at Bio-Tekk were working undercover to expose Jay and T. The plan was to recover the information more delicately, until I came along and got in the way. I consider that Roy is only telling me these things to keep my mind occupied. To keep my thoughts off the void.

I try to tell him I'm sorry about his partner, that I didn't mean to kill them, but he reassures me it wasn't my fault. That the tech they had implanted was corrupted by the contagion virus too and it was my last-ditch effort to save them that tipped Roy off. He said when his partner's cosmetic augmentations were rebooted, a signal was sent to Roy.

"You obviously can't stay here," Roy says.

And that's good, because I don't want to.

"I took care of as much information T and Jay collected on you as I could," he says. "But you need to leave."

"We are but the choices we make," I'm saying. Maybe I'm just thinking it. "Despite the opportunities we're given."

Roy pulls the mod from my wrist and says, "Should have enough painkillers in your system for a while, but find somewhere cozy. It's going to be a hell of a come down."

I tell him thank you and drift out the door. As I reach the stairwell, I pause and look out the window. There's nothing but concrete haze on the horizon. Rain beats down on the glass, awash with the faint glow of dying neon lights, and I swear I hear the building sputter. I start down the steps and there are too many to count, but this time my knees feel nothing. Doesn't surprise me. This city takes everything and leaves the dregs behind. And me? I'm just a stumbling pile of flesh.

The Emerald
John Cramer

Hailing from the apocalyptic wastes of Cleveland, Ohio, and raised in the swampy hell that is Houston, Texas, John Cramer has spent the bulk of a lifetime lurking on the outskirts of normalcy. He has eschewed the predictable white-American-male pathways for the instability and mayhem of a creative life. Whether through music, the visual arts, or music journalism, John has managed to remain unfamiliar with the comforts of wealth. However, now taking up horror fiction well into his 50s, John is almost guaranteed to reverse his fortunes for the better. You know, or not.

~

I'm driving in a motherfucker of a downpour. Biblical shit. And I love this kind of weather—as long as I'm not driving in it. I'm so drunk that I will almost certainly struggle to remember this in the morning. If I survive. Because at this rate that is *not* a certainty.

Here's what I do know: I'm driving down an alluvial backroad somewhere deep in the asshole of the asshole that is Louisiana. They elect Klan dicks governor up in here. I'm in a stolen 1980 Ford F-250, and you're probably telling yourself, *oh cool, those are the shit.* Fair enough. They are indeed the shit—if you were driving yours in 1980. This is 2023, and this thing is bucking like a bull with a strap across its nuts. And the truck, it isn't mine, remember? So I'm in the deluge and this—let's say borrowed—truck is not handling the storm too well. That means I'm having to drive carefully. I don't drive carefully. Perish the thought. Life is too short for that shit.

Anyway, here's what's important—there's a young woman in the passenger seat who is surprisingly calm about all this. What does she think, that we're on a sightseeing tour? She seems totally oblivious to the fact that we were running for our lives out of a Bogalusa backwater and into the dishpan of the Lee's Creek Mississippi floodplain. *Wait,* you scream, *is that a safe thing to be doing?* Well, no, but this is Louisiana. We aren't known for safety. In Louisiana, this might just be a Tuesday. Now look, I've got a story to tell here. Save the fake concern because we're just getting started.

You know how sometimes you're between vehicles so you walk to a bar in Bogalusa on a Tuesday night instead of working because you just told your shift leader to go fuck himself because he wants you to care about your job, which is really *his* job, as if it leads anywhere other than an early grave anyway, and now you need a drink or ten just to keep from going back there and burning the fucking place into the swamp from which it came? Of course you do.

Let's sweeten the pot. Some True Detective season-one biker-bar death-cult meth-priest motherfuckers walk in and you're on pitcher three, and you're busy being impressed with yourself because it's looking increasingly likely that you might just go home with the lady who has given you the I'm-going-to-fuck-you hall-of-fame looks from across the room. You don't even realize she's in the bar until you happen to look up and lock onto her emerald laser gaze as it instantaneously consumes all your attention. Right away you decide that she is your best friend. So by the time you are beginning the opening bars of the dance-the-sticky jig in your booth, guess who has finally laid eyes on us?

Oh good, you have been paying attention!

And oh good, the head honcho of this group looks like he used to bitch-slap

Ed Kemper around with a velvet glove to keep him in line. And oh better, because this Andre the Giant impersonator just found what he was looking for—his old lady. You know, the one with her panties on the table and your hand between her legs? Yeah, that lady. And here you were thinking you would soon be balls-deep in a mossy life-affirming snatch so powerful it could run a reactor. Turns out, you might spend this night watching your life flow by as a pile of knotted meth-muscle peels you like a banana.

Yeah, no. I'm not into that plan either. That's why I stuff her panties in my vodka bottle, light them, and toss it at the boys. While they're distracted trying to not be on fire, I hop over the back of the booth and snag the keys off the pool table from the guy who was gonna 'teach me a lesson' once we got around to our game. Here's a lesson for *you*, my man—don't leave your keys out in the open like a wad of $100 bills soaked in gold.

I lift old green-eyes out of that booth like she is nothing. She is just sitting there like a bump on a log, eyes unfocused and glassy and intently looking nowhere. I scream at her to get up, but she just sits there and looks at me all funny—no, wait—through me. Don't have the time to question where she is coming from. Wish I had, but I don't. And I also don't have the luxury of being uncomfortable with it. We need to get out of here pronto. I am surprised to find I am not only capable of picking a full-grown adult off the ground but that I am also capable of carrying them and running out of a door into a blackout downpour and then spotting a Ford F-250 way in the back of the parking lot. How do I know *these* keys start *that* truck? Fair question, so glad you're still paying attention.

It's simple—his keys were on a Ford keychain. Oh, *and* he smelled like Skoal. Do the math. I carry her to the old truck with my name all over it, open it, toss her in, and bolt out of the parking lot at record pace, all before I am nearly murdered by a man who might or might not be currently on fire. Schrödinger's lunatic.

You'd probably say I am in a bit of a pickle, but here's where things really go briny. I know these roads like I know how to stuff a steak down my pants and walk up to the counter of a Pyburn's Grocers and buy only a box of Dorals. Even in this endless rain, I am a pro out there. And I know that those movie villains are coming up behind me because I can see their headlights and hear them crawling directly up my ass.

And fuck me if they don't catch up to me and now it's just one frantic line of desperation and rage that is heading nowhere good obscenely fast. I take turns as fast as I can, not sparing a fraction of an mph, and oh the tail of this vehicle is weightless, which means that these turns have an added level of difficulty. And here I am, much preferring to play on easy mode.

While I'm putting most of my everything into staying on the road, I save just a tiny piece of myself to try and find a way out of this. Don't get me wrong, it's been real. *Too* real.

I'm racking my brain trying to think… Think… *Think!*

That old house on Fontenot, way back off the main road, with the overgrown driveway. The one that was fixed head to toe with prohibition backdoors and passageways. Yes! Only guys like me who have spent their wretched lives in this area counting roaches and washing their balls five times a day would know about this place. I never saw these guys before, so they must not know these roads as well as I do. Or at the very least, maybe I could get far enough ahead of them to cut down the drive to that ramshackle ruin and hide out until it all blows over. Here's to hopin'!

They can spend the night driving in circles and end up with lungs full of swamp water because they don't see a hard turn around a swollen bayou and go for a final bath for all I care. To be fair, I'm sure they need one.

If I thought I was pushing my luck before, now I'm deathwish-driving with abandon. I have to lose the murder caravan. Every straightaway gives me a tiny window, and every turn that I know is coming through the morass is taken just fast enough to gain a few feet here and there. In time I find it's beginning to add up. I'll just keep eking out this lead, winding through dense marsh and thick growth, high enough to become your accomplice, shielding your taillights.

After what feels like my lifetime—yours, and everyone else's—they just aren't there anymore. I have shaken them. They are going to have to go back home and fuck each other to sleep in a heap of tears, or whatever it is addict-sadists do in the privacy of their own shed.

I work my way back to where the old house is tucked away on a branched-out network of forgotten side streets. I'm suddenly really happy that I'd chosen to steal this big-ass truck because I hit a spot where the drive was washed out and blast right through like a fucking champ.

When my friends and I were kids, we used to walk up this driveway on the way down to the old plantation house. We'd run through the place, throw rocks at the windows, and tell stories about how the oak out front with all the Spanish moss was a hanging tree—standard stuff. It was in rough shape even then, and it had been years since I'd laid eyes on the place. I inch the truck down the muddy drive, and in the sheets of rain slapping against the windshield, the house shows itself to me. My headlights excavate this memory burial site and drag it back into rainy focus. My favorite Antebellum throwback is looking the worse for wear. It wasn't exactly turnkey decades ago when I piled up an impressive list of firsts among her musty halls: first kiss, first copped feel, first beer, first shit in the woods, first acid trip—but now the place looks downright janky. The once-white outer surface is now coated in dingy mildew. The five big gaudy pillars the rich racist dickheads planted across the front of the facade to make themselves feel all Greek revival are now down to only four. The lawn is so badly overgrown that Ronnie James Dio himself might not be able to even see the place on platformed tippy toes. *I* can see that there are now gaping holes in parts of the sprawling roof. The girl needs a good plastic surgeon.

I want to park around back, just in case Man Mountain Dean and the boys find the place after all. I drive around the far side of the house, opposite the driveway. It isn't just the lawn that's overgrown. The oaks look like giant beasts reaching over the house to try in vain to protect the place from the harsh Gulf Coast weather. The once-painted fountain out back is wind-worn now, and most of the paint is gone—a victim, no doubt, of decades of brutal sun and countless hurricanes. I suppose I have to hand it to the girl, she's still standing. Shit, several of the friends who joined me in our escapades back then are long gone. Bogalusa is a harsh mistress.

The rain is unrelenting, which given the circumstances is welcomed. Anything to deter my followers and lead them to throw in the towel is much appreciated. I park the relic, check the girl—still wide-eyed and unbothered—and dart out of the cab to see if there is a way in.

I do that stupid rain hunch pose where you raise your shoulders, scrunch your head down, and squint your face, all serving the stupid fucking idea that this might be a magic spell that repels rainwater. I reach the overhang against the back of the house, sad to report that I am fucking drenched. The back door is unlocked—that was easy enough. Once I have the door open wide, I run back (yes, hunched again) to the truck and start trying to get her to snap the fuck out of it. Apparently she's still not ready yet for prime time, which means I get to carry her again. Great.

I run her up the two stairs and in one sweeping motion turn her so that her feet go in first, followed by everything else. I pulled that one off on sheer booze-fueled escape-adrenaline. I set her down on the floor in one of the rooms and close the door. Open for a minute at the most, the doorway has let in a river of rain which I see is beelining for my friend on the floor. Low spots. Old houses. It figures. I go to move her. In my drunken logic, I don't want her to get wet. You know, the drenched woman on the floor.

I pick her up for the third time (which had gotten old the first time). I carry her through the dark house, looking for, well, I don't know what I'm looking for, but I find it anyway. The central stairway. *Go upstairs*, I think, *and then you can get, and stay, dry*. Good idea. Except for the carrying-her-up-the-stairs oversight. So I pick her up a fourth time and I start tackling the stairs. I start weakly, and then it gets harder by the step. By the top stair, I'm dragging her from her pits. I'm not ashamed to admit it.

I get her to what I believe is a bedroom (it's hard to say because apparently the house was built to accommodate a small nation) and sit her ass back down. And then I take the spot next to her on the hardwood floor. I crudely flop down because I'm not exactly in top form. Now I'm on my back gasping for air, trying not to start coughing—as a smoker I know where that will lead—and I stare up at the ceiling, at an impressive display of rain stains covering most of the surface.

I don't know what the story is with her. Back in the bar she was all lustful fire and laser light focus, but when the circus arrived, it was all bag-of-sand the rest of the way. The whole drive she gazed out the window not seeming to have the slightest clue what was happening beside, behind, and all around her. Drugs? Had to be. She dropped a little something back in the infernal bar and now it was hitting her hard like Jack Johnson on the comeback trail.

I must have dozed off because the next thing I remember is the sound of car doors outside. Fuck me sideways. They found us. I hear the head pituitary mutant directing his crew, though I can't quite make out what he is saying because of the rain. But I have a pretty good idea it includes stuff in the let's-not-make-friends sort of vein. I need to think. If I don't think, I might as well strut down the stairs and challenge the whole gang to a slap fight and just get it over with.

Bangs and whimpers, you know the scene.

Ding goes the lightbulb (LED, of course, I'm not a savage). *Hey, fuckface, you've been here before…* Yeah, it's been years, but I know the layout of this monstrosity well. A summer acid trip in the bank *will* implant things in your memory. That's just science. I can hide in here for hours—maybe even come up with a plan that includes our survival. The sky's the limit, bitches!

I notch my pickup-the-vegetable belt and haul the girl over my shoulder. It's time to go deep. And hide, baby, *hide*! I can hear the boys lumbering around the bottom floor, searching all the rooms for the easy win. And all the while I carry my precious cargo into the belly of the beast.

My leviathan is a treasure trove of hidden doorways, inner-wall passages, dumbwaiters, and hideable nooks and crannies. Our hide and seek games back in the day were the stuff of legend. We mapped this bitch *out*.

One time, Derek Fontenot (no relation) got stuck in a hatched crawlspace way back in the last room of the third floor and had to spend two days in that fucker until the parish cops finally located him, overheated and dehydrated. Two weeks later and he was back at it. This may come as a surprise, but he is no longer with us. He had what one might call 'poor judgment,' which is not something you want when you've been driving heavy cargo cross-country and you've been up for fifty hours tanked on NoDoz and Mini Thins and you find yourself racing the clock through the Appalachians and losing. As in—*real bad*. They had to scrape him off a hundred-yard stretch of highway with a spatula.

I know that the fourth door on the left up here on the second floor—*wait, is it the third? No, the fourth, that's right, because the third door was missing*—has an old armoire with a false back. Just another of the prohibition features they added to this place. If only they'd known how handy they would turn out to be. I can surely cram what's-her-nuts in there and buy myself a little time. I haul her down there, thankful that the rotten carpet is still mostly in place through this area. Hard to be graceful drunk off your ass and about a hundred pounds heavier above your center of gravity (which gets lower by the second). Gingerly I crank the tarnished brass doorknob and am relieved to see that the armoire is still there and in one piece. I pull out the bottom two drawers, and remove the unfinished pine panel, revealing the secret space. In you go, you emerald temptress. I'm not sure how strong I thought I was gonna be for this little exercise, but I clearly overestimated it. I've pretty much used most of my juice lugging her around and this is proving to be my undoing. I get her feet in there, and I'm lifting her hips now, just to get them over the lip. I sit down on my ass so I can try and leverage myself and push her in with my legs. I'm giving it the heave-ho, shaking, and suddenly she turns her head and those eyes are all up in my shit.

"What are you doing?" she asks, sounding groggy.

"Shhhh," I whisper, while putting my finger up to my lips like an idiot. "I'm trying to hide you."

"Hide me?" she says.

"There's a whole steroid customer base down there and I'm certain they aren't here to make friends." Still whispering.

"Don't let them hurt me," she pleads in a tone that is instantly intoxicating, and I also get a dose of emerald so intense that at this moment I would do any-god-damn-thing for this woman.

"Nobody is getting near you while I'm around. Don't worry," I add, about to bust out a major boast. "I know this old lady inside and out." I'd say it was a panty-dropper but, well, you know.

She reaches her arms around me and hugs me with surprising strength. She smells like moss, like the earth, like rain on pavement, like I would kick puppies for this girl. I've read that smells hang around up in your craw and come right back out as fond memories of moments in your own personal timeline. But what if the smells intensely bring you back to memories you never had to begin with? She's good, this one. I'd want her back too.

Her voice is quiet but it's conducting some powerful energy from her mouth to my ears. "If they catch me, I will die." Her words soak into me like I'm a sponge in a bubble bath—the good stuff, like Etsy shit.

"Don't worry, baby," I assure her, and believe it, "that's not going to happen."

I can still hear the goons downstairs stomping around, turning stuff over and grunting back and forth like Kubrick's apes. *Man, I sure hope they find a monolith and a pile of femurs.*

What I want to do is get down the hall to another little hideaway, but I'm not sure if this one here can even walk after the shenanigans we've been through tonight.

So I ask, "Can you walk?"

"I think so," ever so gently.

I help her to her feet. Now that I'm starting to sober up I notice that she is wearing a mish-mash of clothes that barely fit and look like they were grabbed at random from a fourth-hand resale shop. She's got an oversized denim skirt that's falling off of one hip, a child's Alvin & the Chipmunks Christmas t-shirt so tight it looks like it came off of a Barbie, and then she's barefoot. Her lips are painted a nuclear shade of magenta. Her hair is filthy, visibly matted, and she has bruises all over her legs. And then there's her skin. She is the palest person I have ever seen. Her skin is like translucent onion skin, thin and delicate—no visible birthmarks, no freckles, no moles—it's the kind of thing you only notice because of what you don't notice. She's milky white like fresh bathroom tile. She has what I call the Baader-Meinhof haircut—choppy all-around, unnaturally black—and while it's a look that tends to hang a bit heavy on the ugly side, with this one it's motherfucking charming. I would follow her regal pall into the ocean if she asked me.

"Okay," I take her hand, "let's go, I know where we can go." And we slide out of the door and tippy toe our way down the hall almost to the end. We stop and I have her stand against the wall so I can pull back the carpet and lift the hatch that is cut into the floor. My friends and I found it back in the day. It is the entry point of a secret stairway that runs down the side of the house, along a chimney, and opens into a door built along the back wall of the pantry. I help her step down into the crawlspace, tell her to wait on the far side so I can lead the way out, and then I mojo the carpet back over the hatch so that it covers the floor again when I close up.

You have to crawl through here, but it should still be pretty solid. I pull out my phone and turn on the flashlight. As I suspected, it's like a museum of natural science in here. I can see the roaches bolt at the first sign of light, and there are spider webs on webs, all of them full of the carcasses of other spiders, roaches, and a litany of other bugs. I tell myself it's just temporary and that if I want to live to tomorrow then it's a small price to pay, but I'm getting the willies something fierce. I shine the light at the emerald girl and she's cool as a cucumber. And hey, her pupils don't dilate. What the fuck did she take, anyway?

I grab her shoulder. "Hey," I ask," are you okay?"

"I am," she says, unblinking.

"You sure?" She nods. "Alright, follow me, there are stairs ahead." I start to run the gauntlet. I can feel the denizens of this hellhole crawling all over me as we crawl all over their homes. *Just passing through, fellas,* loops through my mind, *just passing through.* I'm hoping it'll work mantra magic on me, but as I'm thinking it I'm also swatting and swiping all over my skin because it's fucking horrible. We finally reach the end of the line, and I have to jimmy myself around so that I can get my feet down to the top stair. I wiggle my leg around until it finds solid wood, and carefully let my weight settle. I turn back and help her turn herself around as well, and I go down a few steps to give her room to enter the stairway. Did I cop a quick look uptown? A lady never tells.

I keep calling this a stairway, but if you really wanna see what the deal is, imagine three stairs, too far apart, and then a big drop to the next three stairs turned the opposite way around. So it's three and then three and then three and all the way down. Fuck, a ladder would seem a better choice, but hey, what the hell do I know? When we reach the bottom floor there is just enough room for us to both crowd together, and I listen to see if the coast is clear. Fortunately the mook squad is heavy of foot, and as I don't hear anyone in the immediate area, I tell the emerald to "Wait here," and give the shelving a push. It doesn't budge. *Stay cool, buddy, it's been a while,* I push again, and still not a jiggle. *Fuck, now what?* And out of nowhere she puts her hand on my shoulder, pulls me aside and pushes the fucking door open with her other. It opens like butter.

"The fuck?!" I mutter, trying to sound—and keep—cool. She steps aside and waits for me to lead the way. With the both of us now in the pantry I move the shelves back in place. It moves easy now. *Now that she one-handed the god damn thing. What's going on here, bud?*

I give a little look-see into the kitchen but it's empty. I give the emerald the old 'wait here' hands and creep over to the door that leads out back from the kitchen. The truck is right outside. We should be able to sneak out there and hit the road before these guys can lay a hand on either of us. I open the unlocked door slowly in case it's creaky, and just as I'm about to walk through I see that the hood is open. Fuck. They're (marginally) smarter than they look. I still need to see if there's something there that I can use so it's hunch time again as I dart through the rain and check out the truck bed. *Oooh, a toolbox, promising!* I open it and right up top is a crowbar, a hammer, and a hatchet. Christmas, baby.

I grab the lot and slip back inside (yes, hunched, goddamnit). I clutch the tools like bullion and ask, "You want any of these?" Without a word she grabs the hatchet. "Okay, we…" And before I can get another word out she has already pushed me out of the way and thrown the hatchet whizzing by my head. I hear a sickening *'tchok'* and spin around just in time to see one of the goons collapsing to the ground, the hatchet firmly implanted in his forehead. He falls sideways, hits his knees, and the asymmetric motion pulls his hatchet-filled skull to the floor for a second semi-hollow *'tchok'* as the guy's head smacks hard enough to spread a gore halo of blood and brain onto the black-and-white checkered tile floor. A piss stain spreads through his jeans and his final breath huffs out of his gaping mouth. The hatchet is still in place.

"Oh fuck," I say, louder than I should, but thankfully not loud enough to draw more attention. "Oh fuck, that was close," I gasp, more in control this time. I look back at the emerald and her face shows no more emotion than before. If I hadn't just seen her play hipster bar games into this poor guy's skull, I never would have believed it. But I saw that shit.

"Wh-what happened?" I ask her. I'm as freaked out as I am impressed. And in retrospect, maybe that was a dumb question. I know what happened, she just brained that homunculus. And it was GLORIOUS. "God damn, girl, I think I love you." And I mean it.

By my count this means that we are now four to one, and I'm suddenly liking those odds. This flips the script. "Alright," I tell her, feeling energized now, "looks like it's last call."

I step around the meat puddle and before I reach the way out of the kitchen she has pushed me aside with startling strength and taken the lead, her head poised straight up and her body moving like a goddamn shark. "Stay back," she murmurs like sheer sex, and takes the hammer out of my hand so fast I didn't even see it happen. I'll be honest, I felt that one down with the fellas. She's good.

She is silent on her feet, and I can tell she's not even trying. Me, I have to put like 90% of my focus into not creaking floorboards, breathing too hard, and generally blowing our cover. We clear a few rooms, nothing doing. I see the puddle of water from when we first came in here, and already it feels like a lifetime ago. Ah, the days of our youth. *Focus, dumbass.*

Before I can even react, she high-steps it around a corner to one of the palatial rooms at the front of the house and out of my sight. I don't know what to do, and I don't get long to think about it because within seconds I hear a slight yelp—a pathetic little yelp—followed by the sound of someone getting hummingbird-smashed in the noggin. It's more of a vibration of blows than a series, like fully auto. *D-D-D-D-D-D-D-D-D-D-D…* It sounds wet, crunchy, and super fucking fatal. I have to brace myself because what I see in my mind's eye is fucked up. And it's still not enough to prepare me for what I *actually* see. Dude's entire skull is caved in from crown to chin—crushed, pulped, and annihilated, like a flattened soccer ball, but made of meat. His bottom jaw is mostly intact and still working itself, and I can't tell if it's because he's still alive, or it's because he died so fast no one had a chance to tell his jaw. I should be disgusted by this, I'm not an animal. But god damn if I'm not at full mast, I mean I am working a rager. What is wrong with me? As I'm standing there reckoning with my murder boner she lifts the hammer to her mouth and licks the fucking thing clean. Even my cock wasn't ready for that one. When she turns to look at me I get full emerald. Those eyes are the end of time. I'm telling you, man. She closes them just long enough for me to snap out of it and notice the blood, bone, brain, and tooth all dotted across her porcelain mug. Can we get a minister in here? I'm ready for my vows.

That's two down and three to go. But it's no longer a question of if we're getting out of this, but when. She drops the hammer on the ground, and the sound echoes through the entire ground floor. They are absolutely on to us now. Poor guys. You have to almost feel for them. I hold the crowbar out and without even looking back she takes it. I'm her fucking murder caddie.

And like clockwork, dipshit number three barrels out of a room down a long hallway heading directly at us. And oh, behind him is another! A twofer! Glory be praised. We stop and watch as they are coming up on us, and as dolt number one lifts his gun, the emerald closes the twenty or so feet between her and them and in one primal sweeping stroke goes low with the bar and up, and in the process cuts this motherfucker in half vertically from the taint to the paint, and the cleaved halves of his body explode in internal goop as the guy behind him runs directly into the bisected man, slips and falls headfirst on the ground, prostrate before the emerald. He starts to scream while she lifts the crowbar about her head and spears this guy to the floor like a fish. She leaves the crowbar in place, like a mile marker for the most dangerous marathon ever, and stands there. I realize that she is done hunting. She is waiting for her dude to come home—back to her loving arms.

She must have heard him coming, that or she *smelled* him, because she turns her head to the right and there he is, on cue, that big meat pile of a man, beard singed, clothes half burnt. *Well I'll be damned*, I think, *I got him after all.* She sidesteps him just as he gets to her, and she realizes immediately that this is exactly what he wanted her to do because with her still pivoting, dude lifts a sawed-off and blasts my fucking leg off in the middle of my thigh. I'm not gonna lie, that shit hurts. Things get fuzzy for me, but I clear up a bit when the guy grabs me square in my John Thomas and lifts me off the fucking ground. It hurts so bad I almost forget about my leg. I mean, if I have to pick one to give up. Well, you know. I hear my own voice kick up several octaves, and consider challenging Mariah Carey to a sing-off.

Holding me like a sack of flour, the big boy faces the emerald. Surprisingly she hasn't murdered him already. I have no doubt that she could. And he is faster than I expected him to be, but he isn't as fast as she is. He has the end of his sawed-off pointing directly at my mixed nuts.

"Oh baby, don't get cute now," he tells her, "and don't give me them eyes, you know I don't fall for that shit. Your kind has always known that. We've kept watch on you folk for centuries, and you don't get to just come out of there and pluck some poor asshole out of one of *our* fine drinking establishments. There's rules, sweetheart, you know that. It ain't news." She is giving him full emerald, and the fucking guy doesn't flinch. "Aww, come on now, girl, you know that don't work on me!" And then, still eyeballing her he starts talking to me, "This girl here, this one that's got your cock all in knots? Not what you think she is, son. Not by a long shot. You don't know what you're getting all excited about, do you? You don't have a clue why four good men had to die to try and save *you* now, do you? I tried to tell you in the bar, but you were too busy shoving your hand up her snatch to listen to reason. The panty bomb though, I gotta give you that one, that's new on me. This 'girl' is a Mississippi river wraith. Which is improper no-menclature, but it's Louisiana, so one can be forgiven for mixing their lore. She's a succubus, a sperm farmer. She wants your seed, son. And when she has it she will be 'with child,' though I hesitate to call what comes out of her rotten womb a child. Her kind don't survive without our precious lifegiving goodness. And that ain't the half. When she's done with you, you're, well, let's just say you're lunch.

"I don't blame you for not knowing, that means I've been doin' my job as God intended. Problem is, we wouldn't be in this predicament if I'd finished the job. And *that's* on me. And now we find ourselves in this situation. She won't touch me because she knows I can end her family line as we stand here today. If the sun comes up and catches her out-river without your seed, well, that's one less of a dying breed, and another day closer to a safer world. I'm all for tradition, but sometimes you need a little progress, you get me?" And he squeezes my balls for emphasis. And I pass the fuck out.

When I come to, I am lying in the spot where I'd lost my leg, and my blood has thickened and glued me to the floor. I'd lost a lot of the stuff, but I was still in it to win it. I cock my head up trying to get the lay of the land, and there before me is the big boy, torn limb from limb, and the emerald on her haunches eating like the buffet was about to close. I don't know where it is all going, but he is at least half gone. And the fucking smell, Jesus fuck me sideways, his intestines are ripped open and there is fecal matter all over the floor and the metallic tang of blood fills any gaps in the air around me. She has piled his bones up like she is at a wing joint. This is happening.

I just watch her eat, mesmerized. I mean it is really something. She takes her time, savoring every bite. And when she is good and done she wipes some of the chunkage from her face and sucks that down as well. Waste not, want not, I guess. And on came the emeralds, and all I know is her. I feel another blackout coming, but before that happens I realize that my flag is full mast.

I awake to the smell of the river. You grow up around here, you know the smell of the river. It's in your blood. You breathe it in night and day. And it just keeps rolling on by, the jugular of a broken nation. And I am in her arms, the emerald, my emerald, and she kisses me so hard and so deep that I almost blow right there, but she has bigger plans for me. And the last thing I see is the sun cresting over the eastern shore of the river, and then it is all wet, and brown, and Mark-motherfuckin'-Twain.